It was as if one shoe had been dropped, in the king-sized expanse of their marriage, the day Geoff began his new career and left her behind with the other faculty wives. And now she had to make some decisions:

She would be bereft if she had to give up Mike Vogel.

The children and her husband aside, she had never felt better in her life.

She could never give up Mike.

If she persisted in seeing Mike, Geoff would surely catch her and all hell would break loose.

To forget Mike would be to forget herself.

> LIMITS OF EDEN—A love story about Abby Mullen, her husband, her lover. A love story about people who think they have everything when they don't; who think they've lost it all when they haven't.

> LIMITS OF EDEN: A Love Story.

Another Ace Book by Joyce Keener:

BORDERLINE

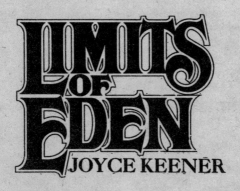

LIMITS OF EDEN

JOYCE KEENER

ace books

A Division of Charter Communications Inc.
A GROSSET & DUNLAP COMPANY
51 Madison Avenue
New York, New York 10010

LIMITS OF EDEN

Copyright © 1981 by Joyce Keener

An ACE Original

"Take Me" by Leon Payne. Copyright © 1965-1979 by Glad Music Company. All Rights Reserved including the right of public performance for profit. International Copyright Secured. Made in U.S.A.

"We Must Have Been Out of Our Minds" by Melba Montgomery. Copyright © 1963-1979 by Glad Music Company. All Rights Reserved including the right of public performance for profit. International Copyright Secured. Made in U.S.A.

First Ace Printing: July 1981

Published simultaneously in Canada

2 4 6 8 0 9 7 5 3 1
Manufactured in the United States of America

for Henry
Elsie
George
Nancy
and Janet

There's not any mountain too rugged to climb
No desert too barren to crawl;
Somewhere if you will just show a sign
Of love I could bear it all.
Take me to Siberia
In the coldest weather of the wintertime,
And it would be just like spring in California
As long as I knew you were mine.

"Take Me"
G. Jones & L. Payne
Glad Music Co./BMI

CHAPTER ONE

Abby Mullen was the one with the eyes of bruised blue. And a quick smile. She was the sort yearbooks used to praise for their pep. Tonight she was sitting quietly between two parties of women at the far end of Maxine Gerber's overwrought living room. At thirty-six Abby was just old enough, settled enough to be welcome in the group on the right—wives distinguished by old gold, fresh drinks and renovated hair. Their husbands all had tenure.

She sort of tuned out when Doctor Mazur's wife —"Mrs. Doc" they called her—started talking about the Friends of The Museum. Abby already knew more about art and charities than she thought was necessary. But this was the group she had the most in common with. They still wore stockings, which whistled whenever they recrossed their legs. They themselves did not whistle, and neither did they work. They volunteered.

The women to Abby's left looked younger, but partly because of the cocky way they stood around in tight jeans—no matter what the occasion. They did not drink much, and tended to pass one cigarette among themselves. They kept an evening a little off balance—often showed up without escorts. Few of them had tenure or breeding. They worked hard at everything. Maxine was always inviting these women in hopes one of them would make a scene. Maxine was like that.

Abby never invited them to her own home, but that was simply because she and Geoff enjoyed other couples, not because she found the women unappealing. She was especially fascinated by Thea Kaltenborn.

"Of course it's racist," Thea was insisting. "You expect them to bus in white jailbirds from Minnesota? Keep the prison population balanced? It reflects real life in the tri-state area, that's all. Blacks still have the fewest options. They're the ones that get caught, usually the ones without the price of a legal fight."

Thea did not seem to notice their hostess bearing down on them, dispensing champagne glasses. Abby saw, and could not help hoping Maxine would not interrupt.

"There's only one white woman in there right now," Thea continued, accepting a glass. "Remember a Mrs. Rainey from the South Side last year? She was in all the papers, for a day. Been married for something like forty years, but one night she just leaned across the supper table and stabbed her husband through the heart with a steak knife."

"Whew!" one of the listeners marveled. "Talk about options!"

"Why did she do it?" Abby asked.

"Why not?" Thea snapped. "He may have been blackening her eyes ever since the honeymoon."

Abby objected, "But she would have moved out

long ago in that case."

"Not necessarily."

"Of course," Abby insisted. "That's what divorce is for."

"Don't be so sure," insisted another woman whose face was obscured behind huge photo-grey glasses. "You never know what all goes on between couples. Not even if you live downstairs from them, believe me."

"But to murder him like that!"

Thea shrugged. "Maybe she just went into a rage. She'd had symptoms of arteriosclerosis for more than a year. Or maybe they never talked. She told me once Mr. Rainey had no idea she was pregnant until the night their first son was born."

Abby did not know which she found more astonishing—the milltown housewife who finally allowed herself one homicidal opinion at the supper table, or Thea. Thea was a graduate teaching assistant who ought to have been smart enough to stay out of prison and out of the South Side, Geoff said, but she frequented both places nevertheless. For her dissertation.

Like most of their circle, Abby and Geoff crossed the bridges to the South Side of the Monongahela River no more than twice a year. Every now and then for a dinner of Slavic food. And once at Easter, to attend one of the onion-domed churches for the spectacle of ethnic holidays. (After all, Geoff said, their children ought to enjoy the advantages of growing up in a melting pot city.) The rest of the year, however, they left the South Side to a peculiar lot of specialists—priests who were allowed to marry, cops who spoke two languages, and Thea Kaltenborn, who seemed to be afraid of nothing. Abby envied her.

She listened avidly as Thea described a recent interview with Mrs. Rainey, the steak knife wielder. It seems she had had the brass to ask that woman, "What was going through your mind just as you picked up the knife?" Abby wanted to know herself.

A *ting*-ing of glass sounded from the fireplace end of the room. She dragged her attention away from Thea, knowing that tonight was rightfully Geoff Mullen's. He was going to make an announcement. She knew it well. He had rehearsed it this evening while zipping her dress.

Geoff was standing on the white bricks of the hearth. Maxine stood there too, still banging on a glass for silence. No one but Abby had turned their way yet.

Her husband was an eyeful—still lanky at thirty-eight as he had been as a starving student. With those long limbs and scant hips he was the perfect clothes horse, and she did dearly wish he would agree to wear one of those luscious velvet blazers such as the poet-in-residence always wore. But youthful as Geoff's figure was, he insisted on the most presbyterian suits. He had too much taste to wear anything stylish. Only the rich growth of his mustache hinted at any personal vanity. As he reminded Abby more than once, the boardrooms of Pittsburgh were pretty sober places and he did not want to be known as another arty flake from the University.

Abby knew he was thrilled right now, despite his poker face. She knew that in another moment all the brainy people in the Gerbers' living room would have to give up their notion of Geoff as the campus crank. He had suddenly outgrown his obscure little teaching job. Through the magic of an enormous foundation grant, he had been transformed from a mere professor of statistics into an intellectual jet-setter.

When Geoff popped the first champagne cork everyone hushed. Heads pivoted. "I'd like to share a bit of good fortune with you," Geoff began. He was expertly modest.

While he spoke, Maxine darted from group to group, pouring champagne. The men at Geoff's end of the room glanced at each other. The wives at Abby's end looked at her, already jealous before they knew what their congratulations must be about.

"Some of you know I've been running around in circles looking for funding to finish my cycles project," Geoff was saying. A few of his closest friends chuckled sympathetically. "This week I got lucky. The Bessemer Foundation has decided to take a chance on me at last. Not only that, but two—count 'em—*two* oil companies are pitching in with matching funds so that we can make a very classy film documenting our findings." Geoff grinned at them in triumph and drained his champagne with one swallow. "To cycles!"

The news was stunning. For a moment no one else drank.

A whole room away from him, down through an obstacle course of cantilevered chrome lamps, potted cacti, gleaming parquetry, Abby tried to catch Geoff's eye. He was grinning widely but not toward her. She lifted her glass. This is full of wine, she reminded herself. Not hemlock, not a spongeful of vinegar. Geoff had splurged for this toast in his honor; she knew it was Dom Perignon buzzing at her lips.

Abby held the wine in her mouth until it went flat. She was not sure she was ready for this exciting new future Geoff had earned for her. She was scared stiff, and too loyal to know it.

The others were staring at Geoff. What he said, in essence, was that he was choosing to defect from their privileged ranks. By accepting a Bessemer grant he was claiming that there was honorable work outside of academics. A whiff of brimstone was almost discernible amid the tulip glasses.

The next instant Maxine's nice husband was lifting his glass. Slipping an arm around Geoff's shoulders, Jerry Gerber led the group in a toast, "To corporate bucks." Everyone drank. The mood lightened. Good sportsmanship returned on a tide of champagne. After all, Geoff's coup was a variation on winning endowments, a process they all attempted. "To corporate guilt," somebody cheered.

Abby soon gave up trying to find her way to Geoff's side. Standing up as tall as she could, she did manage to see his face—shining cherubically within a hedge of jealous mustaches—and she could see how much he was enjoying the astonishment of his colleagues.

"So what about your book?" Jerry Gerber asked, moving into the circle with another champagne bottle.

"It's all but finished anyhow," Geoff said. "I'll take the galleys with me. We're shooting all over creation—the Philippines, the Yukon, Ascension Island. . ."

"Very nice," a spoilsport interrupted. "What about your classes?"

Geoff winked at him. "They'll have to settle for some starving assistant. I am on sabbatical as of this semester." The playful lilt in his voice was one Abby had never heard him use in public before—only in the master bedroom at home. And that laugh. After years of begrudging any moment their social obligations took away from his work, he was thriving on being the life of a party. Abby knew she should take this as a good sign of even better things to come. Instead she was spooked by his glee. She left her champagne glass in a bookcase and went looking for a seat.

"I've been asked to address the Royal Zoological Society in Oslo," Geoff's voice continued. "They're having a special conference to kick off their endangered species census. So I'll give them an update of my timberwolf population projections, just to get things rolling. Really I'm going in hopes of getting cooperation from the scholarly community in Scandinavia. While I'm in the neighborhood I can grab a quick meeting with local film crews, get a leg up on our spring shoot of the seventeen-year cicada migrations."

Anne Fellows was probably the best wife in the world. Now, as always, she was gracious. She leaned across an end table, fingers twinkling, to touch Abby's dress. "You must be very proud."

"Oh, I am. He's worked so hard."

Following Mrs. Arnold Fellows's lead, other women leaned close to say the gladdest things they could think of about Geoff's research, his resulting new job as a filmmaker, and his presumably glamorous future. Abby knew exactly how to respond;

she had witnessed promotion parties for years.

One woman who was shackled with pounds of sand-cast silver barked at Abby, "I've been teaching here for three years and never heard of his studies."

Abby smiled generously. "I'm not surprised, really. The few who did swore he was selling snake oil. Statistics hasn't been a very adventurous field."

"You're so lucky," the dean's wife burbled. "Traveling to all those curious places with Geoff."

"I think I'm looking forward to Oslo as much as he is," Abby replied. "I won't get in on all the trips, of course. The children have school, and there's such a thing as too much Grandma, you know."

"Excuse me?" Thea was offering a joint to Abby. Rank smelling thing. She did not know the polite way to refuse so she just smiled. Thea took another hit herself. Passing it elsewhere she rasped just between them, "Cycles! That's pretty organic stuff for somebody as tightassed as Mullen. Come on, Abby, admit you gave him the idea."

"Oh no," said Abby. In fact, she had. But only technically. It was Geoff's abilities that made the idea work. He was an unusually gifted man—capable of ecstasy over statistics. Always had been. Simply out of devotion she sometimes sat with him at their paper-strewn dining room table when she brought fresh coffee. He seldom answered her questions so she would proofread or browse his charts for interesting words. One night it was not a word but a number that struck her eye: 5-point-6, the same as her height. Here was one item showing peaks in the Yukon's timber wolf population every 5-point-6 years, and another showing slumps in the commodities market every 5-point-6 years. Elbows splayed out on the table, holding the hair from her eyes, Abby had read deeply in columns of numbers and found some peculiar 5-point-6's. Geoff had dismissed her observation. But 5-point-6 rolled around in her head until the day she mentioned it to a retired lecturer, a man she met by the Xerox machine in the economics tower. She had come to drive Geoff home, but the old man followed her to Geoff's office in the basement and all three of them ended up staying out most of the night. They missed dinner together, sneezed over a lot of neglected file folders reading aloud to each other, and before morning Geoff had begun carving out new territory for himself.

Developing a discipline was painfully slow labor. But little by little Geoff's scholarly papers on the cyclical analysis of recurring phenomena were revolutionizing the field of statistics. His department was suddenly granted a lion's share of the university's computer time. He began to attract disciples—Geoff Mullen, at his young age. He was invited to speak on other campuses. The study of cycles began growing so rapidly that not even Geoff could keep abreast of all new developments. Even in the financial district taverns downtown, brokers and pollsters had taken to gossiping about the super-forecasts these studies generated. Still, the public sector remained officially disinterested.

Geoff ran out of money twice. Finding outside support drained off more of his energy than his actual studies did. Abby listened to him rehearse his arguments until every point was airtight. And then she encouraged him once more. When he began losing faith, she would ask him questions until the sound of his own proposals instilled determination again. He began losing weight. One grim weekend he and Abby feared his sex was turning dysfunctional. During the next two years Abby had numerous occasions to wish she had kept her mouth shut. By the time of his breakthrough with Bessemer Geoff had almost suspected himself of promoting snake oil. After all that, Abby was only too glad to let him have the spotlight to himself. He was the brainy one. Let him be the star. She did not have the stomach for that sort of pressure. Anyhow, she reminded herself, she already had everything she wanted.

Abby shook her head. "I'm just his cheering section," she smiled.

Thea looked at her hard, then turned away with a groan. Their hostess was growing quarrelsome on champagne and had picked Thea to bait.

Abby watched with interest.

Maxine lounged on a sofa between pillows she had needlepointed with portraits of Susan B. Anthony and Mick Jagger. She was peeling lead foil from the neck of another bottle and sneering. Thea was insisting that violence has always been the only eloquence available to the poor.

"Bullshit," Maxine objected. She was married, so in feminist circles she made an effort to be vulgar—a show of solidarity. "It's just another result of the callousness we've all picked up from runaway prosperity. You know what Dylan said the other day? I was driving him home from nursery school and, you know, he was bouncing around in the back seat like any respectable toddler. And the next thing I hear from this child of mine is, 'Bang, bang, you're dead . . . fifty bullets in your head'."

Thea giggled. "It's the Y-chromosome."

But Maxine was indignant: "It's that goddam television."

"Then don't let him watch it."

"Oh ho ho, a closet fascist," laughed Maxine.

Delaney, who was separated, threw in bitterly, "Just try to stop them. It only makes the whole nasty business more alluring."

Thea tried to draw Abby into the controversy. "Do you let Toby and Gabrielle watch whenever they want to?"

"We don't have a TV," Abby said. "But I suppose television should be handled like any other appliance. I wouldn't think of letting either of my children use the Cuisinart without supervision, or the steam iron, and the same goes for TV." Thea flattered her with explosive laughter. But Abby did not have the heart to go on debating. She was tired.

Just as she managed to slip away into Maxine's fern-shrouded breakfast nook, a hand caught her by the elbow.

Anne Fellows led her smoothly into a circle of art-lovers. "You know, with your new position in the community," Anne was advising her, "you'll probably want to take a more active interest in volunteer work. There is so much to be done. I would be happy to sponsor you into one of my committees."

Abby's heart sank. Last year she had volunteered at St. Brigit's-Acmetonia Regional Rehabilitation Center for several months until she was driven out by the defensive scorn and jealousy of the paid staff. She still gathered pledges for them every Christmas, but avoided community-spirited committees.

"Get yourself some capital campaign work for the educational channel," urged one of Anne's friends. "I just love that station, it's my favorite charity. They're such exciting people down there." Another woman added that the public TV station was even using volunteers on screen sometimes.

Anne persisted. "I only started being active in the Museum five years ago, and already they've put me in charge of Corporate Giving," she said proudly. "It hasn't hurt Arnold's position one bit, either."

For the first time then it dawned on Abby: she was no longer a simple faculty wife whose husband did well enough so they could both be comfortable. Geoff's new connections had made her a Foundation wife overnight, a Corporate asset. He was the whiz who had figured out how to tap into Corporate Giving and there was status for them both in that. But something was going to have to be given back. Not by Geoff. By her. That's the way it worked.

She was going to have to memorize new feminine duties, perfect the labyrinthine protocol of being prominent. She winced to think of the price in additional Christmas cards alone. Her good nature shut down for the night. Suddenly aware that her feet were aching, she nodded hastily in response to an invitation to luncheon next week and went looking for Geoff.

CHAPTER TWO

Something like heat lightning flickered behind the twin snow-capped peaks. Mike thought at first he had blinked. Narrowing his eyes he watched the panorama before him. Everything was still. Off toward the south a hawk might have cried out, because an elk had stopped grazing and lifted his head to stare in that direction. Shank-deep in wild flowers the rangy old buck looked sort of tame.

Again the light flickered. Mike sighed, got to his feet and, reaching behind a frame the size of a picture window, switched off the light. He would have to replace that bulb soon. Watching the elk picture usually soothed him pretty well after a hard day, but not with lights jittering like crazy.

He looked around the room impatiently. Nothing much to do here. He had eaten supper from the packages he brought it home in, so there were no dirty dishes. No point in spending time repairing that butt-sprung chair he just heaved himself out of; when it finally came to be uncomfortable he knew he would bring home a new one. No television to watch. There was nothing left of his black and white TV console except a mashed place on the carpeting. Been on the fritz ever since fourth game

13

of the World Series last year, but he had not taken it to the dump until it stopped delivering sound, as well, during a Steelers game. He liked his home better without a TV anyhow—just fall asleep in front of the damn thing and wake up feeling doubly lonely hearing the hiss that follows sign-off. He'd take live company over canned, any day.

Mike fingered the switch of his record player thoughtfully. He did share the Vogel family failing of restlessness, no doubt about that. In Pop's case it took the form of hobby work at the power lathe. In Mike's more often than not it came out in the form of loud singing. But he did not feel like singing alone tonight. He lifted a disc from the record player, dusted it off with his sleeve, and returned the same record to the turntable. Rolling the sound high, he stepped into the bathroom for a quick shave. No neighbors were apt to complain about the noise.

His shirt went into the plastic basket on first try. Two points, he grinned to himself in the mirror. ". . . The very moment," he warbled along with George Jones, "I saw your smile it'd be like Heaven to mee-ee-e." Singing along under his breath, he slapped water onto his cheeks, started smearing lather from ear to ear. A quick rinse of the hands, then he lifted a shiny length of leather away from the wall where it hung, and began stropping his straight razor. The flexible L of steel balanced just so in his hand. He whisked upwards on one side of the blade, down the other, sharpening it with faint liquid hushes. Just the way Pop taught him. Made him smile to recall how the Army could not tolerate it that this kid shaved with a straight razor; the sergeant took it away "before somebody gets hurt" and issued him a safety. But as soon as Mike was his own man again, he went back to the straight. He almost gave a hoot what anybody else thought: this was how he learned to shave at age thirteen— practically twenty-seven years ago now. He expected to continue that way at least twenty-seven more. It was something real, a little bit difficult, in a world full of convenient junk.

Keeping up with the tenor on the record he lilted, "I can get overhauled, get high, wired, and bald," into his closet. "But I don't guess I'll get over you."

He did not care for the chilly slickness of the shirt he was pulling on. Made him feel sweaty. He had a raft of them anyway; stocking up on synthetics was his way of breaking Mom of her habitual sneaking in to iron his shirts. He rolled the cuffs back. You'd think they could make shirtsleeves long enough to fit a grown man, he grumbled to himself.

Wondering who might have shown up before him, Mike patted his pockets. Yes, there was enough to pay for a night of elbow-bending even if that guzzler Web came in.

He turned off the record player, doused the lights and stepped outside closing the door softly behind him. His breath wafted up in plumes. Not that the night was so very cold; last week a half-hearted thaw had started and there was plenty of moisture in the air. Looking down toward the lights of Mom's kitchen he could see frost shimmering on the bare branches of apple trees surrounding him. Still, he decided, if rain came after midnight it was likely to be an ice storm. Contrary time of year.

Kicking some mud off the rocker panel, Mike sat into the El Camino and turned over the engine. "And reap together the wild seeds we've sown," he sang.

CHAPTER THREE

Their gingerbread house would be quiet, inviting. The antique furnace snoring quietly, the new refrigerator humming. Tomorrow morning's juice was thawing slowly beside nice brown-shelled eggs. (Oh yes, Abby remembered, that eggplant in the hydrator would have to be used before it turned runny.) In the darkest reaches of the garage the latest kittens were probably prowling their nest inside a tire, peeping and searching for a handle on their harlot mother. Not awake really, just greedy.

High under the carved, scrolled eaves their children would be asleep—Toby sprawled and drooling, Gabrielle fetal. Esther Sipe, young mountain stock who mothered all four Mullens from time to time, would be dozing on the chaise longue under the living room bay window—dozing or working on another afghan in her endless series of crocheted afghans.

Abby loved their house. She and Geoff had made a down payment on it in the first year of his tenure, rescuing it from the neglect of a retired couple who were moving to a condominium in the Sun Belt. It had everything wrong with it—paint over embossed tiles, shag carpeting over oak floors, stained glass windows sagging and buckling. But the kids loved its three-story bannisters and sliding doors. Geoff did the right thing at once—had numerous bathrooms installed where none had been, removed false ceilings that harbored awful flourescent lights, and had all the chimneys swept. Abby refinished fine old wood a few feet every month, offered weekly the incense of quiches and cookies. By now the house was perfect.

She never looked back at the married-student housing where Toby was born. This was her first real nest, she reflected. She meant to keep it forever, although Geoff had pointed out often enough that it would be entirely too big for them when the kids began leaving home.

Abby recalled how carefully she had planned both births, and remembered Thea's deadly Mrs. Rainey again. Thank goodness she and Geoff had always discussed everything. They had been half-grown when they met, really, and done all their dreaming, maturing, planning together. Secret grudges were unthinkable. She put Mrs. Rainey out of her mind.

Abby moved her feet away from the heater and looked out the car window. Even this late on a wintry March night she could see barge traffic out there ruffling the Allegheny River. Black trees along the banks cut her view into slabs, but she could see the wake fanning out behind a tugboat until a sharp turn took their car away from the river and plunged them once more into woods. She wished Geoff would watch the road while he talked. Out here in Farley Landing a rabbit, or worse a deer, might run in front of the car.

". . . Will take a lot of organization, you know,"

he was saying. "I'll have to whip my conference paper into shape on the way to Oslo. To tell you the truth, I could have done a better job with a little more time. And how I'm going to have a film crew picked for Spitsbergen by the end of next month is beyond me, although the Foundation guys say they have people standing by." Geoff was saying fretful things but his voice was full of satisfaction.

Geoff was going to be on the move constantly this year, Abby remembered suddenly. Worse than that—on the move all over the world. She wished he had already thought of inviting her along, in so many words. It would have been more romantic than her having to wonder how they might work this out. She wished he were showing some tiny bit of sentiment about how long he would be away from the children. She assumed he could not look forward to these trips so much if he gave any thought to traveling alone. He seemed to forget how little they had been separated.

Besides, why was he so excited about living on the run for a year? Maybe he did not realize how finicky he was.

"Do you want me to go along?" she asked. She would arrange his personal amenities at least. Abby applied her imaginary pencil to a list of arrangements that would have to be made.

"Sure," she heard Geoff smile. "When I've worked out something like a routine you ought to come, too. No reason why we shouldn't see the Great Wall together, is there?" He squeezed her knee. Abby's list grew: much as she hated hair dryers, better to carry one for drying emergency laundry than go looking for a laundromat in Pe-

king. And a voltage adaptor. "But," Geoff continued, "there's no point in your going along for these
first few trips."

"No point?" Abby began. But she did not want
to argue. Most of all she had wanted him to say an
unqualified yes.

"What kind of fun would you have alone in Oslo
without anyone to show you around? I'll just be
wild, myself," Geoff said.

What kind, indeed. She recalled the time she
went to Cincinnati alone. It had been nice in a way,
except for the mess her father had left for probate
to decipher. She felt mischievous. She had taken a
wicked pleasure in wasting time and hotel toilet paper. She had spoken to strangers. She had dressed
for dinner as carefully as she did back home for the
Symphony, and then walked out of the hotel dining
room rather than argue with her waiter. She never
did figure out what an all-night bakery was doing
vending perfect cream puffs in that neighborhood
straight from a Fellini movie. Safe in her clean hotel room again, naked except for her pearls, she
had eaten three cream puffs, then slept all over the
bed. And felt silly in the morning. What, now that
she thought about it, would she do in Oslo alone?
Probably what she had done at the end of the Cincinnati trip—race through a museum one afternoon so there would be something worthwhile to
report to Geoff.

Abby resolved not to ask him again. He would
certainly invite her when it suited; besides, better to
let him find his own version of these places first.
When they had become his personal territory, he
would be very happy to show them to her. He was
good at exploring, generous as tour guide. Abby,

they had often agreed, was a highly accomplished audience.

She considered that notion. At the moment she felt grumpy, not receptive. The prospect of being groomed as a Corporate wife grated against her bones and she wanted to be taken away from it all. She wanted to curl up with her nice husband, spoons-style, and eavesdrop on foreign voices below their hotel window. And in the morning find out all the rest of his work could be done at their dining room table at home.

Geoff bounced the car across the roadside ditch —nearly a moat these days—then sloshing through icy puddles, rolled down their driveway to the garage door.

The house was not asleep. In yellow light from above the sink, Esther waved, vanished. Such a nice, safe place—it looked like an advent calendar. The light was still on in Toby's room, too. Abby yawned, "You'd better let me take Esther home. Have a talk with Toby. . . . He seemed anxious about something at dinner."

Geoff pulled on the hand brake and reached into the back seat for a grocery sack of leftover champagne. "Okay," he grunted. "Do you want to send one of your loaves of carrot bread home with her?"

"No, they're frozen now," Abby said. "I'd like to give her a bottle of this."

Geoff made a face. "Well, for Pete's sake tell her not to use a corkscrew."

Abby slid over to the driver's seat. While she held her fringed shawl away from the door, Geoff shut her in. She rolled down the window to say, "I predict his buddy Caleb is the problem. Last week he told all the kids Toby wets his bed." Geoff

wagged his head in vexation. They were both
steaming quietly in hazy moonlight. "He still feels
betrayed."

Esther's feet were thudding down the sidewalk
into the garage. "I'll talk to him," Geoff said. "Hi
Esther. Later," he added, leaning in to say it
against Abby's ear, "if you like, I'll chase you
around the house a little bit." Abby offered no
comment as Esther ducked into the headlights
from the open garage door. "Hi," she said, and
watched Geoff walk inside, trailed by the erect
tail of a hungry mother cat.

Esther was better off getting a ride home with
Abby. Either Geoff truly could not find his way
through the back roads of Allegheny County or
some Freudian miscalculations prevented his
straying so far from town; whatever it was, both
times he had taken a turn at giving Esther a lift he
had ended up on the far side of Natrona Heights.
Now they had a tacit agreement that it would
seldom be convenient for him to drive Esther
home. Abby did not mind. The distance was not so
great; it was simply a far cry from the campusy
climate of Farley Landing.

Out toward Esther's place the pastures and
woods remained undeveloped, rank as in the days
before steel. Some people had farmed those hills all
their lives, and it was difficult for stray sub-
urbanites to find their way around. What few road-
signs there were got used as shotgun targets more
than anything else. And in the bickering between
state and county highway officials, none of the
pavements saw much maintenance. Abby didn't
mind, though. The way to Esther's was just long
enough for a chat, unless the kids had done some-

thing vile. It took them past railroad sidings
choked with frosty burdock. Toward bluish islands
of light that turned into filling stations, then into
blue lights once more absorbed by the darkness in
her rearview mirror. Between orchards and produce stands boarded up for the winter. Past school
bus shelters where "Steeler Defense" was proclaimed in spray-painted scrawls. Abby's sturdy little car zipped past all these landmarks, but neither
woman noticed because Esther was talking.

"So there's me and Web, squunched into this
teeny little place under the sink, hauling on our
wrenches. . ."

Esther was younger than Abby but she spoke
with a hoarse growl befitting the harridans of a
carnival. It sounded as though she screamed too
much, although Abby had never heard her so much
as raise her voice to the Mullen children. In fact she
seldom spoke at all. Except when alone with Abby.

"And Web's wrench lets go, smacks me right
here on the wrist bone." Esther pointed to a spot
on her cast. "It blew up and got purple right away.
Boy," she laughed. "You shoulda seen the face on
that doctor. At the hospital? He came out with my
X-rays looking like he'd seen a ghost or something.
'Your fingernails,' he kept saying. 'They show up
on the X-rays. Fingernails *never* show up on X-
rays!' And they did look like claws—claws at the
tips of these skeleton fingers. We finally figured out
it was all the polish I had on." Abby glanced at the
iridescent manicure Esther held out toward the
dash lights. "I hope you don't mind, I took a bath
in your tub."

"Of course not."

"All we have's a shower out home, and it's hard

to keep the cast from going all slimy on me."

Abby smiled. She was too decent to point out that since Esther was the one who cleaned the tubs on Farley Landing Road, there could be little harm in her bathing in them as well.

"How was the party?" Esther asked. "You sure looked nice when you left."

"Thank you. Okay, I guess. A lot of Geoff's colleagues."

"Didn't exactly light your fire, huh?"

Abby's eyes were busy scouting a slalom through the potholes, but she did grin. "I was a little uncomfortable," she admitted. She was somewhat surprised how it relieved her to say so. Alone in the countryside with Esther, she permitted herself the luxury of disloyalty. "Well, they talk so much. The men get together and talk about work, and the women are even worse. Nobody dances," she complained. "Except every once in a while a couple of libbers will dance together. Maybe that's a prerogative of sisterhood, but I don't care for it myself."

"Oh, I don't know," Esther shrugged. "We used to dance girls-and-girls in junior high when we couldn't get the guys to dance. Wouldn't bother me."

"Geoff danced at our wedding, period," said Abby. "I wish . . . you know what? Couples never even *talk* to each other at these parties. From the moment they come in until it's time to go, they only talk to other people. Doesn't that seem silly?"

Esther could not make any sense of that oddity: she shook her head. "Tell you what. You wanta have fun sometime, you and Geoff go out dancing with Web and I. We know lots of places," she said.

"Nobody much talks. The band's too rowdy."

Abby pictured herself in a hicktown ballroom. Oh to be tonguetied again. It would be so peaceful to travel in circles where nothing was "fascinating," where precious little was "discussed". When was the last time she had really danced, Abby wondered. That time she had drunk enough to learn a few disco steps did not count: she had been mortified in the morning. But the sort of dancing that led to sweaty palms. With boys who would rather hold her hard and fast than talk. When festoons of crepe paper . . . She reminded herself of the misery, too. Adolescence was Past Lives, as Maxine would say, and bungled at that. Amateur nights.

"We went to the Elks last Saturday," Esther was saying. "They're polka crazy."

Abby turned right past the sign that bitched "Not a County Maintained Road". She began watching for the rutted lane that led to Esther's home. Carefully she drove with one side treading the center ridge and her righthand tires crunching through frozen weeds on the shallow bank. No doubt the owner would grade here again after the worst of spring weather had passed. Ahead the trailer park was aglow with strings of colored lights. "When are you people going to take down the Christmas lights?" she asked.

Esther said, "Think it makes the place look cute."

Abby put the car in neutral and handed her the bottle of champagne. "Geoff bought more than enough champagne for the party," she said. "Would you like some?"

"Sure." Esther held the bottle into the light and looked at it speculatively.

"If you still have car problems next week, just
say so. Geoff's going to be traveling quite a bit and
I'll have the car every day."

"That's nice," said Esther. "I'll let you know.
You gonna be lonely?" She tucked the cash Abby
paid her into a shopping bag of yarn.

Abby unflinchingly recited a little something she
had made up earlier tonight. "Lonely?" it went.
"Without Geoff underfoot I'll be busier than ever.
I may finally get on with some projects I've had
waiting since Gabey was born."

Esther nodded soberly. "Yeah," she said. "Well,
if you need a change maybe we can do something
together. Too much time in a house as big as
yours'd give me the heeby-jeebies."

"Maybe so," Abby said. "Thanks again. See you
Monday."

Esther slammed the door, waved and made her
way toward the party which was blaring from a
trailer next door to her own. Abby watched for a
moment, wondering what that party might be like.
She felt an impulse to roll down the window and
invite herself along.

Why should she feel like an outsider, when it was
time to go home?

The trailer park had no parking lot. Or rather,
Abby supposed she was in it—a patch bulldozed
out of pastureland, sprinkled with cinders and
now, jammed with cars. There was no place to turn
around unless she cared to try springing her fender
off the bumper of that 280Z. She decided not to.
Geoff was pretty fussy about dents and she could
not be sure her strategy would work. Instead, she
began backing down the lane.

Backing did not work too well, either. In the first

place, the only time she had enough light to see was
when she applied her brakes. Slow going. And she
already knew—on Esther's advice—that this car
rode too low for her to follow the deep ruts; she
must totter along the bank as she did coming up.
Eventually, after running over a section of old barn
siding, she made it back to the road.

Shifting into drive Abby headed for home. There
was no difference she could discern between the
road not maintained by the county and the one she
turned left onto, presumably county-maintained.
They were both humpbacked with frost heaves and
pitted with holes. But she made the most of the
ride. She drove slowly. Without actually thinking
so, she felt a superstitious fear rumbling through
her guts that tonight might be the last time she and
Geoff would be together exactly as they always had
been. Any day now the future was going to begin
and the future might easily get out of hand. From
now on, women she had never met would be meeting Geoff. And he would be meeting them back.
Then what?

She did not want to think about it. She pictured
instead the good normal things she would be seeing
if she were driving this road in daylight. There, just
after that leaning mailbox named Nincovicz, there
was sometimes a muddy white horse hanging his
head into the tufted acreage he shared with some
bandy-legged Herefords. Her daughter called them
"Teddy Cows". That cheered her. Also out there, if
it were not for the dark, she could see the scruffy
birds who seemed to live in roadside brambles all
winter long. Loners living on seeds. Until May,
when the insects came back and a red-winged
blackbird would be holding down every fencepost

she passed. Around the front of this knoll, a distant view of the river. Then the mailbox Dubbs. Next, the sign announcing fresh mushrooms. A huge subterranean mushroom farm. It did Abby's heart good to think about something growing steadily under these pastures, live, even if it had to be fungi, in the catacombs of an abandoned coal mine.

Daughter of a man who used to come home from work at least once a year announcing, "We're moving next month, I've been transferred," she treasured every homely detail of the landscape she had come to consider hers. So maybe she would be left out of Geoff's first thrilling trip. She had all this to browse. She could still tour Route 489 whenever Esther needed a ride.

Abby swerved to avoid a new pothole and felt an odd stiffness in the steering. She waited until a fast-moving car swept past her. When it was gone she pulled as near the ragged shoulder as she dared and got out.

She groaned. The right rear tire was going flat. That board she had backed over must have had a spike in it. And here she was, in the middle of basically nowhere. Late at night. The headlights of another car bobbed up over a rise in the road. Abby hurried into her Gremlin again. The last thing she wanted was to have the dubious help of anyone else who was abroad out here at this hour.

She had never had a flat before. The competent male voices of assorted friends, husbands, advisors accompanied her down the road. Yes, she was trying to drive slowly, giving the rougher sections of pavement a wide berth. No, she did not intend to drive any further than necessary on the rim. But how far was necessary? Abby had never bothered

to acquire the habit of checking odometers, nor the
skill of estimating distances. In fact, she would
have been utterly unable to give directions to someone else for following most of the routes she trav-
eled in a routine week of homemaking, because
Abby found her way by reacting to landmarks as
she got to them. For the life of her she could not
remember how far the first filling station might be.
Or guess whether it would be open.

At the top of the rise she saw help. At least she
saw the bleary neon sign of The *Friendly* Rising
Sun. It was a roadhouse she and Esther had passed
some five hundred times. Until tonight she had
never wondered what it was like inside. No doubt
it had survived a colorful past; under its whitewash
she detected the form of a nineteenth century inn.
But it probably offered modern conveniences, such
as a telephone. She pulled in among the puddles,
pick-up trucks and cars. There was not a single foreign car in sight, let alone a ski rack. Wishing
Esther were still with her, she grabbed her purse
and got out. Crunching her way carefully across
the gravel, she felt as self-conscious as she would
have felt entering church during the reading of the
first lesson.

CHAPTER FOUR

There was no pneumatic hinge at the entrance to The *Friendly* Rising Sun. It was fitted with an ordinary front door discarded from a dismantled house. So when Abby opened the door to come in, it slammed into the wall with an emphatic whack. Everyone looked up.

Instead of a half-drunk second-shifter stomping in with a chip on his shoulder, they saw a slender woman balancing uncertainly on the threshold in dainty high heels. One who had never been here before. She was peculiarly fresh-faced for a woman going drinking alone. They all stared for a moment. Mike Vogel wondered what cloud this one had dropped off of. Her old man must have dumped her outside; he hardly thought she could have driven here herself swaddled up in that huge shaggy shawl. He appraised her as one of those hothouse plants from the ritzy neighborhoods near the Turnpike. She was too short to come from that horsey bunch down the road. He turned back to his glass of beer.

The sudden warmth of the tavern stung Abby's cheeks. She hesitated, unsure what to do without a headwaiter, an escort or usher. A waitress wearing

a black bra under her white uniform, and elastic
stockings, strolled out of the kitchen toward her.
Abby was wondering how to explain what she was
here for when the waitress told her, "Phone's in
back, by the little boys'," and carried her tray of
steaming soup bowls elsewhere.

Abby almost smiled to think how obvious it
must be that she was out of place. Well, then, she
must get on with her business. Groping through
the bottom of her purse for a dime, she moved in
the direction of the phone. Eyes followed her. She
pictured Geoff at home in their cozy bedroom. If
he was still awake she knew he was sitting up in bed
rewriting the notes for his conference speech, or
proofing galleys, or both, papers spread all over
the maroon herringbone sheets. On the other hand,
if he had had as much champagne as she thought,
he was seriously asleep. The phone would wake
Toby and Gabrielle before it woke him.

Abby paused by the sheet rock partition where
the pay phone hung. She reconsidered the importance of waking Geoff. There was nothing he
could do to help her unless he called Jerry Gerber;
she had their only car. The clock in the plastic Rolling Rock panorama indicated two-thirty. She considered that it was late enough to try another solution before they routed Jerry out of Shadyside. A
refrigerator-sized man, smelling of hops or indiges-
tion, squeezed past her. She decided to have a
drink while pondering Plan B.

Abby slipped into the nearest empty booth and
surveyed the clientele. Maybe there was a way to
approach someone here about changing her tire.
There was obviously no shortage of people who
understood hard work. Although it was Saturday

night most of the men still wore uniform wash-pants and shirts with sleeves rolled up. The bar bristled with hairy forearms. There were a few women. They were wearing high hair and low necklines. Unlike the women at Maxine's party, these women were not clustering together—not trading consumer triumphs or sharing insights; they were busy joking with the bartender or listening to the men they were sitting with. The women's hands looked almost as thick as the men's.

A primitive cartoon was attached to the cash register with a yellow smiley-face magnet. It depicted a frog slumped on a bar stool. The balloon coming out of his head said, "I'm so happy here I could just shit." Abby would have given the contents of her purse to know which one of the regulars had dreamed it up. She looked around and noticed the waitress ambling toward her. She took a deep breath, made a wild stab at what she might want to drink.

"Were you in here, oh, say, like Christmas?" the waitress wanted to know.

Abby smiled nervously, shaking her head.

"I been out so much lately I don't even know all the faces any more. Doctoring," the waitress explained.

"Oh," Abby said.

"Female troubles."

Fearful that a full organ recital might follow, Abby suggested the summary: "Feeling better now?"

"Fit to kill," said the waitress. "Whatcha drinking?"

"A bloody mary, please. Without the vodka."

The waitress headed back to the bar, ordering in

an outdoor voice, "One Virgin Mary." Heads
pivoted to see who was ordering a Virgin Mary.
Abby wished she had ordered an anonymous beer.

The bartender did not miss a beat. He shook
some Tabasco into a glass. A crusty can of tomato
juice stood atop the refrigerator beside a gallon jar
of either pickled eggs or something imported direct
from a pathology lab. He poured some tomato
juice. Abby willed her attention to wander
elsewhere. Blessedly, other customers had lost interest in her. But interest was growing in an argu-
ment near the pool table.

Two men over there sounded as if they might
begin slugging it out. A gallery of men at the bar
urged them on. The big one the bartender was calling Mike looked nice enough—about Geoff's age
but beefier, wearing a silky flowered shirt. She
could tell from the way he had rolled the sleeves
back from his sunburned wrists that his arms were
too long for cheap shirts. She supposed he sold
aluminum siding. The other—were they calling
him Cletus?—was a fright. He was older and probably had lost that thumb in a corn picker. But how
to account, agriculturally, for the gaps in his dental
work? The two men moved toward the door, past
Abby's booth.

"Tell me about it," Cletus was jeering. "I guess
that piece of shit you're driving will go from zero to
sixty in about a week."

"It gets me to work," said Mike. "I've got no
complaints."

"You got no class," was Cletus's retort. "Hell,
that rattletrap's only held together by all the bug
guts on it."

"You can't paint horsepower onto the outsides,

Cletus," said Mike, winking over his shoulder at their buddies. "We better settle this out on the road."

Abby was unable to make much sense of what was going on. She was stunned at a thought which had just occurred to her. There was no spare tire in her trunk. The Mullens were sensible enough to own five tires, of course, four regular tires and a spare to match. But they were all stowed in the tidy garage off Farley Landing Road. They had been ever since the four snow tires were put on the car in November. The cat was nesting among them. She tried not to panic. There must be another solution.

Abby became aware that the room was now in motion; from dim corners she saw men materialize, drifting toward the door behind Cletus and his challenger.

The older man grinned wickedly, jingling keys and change in his pants pocket. "Attaboy," he said. "Wait 'n' see. I'll drag you's far as Brightbill's access road. Loser buys the rest of the night." A draft of cold air struck Abby's ankles and then the twosome passed behind her booth to the outside. They were followed by carousing drinkers—bets being made, money changing hands.

The waitress brought Abby's drink. "Wanna get in the pool? Cost you two bits."

"What's going on?" Abby ventured.

The waitress shook her head. "Oh those two! Every so once in a while they get at each other. Maybe it's sompin like a period, I dunno. Then they get goin' good and seems like they hafta work it out in the parking lot before another drink goes by."

"Fists?" Abby protested.

The waitress snickered dubiously. "I wouldn't bet on it. Though now't you mention, one time Cletus did paint Mike's dog green and we had to pull 'em apart about that."

Abby shuddered. "I couldn't bet on a fight."

The waitress leaned past her to swipe at the sugar bowl with her dish rag, and her breath was ripe with kielbasa. "Pf-f-f, it's all in fun."

"I'm more spectator than speculator," Abby said.

"Better get a different seat if you wanna see anything," she was advised. Then she noticed that the window beside her was blocked by a massive sheet of plywood. "That thing's been boarded up since Vernon put some fella through it before Christmas," the waitress complained. "Gets my dandruff up, too. Drafty enough in here as it is."

Abby slipped out of the booth and away from the waitress. Everybody in the place was crowded around the doorway. Now was not the time to attempt a discreet exit. She looked at the cartoon attached to the cash register once more. She had never seen anything like it. The claustrophobic frog was a scream. On an impulse, Abby lifted the drawing free and quickly folded it into her purse. She had no inkling what she might do with it, but she wanted it.

"Mike, you rapscallion," someone in the crowd chortled. Everyone laughed. There was no getting past that gallery, Abby knew. She might as well watch. She stood on tiptoe.

Outside two pick-up trucks were revving up, exhausts mixing with clouds of breath from bettors and drivers alike. From what Abby could see, their race to the road in itself would mean disaster, as both trucks would be vying for the same narrow channel amid casually parked vehicles. But no one seemed worried. Not even Cletus and Mike. They were cursing and laughing out their windows at each other, eyes homed on the starter's flashlight. She tottered against two men nearby and heard them saying something about Cletus. When she found another way to balance on her tiptoes again, she could see five of the men who had been betting on Mike now crouching down behind Cletus's truck: they were lifting his rear bumper. His rear wheels were off the ground. Then she stood down to rest, amazed to find she had been holding her breath. She scolded herself for getting so caught up in the contest. Ridiculous! Was she also the sort who would cheer for the lions, thumbing down a Christian for sheer love of disaster? As soon as the parking lot cleared she was going to leave. She did not belong here, and if it meant riding that snow-tread to ribbons she would limp to an all-night service station.

A shout: the signal must have come just then. She was heading back to her seat when flying gravel began pelting the windows. A pebble hit the neon "Bud" in the window nearest her; she saw it flare and go dark. Through the figures of men jumping in hilarity outside, she glimpsed Mike's truck darting onto the road beyond. Cletus was still on the mark, revving his engine amid howls of protest from his backers. The truck was not moving. Shouts were becoming more coarse, more specific. She heard boots scuffling on gravel. Afraid of a fight, Abby hurried back to her booth and the rusty drink awaiting her. No sooner was she in her seat than another piece of gravel blinded an Iron

City Beer sign over the bar.

"Aw!" the bartender began. Then pandemonium broke loose. A squeal of tires, hails of gravel over a roaring engine, followed immediately by the unmistakable crash-tinkle of another vehicle being hit. Silence. Oohs and aahs began drifting in the door. She heard the other truck return, and stop. The bartender started pouring fresh drinks at every stool.

Abby intended to get out of here. She slipped a dollar bill under her glass and stood up, ready to leave. On second thought, she turned back toward the men's room: she would call Geoff after all, let him know she was on her way to a service station. She had just put her dime into the telephone when she heard an uproar from the bar's entrance.

Mike and Cletus were returning to the bar wreathed with the guffaws of their friends. They had their arms around each other's shoulders and were laughing, leaning together, as if some fabulous joke might cripple them both. Money was changing hands again. Someone handed Mike a beer. "Hey!" he called out when he had wet his throat. "Hey, who owns that . . ."

"Used to be a Gremlin," Cletus snickered.

Abby hung up the telephone. A handful of people were mumbling, "Not mine." "No."

The knowledge that hers had to be the only Gremlin in the parking lot spread through Abby like a stain. She was genuinely frightened. Unsure what else to do, she invented a series of dumb explanations, ways she could make Geoff understand what had happened to the car, means to make him see that it was not her fault. But to understand, he would have had to be here. Geoff would never have been here. None of the explanations made sense to Abby either, so it must be her fault after all. Her eyes stung. Bracing herself for one more pass through that gauntlet of stares, she went out to survey the damage to the Mullen family car.

Mike followed her outside. He stood at a distance while she looked around. He saw her see the wide dent in the door on the passenger's side, the window a sagging curtain of pebbled safety glass. He saw the place she was prodding, where steel pressed against the right front tire. He watched her open the passenger's door, winced along with her when he heard its groans of resistance. He was just drunk enough that he could have watched her walk around her car, scowling, until breakfast. Wrapped up in that shawl he thought she looked like a little kid rousted out of bed for a surprise.

"I'm surprised about the rear tire," he told her. He did not want to scare her but plainly he had. She stared at him. "I can't figure out how he managed to hit you in so many places."

"I hope you have insurance," Abby ventured. It was not the money. But that was the only civilized reproach she could think of. She was almost in tears with her desire now to be home.

"Well I do, sure," Mike said. "But it's Cletus's truck has the marks to match yours. Want me to call him out?"

Abby was horrified at the thought of confronting two of these men under the lurid neon of the Rising Sun. One was bad enough. She spoke up in a hurry—anything to keep him at bay. "No, really, it's all right. My insurance will cover it, I'm sure."

Mike pulled out his wallet, saying, "It's probably hundred-dollar deductible. I'll be happy to make up the difference."

Abby backed away from his big hand. Mutely, she shook her head. For one awful instant she could see what they must look like—a strange man and woman dickering outside a tavern.

"I feel sort of bad about this," he was saying.

"You feel bad?" Abby found her voice. "I stopped at this madhouse because I had a simple flat tire."

"I'll change it for you," he offered. He went to his El Camino and started clattering around in a tool kit.

"What if I had been sitting in my car when the truck hit it?" she fumed, following him. "I might have been killed. If it's time for me to die, you know, I'll kill myself, thank you."

"But you weren't," he muttered. "How good's your spare tire?"

"I don't have a spare," Abby objected. "And now I can't even drive home!"

He looked over his shoulder at her. "You want me to take you home?"

"No!"

Mike straightened, bringing a crow bar to light, and a large aerosol can of some sort. "Then give me a couple of minutes to fix your tire, straighten out that fender so you don't get another flat on the way home. You live far from here?"

She declined to answer so personal a question. "I'm going to call my husband," she announced, hoping he would get the point. "And tell him when to expect me." Mike paid no attention but got busy instead wrenching the metal away from her front tire. Abby walked as far as the front door and then faltered. Even if it meant Geoff had to worry ten unnecessary minutes, she could not bring herself to go in again.

Abby stepped as quietly as possible to the Gremlin. Mike was forcing air from the can into her punctured rear tire. She watched his shoulders moving under that unnaturally shiny shirt.

Without looking around to see whether she was within earshot, he said, "If you change your mind, you can reach Cletus in there most nights." He jerked his head toward the bar. "Weeknights." He finished, stood up brushing loose gravel from the knees of his pants.

"Thank you," Abby said. She hurried to the driver's side and got in. With relief she discovered the engine turned over at once. All she wanted in the world was to be gone from here. To be safe at home in her own bed.

A big face appeared beside hers at the window. Abby cringed. Telling herself he was probably harmless, she rolled down the window.

"Take this along," Mike told her, dropping the Spare-In-A-Can onto her lap. "You might need it again on the way home."

Abby nodded grimly and put the car in reverse. She told herself she was not getting out of this car again, not for anything, until she pulled into the warm maw of her own garage. She would drive on the wheels themselves if need be. That man was going back in the tavern where he belonged as she pulled to the edge of the parking lot. She was glad to see him disappear. She slipped her mind into neutral as she drove onto the hardtop of good old Route 489. Everything was going to be all right.

As she searched for a radio station with soothing music, something in the ashtray caught her eye.

She picked it out—paper. Holding it up to the windshield she unfolded a pair of crisp fifty-dollar bills.

Mozart was bubbling quietly from the digital clock-radio on Geoff's side of the bed. Abby felt a pang, remembering what he had said when he left the car. He always turned on Ph.D. music when they planned to make love. The bathroom light glowed around a corner in its accustomed pre-coital way, waiting. But Geoff had fallen asleep. She did not feel like making love anyhow. With painstaking quiet she shed her clothes, switched off the light and radio, and eased into bed trying to make her presence no more than a quirk in the progress of Geoff's dream.

He rolled over. "Find my passport?" Even in his sleep he was full of expectation.

"Yes, love," whispered Abby. She folded herself into the curve at his belly and guided his hand to one breast. Sleep came at once in this position. It never failed.

CHAPTER FIVE

In the scurry of Geoff's departure preparations, there was very little made of the damaged car. Abby told him about the drunk who broadsided her in the parking lot, but he scarcely paid attention. She did not specify which parking lot. They were going through his wardrobe at the time—culling useful gabardines and compiling a shopping list. All that really mattered to Geoff was the bottom line: their Gremlin could still get him to the airport as planned. He muttered about the inconvenience of a shattered car window this time of year, seeming to blame it unfairly on "that riffraff" out where Esther lived, but Geoff always did suppose the worst possible things happen in trailer parks. He even half-believed trailers attract tornados, and when feeling playful could cite the statistics to prove it. At least he did not seem to blame her and there was no point in arguing about details, Abby felt, when they had more pressing business to deal with.

There was no time to dread missing Geoff. Right now she was immersed in her own competence as a helpmeet. There were two climates to pack for, dress for everything from cross-country to ceremonial dinners. And a fairly complicated itinerary to consider. Geoff's travel agent and the department secretary each called the house at least twice a day until Abby got on the phone and asked them to call each other. In fact it was Abby who suggested that the Foundation assign Geoff a secretary now, which simplified matters from then on.

Esther Sipe came in every day for one week straight and churned out clean laundry, fresh groceries, hot meals. This freed Abby for packing and shopping, and Geoff for prolonged telephone calls. The day Geoff absolutely had to go into town, Esther used her own car to ferry the little Mullens to school. Abby drove Geoff as far as campus, then swung downtown to find him some new Oxford cloth shirts. The night Geoff was rehearsing his speech to the conference, she farmed out Toby and Gabrielle to Maxine Gerber, and stayed up late with him organizing his slides.

She made lists. Her mind clicked along with admirable precision. She remembered to re-stock his shaving kit, which had not been used since their last ski trip. She went to the bank and got enough British currency to spare him the trouble during his brief stopover in London. Only once did she draw a blank: leaving Mellon Square she found two fifty-dollar bills in her wallet. Oh yes. She promptly transferred them to her pocketbook sewing kit and put them out of her mind. Then there was an uncooperative dry cleaner to contend with, which she did once and for all. She even fielded a couple of student inquiries in Geoff's office while she waited for him to slip down to university hospital for a fast check-up.

She made appointments. Some dinners could not

be avoided. It would be positively rude, Geoff felt, to leave their social life untended when he was going to be gone so often this year. Abby saw his point. So Professor Mullen's staff at the university came for an informal evening of fettucini and charades, which they all pronounced fun when they wished him bon voyage at the door. His new secretary at the Foundation had to be taken across town for Lebanese. Then the couples who always had Symphony seats flanking the Mullens' went with Abby and Geoff to a wonderful new place in the East Hills, where they tasted each others' entrees. Geoff's yellow pike was the best choice, they agreed. Abby tried to squeeze in a morning meeting of Geoff and Toby's piano teacher, but their schedules clashed hopelessly. There were not even a couple hours left over to see Jerry's pride and joy —plans converting the Gerbers' back yard into a tennis court this spring. Even as long as the four of them had been waiting for this blessed event, Geoff could not concentrate on tennis now. He nearly despaired of getting the essentials covered before he left. Not Abby.

She knew Geoff's departure was superbly organized. After all, this was her profession. She even had enough energy to spare for surprises. At a bookstore near her hairdresser's shop, she chose a good-looking new appointment book just the right size for a man's inner pocket. While she was at it, she chose one volume of light reading in case the time difference disrupted his sleeping habits, and a present for him to give the children.

Having her hair trimmed and protein-treated was one of those essentials she saved for the last minute. At the risk of getting home with too little time to spare, she went into Betty's for the works. She wanted Geoff's freshest picture of her to be a spruce one.

"Isn't she darling," Mrs. Curran told Betty as Abby hurried out once more. "You'd never guess she has two school-age children." Mrs. Curran exaggerated: Gabrielle Mullen was in nursery school.

The beautician reached a quick feel under Mrs. Curran's dryer, then moved on to unravel Mrs. Lewin's rollers. "Yeah. Sweet face," she said. "I only wish I could talk her into letting me rinse the hair. She's got a few grey ones coming in now and it doesn't go with the look at all."

"I noticed that. I sit behind her in the choir at church," replied Mrs. Curran.

"Now her husband—you know Geoff?" Betty asked. "He could use a little grey around the temples. He just doesn't look the part of a professor. Almost too cute, you know?"

Mrs. Lewin lighted a cigarette, talking around the filter. "I heard he quit the university."

"Not on your life," Mrs. Curran begged to disagree. "He's got tenure. He's much too responsible to walk out on that kind of security. With those kids, and Abby?"

Abby could not help being a little bit tense about dinner the night before Geoff left. He insisted that the whole family should have dinner together—sort of an observance. He claimed it would help Toby and Gabrielle comprehend that he was not deserting them or their mother. That he should even mention such a thing was distasteful to Abby,

but she knew the kids would appreciate the party
aspect of dinner. They seldom ate together. Abby
had started feeding the children separately when
Geoff first began working odd hours, but even
those nights when he was expected on time she continued the practice. It was easier: Geoff tended to
get upset at the sloppy way children naturally ate.
He upset them sometimes too, never having
learned the funky logic of childish conversation.
Often, until the dual dinners policy was estab-
lished, Geoff corrected their manners or their English before he heard what was on their minds and
spoiled the climate for kid revelations. But if Geoff
wanted to have dinner with their children tonight,
Abby would not demur. Besides, she could not
help welcoming this sign that Geoff did expect to
be homesick while he was gone.

She worried briefly that Gabrielle would spill
something on him. She did not want a scene to mar
their last supper.

Then she felt silly for thinking in terms of a "last
supper."

Then she realized that Geoff was just vain
enough to think a last supper climate was appropriate. He would be leaving his family to fend
for themselves for two whole weeks.

Smiling at Geoff behind his back, she put bright
linen on the dining room table. She put full place
settings at all four places—soup spoons, salad
forks and all. She got out a wedding present can-
delabrum and added eight different colored
candles. She called her family for dinner promptly
at six-thirty.

Toby had decided on his own to "dress" for dinner. Abby was astonished when he appeared downstairs promptly—blazer, clean socks, hair more or less brushed. Gabrielle took her cue from him and made her entrance a moment later wearing one of Geoff's ties.

For the most part dinner was a success. As it happened, the day's crop of stories from school was blessedly devoid of cloakroom bloodletting or mouse placentas. Neither child balked at tasting Portuguese kale soup. In fact, they both appeared to be engaged in a contest for the good manners championship of Farley Landing. Better still, Geoff seemed to have left all his preoccupations in that attache case upstairs and really listened to the kids talk. He was as accommodating as he would have been in a seminar. It was easy: tonight he did not have to compete with them for their mother's attention. Tonight everyone agreed on who was the star attraction.

Toby had lots of questions about airplanes— would Daddy be flying back in the same 747 or did he think there was any hope of getting a ride on Concorde? Would there be any chance of seeing the cockpit?

Gabrielle wanted to know about bugs.

"Will they have bugs there, Geoff?" she inquired, salad fork gripped firmly in one fist and a dripping spear of romaine in the other.

Abby watched to see what would happen. Gabrielle had acquired several presumptions since entering nursery school; one of them was addressing her parents as equals and it infuriated Geoff. Abby had counseled waiting until they might learn what this quirk meant, but usually Geoff played

deaf until Gabey relented and called him "Daddy."
For the moment, however, he was letting it pass.

"Bugs?" he answered. "I'm not sure, to tell you
the truth." Bravely he kept his eyes from the salad
oil running down her elbow. "Norway's pretty far
north, so they may be all covered up with snow."

"But later," she insisted.

"In the spring? Maybe so. Every country I've
heard of has its own insect population."

Gabrielle was looking cagey. "Will they have ladybugs?" she asked.

Abby could not account for this interest in *Coc-
cinellidae,* but she said nothing, waiting.

"I'll find out and write you a letter, how's that?"

"Will they have Avon ladybugs?" Gabrielle
grinned.

"Avon ladybugs?" Geoff repeated. "Do you
think you might mean aphids?" He was plainly
baffled, concentrating too hard on being a good
father to get the joke. His attention wandered back
to the dripping food in his daughter's hand.

But a pang of delight ran through Abby. This
was Gabrielle's first wordplay. Their youngest was
now inventing jokes, and Abby thought that deserved a party in itself. Gabrielle was definitely
growing a mind of her own. Abby and Gabrielle
both were enjoying this change far more than her
previous, literal weaning.

Only half-hearing Geoff's discourse on insects,
Abby served baked clams and rummaged through
her feelings about her daughter's blossoming
private life. But much as she envied Gabey the
fresh start, she could not discover any regret, no
hint of that empty-nest depression she had felt
when Toby began growing away from her. This

time she would probably not be homesick for a baby. With pleasure she tucked away "Avon ladybugs," simply looking forward to more.

Dessert was a splurge—Mexican raspberries drenched in cream. They all had a good time watching the cream slither around each seed. Geoff made licentious eyes at Abby over the children's heads. There was espresso and, for some, cocoa in tiny gilt demitasses. Then Abby brought out the present she had bought for Geoff to give to them— something he would have chosen himself if he had thought of it—a book of photographs picturing rural Norway. He was very pleased. He led Toby and Gabrielle into the family room for a look at the globe.

Smiling, Abby cleared the table. Through the doorway she enjoyed the sight of her husband, an unlikely madonna, ensconced between her children. They were leafing through the book together. Geoff was deliberately being patient with them. She appreciated his special effort. He probably was worried about going away after all. She fought down the knowledge, which ungraciously suggested itself, that the Mullen household would not be plunged into utter disarray by Geoff's absence. No matter what he thought. But she would never embarrass him by saying so.

She moseyed back and forth between the dining room and kitchen, listening to Geoff's tenor voice gently droning on about fiords. Bedtime stories had become a rare treat in her life. She wished it would go on forever. The dishwasher practically loaded itself.

Abby knew their special-occasion lovemaking

ceremonies by heart, which made her a good lover, Geoff thought. He folded down the covers while she got into the shower.

He took pride in how much he was going to please her, and methodically hung up his slacks.

He looked forward to the cheerful ways she found to please him. He joined her in the shower.

"Do you want me to shave?" he asked her.

Abby made room for him under the water, turning to squint into his face. "Oh, I don't know," she burbled. "Doesn't look very scratchy to me."

He nuzzled his face around her cheeks and all she did was smile, so he decided not to bother shaving. Obediently he stood still while Abby lathered his back. God love her, she made it a massage.

"Turn."

He turned around. She looked like a pastry chef in that shower cap, but at least the pillows would not get wet later on. He looked down at her with affection. It tickled him the way she gave him what they had always agreed was a perfectly dirty lathering. Nothing like these homey bouts of bawdiness; Geoff could not imagine why bachelors would want to bother with random couplings—full as they must be of predictable discomforts, surprise disappointments. Abby was just right. A sweet little body, a steady and attentive match for him. There was nothing mysterious or scarey about making love to her, he thought, and she had long since outgrown those eerie moods of aggressive randiness which used to crop up periodically. Sixteen years of marriage had groomed her into a very considerate sex partner. She never left marks on his back—something Jerry Gerber suffered at

Maxine's hands whenever they were on speaking terms. Even with her knees pressing into his ribs, Abby was a woman with her feet solidly on the ground. Tonight he meant to convey his gratitude for all that. They toweled dry quickly.

A wave of pity churned in Geoff's pelvis for this good woman who would sleep alone so many nights this year. She deserved better. But then he reminded himself that the cycle of her appetites had wide loops in it; he smiled slightly to think she might actually welcome a vacation from his courtships. And she was going to appreciate him so much the more, afterward. Let's see, he thought, counting every trip out of town that will make about five honeymoons this year, at least.

He started at her toes. Abby loved nothing better than a definitive foot rub, he knew that. Her eyes were drifting shut when their bedside radio began to exude the passionate first movement of *Sinfonie Pathetique*. Perfect.

Morning, on the other hand, was mayhem. Just as it was time to leave Abby took a telephone call that she should have let go. Geoff paced between breakfast nook and sink, carrying his dishes, Abby's dishes; the kids were still dawdling over their breakfast. He looked at Abby for help. She was still talking and turned her back to him. "No problem," she was saying. Phone tucked under her chin, she was taking foil-wrapped loaves from the freezer. "I'll stop by this morning."

At last Geoff caught her eye, pointing to his watch. She mouthed "milk money" at him.

"Do you need milk money?" Geoff asked Toby. Toby was in the third grade and already suspected of buying colas in vending machines. Toby shook his head no.

"Do you need milk money?" Geoff asked Gabrielle. Gabrielle shook her head. She reached for the quilted purse she had hooked over the back of her chair. She dipped it into her cereal bowl in the process, but the spill did not faze her. She scooped a large quantity of milky money onto the tabletop.

"Where did you get all that money, Gabey?" Geoff wanted to know. Gabrielle shrugged. She was busy mopping up milk with her placemat. These kids were becoming rather unruly under Abby's laissez-faire conventions, he thought, and anarchy would probably be the house specialty by the time he came home again. "Have you been taking money from my dresser?"

"It's mine," Toby bellowed, lunging at his sister.

"Not!" wailed Gabrielle. She jerked away from Toby and sent her cereal bowl, spoon and all, skittering to the floor.

"Abby!" Geoff insisted. "Where does Gabrielle get all that money?" Something would have to be done.

Abby hung up the phone and reached for her parka. "She sold one of her kittens to the meter reader." Gabrielle was in tears, but Abby calmly wiped milk from the little slacks and handed her daughter into a parka. Geoff gave up trying to referee. He stood by the stairs to the garage with his luggage—reasonable vanguard of a daft tribe.

"Write notes excusing the kids," he told Abby. "We'll have to go to the airport first and they'll just have to be late for school."

But Abby had it all figured out. With a few fluid gestures she directed Toby into his windbreaker, Gabrielle downstairs, two foil-wrapped loaves under one of her arms and Geoff's attache case into his hands. "We'll go the back way," she said. "There's plenty of time."

What a woman, he congratulated himself.

The kids had already forgotten that today was special by the time they pulled into the school driveway. Geoff took care to get out of the car and kiss them goodbye so they would not feel sad he was going. Toby pecked his cheek fast, then ran up the pavement to a small swarm of boys. Gabrielle chose this morning to do her dying swan number in his arms when he tried to hug her. She was still curtseying at them as the car pulled onto Chatham Road.

Geoff was an irritable passenger. Abby steered their course expertly through the potholes and bottlenecks of Allegheny River Boulevard, but he found the ride too rough for studying his itinerary. And the crazed window on his side permitted very little sightseeing. "Did Esther get you that fellow's number?" he asked.

"What fellow, love?" She finessed a yellow light and gained the left-turn lane of the Highland Park bridge without missing a beat.

"The drunk who ran into you at the trailer park," he said. "You thought she might be able to find out who it was or something." Abby was maddeningly opaque this morning. If he didn't keep after her, it occurred to Geoff, she would probably drive around with a shattered window and bashed-in fender the whole time he was gone. The woman had no respect for equipment. Almost as bad as the kids on that score. Like last Easter when she and Toby tried to incubate an orphaned wren's egg in the electric crockpot he had just bought her. That was his fault, really. She lacked his technical appreciation for state-of-the-art anything, he should have realized, and she cried for hours when she found out he'd tossed that louse-ridden nest down the Dispos-All. He knew now his pride should not have been so bound up in the gift of a simple appliance; he tried not to let Abby's daffy priorities ruffle him any more. After all, she was pretty sensible about what mattered most. "I want you to have it repaired before I come back. I'm not going to look like a yokel in the Foundation parking lot," he grumbled.

"I'll call Frank Wechsler about it today," she said. "It'll come to more than enough for our deductible."

"Um," Geoff said. "But we're stuck for the first hundred, right?"

Abby was soothing. "And this year you'll be making twice what you were before," she reminded him. "If you fret more than a minute on this it's time wasted."

She was right; he did have more important things to worry about. "While it's in the garage," were his final words on the subject, "make sure they fix the windshield wipers."

He consulted his watch as they whizzed past traffic stalled in the inbound lanes from Greentree. Abby was going to get them to the airport on time, as promised, so he tried to relax. He rechecked the pocket where he knew his ticket was. "Now," he told her, "don't forget to get an estimate from the septic tank man." She was paying attention—he could tell by the lift of her chin. "Toby's music teacher can wait 'til I get back. Don't even discuss it with her. She needs to come to an understanding with me," he added sternly.

"If you need to get in touch with me, Sylvia at the Foundation will have a constant update for every stop on our itinerary. If you need anything minor, just call Jerry Gerber." Abby nodded. "Are you sure you won't be lonely?"

"Of course I will," Abby reassured him.

Geoff thought of a favor to ask, a sort of time-release obligation to make sure she would mind his absence. "Do you think you could do a little something with the Fairchildren while I'm gone?" he said. He meant Chris and Kit Fairchild, of course; in private he and Abby always called them that. "They've been after us since before Thanksgiving, and he's such a relentless twirp."

"I've promised her Gabrielle's stroller," Abby offered.

"Good. Take it over on a Saturday and stay for coffee a few minutes. That ought to hold them for a little while. He wants me to politick for his tenure," Geoff complained. "And I haven't decided I will. He's a sloppy scholar." He glanced at Abby. She was nodding gravely.

He marveled at what a good sport she was, his Guid Wyfe, and at how wise he had been that first year in grad school to pick her out of all those juniors working the reference desk. The opulent charms of college juniors. Another ten minutes in bed this morning would have been nice. But no, just as well; they were only now pulling to the curb at Foreign Carriers, and look at those lines.

Abby got out to help him lift his bags to the curb. "What do you want me to bring you from Oslo?" Geoff kissed her.

"I don't know," she smiled. "A first edition of Selma Lagerlof?"

He approved and kissed her again.

"Have a good trip," she called after him.

CHAPTER SIX

The Allegheny River was busy this morning. Not that it ever seemed to move fast. It was too wide and deep for that. But winter was decaying these days and the river was hauling it away. There was already a hint of spring in the way its smooth current was bearing shards of rotten ice downstream. Where the ice caught against last year's defunct growth the rubble was being torn clear, plowed under in a steady sweep. On to Ohio and longer days. Ice still corseted twigs wherever branches touched the stream, but the dark soil of the banks was soaking up more sunlight each day. Soon every maple along this road would break out in chartreuse fuzz. About that time the river would rise, flooded with melting ice from its mountain tributaries and with warmer rains. The river would turn brown while everything else was turning green, brown to its five-fathom depths. Then would come the fish—mostly scavengers—up from the mud, followed by men from Blawnox. Darker lumps in the dark the fishers would sit out spring evenings with their beer and dead catch, no more than the undersides of their noses lit up by sparks in the bowls of their pipes. And then the blare of summer sun, summer

thunderstorms. The river would be gaudy with
speedboats and waterskiers. Abby would be glad
for the arched foliage that would be veiling these
banks as she passed. Now was the river's best time.
Unruffled by traffic this morning, it simply went
on. The quiet was almost palpable.

Abby took it to heart. Turning off Allegheny
River Boulevard into town, she promised herself to
sit in the middle of her quiet house today and feel
like that river. But first she had errands to finish.

Into the Presbyterian church basement with two
loaves of carrot bread for the Fresh Air Fund bake
sale. Many thanks. "Any time."

Into The Ten O'Clock Scholar for coffee, by
chance, with Kit Fairchild. Maternal inquiries, arrangements concerning Gabrielle's stroller. And
"Don't let anyone tell you it doesn't hurt. Especially afterwards, with the hemorrhoids!"

Into the Holiday Inn up to the car rentals desk.
"Mastercharge."

The garage. "How long do you *think* it'll take to
get a window?"

Lunch at the zoo. (She was the only mama without a snowsuited toddler lunging along at the end
of her arm.) A phone booth, an insurance-adjust-
ing voice: "Frank Wechsler, please?" The grocery
store. Italian meat market. The school (almost
home).

Maxine Gerber left her car and walked over to
lean on Abby's. Any moment now the school doors
would open and gush children. "New car," she observed. "To go with the new job?"

Abby shook her head. "The Gremlin's on sabbatical."

They contemplated the stairs to Ellsworth

Academy in silence for a few moments. "He's going to sleep around, you know," Maxine announced. Abby did not budge. "You're giving him the perfect opportunity by staying here."

"I'll be going along later," Abby said with a smile. "When things aren't so chaotic."

"*Later* he'll have one in every port. He's at that age, believe it."

Abby made a face. "Not Geoff. Everybody's got Herpes II except you, me, and our mothers. He read me the statistics from one of Jerry's journals last year. The odds are very bad for casual contact."

"Which reminds me," Maxine said. "What are you going to do with yourself while Geoff perfects shuttle scholarship? Read?"

"What's the matter with reading?"

"If you're going to do that," her friend urged, "you might as well go back to school. Finish your degree. Get another one!"

Abby could not resist laughing. "Please no! I already have the equivalent of two Masters in faculty parties alone," she protested. "You're selling Frigidaires to Nanook." This was an old contest for them. Maxine considered herself Abby's dearest friend and she could be very stern about what a junkyard of potential Abby was.

"What are you gonna do?" Maxine demanded. "Without Geoff to take care of, you'll start chewing your tail!"

"There's plenty to do," she responded in her most reasonable voice. But she hoped she was not going to be invited to itemize.

"Hah! You can only shampoo the carpets so many times. I know you. Abby Mullen, don't you dare waste this whole vacation brewing up home-made vegetable stock. *Do* something for yourself. Get a job."

Gabrielle spared Abby by jumping between them and madly waving a finger painting. "That's lovely, Gabey," she said. "Is it an Avon ladybug?"

"No," Gabrielle huffed, climbing into the back seat. "A nangel."

Maxine peered in at the little girl. "Did Dylan come out with you?"

Toby vaulted into the front seat, hands instantly all over the dials and switches. "Far out," he rejoiced. "We got a new car?"

"Over here, Dylan," Maxine called. Then she leaned in again to hear Toby's story.

He was saying, "Mrs. Hinkle's gonna have a baby. She told us all about it."

"That's good," Abby said. "We talked about that too, remember?"

Toby nodded. "About how first it's like a little fish, and then it grows fingers and stuff. And how you get one." Abby nodded.

Dylan's tiny fingers were turning white on the car door as he tried to lift himself far enough to see inside.

"But I still don't think it'll work," Toby continued. He pointed to the wrinkled corduroy at his crotch. "I don't think that's long enough to get way up inside a mother's uh . . ."

"Womb," Abby finished for him. "Don't worry," she added comfortingly. "That develops automatically as you get older."

"Right," Maxine muttered. "Along with the taste for gin, power, and jalapeño dip." She took

Dylan's hand, turning to go. "Call me when you get them to bed."

As it turned out Abby was in no condition to do so. Her curious mood of recent days resolved itself into a bout of flu that same evening. She felt vaguely guilty about getting sick; her father had always told her that illness was an attitude problem and he ought to know, having finally died of one. But she ached too badly to keep moving on a matter of principle. She crept into bed as soon as the children were tucked in.

Toby must have called Esther early in the morning. At any rate, she was there when Abby opened her sticky eyes. She put a hot mug of coffee in Abby's hands. Then she must have taken the kids to school. Abby was not sure: it took all her energy to get that mug close enough to her face so that she could breathe the steam.

When Abby next opened her eyes, Esther was sopping up coffee from the bedspread and asking her if she could eat some breakfast. Or maybe it was lunch . . . Abby was not quite sure, because the canned cream of something Esther spooned into her mouth smelled a lot like the lunches she used to eat long, long ago when children still walked home from school at lunchtime.

A tottery trip into the bathroom exhausted her resources.

That evening—or maybe it was another evening—Esther brought in some mail and pulled the covers into place for Abby. The mail consisted of a few extremely heavy periodicals, a garage sale flier, and a form her insurance man wanted her to fill out. Esther plumped up the pillows in case she wanted

to look at magazines, and brought an extra comforter in case she got chilly sitting up. But Abby did
not feel like reading. It seemed terribly important
to her that she fill out this form for Frank
Wechsler. When Esther was gone, she dragged
herself all the way across the bed to the drawer
where Geoff stashed writing things for his midnight brainstorms. She spent minutes, shivering,
choosing a blue felt-tip pen. At last she fell back on
the mound of pillows, dragged her knees up and
spread out the insurance form to take a look.

It was not the questions that confounded her. It
was the drawing these insurance people wanted her
to make. Abby sighed. Her eyeballs ached. They
wanted her to squeeze in all the vehicular chaos of
The *Friendly* Rising Sun parking lot—the pickup
truck with its rear axle held off the ground by four
drunken men, the El Camino driven by an
enormous grinful of white teeth, the spectators
crowding about and waving money—they expected
her to indicate all that commotion within the con-
fines of a tiny, symmetrical crossroad printed on
this form. It could not be done. "I might be a
modest little faculty wife," she found herself thinking, "but when I have an automobile accident it is
something grander than Geoff's insurance man can
imagine."

Giggling, she balled up the insurance form with
her last iota of strength and let it roll out of her
fingers onto the garage sale flier.

As she drifted off to sleep it occurred to her that
she had a very high fever. "I must have," she reasoned. "Because here I am hallucinating wild
parties in a roadhouse I do not patronize, and wor-

rying that some invisible authority wants me to draw pictures about it."

Esther called a doctor some time while Abby was sick. The only phone number she could find was a pediatrician the Mullens used for Toby and Gabrielle. He listened to Esther's recitation of Abby's symptoms, assured her it was something that was "going around", and left instructions to get as many fluids into the patient as possible. Esther did not go home much during that time. She might have called Abby's mother and asked her to fly in as a sort of relief housekeeper; a lesser woman would have done so. But Esther considered herself Abby's friend. Abby had always been decent with her and now she simply did what needed doing.

The children were quiet. It seemed to relax them to have so little traffic through the house. And from the night Web showed up with a six pack and Esther's portable TV, they were even more contented. She put her little television set on the table in the breakfast nook, instantly making the kitchen the center of the household. They watched avidly, even local news.

The house was very easy to keep clean. Living room, dining room and family room stayed dark and quiet for days. Nobody used the front hall, except when Esther shooed Toby and Gabrielle up to bed. No one opened the sideboard at six-thirty each day and poured Scotch with a clink into a perfect Dansk tumbler. (Nobody used the Dansk glasses at all.) No one filled the telephone pad with intricate geometrical doodles. No one lit fires in the fireplaces or straightened pictures on the walls.

There was no one to light up the slim green pilot of the sound system and fill the house with loud horn concerti. While the lady of the house wrestled with flu, in the absence of the lord, at least Esther kept vital signs going. There was always a light on in the kitchen—the ceiling light or TV—and by turns the dishwasher, washing machine or dryer made comfortable little noises. One night, to the click of pant snaps slapping against the clothes dryer drum, Web made hurried love to Esther in the utility room while they waited for a frozen pizza to finish baking. So although the climate in the rhododendron-hedged house on Farley Landing Road was not precisely the same as usual, it did stay warm enough to shelter two kids and one delirious woman.

Abby abandoned herself to the virus completely when she realized that she did not have to be in charge of anyone's welfare. Then being ill was no longer a fever so much as a narcotic. It was almost pleasant to drift from the yellowish sleep of daytime to the blinding sleep of nighttime, and back, feeling her body fight on its own account with no interference from her. The most her mind did for her in four days was to identify the male voice she heard rumbling downstairs one night. Even that was invalidly done: the voice belonged to Esther's Web, but Abby felt certain it emanated from the man with the long arms and short shirtsleeves who fixed her flat tire.

Her first coherent thought in six days came one rainy afternoon when the bed seemed to be moving. Odd, the bed actually *was* moving. A midget was climbing onto it lugging a huge volume of iconography. Abby opened her eyes wide. "Abby!" it hissed at her.

"Gabrielle," Abby murmured, slipping further under the covers.

"I'm going to read you a story."

"A bedtime story, baby buzzard. Abby's very tired."

"About a bad little boy," Gabrielle said firmly, opening the book.

A bad little boy. Abby came awake in a hurry. "Where's Toby?"

"Downstairs. With Esther. They're talking to Geoff."

Downstairs? Abby sat up trying to clear her head, then eased her body stiffly toward the bedside phone. "Hello," she tried, then cleared her throat and tried again. "Hello? Geoff?" she managed to say brightly enough.

Geoff's voice thanked Esther again, waited for her to disconnect, then repeated for Abby's sake the explanation for his change of hotels. He hoped she had not been worried. He had better accommodations now and was quite enthusiastic about his work. Abby lay down on her pillow, wedging her ear into position with Geoff's pillow. His progress report warbled cheerfully out of the receiver.

She was bone tired.

"No, really, we're doing fine," she said. "I caught a bug, I guess. A ladybug," and she chuckled weakly. She added a few more "fines" and "that's goods" wherever she heard a gap in Geoff's voice, and watched Gabrielle slide from the bed dragging the comforter behind her. Geoff was saying how much she would enjoy seeing the steep roofs of this little town, their chimneys aflutter with sea gulls. He said something else too.

Abby woke up later feeling better. She felt well

enough, in fact, to attempt a shower. Water felt harsh on her skin, but once she got used to being wet she was glad for the cleansing. Lifting her chin, she let the water beat down on her breasts and belly. She stood that way a long time, breathing steam, letting her mind drift pleasantly to sensuous things. She fancied herself standing under a waterfall in a pool with a young man who wore nothing more than one hibiscus behind his ear. He was all skin, no face. Then a face came to her—a nice manly face belonging to that stranger out at the *Friendly* Rising Sun. Suddenly she remembered the two crisp fifty-dollar bills again. They were somewhere in her pocketbook, awaiting disposition. One hundred dollars was still a substantial sum, regardless of Geoff's new fortunes. It was unbudgeted cash.

Washing vigorously between her toes, relishing the good feel of restored circulation, she pondered that money. She was tempted to do something silly with it, something festive. It was the first money in her possession that was not community property.

But to play fair, she should spend it on something Geoff would not enjoy anyhow, something he could not possibly feel left out of. She thought of spending it all in a posh cosmetics salon downtown. Abby had been wondering for months whether she might be approaching that age where makeup disguises more problems than it creates. Maybe this was a good occasion to take up painting her face.

One hundred dollars might buy a definitive cashmere sweater (too practical), or a St. Bernard puppy (too impractical).

She would spend the money flying to Montreal for dinner with an old friend—if she had an old friend in Montreal. Or if she had a friend who was not also Geoff's.

Toweling off, she thought it might be better to give the money to charity and get it off her hands. Still, the opportunity of one hundred dollars nagged at her.

As she crawled into bed for a rest, she gave up trying to divine just the right way to handle it. Ridiculous, worrying about it so much. Going to sleep she dreamed, or reasoned, that the only thing to do with two crisp fifty-dollar bills was to return them to the poor working stiff who had troubled her with them in the first place. She did not want to take his money. No doubt he could ill afford to spare one hundred dollars, regardless how reckless he was with other people's property.

When Abby woke up next she knew she was well. She came alert light and dry under her covers, fully aware that she was wasting time somehow, and that the thermostat was just switched on. She sat up and looked around. From here the house seemed completely dark. She dressed deliberately, taking pleasure in the rough, adult feel of her slacks and sweater after days of helplessly soft, crumpled nighties. Scratching an itchy spot on her hand, she wandered toward the light of her children's rooms.

All was peaceful. Toby, wet-haired and pajamaed, was making faces in his mirror. He did not see her. Gabrielle was slack-jawed with sleep, surrounded in her bed by coffee table books, a bean bag bunny, and a small bronze Giacometti reproduction jammed into a Barby Doll dress. She retrieved her woolly slippers from Gabey's closet floor and stepped into them.

She moved downstairs where cozy sounds were coming from the kitchen.

Esther was scrubbing mud from Toby's sneakers with a vegetable brush. She smiled into the window above the sink when Abby's reflection appeared there. "Jeez, you must be starving," she said. "Want me to fix you something?"

Abby shook her head and opened the refrigerator. It was full of exotic things with names that sounded like Andy Warhol stars—Dream Whip, Wish Bone French, Velveeta, Brown N Serve Parker House—not the plain produce Abby usually brought home. Diet Rite ginger ale looked delicious. She poured some into a mug.

Esther blotted water from her cast thoughtfully. "You feeling some better?"

"Yes, thank you," said Abby. Then coming to herself, she added quickly, "I'm so glad you're here, thanks much! Have you been staying over?"

Esther nodded. "Hope you don't mind, I fed Web here a couple times. When he got off work this morning I went home with him for a while, too. We returned the rent-a-car for you on the way. Picked up your Gremlin on the way back." Her good homely growl went on about similar facts of Abby's life while Abby nodded her thanks, thinking this must be what it is like to have a wife.

"The bill's up there in the cake saver," Esther continued. "Along with the grocery store receipts."

"Good. Thanks."

"I filled up the tank on your credit card, by the way. So your car's all set to take the young'uns to school tomorrow. And drive to the airport Friday if I don't come in for a few days, right?"

"Friday?" Abby misunderstood, thinking only that Esther certainly deserved to have Friday to herself. "Surely, why not?"

Esther grinned knowingly. "I *thought* you fell asleep before he hung up!" she said. "I came upstairs to check on you—you know, after Geoff called that time? You were sound asleep on the phone. He'll be home day after tomorrow. He just called again this afternoon to make sure."

It was all coming back to her now. Geoff *had* called—something about seagulls. She scratched her hand reflectively. Already Geoff was heading here from Norway and she had had no time to really miss him. She had missed something, however. All that private time she had worried about, all the loneliness she had intended to sample, the river thoughts.

"What's wrong with your hand?" Esther wanted to know.

Abby answered "Nothing" right away, just as Toby might have done, and then looked down at her hands. She had scratched raw the skin between three fingers on her left hand.

Esther looked closer. "Doesn't look like nothing to me," she muttered.

"Actually it itches like crazy," Abby admitted.

"Don't touch it!" Esther hissed. Abby looked up in surprise. "Don't touch anything that looks that bad. And don't get any soap on it. Here," she ordered Abby.

The bath of baking soda and water that Esther trickled over her fingers helped for a while. But the rash did not heal.

CHAPTER SEVEN

The El Camino jolted across a frost heave in the road as Mike Vogel swung into the crunching parking lot outside The *Friendly* Rising Sun. Lunchtime, and for a change he was within range of a decent bowl of chili. He had washed the truck at Gladney's a minute ago. Now he hopped out, took an old T-shirt from the glove compartment, and wiped a few waterdrops from the shiny chrome of his bumper. He reached into the pocket where he kept his wallet. Squatting down behind his truck he gingerly peeled the protective backing from a bumper sticker. One side of his mouth wriggled in amusement as his long, flat fingers smoothed out the message in hot pink on khaki: Fish and Game Commission Personnel Make Better Lovers. Jamming the leftover papers into his pocket, he went inside for lunch.

Abby quickly looked down when he came in. She was having lunch in an out-of-the-way booth, and had been enjoying her anonymity until then. The bar was quiet, comfortingly dim on a bright spring midday. Stopping here for lunch rather than at the Brackenridge Club, where she usually met someone after errands, was something like Gabey's baby game of "You can't see me," a wickedly safe feeling of being hidden behind one small hand. She was outside the house, but out of social circulation still. No one here knew her. It was a refreshing change. True, this place lacked leaded glass windows straining sunshine down two-story-high walls onto her while she had her soup du jour. In fact, the Rising Sun waitress had wisecracked, she didn't have any du jour today, only a fresh pot of navy bean. And there would surely be no cappuchino for dessert. But then neither did she have to crowd in with legions of students, teachers and professors all babbling about their own progress through the stations of erudition. Here two people were arguing quietly, pointing at the TV. Their ire at the game show in question made no demands on her. Two others bent over the green felt table where billiard balls clacked softly together and rolled down troughs. Nobody seemed to be on a schedule. The sense of detachment she felt was restful. Until he came in.

Go on, she urged herself. This is your chance to get rid of those two fifty-dollar bills. She knew standing up would make her conspicuous. But the money was her legitimate errand here. The right thing to do was to walk straight up to that man, explain simply in her most well-bred tones that his courtesy had been much appreciated, however unnecessary, and to excuse herself promptly. She did not move.

"Come on, Vernon," the waitress called out to a young giant in a Purina Feeds cap. She thumbed a series of quarters into an iridescent juke box. "It's my birthday, you know."

Abby watched dumbly as the waitress pulled on

the giant's elbow. Mike was not paying attention to them. Neither was the bartender. But Abby found this couple mystifying. The waitress had twenty-five years on that boy, and no waist. Nevertheless she obviously did have prurient interests.

"It was your birthday last week," Vernon grumbled. "Remember? Bought ya 'nough black-berry brandy about it."

"Apricot. One measley shot."

The waitress tugged at his arm again. When he turned on his barstool to brush her away, his small beef-shrouded eyes fell on Abby's for a moment.

Abby promptly took a deeper interest in her soup. The curious pair of voices continued.

"It wouldn't kill you to dance with me once," the waitress said. She must have made her selections now, because a pair of hillbilly fiddles gashed the air.

"Don't want to dance with you," Vernon said, getting to his feet slowly as a bull does.

"Sure ya do."

Vernon was weaving across the linoleum to Abby's booth. There was no one else nearby. She knew he was going to speak to her. Small hairs on the back of her neck stood up. She could not get around to the door without making a scene. An adenoidal female voice was keening out of the juke box and Abby wanted to slide under the table.

"Dance, miss?" Vernon asked, holding himself up by the bill of his cap.

"I don't know how," Abby said.

Vernon leaned heavily on his hands, propping himself against her table. "Follow your heart," he advised.

Abby could think of nothing to say. She made herself smaller.

Vernon leaned closer.

"Come on, tiger," she heard Mike's voice say. "I bet Ron you could sink three more balls than him on the first break. Don't let him make a liar out of me."

Vernon swung his head around with a happy smile. "How much?"

"Enough."

The giant took the cue his friend handed him and lumbered off toward the pool table, just as intent now on racking up as he had been a moment before on making out.

Mike stayed behind, looking bluntly into Abby's face. "Come dance," he said, and held out his hand.

She was astounded. Of course he was crude. If he hung out here he was no finer than the rest of them. But she had guessed he would have been too intelligent to make presumptions. She shook her head a tiny bit.

Mike was not coaxing, simply stating facts. "You might as well, if you want to be left in peace."

"Excuse me?" she said.

"You turn down Vernon, any of those clowns, too many times and you'll get to be a challenge," he told her. "A single girl, you know?"

Abby had no intention of dancing with Mike when she came in here. At the very most she was going to chat with him a moment, return his money and move on at once. But there was dignity in the way he was offering her the odd delicacy of his personal protection. She had no wish to insult him. This might be the easiest way to broach the awkward subject of money, after all. And it would certainly look better than her approaching him where he sat at the bar. She glanced around the room uncertainly. The bartender was staring but everyone else was drinking, arguing or shooting pool.

"I suppose," she began.

Mike smiled a little bit. "It won't take long," he said, stepping back from the table. He wagged his head slightly toward the bar. "Gary'll watch, and tell everyone about it for days. Then you can come in and drink your head off if you want to." A simple enough bit of logic.

Abby did not have the gumption to say "no" twice in one day. Reminding herself that this man was more presentable than the young giant, and no worse *au fond* than Esther's decent lumpish Web, she slid to her feet.

His hands were cool and dry. He held her at a proper distance, moving lightly on his feet. But there was something shocking about being able to smell the starch in his warm khaki shirt. She flushed wildly at the knowledge that the top of her head was brushing whisps of her hair across the underside of his chin. She could feel it in every follicle. And it did not calm her to be dancing to a lamentation that sounded like "Take Me".

"My name's Mike," he said, pulling back to look at her.

"I know," she answered. It was the best she could manage. To volunteer, in return, the name of Toby Mullen's mother was an absurdity of which she was not capable. She stared instead into the embroidered insignia over his breast pocket. She tried to think what it reminded her of. Gliding speechlessly around the linoleum with Mike, she came to realize that he could not be an aluminum siding salesman as she had thought, because he was a state employee. The keystone insignia on his sleeve made unmistakable sense: she saw it every time she took the car for its annual inspection, every time she went to the State Store to stock up on Scotch and sherry. But he certainly lacked the stale quality she would have expected from a civil servant: come to think of it, the way his neck smelled reminded her of lumber—a bare wooden windowsill on a summer morning. She began remembering mornings from very long ago. The music addled her further. It reminded her of fly-specked radios in dairy barns. And big Dutch yokels. She found the slight dip and spin of Mike's dancing a perfectly easy, mindless thing. Had she not known better, she would have said she liked it. In this delicate condition, she did not dare to speak.

"There," he told her, as soon as the record stopped. He dropped her hand abruptly, leaving her dizzy with sudden stillness.

He did not thank her for the dance or, as she crazily anticipated, see her to her seat. Without any show of rudeness, or interest, he returned to his glass of beer at the bar, mission accomplished.

Abby watched him slide onto the red plastic barstool under the Rolling Rock clock. By the sound of the more articulate grumbles to reach her ears, he already seemed to be discussing the coming Pirates season.

At a loss, Abby studied her watch. She had less than forty minutes to make it to the airport. She grabbed her purse and fled. The front door gaped behind her.

"You getting any of that?" the bartender wanted to know. He scooped some change from the bar, jabbed a key on the cash register and dumped the money into its drawer. Bringing a fresh beer for Mike and one for himself, he leaned on one broad elbow. "Hothouse tomato, eh? Nice and sweet."

"Come on, Gary," Mike said. He was studying the tailoring on the TV game show host flickering behind the house whiskeys.

"She likes you," said Gary.

"Hey. I come in here for lunch because it beats a baloney sandwich in my truck. Most of the time, that is," Mike scowled. "Stop chewing my ear, okay?"

The bartender did not mind either way, talking or not. He leaned on both elbows and watched the TV. The game show host had a great wink, perfectly deadpan, but he did use it too much, as Mike said. "Which one you rootin' for?" Gary asked.

Mike didn't care much for any of the contestants, he claimed, but he did wonder how that host got his job. "Seems like to me," he said, "that guy's not much slicker than my mechanic down at the Chevy dealership. Nor any easier to look at than you."

Gary nodded. "Hell's bells, even you're better lookin' than him!"

"Where do they find those guys, do you think?"

"They never tell you that," Gary said sagely. "I mean they probably start out as preachers or something else they'd be ashamed of."

"No," Mike shook his head. "I got a sneaky feeling they're college boys. You can study TV in college now, you know. I saw a lot of guys looked like they were gonna turn out like him that summer I was up at Penn State."

"College *and* TV," Gary tsked. "Bet they get an awful lot of leg."

"Probably more than they can use."

That remark folded Gary up. How much sex might be more than a man could use, was more than the bartender could imagine. He turned back to Mike, still laughing. "You're some card, you know that? You ought to get on TV like that guy, what'sisname. The fella that visited one of these game shows and now he's got his own comedy series. You're smarter than him, I bet."

Mike was flattered but he brushed off the suggestion. "Hmm," was all he would venture on the subject.

"You'd be hot stuff on the television," Gary persisted. "You look good. You're handy with women. Look at the way that little stray took to you, the one was just in here."

Mike considered the lady with the Gremlin. He wondered what she thought she was doing in here. He had never seen her before, then all of a sudden she showed up twice in two weeks. Obviously she was no barfly, but damned if he could figure out what she did want, exactly. Only one other time had he seen a thoroughbred like her knocking around in bars. That was up at State College, too, when he was taking a summer school course in estuary populations management. For a while there he was seeing the same pretty little thing in every joint he went into. He left her alone until she sneaked up on him and a couple other guys with her tape recorder. Turns out she had been studying them. Mike had never been studied before then, so he never forgot what she had told them. She was gathering material for a paper—a paper!—on the non-verbal transactions of working class public houses. She got to hear some verbal transactions before she felt unwelcome enough to clear out. But this Gremlin lady was up to no such shenanigans, he could tell. She was a scared little rabbit, was all. He wondered what she was so scared of.

CHAPTER EIGHT

Abby darted through people wandering under the vast Calder sculpture in the lobby of Greater Pittsburgh International Airport. She had had to park in the expensive lot because she was cutting her time so close. There was not even a moment to stop for a bouquet of pussywillows on her way to Geoff's arrival gate. And the employees who were hand-checking luggage delayed her further by asking questions about a scissors in her sewing kit.

The nylon taps on her boot heels clicked rapidly as she hurried down the long corridor to Overseas Arrivals, and just about the time she stepped onto mottled red carpet she could see the first passengers crowding out of a chute.

Abby was worried as she searched the faces coming at her. She felt self-conscious thinking what had delayed her, mortified to realize that she had had fun besides.

She wondered if she looked like someone who had stopped at a roadhouse on Route 489 on her way here. She tried to shake the feeling she had been unfaithful by going someplace she had never been with Geoff. It was unusual, she admitted, but not what anyone could call wrong.

She realized with a start that dozens of people had already flowed around her. Had she changed so much that she did not even recognize Geoff? In a moment of panic she scratched frantically at the black kid glove that covered her left hand. A man over there seemed to have the back of Geoff's head. "Geoffrey," she called out the moment she was sure.

It was quite a shock. She had expected him to look tired after all that travel, tired and in need of attention. In fact, he never came back from a tennis match looking so invigorated as he did now.

"Abby!" He *did* recognize her. He halted his headlong race toward the lobby, smiling broadly. Everything was still the same, after all. She went to him and collected her kiss, relieved.

"We've got to get into town right away," Geoff told her.

Abby held his coat while he shouldered into it, then strode down the corridor with him. "What's the hurry?"

"The Foundation is having a budget meeting this afternoon, and all they have from me is an estimate I rigged out of no more than enthusiasm. This trip has been an eye-opener. Now I know what we're about. And I don't want them moving-seconding-approving an ironclad budget that would shortchange our film shoots," Geoff explained.

"Let's find a phone booth," said Abby helpfully. "You can call them about it right now."

"I don't want to seem worried," Geoff said, shaking his head. "I am worried, but I think the best way is to just drop by on my way home."

"Suppose we get stuck on the Parkway?"

"We won't," he said. "I can't." He flashed her another exuberant smile.

Abby hurried along toward the baggage claim area, nearly running to keep up with him. Had she not, she would have missed most of the greetings he was lavishing on her, or on the strangers who mistakenly came between them.

"I missed you a lot. Listen, one thing I learned on this trip was how important it is to get out in the field. There are variables on site that make really fine tuning possible," he told her.

"What?" she asked when she caught up.

"I've got to *be* there. This stuff can't be farmed out."

"Oh."

"We've got to be in Sulu Province for a survey before spring, spend a week or so on a fishing boat."

"Where?"

"In the Philippines. There are these nomad fishermen who know everything there is to know about fish migrations in the Celebes Sea, and . . ."

"That's going to be a tough one, Geoff."

"Why?"

"Because I'll need more time to make arrangements. We'll need someone to stay with the kids. I can't ask Esther," she said, preceding him through the doorway to a drafty baggage claim. "She's been working constantly for us. While I was sick. Yesterday was the first full day I felt . . ." She was interrupted by a flying wedge of businessmen intent on catching the cabs outside.

"No," Geoff corrected her. "I don't mean you and me. I mean Neville."

Abby did not have the faintest idea who Neville

might be, but she had every confidence she was going to find out. Geoff was so full of himself she knew they were going to be up all night talking, if that was what it took to get everything told. She stopped beside the luggage conveyor and treated herself to a good long look at his face.

"Neville Carpenter," he was saying. "I told you about him on the phone. He's this unbelievably knowledgeable cameraman I met at the naturalists' conference in London. Used to work exclusively in time-lapse."

"And *he's* going with you to the Philippines," she guessed.

Geoff nodded. "That's one reason I have to sit in on that budget meeting. Neville's showed me how important it is to have a cinematographer along on a survey. That will raise our travel expenses a lot, but it's essential."

They each grabbed one of Geoff's suitcases and bolted for a pair of glass doors that led outside to the bleak pocked expanses of the parking lot. A sour low front had oozed in. Every step was another puddle.

Fortunately Pittsburghers are used to inclement weather. The drizzle did not slow Abby's driving or the driving of other cars and trucks crowding the parkway. They barreled along toward the bottleneck of the Fort Pitt tunnel. There was no short cut or back way between the airport and the University. A dogged head-on approach was the best she could manage. Whisking her Gremlin under the ominous sign warning "Overweight Trucks, Flammable Loads Must Exit" she plunged them into the honking twilight of the tube. Keeping her

eyes six cars ahead, she kept to her lane and let
Geoff do the talking.

He paid no attention to the spectacular view of
the city as they burst clear of the tunnel onto the
bridge. The rococo masonry of Pittsburgh's Victorian industries and the sheer steel cliff dwellings
that modern corporations erected for themselves
were lost on Geoff, who had vistas of his own to
describe. He was not talking about the trip to Norway via England, however. Not a chance. He was
full of news about his *next* trip, about the Bajau,
the nomads who track an individual species of fish
through uncharted expanses of open sea. The live
data he was going to gather from aboard their
boats, Geoff rhapsodized to Abby, was going to be
richer than anything the scholarly journals had
ever dreamed of providing. Plus the experience of
hands-on research. Plus the excitement of meeting
the natives, living as they live. Not to mention
planning a film on the subject. Sailing thrown in as
a bonus.

Abby did not have the heart to ask anything
about Oslo.

By jumping out of the car at a light, sprinting
across Forbes Avenue against traffic, and skipping
the elevator inside, Geoff made it to his
foundation's budget meeting before the agenda
was exhausted. Abby took her time about parking
the car. She waited in Geoff's old office, chatting
for a while with a Sikh mathematics major who
was waiting there to see the department head.
When he left, Abby dialed nine and then Maxine
Gerber's number.

Flushed with satisfaction and still sophomorically energetic, Geoff showed up in the doorway two hours later. It was dark outside. Abby had not bothered to turn on lights against the gloom, but by the glow of the hall's fluorescents she could see her husband had gotten his way. She smiled too.

"Maxine picked up Gabrielle and Toby for us," she told him. "Would you like to have dinner in town?"

"Alone?" Geoff urged.

She kissed him and led the way down to the wet streets of the campus he had outgrown. Everything was better now. Paolo's was precisely the right place for getting reacquainted. The restaurant had a gratifyingly sensuous menu from a Bolognese chef and food served discreetly by an old waiter with Gallic pretentions. Paolo's was that rare Italian restaurant in town where it was not necessary to call ahead to arrange for room-temperature red wine.

The waiter fawned, and vanished. Geoff reported over the soup course about his victory in the budget meeting. He told her how his status on campus would be rising with this vote of confidence from the Foundation. As a plum, he told her gleefully, he was to be offered a consultancy besides—a fringe benefit of getting to know the board members. He garnished every item with tens of thousands of dollars, with the names of powerful men.

When the cannelloni was served, Abby took advantage of the interruption to fill him in on the children. "Mrs. Hinkle is finally winning Toby over," she began, intending to regale him with his son's description of the pregnancy process.

"Who?"

"Mrs. Hinkle, the teacher who handles science and music for Multi-Age," she said.

"Good," said Geoff, turning to signal for the waiter.

After he had his entree modified to perfection, Geoff turned his attention back to Abby. She decided to save the Mrs. Hinkle story and get to more pressing matters. "My mother called last night. From Sugar Bush."

"Good," said Geoff, and made it sound like "Next?"

Abby persisted. "She wants us to make a decision about dancing lessons for Gabrielle, she says." Geoff watched her, chewing, waiting for the crux. "I already told her I didn't think ballet was important enough for us to even consider the problems. But she wants to give ballet lessons to Gabey for her birthday."

"What's wrong with that?"

"She went over our heads, so to speak," Abby complained. "She's been talking to Gabey and has her raring to go."

"Fine," said Geoff irritably. "Then let her do it."

Abby could tell these items seemed like so many extraneous details to him, and why not, for a man who had just pulled off a six-figure *coup*. She wished she had something exciting to say back to him, to welcome him home with. She decided to keep for another time the matter of having the pot holes graded from their driveway. And there was nothing else she cared to report. Naturally, Geoff took up where he had left off, with more grand plans. Abby listened carefully.

While they waited for dessert Geoff dug Abby's

present out of his attache case.

It was an enticing package, book-shaped and swathed in blue-and-white plaid tissue. Abby was thrilled to have it. Already she could smell the little antiquarian bookshop where he must have gone to search out a first edition Lagerlof. She could almost hear the lilting tones of the spectacled proprietor calling up a ladder to the assistant who must have helped him dig for a certain precious volume, just the right gift. Abby loved the diabolical naivete of this Norwegian storyteller, and she knew just how to enjoy her book. Sometime when Geoff went traveling without her again —this imminent trip to the Philippines might be a good occasion—she would curl up with Lagerlof and sniff the Norwegian air her husband had been breathing so recently.

She opened the box. Inside she found, not a musty old book, but a devastatingly bright gold medallion. It was gorgeous, there was no doubt about that, with the distinctive tastefulness of Scandinavian designers—the sort of thing Geoff loved. It had "duty-free shop" written all over it. He had bought it at the last minute. Unreasonably she felt tears under her eyelids.

"I paid more for that than anything I've ever bought you," Geoff said, leaning toward her happily. "But it's about time I could afford to buy you expensive gifts, don't you think?"

Abby did not know what to think. What stuck in her mind was that something significant had shifted in Geoff. He was now saying "I" when he spoke of what they could afford, and "We" had lost its old meaning entirely. Now "We" meant Geoff and Neville, or Geoff and the foundation, but not, unless so specified, the Mullen family.

When Abby raised her eyes to Geoff's again she saw that his were shining too. Not from tears. Drinking red wine always made his face flush, giving him a histaminic twinkle that looked especially sexy in the candlelight of Paolo's.

"I don't know what to say," she said.

"You could tell me how much you missed me," he suggested.

Abby parted her lips, ready at once to give him the answer he wanted, then blurted, "I was sick the whole time you were gone!"

"I'm sorry," Geoff said. He reached past the wedges of sugary genoise cake glittering on the china between them. "And I wasn't there to take care of you." He took her left hand and gently pressed each fingernail, sending quick, bright signals through her. To think she had feared things would be different. Her fingertips grew warm nestled in Geoff's attention. It felt very good to have things normal again. She was relieved. All the missing she had not done flooded into her at once. Now that he was here, she needed him.

"Let's skip dessert," Abby whispered wickedly across the cake plates. "Better yet, let's ask for doggie bags and eat dessert at home in bed. With brandy." A giggly feeling tingled in her lap. "In the nude. Let's have our cake and eat it too."

Geoff usually squirmed when she said suggestive things. But this time he did not seem to hear what she had said. He was frowning at her left hand. "What is that?" he asked.

Abby frowned too. "I don't know." She tried to withdraw her hand, not caring for the way he was scrutinizing it.

The palm of her hand had shiny patches of skin
that looked pale with an unwell halo of pink.
Crawling up the middle fingers from the scaly place
were two red hair's-breadth trails of blisters.

"What do you mean you don't know?" Geoff
asked.

Abby shrugged apologetically. "I just discovered
it a few days ago." He may not have noticed but
she did: he was wiping his hands rather thoroughly
on Paolo's napkin.

"Are you allergic to something, or what?"

"I can't be."

Geoff was annoyed now. "Of course you can.
Everyone's allergic to one thing or another."

"I didn't eat anything for a week," she protested.
"You mean you think I'm allergic to malnutri-
tion?"

"Of course not," Geoff mused. "Although, you
could be allergic to the flu, or whatever bug you
had. Have you shown that to Jerry Gerber?"

Abby shook her head. She looked at the irritated
extremity. He called this poor wild hand of hers
"that". It did itch like crazy and she wanted to
scratch it, but she did not dare. She hardly knew
what to do with it. "Don't scratch," Geoff
prompted. She moved to rest it on the table, but
the way he was frowning stopped her. No room in
the dainty patch pocket of her suit. The hand was
throbbing now, with infection or embarrassment.
There was no place for it. She imagined sending it
out to the kitchen along with the empty plates and
smudged glasses. She was mortified.

"Relax!" Geoff instructed her.

He was digging into his cake, so Abby went
ahead and ate hers, too. Shards of praline icing dis-

solving on her tongue took her mind off the fiend-
ish itching. By the time they had finished dessert
and coffee, collected their check and exchanged
niceties with the cashier, she had forgotten the urge
to scratch. She had also forgotten that stab of need
for Geoff.

Even though they could barely keep their eyes
open by the time they drove home, she knew that
he would have to make love to her. She understood: it was a territorial matter. With so much jet
lag, dinner and drink in him she could not imagine
his spunkiness was as genuine as his relief at being
home, but he insisted on walking through all the
rooms, straightening pictures, *and* having his way
with her as well.

"How many times do we have the whole upstairs
to ourselves, after all," he reasoned with her. "You
can moan out loud if you like. We can swing from
the chandeliers.'"

Abby never was as stimulated by the sheer
absence of their children as Geoff was. Any more
than she was oppressed by their presence. It
rankled her that sending the children away insured
their father's sexual vivacity. She would have preferred to curl up inside baggy flannel nightclothes
herself and hear a bedtime story or two, not moan
with domestic passion. But she deferred putting on
her nightgown, for him.

Geoff was affectionate. And Abby quickly grew
more willing. The courtly conventions by which he
took her again were more appealing than ever, because this time he was eager. He fumbled. And his
fumbling was so much like the earnest virgin he
had been—each of them had been—'way back in
college days.

* * *

Satisfied, grateful for the warmth of his furry
legs against her legs, Abby turned over. She heard
one more of Geoff's stories before she drifted off to
sleep. He was telling her about the bomb threat at
Heathrow that nearly caused him to miss his flight
to New York, about the tragic way innocent people
are becoming embroiled in the Irish doings, how
saddened Neville was by Ireland on his last film
shoot there.

To Abby's drowsy ears it sounded like old times.
The days when Abigail Hays and Geoffrey Mullen
were discovering each other. Two prematurely
grown-up kids, working soberly toward degrees
just before diplomas went out of style, mothering
each other, heirs of Freud and Meade and Horney
and Spock studying how to acquire minds of their
own, making themselves safe for democracy.

Love was different in those days. Hang-ups still
haunted segregated dorms. Pre-marital sex was still
considered dangerous, love was a political issue.
Geoff and Abby got together to read *Tropic of
Cancer* as soon as the bookstore stocked its first
paperback copies. They were the last of a generation that would underline the good parts. Reading
it was a blow for freedom. It turned them on.

They first made love in the chapel vestibule after
an on-campus memorial service for JFK. They had
been overwhelmed with feeling after three days of
grieving with other students and faculty. They had
only slipped away for a moment when the consol-
ing urge to make it sneaked up and got them. Sex
had a poignant tang then that stayed with them the
rest of the semester. Before President Johnson's

first State of the Union speech they knew they were in love.

Geoff put a down payment on matching rings.

Abby's idea of being sure was to remain in her dorm for another semester, instead of moving into Geoff's apartment. But they were mostly inseparable. They sat up late in the library stacks whispering about love's responsibilities, resolving to be honest—never to live out a loveless charade such as their parents and their friends' parents had been doing. They would be creative, like the lovers in the Donne poem Abby typed out on origami paper. They were liberal. Getting it on was a by-product of their yearnings for global brotherhood. When they went at each other they felt at one with mankind. When they did it, it was with the conviction that it was one small act of piety defying a society crazed with puritanism, cruelty and stupidity. They had more than enough love to go around. So much so that nothing less than abrupt monogamy could express it. They were the last couple in that decade to be married in the university chapel.

They devoted their honeymoon to chaperoning a group of delinquents on a camping trip through the Adirondacks. They were wholesome examples.

Abby did not return to her studies in the fall. She learned to have orgasms. She became something of a menace for a while, but that was no real problem for a pair of intelligent young people. They furnished the bedroom of their new apartment with sleeping bags, a Japanese pillow book and one small bottle of Kama Sutra oil. They worked it out. They read abnormal psychology aloud to each other and resolved not to make any of *those* mistakes with their children. They decided Abby was perfectly designed for motherhood. (She busily began planning her pregnancies, little knowing the perfect mother was cursed with an incompetent cervix.) Once they made love after a night of picketing, slippery with a sense of danger and righteousness, in the back of a bus named American Friends Service Committee. Twice in their own bathtub, experimenting. And then once—just once when they might have been seen—in a storefront campaign headquarters. They had been rushed there to grind out hurried press releases whitewashing the untimely death of a congressman they had been canvassing for. Gus Tallo was heading for a brilliant career challenging the Establishment from within when his career, campaign and life were blown to hell all at once by the deranged husband of his campaign manager.

The night he died was the last time Abby could remember making love with tears in her eyes. This time it was from a sense of disgrace. The poignant tang was gone from politics. It was getting rough out there for dilettantes. It was also the last time she and Geoff went to bed somewhere other than bed. They needed their rest. She already had had two miscarriages. Geoff was finished with graduate school—all but the oral defense of his dissertation. And it was time they got on with finding a place for him to teach.

Geoff was subject to terrible anxiety attacks in those days and Abby was the only thing that kept him steady. Some sleepless nights she turned on the light and read eerie, thrilling stories by Selma Lagerlof to help him purge his own devils. Other nights she would awaken in the dark and find him absentmindedly rubbing her back, rubbing and rubbing as if the trouble were something he could erase from her hide. She was gratified by the way he needed her. At those times some atavism in her prayed—a mumble opposing change.

Now something *had* changed, and against her will. But if tonight was anything to go by, she would have little to complain about. They were such old lovers by now that even various jerks and turns, as Geoff grew more possessed by sleep, did not disturb her.

What did disturb Abby's sleep was having her children somewhere else on a night like this. She dreamed, accurately, that winter was coming back. Through a thin muffler of sleep she could sense slushy rain washing down the storm window panes. The furnace kept running. And the babies were not here with her. Toby and Gabrielle both. She had gone to bed, after three miscarriages, to keep those tiny babies growing into something full-term that she could have, hold and raise. Reclining for nine-plus months, clenching her bumbling cervix shut she had tried to keep them warm and growing. Now they were not here. The absence of Toby and Gabrielle kept her nearly awake all night. The emptiness of their little bedrooms across the hall was as chilling as the wind outside.

Throughout the small hours, the drizzly warm low from Virginia was gradually crowded out by a colder low blowing down from Lake Erie. The daffodil shoots volunteering along Farley Landing Road were in for a rude awakening. Spring had reneged on its promise.

By morning blobs of snow were stuck to every-

thing in the Mullens' clearing. The woods appeared
to have been sprayed with styrofoam and all the
cultivated things in the yard were bowed. Geoff
was in his robe, having a fit by the window when
Abby came to.

"Dammit, dammit, dammit," he gritted into his
mug of coffee.

A limb had broken away from the upper trunk
of their tallest and most pampered planting, a sugar maple. It had failed to break cleanly, however,
and was dragging bark down the trunk, a gigantic
hangnail exposing four feet of cambium. The tree
was doomed, as were lots of buds throughout the
yard. And the driveway would have to be dealt
with before they could pick up the children.

Abby sat up. Geoff had left a second mug of coffee steaming on the end table beside her watch. Sipping from it, she studied the storm's grey leavings
for a moment. Even in this bleak light Geoff's medallion managed to glow on her dressing table. She
would have to find the right chain for it. She would
be expected to wear it to the Gerbers' for dinner.

Some things in a marriage never change.

CHAPTER NINE

"And you had no idea what was up, so to speak?"

"No," Geoff protested. He was regaling the table with the most outrageous from his collection of London stories. "I've never seen one before in my life. Not to my knowledge anyway."

"Who was with you?" Maxine asked, nudging the cheese board away.

"Neville Carpenter, my cinematographer." Abby noticed that Geoff was getting a little bolder with his newfound technical jargon every time he discussed this first outing. "And you know, the funny thing is, she never said a word to *him*."

Jerry asked, "What exactly did she say?"

"I'm not sure, I was so surprised. It must have been something fairly common . . ."

"Oh, come on," Maxine fumed. "Try! Nobody else here has been propositioned by a working girl. We need to know these things."

Jerry interrupted, saying, "Speak for yourself."

Maxine narrowed her eyes and sighted down her fruit knife at him. "You mean you were?"

He chuckled happily, annoying his wife. "Sure. But she wasn't a prostitute."

"So anyhow," Maxine said, urging Geoff on.

"I think what she said was, 'Are you new here?' Yes, I remember how it went now. I was surprised that a stranger was talking to me at all. And of course Neville and the guys didn't offer a lick of assistance . . ."

At this Maxine and Jerry both burst out laughing. "He uses language like that," Jerry chortled, "and then he wonders why he attracts whores."

Geoff was laughing too, modest and gleeful. "Well, they didn't say a thing.

"So I said, 'Excuse me?' She said, 'Are you new here?' And I said, you know, thinking that I was neither new nor old but just passing through, I said, 'No.' Well! You should have seen the way she looked at me. Her eyebrows would have gone all the way under her hairline, if she hadn't plucked them completely bald already. And she said, 'I come here all the time and I've never seen *you* before.' " Her sultry tones sounded comic in Geoff's voice. Everyone laughed again. "And then," he added the last touch. "Then she said in this perfectly matter-of-fact tone of voice, 'I don't know what I'm doing later.' "

The Gerbers loved it. Geoff's story was a shade racier than anything likely to happen on the well-beaten paths from University to Shadyside to Symphony and back. Abby was not so entertained. She was pondering how it happened that Geoff remembered so little of the incident at first and then the next minute was able to recall it in uproarious detail. She wondered if he had deliberately withheld this anecdote until they were safely in Maxine's dining room. In any case, she didn't care for the subject. "Now tell them about the foxes," Abby suggested. No one heard her.

"I have no inkling why she would have singled me out," Geoff mused mildly. "The place was crawling with men, most of them younger than me."

"Because of your looks," Maxine explained. "Of course."

"But Neville's much more interesting looking than I am. He's younger. He's got this very full curly beard. It's orange as a calico cat. And he always wears an old leather flight jacket that's practically a museum piece."

"But you look prosperous, you ninny," said Maxine. She had just quit smoking again, and was chain-drinking. "If I were a hooker, I wouldn't be looking for young men. Young men expect to get everything free, for one thing." Jerry's smile wrinkles creased but he did not say a word. "Besides that," she continued, "you wouldn't want some freaky *interesting*-looking guy. He'd probably take too much time or want to hear the story of your life, or some such kinky business. A hooker would probably prefer doing business with somebody old enough to have manners, someone who was already out of circulation by the time the superbacillae started coming back from Vietnam. Somebody in an expensive suit who wouldn't dillydally because he would have an appointment book ticking away in his attache case all the while." Geoff was looking slightly less pleased now, but only Abby guessed how hard Maxine's last punch would be. "In short, if I were a tramp," she finished him off, "I'd be looking for you, love."

Jerry got between Geoff and Maxine at once. Fishing a bottle of Kahlua from the bar cabinet, he waved everybody toward the living room. Geoff made a beeline for the sound system.

"I'm sorry you were sick the whole time he was gone," Maxine said to Abby. "We could have had some fun, just the two of us."

"Oh, I had a marvelous time," Abby replied.

"What?"

Abby did not know just what she had meant. "It was restful, I think. Being completely alone and out of my head."

Maxine raised her eyebrows and, pouring herself half a coffee cupful of liqueur, danced serenely around the rim of the rug to some Haydn Geoff had found. Abby took her customary after-dinner seat, nestling into cushions that sloped down toward Jerry Gerber's weight. He lay an arm across the sofa behind her shoulders.

"No Kahlua tonight?" Jerry murmured to her at a pause in Geoff's account of the conference. Abby shook her head. "A little Dry Sack?"

"She's steering clear of caffeine and other stimulants," Geoff explained across the coffee table. "We're trying to figure out what's going on with that hand of hers."

Jerry looked questioningly at Abby. Before she could say a word, Geoff was on his feet. "Have you shown him?" he asked, coming around to her other side. He tugged her left hand open for Jerry to see. "Look at that."

Abby looked at the rash. Tonight the paired threads of blisters had retreated somewhat toward the palm. She thought it did not look so bad. At least in this light. Jerry did not look very worried. And she did not care for this sort of attention—two men hovering over her, talking to each other as if she were a problem for them to solve.

"What is it?" Geoff demanded.

With his thumb Jerry slid her ring out of position. She had been avoiding doing that. And sure enough, red pinpoint blisters raged around her finger in perfect replication of her pretty hand-wrought wedding band. It was spreading then, not healing after all.

Jerry looked into her face. She looked back levelly, hoping he would say something to calm Geoff. "Some sort of dermatitis," he said to her. "Could be the virus you had, could be any number of things."

"Is it contagious?" Geoff wanted to know.

Jerry puffed through his lips and shook his head. "I think not." He was more interested in examining the rest of her hand and wrist, it seemed. Pushing up the sleeve of her sweater, he added, "You're more likely to catch freckles from her."

"Oh. It's gender-related?"

Jerry laughed briefly. Satisfied with the look of Abby's skin all the way to the elbow, he winked at her and, gently rolling the sleeve into place, told Geoff, "Of course, the treatment of choice in these cases is two weeks on the Riviera."

Geoff scowled.

"Or traction," Jerry added. "Whichever will keep their hands out of dishwater."

"I haven't washed a dish by hand since I put away the punchbowl after Christmas," Abby objected.

"Take that ring off," the doctor prescribed. "And whatever you do, don't *worry* about dermatitis. Just leave it alone. It'll probably go away when spring settles in and your skin isn't so dry."

Abby turned to Geoff. "Maybe when you get back from the Philippines we can go away on a steamy little trip together," she suggested. "Some place opulent."

"Good idea," he said. "Although come to think of it, after gadding around the remoter regions of an underdeveloped country, what I'll probably need most is a big dose of home."

"They running you pretty hard?" Jerry asked.

"Yes," Geoff sighed. "Field work takes more out of you than I ever realized."

Maxine spoke up from the alcove where she was dancing. "You're not exactly a Boy Scout any more, Mullen."

It was one of Maxine's Kahlua-induced taunts, but for a change Geoff did not mix it up with her. Eagerly he leaned forward, explaining to his wife and his friend. "I think I must be a late bloomer," he said earnestly. "I've never gone anywhere without Abby to smooth the way. I thought I'd feel exhausted. Foreign currency, different customs and protocol. Not to mention personalities! Now, I do have to say all the new people I've met so far have been fascinating types. For instance, this one naturalist we met used to be in Bergman films. Good-looking, in a weird sort of way. And he knew as much about art as he did about foxes. But still, it's a whole parade of egos to thread your way around while trying to accomplish some difficult task. And then when the day's work is done, that bunch of footloose bachelors from the survey want to go out drinking!" Geoff threw up his hands in mock despair.

Abby watched him quietly, wondering whether she was going to cry.

"Some people acquire more energy the more they try to accomplish," was Jerry's simple reassurance.

Geoff nodded. "I do. I know now that I can never go back to full-time teaching."

"Scuttling between your office and the classrooms, you mean?" drawled Maxine. "Like a little tweed mouse. Who the hell would want to?"

"I was getting stale," Geoff agreed. "But this project is really getting the juices flowing. It's calling up resources I'd forgotten I had. If I ever had them," and he dimpled at Abby. "Only my wife knows for sure and she'll never tell."

Abby had nothing to add.

Jerry allowed that Geoff certainly sounded like a man who had found his calling.

"You can't help getting drawn into it," Geoff said. "Behind every datum there's a whole fascinating microcosm." And then he finally told the story Abby had been requesting all evening. About all the sugary things they drank—Geoff, his guide and the film people—all the greasy and sweet things they chowed down on in Norway. They had to, to keep warm and spry while doing their tundra survey for the film on the Arctic fox. He said he went without brushing his teeth for several days and it was the greatest emotional hardship of the trip. By the time the crew got him to a small village of hunters and trappers, Geoff claimed each of his teeth had its own individual fur coat. He could hardly wait to get to the tiny general store and buy some toothpaste. It was driving him crazy to have dirty teeth. He had seen the last Arctic fox he cared to see until he could restore some hygiene to his mouth, he said. And then, when he finally got a chance to shop for supplies, the storekeeper told him the store was fresh out of toothpaste, again. Why? To Geoff's horror and ultimately to his merriment, the trappers had bought up every last tube of toothpaste because it makes prime bait for Arctic fox hunting. It seems the little devils actually prefer it to meat.

When the chuckles subsided, Jerry inquired, "How'd it happen that you decided to go up there?"

"A biologist at Royal Zoological told me about the foxes. He claims they share a density-dependent population cycle with lemmings." Geoff was enthusiastic. "We're going to get some very fetching film footage out of the little critters."

"No, I mean why are you putting yourself through all this wilderness business now?" he asked. "I don't understand why you're taking on another sub-specialty in natural history. Aren't you doing things the hard way?"

Now there was a thought. Abby had not gotten around to counting the ways Geoff might be wearing himself out. She glanced from Jerry to her husband. He looked healthier than he had in years, windburned and wide-eyed in fact, and not so middle-aged as he had when he was a doctoral candidate.

"I'm still a statistician at heart," Geoff was saying. "But I've got to use wilderness footage to illustrate my points. If we want anybody to watch these films. It's easiest to visualize a concept like cycles with natural phenomena. Besides, a little white fox is cute. Much more charming than a bunch of charts about the commodities market."

Geoff talked until it was past time to go. He was that rare thing—a man utterly happy in his work. He griped about logistics, but it was obvious that he loved the commotion of traveling with a small pack of men from site to site, roughing it one day and black-tie dining the next. He talked until even Jerry's eyes glazed over.

"We ought to be going," Abby suggested gently.

Digging in the hall closet for the Mullens' coats, Jerry asked, "So you're off to the Philippines next? Why don't you take Abby along?"

A flurry of protestations followed about how lovely yet how impossible that would be, until Abby broke away to say goodnight to Maxine.

Geoff muttered to Jerry in the doorway, "Make sure she gets invited out while I'm gone, know what I mean?"

Jerry promised.

The first Sunday after the snowstorm, Mike Vogel groaned into his roughout hiking boots and went to work. Ordinarily he took Sundays off. But the sun was out and he knew that the game lands out behind Route 422 were going to be swarming with snowmobiles. This morning was as good as any for making himself unpopular with a lot of overgrown boys, and just possibly dishing out a few profane lessons in conservation. He took the shotgun from under the seat of his El Camino and placed it firmly in the gunrack of his Commission-issue Jeep. Carefully he spilled the boiling water from his thermos, then poured in fresh coffee. He hesitated at the door. What the hell, you never know, he thought. With a cardboard box of supplementary Cheez-Its under his arm, he hauled himself into the Jeep.

His mother waved her pancake turner invitingly in her kitchen window as he jounced past the farmhouse. He waved "No thanks" and made for the road. The county snowplow was out this morning, rearranging slush and fragments of last summer's tarmac repairs. The plow was days late, as usual. He down-shifted and drove around the slush-pusher with a cheerful wave.

Spring was on its way for sure now, whether the winter sport crazies liked it or not. The ground was mostly thawed when this storm came through, and it was only by dumping a godawful amount of snow that the stuff managed to lie on the fields for more than a minute anyhow. Now the surface was thawing again, recovering quickly from the cold snap, softening all the way down to subsoil this time. Snow was melting and running off faster than the mud could absorb it. Every morsel of topsoil would be glutted by tomorrow—snow melting from the sunny side down and frost melting from the dark underbelly. The caves that honeycombed these hills would be quick with subterranean floods. Water was guttering into the culverts already, undercutting the snowy shelves that jutted over the road's edge. About the time the snowplow tore up another hundred yards of blacktop, some of that snow would be part of Onondaga Creek.

Even up in the highlands where the nights would be dipping below freezing for another month or so, the southern exposures were beginning to thaw. To the people in town the storm may have seemed like a relapse of January. But Mike's dad, and other fogeys, knew better. This snow was a guarantee of spring: it was the onion snow. As soon as the melt dried off it would be safe to plant onion sets.

The snow on the Jeep's hood was steaming. Mike unzipped his jacket. Where branches of hardwood trees overhung the road an occasional load of snow slumped, and fell, sometimes bombing the macadam ahead, sometimes thumping on the vehicle roof. He slid his window open. So far it sounded as if he had the place to himself. He turned in at the sign that said: State Game Lands—Trapping Discharging Firearms Off-Road Vehicles PROHIBITED. Parked just beyond the sign was a highly-polished Chevy Blazer with an empty trailer hitched to it. Fresh snowmobile tracks had churned mud into the snowy ruts.

Mike shook his head slightly and geared down. Those guys, he thought, they think "prohibited" means everyone but themselves. This dipshit had apparently gotten up early especially to chase the deer. Probably had his girlfriend with him—big man with a hot machine—and they would likely be roaring, sputtering through a hollow right about now. Soon they would drive a whole herd of does, eyes rolling, right up against the cyclone fence overlooking the Turnpike. He ached to catch up with the fool.

But there was not a single raucous note to be heard from a snowmobile. Mike pulled across the trail to make sure no one drove out of here without seeing him first. When he killed the engine, a squirrel took up scolding from a hickory tree nearby. The rest of the woods was silent. The snowmobile tracks ran off at an angle, across a clearing, then directly through a perilously dense stand of hemlock and out of sight. He could not see where it had headed, but on the chance that it might be tracking back and forth at random, he decided to stroll out a ways in hopes of meeting up. He took the shotgun with him.

Mike struck out around the hemlocks and saw at once the tracks of a big deer the sledder must have flushed out. So help me, he thought grimly, if that bastard corners a panicky buck and gets himself hurt I'm going to punch his lungs out for him. He listened for a rasping engine, heard nothing. He lengthened his stride.

Walking across decaying snow might have been rougher going except for the packed trail left by the snowmobile. Mike stomped along, breaking through every few steps and, hauling his boot out of knee-deep snow, feeling more provoked every moment. A crow floated lazily up from the top of a dead chestnut tree, cawing a warning to the woods in general. Mike squinted, then lost the bird in a shaft of sunlight. If that crow chose this moment to fly off with an alarm, then no one had passed this way in some time.

The deer's tracks disappeared under the snowmobile tracks. The bastard had been right on his tail. And here, where the deer had leapt over a half-drifted thicket of rhododendron, the sledder had actually tried to ride over the top. Tattered twigs and leaves littered the snow. Mike found himself wishing maliciously that he had made it over the top and had landed, sputtering and spewing gasoline fumes, in a fresh sinkhole on the other side. That would be a fit ending—if the forest floor would collapse right over a thin-roofed cave and swallow up the weekend sportsman who terrorized deer.

It could happen, he knew. He had seen a sink-hole down near Uniontown that a farmer kept putting junked cars into. It took eleven of them before the landfill dumped in around them stopped sagging.

But no such manifestation had awaited the sledder here. The tracks continued up the steep side of a swale beyond the thicket. Mike stalked onward, hearing nothing but the drip of melting snow.

It was not until he started down the other side of the ridge that Mike spotted the snowmobile. It was belly-up—silent, more likely run out of gas than switched off. It looked abandoned, another stray piece of urban junk defiling the pristine quiet of the game lands. Then Mike saw the head and shoulder sticking out from under the machine.

He sprinted to it as best he could in sodden snow. The snowmobile had turned over in a rocky downslope where the trees were thin. It looked as though the man had flipped the machine and it had fallen on top of him. He seemed to be sprawling peacefully, his face in the sunlight, but Mike expected him to be dead if he was pinned there for more than a few minutes. He would have crushed ribs, internal bleeding, at least.

Wedging his shotgun between two lichen-scarred boulders, Mike knelt in the pond of snow for a closer look at the victim. This was a city slicker all right—his outdoors clothes were new from the canary yellow windbreaker to the mirrored sunglasses that twinkled in the snow a few feet away. His color was bad—putty. But when Mike leaned closer to feel for a pulse, he noticed that the snow-mobile did not have the man pinned to the ground. In fact it was resting nearly on its handlebars; the driver's legs and abdomen fit easily in the space betwen handlebars and seat. The snowmobile had been turned over long enough for all the gasoline in its tank to have dribbled away into the mush of snow and humus beneath it, but the driver had not made the slightest attempt to crawl out from under it. He must have hit his head on a rock during the fall; he was no doubt dead.

Mike might not have tried a second time to find a pulse except that the man's eyelids fluttered once. Mike jerked the jacket zipper down and, digging brusquely through a shirt and T-shirt, found a weak pulse at the carotid artery. Good: at least it would not be necessary to beat on the man's chest. "Hey!" he yelled at him. "Where you hurting?" The man's eyes opened halfway but did not focus. Mike tried something easier to answer, whatever might stir this guy: "What's your name?"

The man muttered something, then lapsed into a stupor once more. There was no interesting him in his own rescue.

Mike slipped a hand under the man's nape, feel-ing around for rocks or any discernible damage be-fore trying to move him. The windbreaker was slip-pery wet, as was the clothing inside. He was hatless, blue-lipped. And then it dawned on Mike. His snowmobiler had been merely stunned by the spill, was out of it long enough to become good and wet. The longer he lay there the more his blue jeans soaked up melting snow. By the time he re-gained consciousness, this guy had already been too groggy with cold to move, let alone go looking for help. The accident itself was nowhere near fatal. But getting chilled to the core was another story. He looked to be on the brink of systemic collapse—hypothermia.

Mike glanced around the clearing. It was going to be a balmy day. But he could not count on any weekenders chancing by here in time to help. Not this far from the road. And now that he actually wanted a snowmobile smoking through these woods, the blasted machine was drained dry. He would have to carry its driver back to the Jeep himself.

He wondered whether the victim would last that far. His skin was cold. Mike pulled the man's jaw down and, crouching low over his face, blew as much warm air into him as he could in one gust. He had to get his core temperature up. Shallowly the man exhaled. Mike blew in again, hoping his breath was hot enough to do some good. He waited for another exhalation. When the dots stopped dancing before his eyes, he blew into the man's mouth again. After a few minutes of that, he pulled him into a sitting position. The breath continued automatically now. Quickly he stripped off his own jacket and sweater, then stripped the man to the waist of his sodden clothes and replaced them with dry wool still warm from his own body. "Hey!" he yelled again. The man's eyes were open, but there was no one home. Cursing himself for not bringing the thermos of coffee from the Jeep, he hoisted the man onto his shoulders and began staggering toward the trail.

Mike's T-shirt was soaked with sweat before he had gone twenty yards. Each step was difficult—so much weight on his back and the surface so irregular underfoot. He did not dare crane to see the face dangling down behind him but kept his eyes on the tracks left by the snowmobile. His own breath burst out of him in great noisy gusts, and he had to wait until he reached the Jeep to be sure that his patient was still breathing. So far, so good. It was not until he had coaxed some hot coffee down the man's gullet that he remembered he had left his shotgun behind.

"I have a good notion to leave you here while I go fetch it," he muttered, and took a swig of coffee himself. The stupefied snowmobiler did not respond. He was not stable yet—not by a long shot.

Heater blazing, Mike pressed that Jeep for all it was worth. Out on the highway, weekend traffic was picking up—diehard skiers and early bird hikers. Cursing and speeding, he maneuvered a course through the station wagons as far as Donegal, where he jounced to a stop at the community health clinic. He scared up a doctor and stuck around just long enough to get his sweater back. With this transfer of responsibility he longed to wash his hands of the whole offensive business; he was tired and hungry. No food so far today. But for his own satisfaction he had to stop back at the site of the accident once more.

He hiked in with a can of gas from the Jeep. It was no real trick to right the snowmobile and, feeling like a hypocrite, he rode the damned machine out to the trail with his shotgun and the victim's windbreaker wedged into the jump seat. His pants were soaked to the crotch. Snow had somehow got inside his boots. His disposition was deteriorating so fast he thought he had better go home before he came across any other snowmobilers. He could imagine mercy-killing the next carload of them. Munching Cheez-Its he drove straight home. The day was half shot by the time he fried a bunch of eggs and hamburger together. Just once, he swore to himself pouring a dollop of Jim Beam into his coffee, just once he'd like to meet some weekenders who knew how to act right, out of doors.

Just once, he brooded, there ought to be someone to take care of *him* when he needed it.

CHAPTER TEN

"I poisoned Toby's."

"With lizard's blood again?" Abby inquired. She could not look Gabrielle in the eye, not while she was executing the delicate application of mascara to her minute lower lashes. But she trusted her daughter to explain adequately.

Gabrielle was dressed for kindergarten, sitting cross-legged on Abby's bathroom vanity. Two pieces of toast rested butter-side-up in her skirt while she concentrated, open-mouthed, on her mother's cosmetics. "No," she breathed. "I used apple butter."

Abby finished one eye and stole a glimpse at the little girl. "That will teach him a thing or two, won't it?"

Gabrielle was jiggling with laughter. "He hates it," she explained. "He says apple butter looks like . . ."

"Never mind, Gabrielle," Abby interrupted. "I know how your brother feels about apple butter. But you'd better watch out, or he'll do something equally mean to you."

Gabrielle said, "Geoff won't let him. He already tried." She fanned herself gently with one of the toast slices. "Can I have some massacre too?"

"Mascara, girlkin. It's pronounced mas-care-a," Abby said gently, putting the tube of it away. "Didn't Daddy serve the muffins I put in the oven?"

Abby had started the day in a quilted robe, stirring up batter for hot breads. Geoff did not have to rush into town and she fully intended to savour the luxury of a weekday at home with him. She wanted to hear every last story remaining from his first trip. She wanted to help him plan the second. It seemed important that she keep abreast of each new development. She was agitated by a particular desire to keep track of how their marriage was doing, and comprehending Geoff's work schedule seemed the best way to do that. She had already telephoned Esther, telling her not to come in today. But when Mrs. Arnold Fellows called about the Friends of the Museum meeting, Geoff urged Abby to say yes. "It won't do us any harm," he whispered significantly while she listened to Anne.

There would be tea, "elevensies," with a small group of women from the membership committee at 10:30 and then the formal business meeting over luncheon. This was Abby's best chance to ease her way into the most prestigious volunteer organization in Pittsburgh. It was also going to take a big hole out of Abby's day at home with her husband. But Geoff thought it would help. Furthermore, he said, he wouldn't mind having the house to himself for a day of peace and quiet.

Feeling vaguely excluded, and embarrassed about it, Abby had hurried upstairs to dress. If she left in ten minutes she could drop the kids at school, dash downtown to leave her rings at the jewelers for cleaning, choose a gold chain for her new medallion, and make it to Mt. Lebanon in time to meet the museum ladies.

"Geoff's saving the muffins for lunch," said Gabrielle. "I think I'll stay home with him."

The time! Abby hastily pulled a teal blue sweater dress over her head. She made a grab for the suede boots that nearly matched and then, on the chance that today might become warm, slipped into a pair of tan sling-backs instead. Trailing her coat, purse, scarf behind her and herding Gabrielle in front she headed for the stairs.

"Mom!" came a cry of distress from Toby's room as she passed. Toby was dressed and ready to leave, except for his guppies. He was getting nowhere fast trying to net them with her tea strainer. In the interest of time, Abby pushed up one sleeve and reached into the aquarium herself. Scooping guppies adroitly into the waiting jar, she made herself a hero with her son and soaked her left hand with tank water. No time to worry about that now.

"Get in the car," she told Toby and Gabrielle hurrying them downstairs.

"You can't live on muffins," she remarked to Geoff in the kitchen. "Don't you want me to stay home and fix a nice lunch?"

"Thank you," he smiled up at her. He was lounging in two chairs, newspaper re-folded at his feet and his dictating machine in his lap. He wore that cretinous expression he got when he was concentrating on difficult ideas. "I've got everything."

"I could drop back here before I go downtown," she offered. "Whip up a quick quiche for you."

Geoff seemed to see her now. "Abby, the freezer

is full of quiches. If you want to come back and
help me decide whether to warm up the spinach
quiche or the mushroom quiche, that's entirely up
to you. But there's no actual need."

The poor man needed his quiet time, she was
sure of that, or he would get even crabbier. She
kissed him soundly and started on her rounds.

Her progress was hectic. Toby dropped his jar of
guppies just as he got out of the car, and far too
many eight-year-olds were on hand to help sort fish
from bits of glass and gravel. A tank truck loaded
with ammonia overturned on the exit ramp to
Etna, so all traffic was re-routed across the Allegheny. Once she got downtown, it took forever to
find a place to park because the Monogahela River
was rising: all parking lots on the Mon Wharf were
closed. At least the nice man at Hardy and Hayes
seemed to understand how to go about cleaning
her rings. But he had nothing she wanted in gold
chains. She chose a silver mug for the Fairchild
baby, left instructions for a baroque *F* to be en-
graved on it, and managed to inch her way out of
the downtown bottlenecks to arrive, moist and
barely on time, at Anne Fellows's door in Mt. Lebanon.

Her initiation into the Friends of the Museum
was nerve-wracking. Apparently Anne considered
Abby something of a find. At least she introduced
her with profuse praise to the other women. There
were endless amounts of touching being done, the
women who were senior on the committee mostly
touching the newer members. Everyone touched
Abby. One woman noticed the nervous way she
kept hiding her hands and presumed she had recently stopped smoking. Other women presumed,

annoyingly, that she was new in town because they had not met until now. One woman knew precisely how long the Mullens had been residents of Farley Landing and chided her for having allowed her membership in the Garden Club to lapse.

Abby longed to have them stop drawing her into the conversation so she could really get a good look at the Fellows's living room. Not a chance. She was in the company of genteel zealots. The issue which fired them all was how to get that mammoth Alexander Calder mobile away from the city and back in the museum where it belonged. It was not bad enough that the mobile had been hanging all this time at Greater Pittsburgh International Airport, high above the lobby where no one could see it except the ladies at Travelers Aid. But some philistine had had it painted green and gold—the official colors of the City of Pittsburgh—covering the lovely warm primer red prescribed by the artist. "Would they paint the Pieta?" one member raged. Consensus was, probably. Anne Fellows, for one, would not rest until this outrage was rectified. Abby's mind kept wandering all the while. Eyes drifting from the brass sconces framing the fireplace, to a wall crowded with hunting prints, to the Williamsburg fabrics ornamenting wing chairs and windows alike, she kept wondering whether Anne Fellows gave a tinker's damn about Calder's work. Nothing had been done about the mobile's hanging at the airport during all these years while Calder was alive. Any one of his works would clash riotously with Anne's personal fuddy-duddy tastes. But, Abby reflected, maybe the woman was so fervent on behalf of the artist's wishes because he was dead. The really cultured people in town did tend to reserve their highest respect for the dead, and the English.

Abby thought of Toby's guppies and almost cried. She found herself willing lunch to be served, in hopes that she could knock back a glass or two of wine, relax. But lunch was artichokes and, as Mrs. Arthur Fellows pointed out, there just are no wines that go with artichokes. Soon after lunch she began to leave. The act of departure took seventeen minutes, burdened as it was with protocol. Smiling until her face hurt, flashing promises like card tricks, she inched toward the porch behind Mrs. Doc who was leaving early for a committee meeting at the Civic Light Opera.

"I think *too* it should be the color he ordered," Abby wailed into a pay phone at South Hills Mall. "But my God!"

"Are you crying?" Maxine's voice crackled. "Abby Mullen, you meet me at Loco Parentis as soon as you can get there. I want to talk to you."

Abby was not crying. But she knew she might start if she had to plunge into the midst of university traffic. "I don't want to go any place crowded," she said. "I'll pick you up in front of your house."

Maxine agreed. She was just back from her yoga class and, as she told Abby while she settled into her seat belt, she was so laid back it was going to take a nice little emergency like this to get her heart started again. "Tell me all about it," she urged.

"No big deal, really," Abby explained, maneuvering into traffic. "Only that I had a genuinely lousy morning. I don't think I'm cut out to be an influential woman."

"What do you mean?"

Shaking her head guiltily Abby complained, "I haven't figured out yet how to enjoy it. This volunteering in lofty circles, I mean. Getting together with all those well-bred wives and being an influence for good. I ought to revel in it, I'm sure. It's a fringe benefit of being Geoff's helpmeet. But it's not me! There I was dressed in my corporate wife costume and all I could think of was how woebegone Toby was this morning when his guppies died. I don't feel like being a Friend of the Museum. I should have just sent my dress and heels up there, with Gabrielle. *She'd* have had fun."

"Where are you taking me?" Maxine interrupted. They were crossing the bridge at New Kensington. "I'm ready to start drinking Geoff's Scotch."

"I know a better place," said Abby.

"Out here?" Maxine protested. "Let's just drink at your place until it's time to pick up the kids. You can take me along to school, then Dylan and I'll catch the 47 bus back to Shadyside."

But Abby said no. "It's not even two yet. I promised Geoff he could have the house all to himself until I brought the kids home."

"Ooh, I see. Two offices aren't enough for him?"

Abby had never thought of it that way.

"None of his stuff has been moved to his office at the Foundation yet," she defended Geoff half-heartedly. "And he says he can't get any thinking done in his office at school with unfinished packing staring at him."

Maxine snorted. "So he's commandeered *your* office."

Abby decided to let that issue rest. She was much

more excited about the surprise she was planning
to spring on Maxine. She could hardly wait to see
what her friend made of The *Friendly* Rising Sun.
This was going to be fun.

A state motor pool Jeep was pulling out of the
Rising Sun parking lot when Abby's Gremlin
pulled in. Mike Vogel honked his horn lightly as
they passed.

"Who was that?" Maxine wanted to know.

On second thought, Abby considered that maybe the roadhouse would be too desolate in the daytime for Maxine to enjoy. Too late: Maxine had
already jumped out and was picking her way across
the gravel on her spiked boot heels. She slammed
her own door, following. "Friend of Esther's," she
lied.

Maxine waited for her at the door. "I thought
Esther was mixed up with an arc welder."

"Friend," Abby said. "He's a friend."

"Uh huh," scoffed Maxine. "I know all about
friends." They went inside, pausing while their eyes
adjusted to the gloom. A short man whose keyring
jingled at his hip and who reeked of cigar smoke
crowded past them on his way outside. In hushed
tones Maxine added, "Can we get a table in the
non-smoking section?"

"There isn't one."

Enjoying Maxine's disorientation, Abby led the
way to the booth she was unreasonably beginning
to consider her own. A couple was dancing way
back in the corner—dancing or weeping into each
other's necks, it was hard to tell. She let Maxine
take the seat facing them. Under her breath she
hummed along with the juke box—a song she had
never heard before. It was a man and woman sing-

ing in the direst revival-meeting harmony, "We must have been out of our mind".

Without looking away from the dancers for even one moment, Maxine raised an eyebrow to Abby, "Dancing? In broad daylight? Who *are* these people?"

"What's the matter with dancing? Our children are probably doing something much worse to each other by the water fountain right now," Abby pointed out.

"But these are grown-ups." Maxine stared until she saw the waitress approaching their table. "My God, don't they know there's a war on?"

"There is not," Abby shushed her. She wanted to be ready the moment the waitress reached them, the better to make certain that business about the Virgin Mary was not repeated. She did not want Maxine thinking she had a regular drink in this place. "I'd like a beer, please," she said at once.

The waitress nodded. "Budweiser, Michelowe, Stroh's, Rolling Rock, Blue Ribbon or Iron."

"Michelob," Abby said.

"Do you have any red wine open?" Maxine asked.

Abby closed her eyes. If Maxine pulled some stunt like sending the wine back she would never speak to her again. She had done that to Geoff once, in the Mullens' own home. In a roadhouse you'd think that even Maxine would have enough sense to order a beer.

"Red wine?" the waitress nodded. "You want a glass of it or what?"

Eyes wide, Maxine nodded. When the waitress walked away, she leaned across her folded hands and whispered urgently, "We have got to get some-

thing going for you, Abby. You are wasting your
life."

"You're no one to talk," Abby stated as simply
as she could. "You don't have a job either."

But it was not Abby's defiance that sent
Maxine's eyes rolling back in her head. It was the
waitress's setting a large icy tumbler in front of her,
brimming with purple wine. Nobody said a word
until the waitress was gone again.

"I *do* have a job. And so do you!" Maxine said.
"How many times do I have to tell you, it would
cost Geoffrey and Gerald a fortune if they had to
hire someone to rear their children for them. We're
making a priceless contribution to this sexist society, even if we don't command top dollar in the
skilled-labor market. But it isn't a job I'm talking
about. I'm trying to tell you, you've got to *want*
something or you'll be an old woman before you
reach menopause."

"I'll look cute with blue hair, don't you think?"

"Serious, love. Dead serious. If you don't start
going after something, you're gonna be senile by
the time your kids leave for college. Look at Geoffrey. Really! Even he can improve! In fact he has
improved one thousandfold in the last year or so.
In all the time I've known that old man of yours I
have never seen him so nearly . . . sexy . . . as he's
been since he started taking a few risks with his
career."

"But you said I don't need a career."

"I said you need some goals, is what. Don't play
dumb with me."

Abby gave it as little thought as Maxine would
probably accept. Licking beer from her lower lip,
she commented, "I have everything I want."

"Such as?"

"Let's see," Abby began. "I have two beautiful, nearly civilized children. A nice home, good friends. I have padded clothes hangers for all my best dresses. I've had my tubes tied . . ."

"Now you're talking," Maxine urged, and sipped gingerly at her wine.

"I'm joking. You embarrass me."

"Didn't you?"

"Didn't I what?" asked Abby.

"You've had your tubes tied, exactly. Doesn't that suggest anything to you?" Maxine fretted. "Do I have to draw you a picture?"

"It means that I have been out of the baby-making business for more than four years, that's all. I don't want or need another baby," Abby reasoned.

"But you could have a lover very easily because of it." Abby was too disconcerted to respond. Maxine glanced around the bar, then leaned toward her conspiratorially and breathed, "You wouldn't have to worry about ramifications. You can experiment a little. No strings attached! Remember, 'Remove from me the occasion for virtue'? That's you now, kid."

"I don't know what I'd do with a lover," Abby ventured at last. Over Maxine's incredulous hoot, she continued, "No. I mean I don't think that's what's wrong with me."

"But you do admit there's something wrong!"

Abby considered it quietly. "You seem to think so."

"The wife is always the last to know," Maxine said, shaking her head. "Of course there's something wrong. Geoffrey is rapidly becoming a professional nomad and you, his loyal sidekick, still haven't kicked the habit."

"What habit?"

"Of thinking you and old Geoff are in lock step."

Abby felt the need to clarify things for Maxine before she carried this speculation any further. "Now wait a minute," she said. "I know you think Geoff is sleeping around. But I don't, and you'll just have to take my word for it. He wouldn't."

"Okay, okay." Maxine threw up her hands. "Whatever you say. But you're not happy. Don't try to kid old Eagle Eye. This is the lady who knew you were pregnant with Gabrielle a full three weeks before you did. And don't you forget it."

"I am perfectly . . ."

"Hey!" Maxine interrupted firmly. "You are not feeling right about something."

"I was sick for a long time," Abby excused herself. "And naturally I missed Geoff. I have a little adjusting to do."

"I think you're lonely and scared, babydoll. Worried half to death about whether you can keep Geoff in spite of his glamorous new doings," said Maxine, taking Abby's hand. "I suggest you let yourself go. You're at the peak of your sexual powers at this age. Everybody knows that but you. Unleash that lovely little powerhouse and have an affair. It would take a load off your mind, show you that you can still court and keep a man."

"I already have a man," said Abby defiantly.

"You also have more anxieties than a hooker has hickies."

Abby looked back levelly at her tormentor-advocate. "And you think a lover would change that?"

Maxine shrugged. "It's a place to start."

"You're crazy," she objected. "No one in her right mind starts having affairs to keep her husband."

"People do it for all sorts of reasons," Maxine answered. "I do it whenever I need a little fresh air. Cools the blood."

Abby permitted herself a deep appraisal of Maxine's face before drinking the last of her beer. Maxine sounded quite flip, but in fact Abby knew that she had been deeply involved with lovers. The affairs had sounded, at the time, both fascinating and painful. She had always listened thinking of Maxine as a victim of romantic circumstances; never had it occurred to her that extramarital sex was a policy with her friend, and for recreational purposes. At last she said, "That may be what suits you best. But it's not for me."

"How do you know?"

"Because!" Abby was running out of answers that would satisfy this crazy woman. She said the first thing that came into her mind. "I don't know anything about lovers."

Maxine made a wry little face.

"I don't," said Abby. "I don't know anything about sex." Hearing herself say that only added to her distress. "Not *sex* sex. All I know is what I've memorized from sixteen years with Geoff."

Maxine shot Abby a regretful grin. "Geoff is all you know about sex," she said. "That can't be a very great deal. I rest my case."

Abby took it hard. She looked so aggrieved that all the way in to Ellsworth Academy, Maxine was trying to make it up to her. She took back her testimony in favor of adultery, pointing out that affairs could be more trouble than they were worth. One tended, she remarked lightly, to be having one's period whenever a rendezvous was arranged and besides, there was never any emotional progress because each isolated incident meant starting from square one. Abby said nothing. Nearing the school, Maxine suggested that *cuisine minceur* classes or assertiveness training might be more suitable for Abby's purposes.

In another hour or so the sun would be slipping behind the steeples of the city, but the afternoon was still warm. Since morning, buds had begun noticeably to thicken the twigged extremities of every elm along the driveway. Under their bare limbs the first crocuses of this semester were blooming. "Uh oh," groaned Maxine. "First colds of spring coming right up." Not a single one of the children was wearing a jacket and some, of course, had neglected even to carry their wraps outside.

When Maxine opened the car door, the clean moist smell of earthworms floated in. Abby's throat thickened with tears. Entirely too much was changeable, she thought, but at least spring smelled the same every year as it had before Daddy gave up fishing.

"There's Dylan," said Maxine, getting out. "Tata."

CHAPTER ELEVEN

Geoff Mullen was traveling so much now he was beginning to run into people he knew aboard airplanes. He enjoyed that. Not because he was especially interested in people, but chatting helped pass the time and besides, it gave him opportunities to review the recent shocking improvements in his own fortunes.

On the flight to the Philippines, however, the old acquaintance turned out to be someone Abby had known better than he had. Geoff did not enjoy talking about Abby; what was there to say besides that she was the perfect wife and mother? Except of course for this peculiar new eruption on her hand, he could think of nothing new, and the skin condition had nothing to do with him. Pressed for information about Abby, Geoff told how fast the children were growing. In fact, he said with a wave of his Scotch glass, the entire family was doing well. Well, except that it was a shame Abby's doctors had forbidden any further pregnancies. He admitted he had a hunch Abby would have liked a new baby to concentrate on while he was becoming more and more involved with these trips. For his own part, traveling was not turning out to be any hardship. On the contrary, he explained, this new project of his could actually be saving their marriage for all he knew. Not that it needed saving, but he had been in danger of going stale until recognition of his work had forced him into the international intellectual community. Now this was one of eight or nine trips he would have to schedule this year.

Having successfully manipulated their conversation into the area he felt most like discussing, Geoff took off his coat and expanded into an explanation of his cycles project. He talked nonstop until the pilot announced that Flight 19 had this instant lost a day to the International Date Line.

"You're not wearing your rings any more," Mike said. "Did you throw the son of a bitch out?"

Abby plunged her hands beneath the table. A little smile played about her lips without her permission; it was the unavoidable result of his preposterous remark. How little people can guess about each other, she thought, once they venture outside their own circles.

"Why're you hiding your hands?" he asked her. "We might think you been palming aces. Some places you can get in real trouble not keeping your hands above the table." They were alone in Abby's booth at The *Friendly* Rising Sun and they were playing with nothing more than a couple of bottles of beer. Mike was doing his best to tease some words out of her.

Abby tried changing the subject. "Please finish what you were telling me."

"They're pretty hands. You ought to have them out where folks can admire them."

"They are perfectly ordinary," said Abby, lifting her hands as casually as possible and putting them down on the cool Formica tabletop. "See? Just hands."

Satisfied, Mike poured more beer into his glass.

"What about the ground hogs?" she persisted.

"Oh yeah. It's not that they're dumb. They're very quick and alert, but they're gullible," he said, picking up the thread of his story once more.

Abby recrossed her legs, had another sip of beer and, folding her hands in front of her, settled back to enjoy the story.

"You can snare a ground hog by slinging a small wire noose around the entrance to his burrow," Mike said. "He will see it, naturally, the first time he looks out. He sees it and smells it, and a shifty little part of his brain sets off an alarm." Here Mike used a rodent-voice that had a tang of Arkansas in it: " 'That wire wasn't there before, so it is definitely not okay,' and he goes back in. The next time he pokes his nose outside, though, it's a whole new ball game. This time the snare smells familiar. 'Oh,' he figures, 'That was there before now. Okay.' And into it he goes, head first!"

On the last words he grabbed her left wrist so suddenly she nearly shrieked. His hand was hard, but his face remained amiable—a decent man merely emphasizing a story point. She caught her breath, trying not to feel like a ground hog. "That's a poison hand," she warned him, borrowing from Gabrielle. "I don't think you want to hold it."

"I'm not scared if you're not," he said.

"Well. No. You won't catch anything from me, if that's what you mean," she floundered. "But it has its repulsive side."

Very gently he said, "May I see?"

Instinctively she wanted him to see. She imagined that he would understand how this slight eruption wounded her, since he was the first person to know about it who did not take the liberty of scrutinizing her skin unasked. He might even know some elusive folk remedy for it because, she recalled, he smelled of sun-dried wood. She uncurled her fingers into his palm.

He looked, without poking. Cradling her hand in his as if it were some brand new bird or a skittish little newt, he blew a cool breath across the rash. "Hurt?" he asked, looking up.

The sensation of his breath ran up her fingers and into her lap. She shook her head. "It's from a virus, my doctor says."

Mike said, "I bet it is. I bet it comes from the same virus that causes asthma, ulcers and alcoholism."

She watched him. But he offered no further commentary. "Do you know so much about people because you're a Game Protector?"

"Animals are different than people."

"Of course they are," Abby said. "But I think you're right about my hand. And I thought maybe since you're the first one to say something helpful about it you might have found similarities in nature."

Mike signalled for the waitress. "I just made that up," he said. "I don't know anything about people. But I do know that there isn't an animal alive that would stay pissed off long enough to get depressed. Or kill itself. Tell Donna what you're having."

Abby looked from Mike to the waitress. Donna winked at her and said, "If he's buyin', honey, I'd go ahead and have a Michelowe. He never springs for the fancy stuff himself, but I bet he'd do it for you." Slowly Abby took her hand away from Mike's.

When Donna had brought them two Michelobs and a pair of fresh glasses, Abby said eagerly, "That's not true, you know. There are animals that commit suicide. Geoff . . ." She hesitated to give up Geoff's identity, but it was becoming very important that Mike believe her, and she certainly did not expect him to accept this information on her authority. "My husband says there are little rodents in Scandinavia, called lemmings, and they periodically run into the ocean to kill themselves."

It was the most she had said in one breath ever since he had slid into the booth. He studied her face, grinning as if she had thrown him a bouquet. "I've heard of 'em," he said. "But no animals *I* know would do a thing like that. Anything's liable to happen in Scandinavia."

"Have you been there?" she asked, surprised.

"Let's see," he tantalized her. "I've been to Daytona a couple of times. Was stationed near Fort Smith, Arkansas while I was in the service . . ."

Just then an older man left the bar and approached the booth where they were sitting. His leathery face showed something in common with the laborers who lingered in the video glow of Gary's barside TV, but he wore a long wool coat instead of a jacket, and rubber galoshes instead of the leather clodhoppers favored by the others. He rattled the change in his pockets at Mike. "Keeping you pretty busy, are they?" he said.

Mike slid over a few inches on the bench. "How do," he answered. "Sit down?"

The man shook his head.

Mike asked, "Busy yourself?" and moved back.

"Oh they're keeping me hopping, I guess, but that doesn't mean I stay outa mischief. We've decided to remodel some up at the house. Closing in the front porch next to the living room and putting in a bay window," he smiled, implying this was fairly scandalous. As he turned toward the door he added, "Stop by if you see the light's on. Both of you."

Abby liked the idea at once and, surprising herself, waggled her fingers goodbye when he left. One familiarity deserves another, she reasoned. But what she said was, "Harmless old guy, I guess. You know, for one terrible moment I thought he was going to ask me to dance!"

Mike rolled his head back and hooted at the ceiling. Then he looked at her over the rim of his mug and said, before drinking some beer, "You're safe now that I've danced with you, I told you that. They all think you're my girl." His adam's apple bobbed thirstily as he half-drained the glass.

"That old man thinks I'm your girl, too, doesn't he?"

Mike said, "He doesn't know what to think any more. He's my father."

"Truly?" she gaped. "I've never known a grown man who lived with his parents."

"I don't."

Once again Abby waited, hoping for further explanations but none were forthcoming.

"Why did you come in here again?" he asked at length.

Before she could answer, the front door swung open. It was the young farmer in the ventilated cap who had asked Abby to dance. She slunk down in her seat. He was greeted with comradely grumbles and obscenities as he made his way along the bar. "Gar'," he yelled at the bartender. "Hey Gar'!"

"Okay Vernon," the bartender growled back.

Vernon measured off an acre or so of space with his outspread arms. "I been caponizing turkeys since sundown," he rasped. "That turkey shit is dusty! Gimme a beer about this big." Gary got an enormous schooner from the freezer below the bar while Vernon chose a stool and bellied up. "Make it a P.B.R.," he said. "And a V.O. for my date."

The bartender set up Vernon with the Pabst Blue Ribbon and a shotglass of whiskey, which he promptly downed in reverse order and asked for more of the same. While he was smacking his lips, Gary observed dryly, "Your date sure drinks a lot, Vern."

Vernon's laughter was uproarious and set everyone else laughing too. "I know," he managed to giggle at last. "That's why I dint bring her along."

Mike touched Abby's hand. "We can't talk while he's making all that racket," he said, standing.

He did not hold the door for her as they went out, nor did he hand her in to the passenger's seat of his truck. She went along entirely on her own. Abby left a roadhouse one cool night in April with a man she had not been introduced to, and got into his vehicle with him; neither one of them had been cherishing the slightest notion that she ever would. It was not like her. Not that Abby had never been alone with another man since she married sixteen years before. But always they had been her father's lawyers, her husband's colleagues or her children's tutors. She was completely alone with this man from the Game Commission. She looked over and smiled back at him. He *did* have beautiful teeth, even if his sleeves were too short.

"I can't go to another bar," Abby said.

He lay his keys on the seat between them. "We don't have to go anywhere."

"No."

"I thought we weren't quite finished being together," Mike said, "and this seems as good a place as any."

"Except there's no waitress here, and no beer."

Mike flipped open the glove compartment and pointed to a bottle of dark rum. "Help yourself," he told her.

"Do you keep a bottle of liquor around all the time?"

"Just started," he said. "In case the St. Bernards let us down. You never can tell when you'll happen across some poor wayfaring stranger, you know."

Abby took that to mean her. She opened the bottle and smelled at the syrupy contents. "Whew, but that's strong!" she said. "It smells like Christmas— eggnog and fruitcake."

He took the bottle, sniffed at it, then handed it back saying, "I always hoped that was how Cuba or Trinidad would smell."

She sat still, resting the open bottle in the cradle of corduroy made by her skirt. Her companion seemed lost in thought now. He pulled one heel up to the seat by his door and, resting one arm on his knee, began scratching tiny hieroglyphics with his big, blunt forefinger on the steamy window. None of Abby's friends, including Geoff, could sit quietly this way, except of course in the case of concerts and films. Mike looked as if he might be settled in for the night.

"I think the reason I keep coming back here," she admitted at last, "is . . . I don't know. Because I *don't* fit. I know those people in there at the bar think I'm a freak. But that's what I like. No one expects anything from me that way. It's very peaceful."

"Peaceful, huh? Some people might think you were looking for trouble," Mike said.

Abby bristled at this. "The first time I came here simply because I had a flat tire. I was looking for help, but you know what happened to me that night!"

"You got your tire repaired," he remarked. "The collision we threw in for free."

"It was not free," she protested. "I ended up writing a check in the amount of two hundred thirty-six dollars and eighty cents for that prank of yours."

"Because you were afraid to tell your husband?"

"My husband knew I wrecked the car," said Abby, sidestepping. "It's my insurance salesman who never would have believed any accurate account of how it happened."

Mike leaned forward and started drawing out his wallet. "I'll make up the rest for you," he offered.

"Don't."

He shot a look at her, but she was perfectly serious. He settled back against the door this time, draping one long arm over the steering wheel, and looked her full in the face.

"I still have to return your two fifties to you," she added.

"Keep 'em. Get yourself a consolation prize," he dared her. "To make up for the aggravation."

"I might just do that."

Hiding her smile, Abby closed the rum bottle and replaced it in the glove compartment. When she sat back, Mike was looking at her. She looked at him.

Leaning close, he softly lay his hands on her cheeks and drew her face toward his. "I've never seen anything like you," he said. "But I'd swear you're looking for something. If it's trouble," he added tenderly, "I sure hope you take it up with me."

Abby closed her eyes. While they were closed, she felt the warmth of his face coming down onto hers. He kissed her very seriously, thoroughly; when she began kissing him back, he took a firmer grip on her skull and kissed her as though he were looking for something himself. Their lips stuck together for a moment when they parted. Then he laughed. Shaking his head, he hugged her fondly and said, "I bet you fuck like a snake!"

Abby stiffened. "I'd better be going," she said, opening the truck door.

That seemed to be okay with Mike. He opened his door and, pocketing the keys, slid to his feet on the gravel outside. "Guess I'll get something to eat."

Abby looked at him across the glossy roof of the El Camino. He was waiting to hear what was bothering her. "How do they do it?"

"Who? Snakes?"

"Are they especially . . . fierce, or fast?" she ventured. "I mean, what did you mean when you said . . ."

Mike shook his head and sat behind the wheel
again. Abby got in, too. When she closed the door,
he turned on the ignition. "Hell, don't ask me," he
answered, looking over his shoulder as he backed
out between another pickup and her Gremlin.
"I've never caught 'em in the act. It's just a
saying."

He drove on familiar roads until they passed the
Teddy Cow farm, then turned off and started traveling toward the mountains on a dirt road. Abby
sat up straight with her knees together, watching
what she could of the dark terrain outside her window. The hills had to be the same ones she always
passed traveling another direction with Esther, but
everything looked different from the passenger's
side. She rolled down her window and took a deep
breath.

"Be cultivating soon," came Mike's voice from
the driver's side. Abby turned to look at him.
"Alfalfa," he explained.

When he patted the seat beside him she slid over
right away. He shifted into third and put his arm
around her, snuggling her against his jacket. He
was wearing a red and black mackinaw of the type
she had not seen since she cleaned out her father's
apartment in Cincinnati. Its stiff wool chafed her
jawbone lightly when the truck swayed. They rode
that way, cuddling like amateurs and breathing in
the sharp springy darkness, until they drew abreast
of an orchard of gnarled trees. "Okay," Mike said.

Abby pulled away to look at him. "Okay,
what?"

"Okay shift," he said. "Don't you know how to
do this?" He lifted his arm clear, downshifted and

used both hands to turn the truck into a lane that ran uphill beside the orchard.

"No."

"Don't you remember your high school days, the guy driving and the girl shifting? How old are you, anyway?" She could hear him smiling although he was looking away from her, craning to see straight down outside his window.

"I-Ii-yi . . ." her voiced bobbed giddily as the truck lurched up the rutted lane. It made her sound nervous. Enunciating boldly as she could, she said, "I am no older than you."

Mike stopped the truck in front of a farm house. Abby was on the verge of asking if this was his home when he said, "Wait," and got out. He came around to her side, opened the door and said, "Watch your step. The mud's ankle deep in some places." He guided her to a slab of flagstone which led to others, which led toward the cellar door of the deep-porched old house. She looked around. A wheelbarrow full of rocks squatted beside a rearward section of porch that was screened off by plastic tarps. A string of work lights dangled, extinguished now, above a section of unfinished masonry that lay directly below the roof spouting. Mike was studying that. But Abby was more taken by the thicket of lilac bushes at the side of the house.

She was imagining how fragrant their blooms would be in another six or eight weeks.

"Is this your home?" she asked.

"My parents'," Mike said quietly, gesturing toward a light glowing from two upstairs windows. "I live up the hill. But the mud's too slick for us to drive it tonight. If you want to see my place, we'll have to cut through the orchard on foot."

Abby turned to look. The orchard floor appeared to be a knee-high tangle of dewy weeds. Taking her boots off was not going to work; it was still too cold to walk in stocking feet. "I'd like to," she began, looking down regretfully at her pretty suede boots with their narrow heels.

"Why don't you save those things for the bedroom?" he whispered, picking her up in his arms. "They're not worth diddly any place you'd really need boots."

Carrying her as easily as if she were a fawn Mike stepped across the mire of his parents' driveway and onto the shaggy turf of the orchard. Abby glanced over his shoulder as he carried her away. His truck seemed to be sporting a bumper sticker. She hoped it said something iconoclastic, but that might be too much to hope for in a civil servant. She told herself he probably had to post it there because of his work—no doubt it had official significance.

"What would your husband say if you came home with mud on your boots?" Mike was chortling cheerfully.

"My husband doesn't live with me," she heard herself saying.

"You wish," he said. "If that was true, you'd be having dinner dates with guys in suede pants, not drinking beer at the Friendly. What about the babysitter?"

"My housekeeper's staying with the kids tonight," Abby conceded. "*She* would mind if I came in with muddy boots."

Mike said nothing. Breathing softly through his

mouth, he carried her uphill, striding zigs and zags around apple trees. The branches were so squat, so well-pruned that they seemed the black skeletons of enormous prehistoric toadstools. No new growth was showing yet. Nothing moved but Mike. Last year's weeds slushed against his pant legs with each step, and last year's leaves rustled moistly under his boots. There was no moon.

Abby never saw the giant bird that exploded from a burdock tuft as they passed. She only felt Mike flinch and heard its wingtips whistle in the air. Her heart constricted. Mike paused, pivoting in his tracks to follow the big fowl's invisible flight. "Pheasant," he told her. It fluttered to the ground somewhere down the hill. He carried her on.

Her pulse was still jittering when Mike took her to the closest big limb of an apple tree and perched her on it. He stood in front of her, looking up at her face. Through her skirt she could feel the damp roughness of the bark. She asked if he was running out of breath.

He shook his head. "Just patience." Then he stepped beween her knees and buried his face in the corduroy of her skirt. His arms closed around her hips, pressing his features deep into her belly. Suddenly Abby loved him very much. She held onto the jutting collar of his mackinaw, steadying herself, and gazed downhill beyond the treetops. She could feel his breath penetrating her slip.

"Can I have you?" he asked, muffled.

She heard him perfectly. She nodded. When he lifted his face and stepped back, she nodded again, managing a smile this time. "It's after eleven," he warned her.

"Doesn't matter," Abby answered.

Mike lifted her down then, carried her swiftly out of the trees while she clung to his neck, and up-ended her neatly on the concrete slab that made his front porch. The door was stuck on a swollen jamb. He delivered a kick to the lower panel which not only opened the door but left it quivering on its hinges. Inside, his house was even darker than the night outside. Cool as their cheeks were, the air from his furnace was stifling at first. Abby braced herself for crushing evidence of a wife to appear as soon as he would turn on the lights. Box-pleated drapes, perhaps, or a dried arrangement on the cof-fee table. But Mike did not turn on any lights. Without a word, without giving Abby a chance to close the door behind her, he led the way along one wall to a room in the back. She did not risk saying anything either.

By the dim glow of an electric alarm clock, Abby watched Mike's shape hang her blazer over the back of a chair. The bed squeaked once when he sat down. Pulling off his boots, he cursed a little. His clothes followed his boots onto a pile some-where on the floor near his feet. She heard a drawer scrape open and she suffered a moment's misgiv-ings. Oh lord, she worried, so this is what primitive sex is like. She dreaded to guess which one of them he meant to protect with prophylactics. Bracing herself for the indecent odor of high-grade rubber, she told herself she did not belong here. But to leave now, find her own way back from the wilds— she was not ready for that. Determined, she fol-lowed his example and took off all her clothing, boots first. When she stood up again in bare feet he looked terribly tall on the other side of the bed. Tall and exciting.

She helped him pull down the covers. And it seemed the top blanket was still whooshing softly onto the floor at the foot of the bed when Mike took hold of her.

They knelt in the middle of the bed, embracing. There was nothing to interrupt the heat coming off him—no jewelry, no high-grade rubber, no barrier of any kind. He pulled her against his chest. Blindly she straddled him. They rocked back and forth on their knees, clinging to each other, a little stunned to feel themselves naked and disorderly together. He bent down to kiss her neck, nuzzling behind her ears, deafening her. Abby lost her sense of direction until she closed her eyes. Then *down* became the only direction that mattered.

She just held on.

Mike picked her up bodily, a slight thing, and fitted them together more snugly. Abby was already pushing back at him when she felt a pillow collapse against the back of her head.

He was not unselfish so much as relentless. He knelt over her for a long time. He plied her with her own pleasure, refusing to take her first gasping "Yes!" for an answer. Breathing close to her cheek, he egged her on, handled her, made her inarticulate. More. Persisting, he coaxed her out of her wifish breeding: tit for tat etiquette was something he brushed aside. Under Mike's prodding she became a hussy, a spendthrift. Again. She lost count. They both grew slippery. And when he pulled back from her sweaty stomach to lean on his calves for a moment, no doubt for a breather—at

last—before his own final plunge, he surprised her
by pulling out all the way. Her knees went slack
and her heels slid weakly down the sheet. Mike
reached up to take the pillow from under her head
and doing so, blew a soft, cool breath under the
strands of hair pasted to her face.

Nothing would do but that he lift her bottom off
the bed and lick every fold of her that they had
slickened together. Crazily, Abby imagined she
was some sort of foal he had just given birth to, but
the notion did not prevent her from succumbing.
She enjoyed it. All the while his penis lifted itself
heavily, a warm prod her leg sometimes bumped
against. He licked her, nibbled at her, he all but
took her in his teeth and shook her. She began to
cry. And when he asked, into the downy skin
stretched across her hipbone, whether he must
stop, she wobbled her head no.

When she had been buffeted into complete ex-
haustion, he came into her again and quickly gave
up the ghost of his own long wanting. Then he lay
down beside her, panting. Abby did not pant. She
had been through every phase but sleep by now.
She lay very still and looked up—'way up through
the deep well that her eyes had become—and tried
in the darkness to see the ceiling. Gradually she
regained the power of thought.

Abby had turned herself inside out, molted. She
felt like a brand new being burst free from an old
familiar hide. Without touching, her bare skin
could feel where Mike was. Right beside her. She
had the feeling she was going to be impossible from
now on. She wanted to keep him. That was certainly impossible.

At last she felt Mike move away. The bed lifted when he got up and padded across the floor. She listened for the sound of his raising the toilet seat, but heard nothing until the sound of water falling into water. Abby decided with satisfaction that he was used to living alone; she knew that no husband can safely approach a toilet in the dark and urinate without running a risk of wetting the toilet lid. She wondered again what he had been doing on his side of the bed when he took his clothes off. She rolled across the warm patch he had left, found the night table with her fingertips. There was a flat plastic bottle about the size of her hand. She held it close to the glowing clock and read the label: "Solar-caine." Bewildered, she replaced it, then rolled onto her stomach.

Mike returned. He sat on the bed, reached over to lay one broad, cool palm on her buttocks, and said, "Please stay." She looked at the clock. Its orange face indicated one-thirty.

"I must call," she said.

"Okay," he said, getting to his feet. She followed him along the wall until he found a light. The blaze of a sixty-watt bulb was dazzling for a moment. When Abby's vision adjusted itself she was looking at the most implausible living room imaginable. The house must be tiny, she discovered; although the living room was roughly twenty-by-twenty, it ran the full width of the building; uncurtained windows on opposite walls faced each other. Mike saw her glance from window to window and said, "Don't worry, there's nothing out there but apple trees." He went to close the front door.

She found the telephone sitting on an otherwise

empty shelf—no telephone book, no books, no collectibles. There were more shelves—equally empty —running the width of the room and stacked from the mantel of a vast stone fireplace all the way to the ceiling. Like the walls, they had been whitewashed, not painted. Marveling, she picked up the phone and dialed her own number.

Mike stood by the door watching, eyes fondling every slope of her, until someone answered. Then he walked out of sight.

"Esther?" Abby could hardly tear her gaze away from the quilt she noticed on Mike's sofa. It was draped there as recklessly as a drop cloth, but plainly antique, composed of thousands of vivid calico triangles which veered and darted until they resolved into a big basket of flame-shaped flowers. It was a museum piece. And clashed terribly with an illuminated photo mural of grazing elk—the only artifact Mike had hung on any wall.

"This is Abby," she said into the phone, trying to imagine the house at Farley Landing. "I just wanted to ask if you could stay another hour or so without any trouble. Is everything quiet?" Listening, she hugged her breasts. "That's wonderful, thanks a lot," she responded, grinning broadly. Then she added that she was fine, that this was no auto accident; she would certainly be home before the children got up. There was no point in trying to hide her pleasure from Esther. Esther had lost her own innocence at a cruelly early age, Abby knew, and although there were no visible scars, those experiences had left her housekeeper with Strip-Eez eyes. Esther noticed everything. She would see right through anything Abby told her, caring only whether Abby was safe. She asked no further questions. Satisfied, Abby hung up.

Mike reappeared with a quart bottle of beer. This was Abby's first good look at him and she took her time. She thought he was thick-limbed, dense, for someone so tall. That minor softening around the waist must be where last winter's beer settled. He had probably never sunbathed a day in his life; the weathered flush of his face and neck stopped abruptly below the collar line. She meant to ask him about the broad bald dent on his shin.

He told her soberly, "You've got jism running down your leg." It was true. She blushed. "Come lie down," he urged. Draping his arm over her shoulder as if she were a champ and he the coach, he walked her to the bedroom and left the floor lamp lighting a nearly empty living room.

Propped up beside him in the cozy dark bed, she did something else she had never done before. She drank at least six ounces of beer all at once. She tilted the Miller bottle up to her lips and gulped thirstily, bubbling the fluid inside, swallowing without drawing a breath until she felt slaked. Sighing, she handed it back to him. "I was so dry!" she said. He drank too, then set the bottle on the floor by his boots. They nestled down among his wilted sheets. Bellying up against his side was a surprise: she found his ribcage was as deep as hers was wide. To avoid comparing him with what she was used to, she began asking questions.

"What is this place?" she asked.

"Cookhouse," he said. He turned, rumbling contentedly, and began rubbing her skin with long, light strokes. "When my grandpa was running the farm, they cooked fruit up here, canned it and sold the jelly and sauce themselves. Now a crew comes out from Heinz. They machine-pick and truck it downtown all in one day." He pinched her shoulder blade pensively. "That fireplace used to have a fire burning in it from August 'til Thanksgiving, Pop says. That was when he was a little kid. Cider press was up here, too."

Suddenly, Abby was homesick for her own father and filled with curiosity about this man. My lover, she thought, awestruck. My lover's family. She had a dozen questions about Pop, his grandparents, his life here in the midst of an orchard, his schooling, his views. But Mike kissed her silent.

Her mouth was bread-flavored from drinking beer. So was his tongue. But his lips were tinged with a faintly sour taste. She looked at him quizzically, licking her lips. Mike's face broke out in a radiant grin. "Pussy," he explained. "Never tasted it before?"

She buried her face in his shoulder and wagged her head no. He held her close so she did not have to see him while he murmured monosyllables about how much he liked it. She was overwhelmed by this coarse man who insisted on naming the gamiest things about her (things she never associated with herself), a man who discussed nothing and who filled her with inelegant joy. She did not try to talk to him after that. The few words he bothered with were too disarming.

They lay together in the dim room a long, silent while. He touched her so lightly, his fingers roaming steadily over the surface of her, that she became acutely aware of the fine pelt of silky hairs growing from her pale skin. She could smell him now; his skin had worked up a scent of its own. It suggested a memory which tantalized her. Drowsily, she tried to think what it was. The effort, or his touch, was making her very sleepy.

One brooding corner of her mind kept her semiconscious, however. She knew if she let herself nod off she would be surrendering her last fragment of control: she would probably sleep like a glutton and never get home in time to resume her normal life. She would neither be Toby and Gabrielle's mother at breakfast nor Abby Mullen the trusty young matron ever again. The first thought frightened her, the latter made her impatient. The spell was broken. She had to get home.

Mike caught her mood and did not crowd her. He simply got busy rooting in the rubble of a beatup cupboard until he found two old boots that were smaller than the others. Abby dressed in a hurry. Mike hunkered down at her feet and laced the cracked clodhoppers tightly enough for her to walk in them. "There," he said. He zipped his mackinaw shut over his bare chest and took her hand.

An owl hooted briefly as they picked their way down the muddy lane to his truck. The lights were off in the farm house now, and a faint hint of navy blue was seeping into the sky. She and Mike separately let themselves into the truck, separately deciding not to shut the doors just yet. He released the hand brake and, when the truck had rolled fifty yards down the lane he turned on the ignition and engaged the clutch. They slammed their doors then. "Gonna be a warm day," Mike commented.

Abby agreed without thinking. All the way to the
roadhouse, she worried about not being home.

He waited around to be sure her car started.
When the engine turned over, he waved goodbye.
As he was backing onto the blacktop, Abby pan-
icked briefly, remembering her boots. Well, she
told herself firmly, there would be no going back to
get them. Pulling onto Route 489 she glanced after
Mike's departing tailgate and read the bumper
sticker. Trashy, she thought. Disappointing. But it
was funny too in a cockeyed sort of way. Must
have been a prank, one of his pals at work or that
awful Cletus. All the way home she teased herself
picturing the fury that would follow if someone
ever put a bumper sticker on any car of Geoff's.

She left Mike's cracked clodhoppers in the basement with other discards bound for the Salvation
Army. Tiptoeing upstairs to her kitchen, she found
a groggy Esther measuring out coffee. A
murmured exchange. A quiet "plop" on the front
porch as the paperboy went by. Esther left sometime while Abby was waking the children for
school. All the way through breakfast, Abby promised herself she would not take risks like this again.

All the way back from Ellsworth Academy, out-
wardly indistinguishable from the other suburban
mothers who had dropped off their children, all the
way home to the bright, bald-faced daylight in her
own kitchen, Abby felt homesick for Mike Vogel.
She was fragile with the love they had been making
in the small hours. And a little raw. But she did not
permit herself to think about it yet. She thought
only as far as the pot of camomile she was brewing
for herself.

When everything was ready, she took the phone

off the hook, slipped her cheshire-cat cozy over the teapot, put it on a tray and carried it upstairs to the bathroom. Stripping quickly, she turned on the taps, tied her hair up. She was reaching for the lever to start the shower when, on an impulse, she let the tub fill up instead. She never took baths, but this morning a bath was just what she wanted. She wanted to sit in warm water up to her breast bone and consider the shock she had just sustained. With a sigh she lowered herself slowly into the hot water. She looked at her left hand. The rash was still there, itching. She used that hand to hold her teacup close to her face where its nice flowery vapors steamed her lips.

"Solarcaine," she whispered into the steam. What had he been doing with Solarcaine? She could not ask him, because she was not going to see him again. She couldn't. She was not the adulterous type, lacked the appropriate attitude for sleeping around. Last night was something else, she told herself firmly. An isolated squall in the serene climate of her life. It would go away as soon as she put it out of her mind. "Solarcaine."

She stood up, sloshed across the bathmat to her own medicine cabinet and found a tube of the stuff behind her bottle of Sea and Ski. "Water, stearic acid, mineral oil . . ." she read, then found the active ingredients: "benzocaine, triclosan, menthol and camphor." She rubbed a bit of it on her rash. The itching went away, and her skin cooled noticeably everywhere the white paste was rubbed. No doubt it would feel still cooler on erectile tissue. Small wonder Mike had been able to hold out so long.

He had wanted to impress her. Abby was

touched. It meant more to her than anything he could have said, more than his marathon performance itself. Smiling, she eased herself into the bath once more. The chink in his armor was endearing, and fatal to her. She was not going to be able to put him out of her mind. She didn't stand a chance.

CHAPTER TWELVE

"Solarcaine!" Jerry Gerber bellowed at her. Every crease in his face deepened with medical indignation. "No wonder it's getting worse!" He bathed Abby's hand in weak saline solution and patted it dry with sterile gauze, dressing her down all the while. Calling attention to the blisters rampant on four of five fingers, he warned her to wear cotton gloves when she prepared meals—avoiding contact especially with raw meat, fruit, wool, and cleansing agents. He warned her again not to scratch, and threatened her with the possible necessity of prescribing corticosteroids if she did not show greater promise of recovery.

"Can't you give me a prescription now?" Abby asked. "It itches like crazy!"

"Maybe it *is* crazy," Jerry suggested. She returned his gaze without a word. "I could give you some tranquilizers for it, if you want me to. But I hate to prescribe steroid drugs after the trouble you gave me when you were on the Pill."

Abby grumbled, "At least Solarcaine makes it stop itching."

"And that's the only relief you're getting?"

She nodded.

Jerry was scrawling a telephone number on his prescription pad. "Well, keep the patent medicines away from it. And, if you'd feel better talking about it to a stranger, I suggest you stop by to see my friend Byron." He tore off the sheet and handed it to her.

Abby looked at the friend's name. "A psychiatrist," she said.

"He did his residency here some years ago," Jerry said. "Brightest protege I ever had. I'll call him and tell him to talk to you about your crazy hand for a couple of minutes, if you want me to."

He was being as casually soothing as he would for a child's benefit, Abby could tell. Blushing, she asked, "Isn't there a more dignified . . . a medical name for this?"

"Sure. Dyshydrotic eczema."

"And you think it leads to insanity," Abby managed to joke.

Jerry walked her to the door, patting her shoulder. "Of course not. Not insanity, blindness or masturbation," he chuckled. "It *is* going to warp your fingernails if we can't arrest it soon. But I have a hunch it might respond to a little counseling as well as anything, okay?"

Abby was kissing him goodbye as usual, a chummy peck on the lips, when his nurse opened the waiting room door. Abby had never felt a single pang of guilt for kissing Jerry, but she had never done it before three settees full of faculty wives and children before, either. She felt guilty now, walking out toward the entrance.

"He's got a great-looking place," Jerry was calling after her. "One of those restored townhouses up on Craig Street. Go see him," he urged. Abby thought it must appear to those staring people in the waiting room as if Dr. Gerber were either pimping for her, or having an affair with her himself. No, she reasoned. Don't be silly: this is not the face and demeanor of a woman who fiddles around.

Then she remembered, and blushed again. Getting off the elevator, she strode through the Magee Building lobby hoisting her purse strap to her shoulder, getting ready to open her umbrella. The slip of paper from Jerry's pad fluttered inconspicuously under a newspaper rack in the drugstore entrance as she passed. She knew she was not going to go see Jerry's buddy Byron. She was not about to acquire a hundred-dollar-a-week confessional habit just because the skin of one hand was in an uproar. Under pressure to account for the dermatitis somehow, she was apt to dissolve into tears, she knew, and confide to this young authority figure that she had betrayed her marriage for the sake of an impulsive one-night fling; then he would know, the fling would be indelibly noted in a Case History and become fact. Abby had no intention of endangering herself so definitively. It would do nothing to help the eruption on her palm, she was certain of that much. This eczema business had started long before she made that one particular error anyhow. It was probably the result of worrying about Geoff, she decided.

In the parking lot she ran into Thea Kaltenborn, who begged a ride as far as East Liberty and ended up inviting her to a party. Abby was flattered to be asked.

The invitation grew spontaneously from the midst of Thea's harangue about her research at the prison in Muncy. She was still talking when Abby pulled to the rain-washed gutter in front of Woman-Space, a converted duplex with a sagging porch. Thea got out into the downpour, then leaned back in to tell her about the party.

"Fine," Abby called, nervously eyeing her rear-view mirror. "Thank you. I'll be there."

By the time she got the children home from school, stashed their muddy boots on the stairs to the cellar, and started supper, she had completely forgotten about the party. Until Thea called to recite its address.

Telephone clenched under her chin while she grated cheddar cheese, Abby committed Thea's directions to memory. "And if you don't mind," Thea was adding, "please go by the bus stop at Schenley Park and pick up Dennis Vlaski, will you? I wouldn't ask, except he's got the only slide projector we can find on short notice, and he burned his car at the Gulf Oil protest downtown last month," Thea was saying when Abby heard the upstairs extension click alive. "He's about your age, thin, red moustache."

"Do I interrupt when you're on the phone?" Abby demanded.

"Mom, I have to talk to you," Toby breathed into the phone.

A shiver of anger ran through Abby. Today it seemed that everyone was conspiring to get her alone with this man or that, and just when innocent bystanders might happen along to misinterpret. "In a minute," Abby barked at him, guiltily.

She was still on the telephone when Toby came downstairs. He watched her listen to Thea for a moment, accepted a nubbin of cheddar and retired to dillydally at the refrigerator door. For the umpteenth time he browsed the poster Abby had taped up there amid a jumble of finger paintings. The nun's calligraphy spelled out: The best teacher of children is one who is essentially childlike. Abby knew he liked the foil it was printed on best. He was such a sweet little body. She felt like an ogre for snapping at him.

When Abby hung up the phone, Toby was gone. Spelled out in Gabrielle's plastic letters on the refrigerator door was a memo from Toby, saying "Mom C me In bedroOm T". She hurried upstairs to hug him.

"Can I have this?" was what Toby wanted to know. He was trying ferociously to pry with his bare fingertips the lid from a hermetically sealed brass cylinder.

"Oh sweetheart, no!" Abby began, dismayed. "You mustn't take things from my dresser . . ."

But Toby was prepared to bargain. "I'll get you something else, a cigar box," he urged. "I really need this."

Abby took hold of the brass can herself. "It's Grandpa Hays . . ."

"Daddy said I could have it!" Toby insisted.

"As soon as it's empty, I said," Abby reminded him.

"You were supposed to scatter them ages ago, it isn't fair!"

"As soon as the weather gets better," Abby vowed. "I'll find a nice place and we'll all go out together to do it."

But Toby persisted. "That's what you said last spring. I need it now."

Unreasonably Abby felt like crying. She tried to remember that Toby had a third-grader's priorities, and that he had never really known her father. "What do you need it for?" she asked, brushing his hair behind his ears.

"For the barrel. Of the telescope," he added. "We're making a telescope for the eclipse."

"Who is?"

"Everybody in Multi-Age. At *school!*"

Abby hugged him close to one side and gently placed the cannister of ashes on the bed behind them. "How about if we go to the hardware store after school tomorrow, Mr. Science?" she said. "They'll have all sorts of things you can use . . . stove pipe, copper tubes, everything. Okay?" Toby thought well of that notion.

"What are Eek-Lips, anyhow?" she teased.

Mischief streaked around the corners of Toby's mouth blatant as fudge sauce. "It's these big mice, you know? And gerbils, all kinds of other scurry-warts. Every six billion years or so they come around the sun and take bites out of it with their big lips, and it gets really dark outside over lunch break . . ." His own blarney was cracking him up.

"Is that what Mrs. Hinkle said?"

On the way downstairs Toby admitted some of the eclipse theory was original with him. He forgot again about her long-delayed promise to empty that brass cylinder and release it to him. Abby's promise to provide stove pipe for the Multi-Age telescope was good enough for now. In fact, he was in such good spirits that he kept his little sister entertained all the way through dinner with wild speculations about the sun-mice. The three of them had a jolly time. They tucked themselves full of tamale pie while the rain sluiced down their warm kitchen windows.

The last thing Abby wanted by that time was to go back outside in the rain. Potholes would be deepening, gutters overflowing and, besides, Esther would have to slog all the way in from the country. (Bet it was warm and dry inside the *Friendly* Rising Sun tonight.) She wanted to put her babies to bed, then crawl into her own queen-size with a small glass of brandy and recall every single detail from the hoarded morsel of her night in Mike Vogel's bed. But no. Geoff would be returning from the Philippines next Thursday. By then she absolutely had to be straightened out. She would have to be able to talk to her husband without that unspeakable error ruffling her stream of consciousness.

So she picked up Dennis Vlaski, projector and all, and made her way through torrential rainfall to the party. He turned out to be invaluable. It was impossible to read addresses in the dark, drenched streets of the South Side, but Dennis knew exactly which house they were looking for. It crouched on the hillside, two flights of bulging concrete stairs above the street. They climbed to its porch guided by a glass wind chime which kept clittering and pinging in each fresh gust of rain.

Inside, the house fairly steamed with bodies. Abby had been to crowded parties before, but never to one with so much turbulence below eye level. Every third guest, it appeared, had brought at least one child.

There was always an attitude du jour at these affairs. Tonight's must be Single Parent Power. She began threading her way through the crowd in search of Thea. Progress was not easy. Near the bookshelves she almost stumbled over a cherub sleeping in an Infa-Seat on the floor. Recovering her balance, she bumped into a nice young man in tweed who, turning suddenly to note her apology, whacked a bystander with the infant snoozing in his backpack. The commotion set Abby's nerves on edge. Not that the children were noisy; only the few still awake on arrival made any sounds louder than the adults and those, as the party developed, wore down gradually, plopping one by one into larval configurations of baby repose between chairs and floor lamps. But it was important to watch one's step constantly.

Abby felt no more comfortable eye-to-eye with these adults than she felt being ankle-deep in their children. For all she could make of their conversations, they might as well have been speaking in foreign tongues. And her hostess was nowhere in sight.

"Assertiveness training," someone in Abby's path was saying. A fragile beauty, the trainee was going without her prescription lenses tonight, if her vaguely unfocused gaze was anything to go by. Abby thought it made her look as if she was in love. "You learn how to stand up to lawyers, head-waiters and other power freaks."

Abby inched away, heading toward a hall.

"Forget it," snapped the nice daddy in tweeds and backpack as he poured wine for his companion. "Guilt's just another one of those stinking S and M conventions that male supremacists encourage to keep the slave class in line." The woman whose guilt he was dismissing so handily looked impressed, nodded.

Off to her right, Abby heard someone else saying, "Contest their license renewal if they don't put more women on camera."

A nun in a sweater and kilt was describing her work on a rape hot line. She was the only woman wearing nylon stockings.

"Parenting," came almost simultaneously from two separate clumps of people.

"Class action suit."

" . . . Cady Stanton . . ."

". . . brutality . . ."

"The nurturing instinct."

"My grandmother," pronounced a woman with grey pinstriped hair, "said it was essential to have a contract, even more important than a diaphragm. No generation gap there! It's my mother who was the total wimp."

Not until Abby made her way into the kitchen did she begin to see traces of Thea Kaltenborn. A large kettle of batiking had been abandoned in progress on a rear burner of the stove, mauve dribbles of dye now dried indelibly onto the enamel. This was Thea's place all right. All women—feminists included—use their refrigerators for bulletin boards; this one sported an enormous poster depicting a woman whose eyeballs were Earth as seen from the moon, facing out between bars. The poster announced a public reading of works from Thea's drama workshop at the women's prison upstate. "No Holds Barred," it proclaimed, was an event featuring words and music by political prisoners taken in the war against women, and was a co-production of the Feminist Theatre Collective in cooperation with the Episcopal Community Outreach Ministry. No one but Thea could have cooked up such an event, Abby knew.

She brushed past a pegboard in the hallway. It

was covered with hats—a Special Forces green
beret, a bright red picture hat of varnished straw, a
fedora, a sunbonnet, a baseball cap with a Buc-
caneer armed to the teeth embroidered above the
bill, a crash helmet—all of them Thea's. Following
the smell of fresh smoke, she turned a corner and
found herself in Thea's bedroom.

Her hostess was lounging on a pillow-strewn
bed, smoking a joint and talking with another
woman clad in an African caftan. Rain trickling
down the outsides of the many-paned windows
glittered prettily in the bright light. They were each
fingering a corner of what appeared to be a very
old lace tablecloth. The caftan lady's eyes were
glossy with tears.

Thea noticed Abby at once and smiled broadly,
for all the world as if Abby were precisely the person she wanted most to see. "This will interest
you," she said. "Come on in." Thea slid over and
indicated a seat beside her on the bedspread. Abby
was too flattered to question how Thea knew she
would be interested.

"Abby. Ruth," Thea introduced them.

Ruth nodded and rushed ahead with her story.
"It's obvious that all this stitchery was their only
creative outlet. You know that old bugaboo about
idle hands being the devil's workshop? Invented ex-
pressly for girls and women."

"It worked," said Thea.

"Better than handcuffs," Ruth nodded. "Any
notion how much energy it drains off to satin-stitch
all those curlicues?"

Abby made so bold as to point out, "A lot of
that stuff was useful . . ."

"Yes," said Thea.

"Of course," Ruth said. "It was so useful it effectively kept women from learning to read, or think or engineer or philander along with the master of the house." She was bitter.

Thea's voice filled in the gulf between them smoothly. "These quilts and things, they're not just torture chamber relics. They're positive too, the graffiti of an oppressed sub-culture. Very passionate stuff!" she added.

"Really," Ruth breathed. "You ought to see some of the samplers! Wendy found one at a flea market, wrapped around some old tin cookie cutters. It was embroidered all over with teeny-tiny little constipated morning glories and French knots. And the quotation stitched out on it was mind-blowing! It said: Take heed of Mad folk in a narrow place; Foul dirty ways and long sickness; a Prophetess; a reconciled Enemy; a Young Wench, and Wind that comes in at a hole! Can you dig it? The full scope of woman-hating, copied out in dainty stitches."

"A gallery full of this stuff," Thea proposed. "What a show it would make!"

"And she signed herself," marveled Ruth in conclusion, " 'A wench'. It was embroidered inside-out near the bottom hem, and at first it looked like a signature. *A Wench*. But it was this defiant . . ." Ruth added a noisy razzberry.

Thea straightened one argyled foot to nudge Abby. "What do you think?"

Abby said, "I think you're reckless to sit inside a lighted window smoking pot."

Ruth rolled her eyes.

Thea persisted gently. "I mean, you're in with that Museum crowd. Don't you think you could get us a group show of anonymous craftswomen through one of your do-gooder committees?"

Abby thought about it. A couple of women stopped by Thea's bedroom door, looked in and moved on. Thea was no great shakes as a hostess and still people were flocking in to her party. Thea rarely entertained—not even for feminists. She spent more time in prisons and halfway houses than in living rooms. There was a fierce socialist cast to her politics which most of these women found too racy for themselves but nearly aphrodisiac on Thea.

Abby was convinced of Thea's sincerity. But she was touched most of all by her beauty. Everything about the woman seemed exotic to Abby. She was daintily framed, but her voice rolled out in rich dark contralto, especially when she laughed, which she did uproariously and often. Her olive skin gave her a permanent tan, the shiny straight hair that swung around her face was Manchu black, but her cheeks enjoyed a subcutaneous pink that was preposterously milkmaidish. She winked at people. She had a dimple in her chin. Tonight she was hiding her figure within the sort of jumpsuit Abby's refrigerator repairman might wear. And sandlewood perfume was detectible when she leaned close to nudge a response out of Abby. "Come on, Mullen," she coaxed, grazing Abby's breast with her elbow.

Abby liked it. She relished the pressure, having this singular lady want something from her.

"I'll see what I can do," she said.

Ruth sighed ostentatiously and strolled out of the room.

"I'm not exactly in solid with the Friends of the

Museum," Abby amended. "I'm not a committee chairman or anything. And to tell you the truth, I'm not at all that enthusiastic about becoming one, either."

- Thea was not discouraged easily. "Look at this," she was urging. She spread the delicate web of stitchery over Abby's lap, smoothing an especially ornate section across her thighs. Her hands were warm. "So delicate! Just think. Someone like you crocheted this generations ago." Silence. "The kinship I feel for that woman!"

"What woman?"

Thea stroked the tablecloth. "This one. All those little chain-stitches. She poured out her soul through her fingertips." She raised her eyes to meet Abby's, frankly appealing.

"It would make a lovely show," Abby hedged.

Thea only looked at her, waiting.

"The Friends make me uncomfortable. I don't believe there's one of them who would notice if I never showed up for another meeting. If it weren't for my husband. He's a big success with them these days," Abby said ungratefully. "They are constantly telling me how smart he is. And how attractive. I am not permitted to forget my husband for a minute."

"*I* didn't mention him." Thea took a box of matches from the dairy crates that served as her bedside table, relit her roach. She held her breath, speaking with the voice of a laryngectomy victim: "Did mention chains."

Abby laughed, shaking her head no at the offer of a toke. "You know what? You make me feel guilty."

Thea got up on her knees and switched off the

wall light, leaving them in semidarkness. A bedlamp glowed dimly in the closet where it hung from a drawerpull of a filing cabinet. "There," she rasped. "If there're any narcs outside at least they won't get a good likeness of you."

"No," Abby explained. "I mean you make me feel guilty about my husband. About having one."

"That's absurd," Thea smiled, sprawling comfortably once more at Abby's side. "I can't make you guilty, or not guilty, of anything."

"I know." It *did* sound queer. "But around you it seems as if we women who got married copped out. We're missing out, depriving ourselves. Look at you, you make going it alone look so stylish. You do everything, suit yourself. You're working on your thesis *and* active in politics. You're so stylish!"

Thea laughed.

"No, you *are!* You're independent and freewheeling, fearless. Only someone completely fearless doesn't bother to put up bedroom curtains, especially if there's nobody else living here to protect you. I need curtains to feel safe even when my husband's at home," Abby remarked. "I would feel too vulnerable."

"You came out without him tonight," Thea encouraged her.

"I go everywhere without him these days. He's traveling so much." She squirmed into a more comfortable position on the bed, resting her shoulder and cheek against the rainy window.

"Maybe that's really what you feel guilty about. Being a woman alone. In the eyes of society you're not complete when a man's not within reach, you know. Dangerous, a single woman. An attractive nuisance, like an unfenced swimming pool. Nature abhors that old vacuum," said Thea, pointedly touching the fly of Abby's slacks. "Prevailing attitude anyhow."

"It's *when he comes home* I feel guilty. Not when he's gone."

"Hard to kick the servitude habit, isn't it?"

"I have complete freedom. Nothing but," Abby defended herself, or was it Geoff?

"He trusts you, right?"

"Yes."

"Trusts you with what? His children? His house, the care of him? And who is he to go around *trusting* you, anyhow?"

Abby tried to explain the way she and Geoff complemented one another in their household, the aptness and rewards of her career as a wife. How much their home meant to her. How important her support was to Geoff. Thea listened so carefully that Abby began to sound as if she were complaining. She gave up in embarrassment, thinking she had made Geoff sound awful.

But Thea said, "You're right. You don't have any problems."

"I don't," Abby pleaded. "It's just that . . ."

Thea was firm. "You haven't got a problem in the world. Not compared to the women I see in prison. You've got nothing to complain about, and I wish to Christ that partisans would quit recruiting among the ranks of women like you. You don't have enough anger to put up any sort of sustained fight anyhow."

"I get terribly angry," said Abby at once.

"But not really," maintained Thea. "Not deep down worried angry, like Fiona. Now *there's* a lady who's learning the hard way, and she's gonna move some furniture around before they get her on her knees a second time."

Abby busied herself refolding the old tablecloth.

"Fiona's at Muncy. Twenty years old. She's serving three to five years for grand theft. One year down, two or more to go. And she's six month's pregnant." Scratching her left hand, Abby worried what would become of that young jailbird mother. "Growing up so fast!" she murmured.

"Yeah."

"I grew up very slowly," Abby added.

"Naturally," said Thea. "Middle class has that privilege."

"Sometimes I feel I still have more in common with my children than I do with other adults. Remember the Little Mermaid? That fairy tale about the mermaid who wishes for feet? But when she gets her wish, every step she takes feels like stabbing knives." Abby had never so much as mentioned her Little Mermaid complex to any of her close friends.

"I used to identify with the Little Mermaid a lot," she mused. "I thought that when I became big enough to wear high heels, when I could see where I was going in crowds, then I would be a big lady and would understand everything. I used to play Big Lady. Whenever my mother was out at a class I clomped around the house in her stadium pumps. They were my favorites. I must have liked that wing-tip look," she laughed. "Then my legs started growing. They grew very fast, and for a while I was awfully awkward. I didn't mind, though, because I knew I was on my way to being a Big Lady. Now

I am," she faltered, "not so tall after all. It isn't the way I thought it would be."

Thea took her hand. "Why are you crying?" she asked.

And she was. Not tears, but big gulping sobs congesting her voice. "I still don't understand! It's almost painful. As if I'd spent the first twenty years of my life desperately hoping I'd grow up and then I did, finally. But all I've gotten out of it is longer legs!" she raged. Now the tears were gushing too.

"Poor little mermaid," Thea whispered. "She turned out to be a fishwife." Sympathy was the last straw. Abby broke down completely and indulged herself in a long, blustery cry. It was long overdue. She never cried when she was alone; alone, she was always too busy for such luxuries. And with friends —well, she might try on lingerie in the same dressing room with Maxine, or discuss money with Jerry while he conducted her pelvic examination, but weeping would have meant entirely too much exposure. She would always have to see these people again, face them when the heavy weather died down. Hidden here alone with Thea, she could let go, however. And she did.

Thea did not rush her or urge, "Don't cry." Choking, Abby tried once to apologize or explain. Thea shushed her, saying, "You don't have to explain yourself to me. I don't think you know what it's about anyhow." When Abby's sobbing doubled her over, Thea let her weep into her lap and simply lay a warm hand lightly on the small of her back, patting from time to time. Abby soaked the legs of Thea's overalls, stirred to further tears by the piteous sound of her own crying. At last Thea lifted her by the ears, gently, and gave her a

large bandana still warmly scented from an
overalls pocket. Chuckling, she watched Abby blot
her eyes and stop the dribbling from nose to chin.
When Abby supposed aloud that she had made a
fool of herself and must look a sight, Thea assured
her she was beautiful. She said she admired the
gutsy way Abby could bawl when she finally let go.

Abby said thank you. It had done her a world of
good. Rain continued washing softly against the
windows.

Thea took Abby's hand and spoke earnestly
about the importance of honesty, of sharing, and
how it was only through instances such as this that
she found the sort of rapport—"non-predatory
connection" she called it—that she needed with
other human beings. She talked a lot about human
beings and, it began to dawn on Abby, by "human
beings" she meant "women." Men she called
"men." Thea was extolling the ancient quality of
the friendships women were able to enjoy together
when Abby realized she was still holding her hand.
Rubbing it, in fact. And the dyshydrotic exema was
itching terribly.

When Abby took her hand back, it seemed to
break Thea's train of thought.

"Excuse me," Abby began, intent on displaying
her crazy rash.

But Thea did not notice. The whole lovely
climate of womanly rapport dissolved as she
bounced off the bed and went padding around the
room feeling under furniture for shoes, cigarettes,
who knew. She pronounced briskly that she and
Abby were probably missing all the slides Dennis
Vlaski was showing from the "No Holds Barred"
production. Abby felt rather disinherited. She

would have liked to hear Thea talk some more.

It was not until Thea ushered her into the hallway that Abby realized Thea may have felt rebuked when she let go her hand. Oh lord, she winced to herself, Thea thinks I think she's a dyke. On the verge of saying this with a laugh to Thea, Abby suddenly realized the fact of the matter, which was that Thea's belief in sisterhood did extend to lesbian encounters, that making love with women was for her politically natural and morally apt. Abby had felt no pressure but now she knew the inquiry had been made. And she had exposed herself as politically un-hip. In a shiver of curiosity Abby wondered what might have followed, exactly, had she not pulled away.

Heads turned when Thea walked into the living room. Dennis Vlaski stepped aside as narrator and explicator of the slide show. Thea took over the projector. At once that wonderful voice spread into every corner of the room. A born speaker, Thea.

Abby tiptoed hurriedly toward the front door. Watching in the dark for sleeping babies underfoot, she was unaware that she was a giant shadow crossing the screen. Everyone stared at Fiona's angry young profile flickering over her slacks. "Down in front," someone called. She got out of the picture as fast as she could.

In another minute she was splashing away from the curb. The further she drove from the South Side, the less Thea's sisterhood appealed to her. She could never be an independent woman like the lovely and scarey Thea Kaltenborn. She fancied that would mean being like her in every way. A woman's woman.

Attractive nuisance, Abby fumed. Never before

tonight had she been compared to an unfenced swimming pool. She told herself she did not give a rap what anyone else thought of her. She intended to go right on suiting herself as she imagined she had done ever since she went off to college. She looked into the rearview mirror and smiled reassuringly: that was the face of a steadfast helpmeet if ever she saw one, she thought.

Before going to sleep that night she called Geoff —went through the dreadful tangle of long distance and overseas operators—for the sake of making contact. There was no news, she insisted to him. Only that she missed him terribly. That he must start taking her along on these trips. They belonged together, she told him, and she was lonely.

But she was not lonely. Not any more. Since the curious night when she had first poked her nose outside the nest of her marriage, she was something else. And it frightened her. If Geoff did not keep her with him as she had become accustomed, what would become of her? She was afraid she had a pretty good idea.

CHAPTER THIRTEEN

"Let 'im sue," Mike growled, drinking his milk shake straight from the stainless steel tumbler it was served in.

"He might, at that," replied the other uniformed man. He wore a plastic label saying "Tuckerman".

"Bullshit." Mike's concession to the boss in this matter was agreeing to discuss it over lunch when he could have been eating in peace someplace else; he did not see any need to act mealy-mouthed besides. Elbows high, he attacked his hot roast beef sandwich with knife and fork. "For all he knows, I saved his goddam life. Some days I think I did." With a half-grin he added, "Other days, when I have a little more pride, I figure no harm done. The fool probably would've lived anyhow."

Tuckerman pointed and Mike handed him another paper napkin from the dispenser.

Eat-N-Park was filling up with the lunch crowd. Mike watched a weary husband-wife team of truckers choose a booth while the boss had his say. "You're dealing with the public here and you gotta use a little diplomacy. You can't go around acting like the Game Lands are your own personal estate, Mike."

"Boy if they were, things'd be different."

"That's just the sort of attitude I'm talking about," said Tuckerman. He crumbled another packet of saltines, opened it and poured the cracker shards into his chili.

Mike looked up quickly. "What attitude?"

"The attitude that *I'm* patrolling this district and . . ."

"What do you pay me for, Shag?"

". . . And you're by jing in charge of everything in it." A raised hand forestalled any objections. "Hear me out now. I know you're a conscientious man. I appreciate that. But you ought to be public relations-minded, too. It isn't just this one sorehead we're hearing from. What about the time you kicked that birdwatcher out of Raccoon Creek? He was hopping mad."

"He's lucky he wasn't shot."

"He was working on an annual Thanksgiving bird count. We took no end of noise from the Audubon Society after you ordered him out of the woods."

Mike put down his fork. "Lookit," he said patiently, licking a bit of translucent gravy from one knuckle. "It was buck season. The place was crawling with hunters, each of 'em with at least one rifle and a whole beltful of lead they felt obliged to spray around before sundown. They had all paid for licenses, besides. Feeling entitled to a deer apiece. They weren't gonna be looking out for one little birdwatcher. If that fella didn't have enough sense to stay the hell out of those woods then I just had to step in and make him see it my way, that's all."

"He said you were high-handed."

"I may have been." Mike poked at the slaw that came with his platter. Catching the hand of a passing waitress, he ordered double fries.

"Every sector of the public has a right to use these forests, Mike. It's like he said in his complaint, the wilderness belongs to everybody."

"Wilderness." This last was more than Mike could endure. "Don't give me that 'wilderness' malarky. This district is second-growth woodlots and pasture. It's a couple of isolated little throwbacks supposedly off the beaten trail. Okay, it's the closest thing to nature most city slickers are ever gonna see. So they come out to stomp around on it. And I'm a traffic cop. Far's I see, it's my job to keep the birdwatchers, the hunters, picnickers, wildlife, and hikers all from stumbling over each other. Which I do to the best of my ability. At least the hunters cough up for the price of a license."

"The others are entitled to come just for the beauty of it, if that's what they like," the supervisor protested.

"Beauty, yeah," Mike snorted. "Those guys get all dressed up in their sporty duds from the wilderness outfitters and they come out to enjoy nature. It's a beautiful sight, all right. They spend more on a chamois shirt than I make in a week. Swiss army knives dangling from belts, silk liners inside their damn boots. They spend a day in the woods and then go home feeling satisfied from all that beauty. Like they've just snatched a little piece of ass. They don't *live* with the woods," he scoffed. "They don't know what wilderness is. Or how it works. They don't have a clue how nasty, or how fine it can be because they've never stuck with it."

The supervisor sucked pensively at his coffee

mug. "You're not wrong," he granted Mike. "Half
of those guys don't know shit from Shinola. But it
doesn't pay to come right out and tell 'em so. Remember, discretion is the better part of valor."

Mike scarcely listened to the rest of Tuckerman's
admonition. He watched him eating rhubarb pie a
la mode and said nothing. "Maybe in Montana or
something where they have more bears than people," the boss was droning, "but not in this state.
Not my Game Protectors."

"Maybe I'll go to Montana," grumbled Mike.
"Bet you there's some kind of wilderness there.
Rough as a cob, I hear."

He got like this sometimes, Shag Tuckerman
knew. Spring fever was a very real thing. Game
Protectors got it worse than anybody.

"I've come for my boots," Abby announced.

Backlit in the doorway Mike looked even bigger
than she remembered. She suffered a moment's
confusion, wondering if it were possible she had
found her way to the wrong orchard. But she did
not chicken out, and he did not disappoint her. He
laughed out loud. The sound of it was splendid,
making her glad she had come.

"Wait," he said. Inside he found a scratchy old
army blanket, brought it out and spread it double
on the concrete slab that formed his stoop. He sat
down but Abby stood, unsure what to do. He
reached up and took her hand, pulling her gently
down beside him. Okay, she decided. She was prepared to sit on his porch with him if that's what he
wanted. Eager to, actually. Never in her adult life
had she sat on a porch with someone, both facing
into a warm spring night. She knew it was done.

Her father used to sit on the front porch with the neighbor man while Mother kept rattling her old Underwood at the dining room table. Abby had always assumed that only people who had known each other for ages did this sort of thing. All the clever, or brittle, or leading remarks she had prepared seemed inappropriate now, seated as she was within range of his body heat. So she said something homely: "It's a nice night."

"You know that pheasant?" Mike replied. "The one we ran into down there in the orchard?"

The one that had stopped her pulse. "Yes."

"It's a hen," he said. "I saw her this evening when I was driving up the lane. She had a clutch of chicks with her. Nine of them."

"Are they like Leghorn chicks?" she asked.

"More like chipmunks. That's how their markings look, anyhow. Like two-legged, pot-bellied chipmunks." She liked the way his voice fondled them. "When I rolled into the bend they were milling around in the middle of the lane. So I tooted and they scattered just like fuzzy little pool balls. Then the hen gave a signal and they all bounced into line behind her, went trailing off into that bunch of weeds over by that chestnut sapling." He pointed.

It *was* a nice night. She leaned closer and he put his arm around her waist. "I'd've thought you wouldn't know Leghorns from a shoehorn," he chuckled.

She told him a little about her father and Wyecross Laboratories, about growing up in a household where back issues of *Poultry Pathology Journal* and *Holstein-Freisian World* cluttered the clothes hamper in the bathroom. She could not tell whether he was interested or not, he was quiet for such a long time after she stopped speaking. Or indeed whether he had heard her. When she could not stand wondering any more, she kissed him—a light one on the cheek. He ruffled her hair affectionately, she reached up to ruffle his, and in the tussle that followed he bested her holding both her wrists in one of his hands. She ended up stretching out her legs across the blanket, head resting in his lap.

"Anyhow, you're no country girl."

"Myerstown isn't exactly megalopolis," she maintained.

"Okay then, Farmer Jane," Mike teased. "You might be *from* there. But you've been a hothouse plant for a long time now."

"How would you know that?" Abby clucked.

"The boots."

"What?"

"Those boots you were wearing when you were all gussied up and ended up out here," he told her. "But tonight, when you *knew* you were going to the boondocks, you wore these flimsy flat things."

Pressing her chin down on her chest, Abby looked at her seasonably pink canvas shoes.

"I do it the other way round," Mike continued. "My boots are for everyday. Slogging around in the countryside. Just every once in a while I have to get dressed up for some cockmamie do in Pittsburgh or Harrisburg. Then I put on my low shoes. That's the difference between us country mice and you city mice."

"I feel more like country," Abby replied in a low tone. "Guess I've been traveling incognito." She waited. But Mike did not ask her what she meant.

Obviously they were not going to get to know each other the way men and women did on the cocktail party circuit—by interview. Mike's inner workings would not be accessible by words, any more than were the wild, dumb creatures he tended in the state parks. If she wanted to get to know him, she would have to observe behavior just as he did. She wondered if she had lost those powers since childhood.

His thigh beneath her neck was friendly, solid as a log. What else should she know? She watched the underside of his jaw, trying to imagine what he was seeing amid that pale blur of apple buds beyond the stoop.

Almost absentmindedly be began rubbing her belly; then seemingly thinking better of it, he lifted her sweater to the waist, slipped his hand inside and resumed rubbing the bare skin of her belly. Abby closed her eyes. His big palm candidly browsed her ribs, stomach, waist, ribs again. It felt oddly familiar, as if they had been doing this all their lives—sexual yet not sexy, the same as nursing had been. She could not have felt more at home. Abby relaxed, enlarged.

The air smelled moistly of pollen.

An owl swooped past once, wings rustling. Mike warbled a soft owl call after it, then murmured, "Bet she knows every mole within a hundred acres."

Mike reached idly up and, through her bra, cupped one breast. A mild squeeze. A callous caught in the thin fabric then skittered clear to graze further, elastic amplifying every contact. Abby lay very still, wanting nothing in the world so much as more of this. Her breasts tightened.

"Mm-m," he said, and she felt his voice rumbling in his lap. He became purposeful. Without
disturbing her position or garments, he went on
petting her, nipping, nudging, stirring her up
through her scalp and down through her groin entirely by stroking her breasts until quite simply she
succumbed. Without a word. She had miraculously
become an easy woman.

Not daring to open her eyes, Abby saw Mike
striding into the cabin, a slain stag draped over his
vast back—no—carrying at his loins a bushel
basket brimming with winesaps even broader than
his grin. She saw herself pink with steam at a copper cauldron putting up their winter store of apple
butter, their impossibly darling children tumbling
on a rag rug braided from the wool of Mike's old
uniforms. No, there were no children; the first and
last of theirs was still an ovule eternally young and
futureless in the adipose vault of her innards. She
would not be loosing that form of love on Mike.
She dragged her eyes open and faced him.

Mike was not looking at her. Instead, he was
leaning back against the door frame, chin lifted
and eyes closed as if sorting breezes for scents.

Miserable with love, she rolled her face to his
belt buckle and hid it there. He fingered her
earlobe. They stayed that way long enough for her
to feel, beneath the twill of his pants, an unused
erection subside. She knew she had to get back to
Farley Landing so Esther could go home. There
was no way around it.

Walking to the car he was cheerful, so she was
brave. She tossed her boots into the back seat, then
suddenly turned to him and threw her arms around
his chest. "What are we going to do?" she wailed.

"God, I love you so much!"

When he kissed the top of her head she could hear his smile moving in her hair. He said, "Do? Honey, what you oughta do is come see me every night you can get the chance. We'll do anything you want."

"I will," she promised, getting into her car. Maybe this was not so hopeless after all. "Daytime would be much easier, though."

"I work days," Mike told her. "But I'll take you along sometime if you want."

She wanted him to take her and never bring her back.

CHAPTER FOURTEEN

As Geoff took to telling anyone who would listen, Abby was obsessed with his health. More specifically, Abby was developing terrible fears about all this traveling he was doing. She worried that the airliners he rode might be highjacked by malicious liberationists of one nationality or another. She fancied his pilot would one day happen to be a Vietnam veteran, an unregenerate hophead who would roll his 747 just to prove he could do it without spilling a drink in first class, then lose control and drill them all into the godforsaken ground of Tasmania. Geoff was flattered by her concern. He made light of the odds that she should be untimely deprived of her husband. He tried to soothe her with distracting anecdotes about his new sidekicks, the Jajau fishermen. Her lurid fantasies grew more troublesome than ever. It seemed implausible to her that he had escaped death by shark attack while touring the Celebes reefs in anything so fragile as a fishing dugout. Even without sharks, on dry land there was food poisoning or parasites. It was not unheard of, she reminded him, that traveling Americans be taken for spies and quietly made to disappear near the borders of turbulent nations.

Simply leaving and re-entering his own country—
what if one of those vaccinations backfired, suppose his own Immigration service gave him a fatal
dose of cholera? In front of the children she made
it a point not to mention these fears. But they kept
her awake long after Geoff fell asleep at night.

He had been gone more than he had been at
home in the last two months, and Abby was no
longer used to sharing the bed. Now she noticed
how heavy he was; it seemed their mattress sagged
hopelessly toward his half. She felt she had to cling
to the edge of the mattress on her own side to keep
from constantly rolling into him. She kept away.
His body made a furnace under the covers—too
warm for a woman in a long nighty. She had taken
to sleeping nude in his absence, enjoying the feel of
sheets against her flesh whenever she turned over.
But with Geoff there, she could never be sure when
the covers might be yanked off her so she had to
return to swaddling herself in flannel. Nighties
bound her at the armpits when she turned, chafing
her. She turned a lot, wondering whether jockeying
from time zone to time zone would induce a heart
attack in the man sleeping beside her. Until recently he had required the steadiest of routines to feel
well and happy. She wondered if he was changing
as much as she was. Was he getting sick? She worried that he would see how worried she was. Afraid
of waking him, she could not bring herself to woo
sleep by masturbating. He would insist on helping,
and he needed his sleep. She did not feel up to talking about it, either. She hoarded her troubles.

For the first time in a sixteen-year marriage
besotted with sharing, her vote was "no confidence". These worries were hers alone.

Geoff did not notice that privacy was becoming
an issue between them. He did not even notice the
longsuffering spirit in which Abby made space for
his toilet articles on the bathroom vanity when he
unpacked. He did not mind that Abby no longer
invited him into the shower with her. (But then he
had broken that habit himself while sharing bathrooms on the road with his cameraman.) He did
not miss the detailed reports of her days—a custom
she quietly dropped. Mainly because he was preoccupied. There was so much new experience for him
to digest, so much more to plan. Abby listened
when he thought aloud, always said she was
fascinated right along with him, and they both
took her at her word.

He *was* somewhat offended by a new poster he
noticed on the refrigerator door, but he assumed
the thing had to be there because of some stage
Toby was going through. No doubt the less said
the better. Actually, it had been Abby who replaced the nun's silkscreen with the cartoon frog
glowering, "I'm so happy here I could just shit!"

Esther took notice, however. She was always the
first to decipher new fronts in the emotional weather of the Mullen household. Seeing the cartoon she
only snorted, but from then on Abby could feel
Esther running interference for her like a good
mate, devotedly dreading whatever might come
next. Seeing Esther's reaction intensified Abby's
agitation because then she knew these changes
were real, not imagined. Neither of them mentioned it until one radiant mid-morning when the
two housewives were working in the kitchen.
Esther was kneeling atop the counters, head and
arms buried in cupboards she was scrubbing. Nests

of bowls, cans and canisters stacked neatly around her knees, she huffed and rattled spring cleanliness into every nook and shelf.

Abby was preparing a joint tax return. Or trying to. At least she was sucking on a pencil. Sunlight splashed in on the pale wood of the breakfast table where she was working. She should have been contented, if not happy. But concentrating on numbers was beyond her this morning. Their taxes were a mess: for the first time Geoff's income was not based exclusively on tidy little checks from the university's Office of the Comptroller, and she would probably have to income-average for the next five years. Five more years of this, she ruminated. When she could not see past today.

"Nuts!" she yelped at last in frustration, flinging her pencil into a tidy bouquet of bachelor buttons.

Sounding like God, Esther's voice reverberated from a gaping cupboard door. "Why don't you go to one of them tax guys?" it asked.

Abby brightened. "Yes," she said. "I'll ask Geoff if he knows anyone."

Esther boomed, "Why bother?"

"What?"

"I mean," said Esther, pulling out of a cupboard and eyeballing Abby, "if Geoff's too busy to help you with the taxes, why should you bother him about finding an accountant? Can't you do it on your own?"

"Because," shrugged Abby, "he may not want me to do it at all."

"Hey. He likes convenience more'n anybody I know. No reason why you shouldn't do the same. Old Geoff's the one that bought the microwave oven, so you could fix things extra fast," Esther insisted. "And the electric crockpot so you could fix things extra slow. He won't care. Go for it."

"Well," said Abby, arranging and rearranging the bachelor buttons amid the pepper grinder, the sea salt grinder, the stoneware honey jug with Pooh clambering over the rim, and her tea cup. "I can't do it today anyhow."

"Why not?"

Eyes blazing, Abby turned to Esther and pronounced hotly, "Because Geoff took the car into town today. I can't do anything!"

They both knew Esther was onto her.

Grateful for the chance to confess blamelessly, Abby raged on: "I hate being stuck out here without a car! He could have taken a bus, or caught a ride with any one of a dozen neighbors who work in Oakland. I even suggested that to him, but no, he has to take the car on the first really hot clear day all year, so he can come home at his famous *convenience*."

"You can take my car for the whole day if you want to," Esther offered blandly.

"Thanks," Abby said, shaking her head no. "Some other time maybe. Geoff and I both have to be dressed and on the road by four thirty if we're going to make it through rush hour traffic to that damn thing downtown."

Esther reinserted her head and scrubbed away at another cupboard. "What damn thing?"

"An *opening*," smirked Abby as sourly as she could. "Another blessed event in the cultural community. Some brilliant young architects have restored a warehouse and turned it into a gallery. They're having caviar and vodka catered by Bikanka, and sushi that Maxine extorted from the new Japanese place near the Hilton. It'll be a mob scene. They've talked an old blues quartet into coming out of retirement for the occasion. Everyone with any pretensions of gentility is going. All our friends. Shadyside and Squirrel Hill will be there *en masse,*" she complained.

For a moment the cupboards had nothing to say. Then Esther finished the last shelf, hopped to the floor and tossed her sponge into the sink. "Sounds better than a sharp stick in the eye," she remarked.

"Well of course. I'm just not in the mood for a brilliant soiree. I detest making conversation at these noisy things."

"I wouldn't know how, myself," Esther commiserated.

Abby was quick to point out, "There's nothing to it, if you're brazen enough. You just talk about yourself until you're hoarse. No point in listening because you can't hear a blessed thing unless you're the one saying it. And I never have anything to say."

"Right."

Abby studied Esther's loyal back as she emptied her plastic pail into the sink, rinsed her sponge, wiped the sink. She felt like hugging her. Sheepishly she ventured, "You really wouldn't mind if I just went out for a little while? To clear the cobwebs."

"Geoff won't be back before two," Esther assured her. "He's taking someone to lunch at the Brackenridge Club."

Abby did hug her. Accepting the keys and taking the manila folder marked "Taxes", she trotted down the steps and into fresh air.

The parking lot outside the *Friendly* Rising Sun

was empty when she got there. She waited in
Esther's car. Sunlight fell through the windshield
onto her lap adding its warmth to the longing already accumulating there. She lolled her head in
the open window. A breeze lightly stirred the small
hairs around her face. But Mike did not appear.
The shopworn waitress Donna emerged from
within just before the first customer arrived, in
time to prop the front door open. And the regulars
trickled in for their lunchtime drafts, sausage,
soup, until nearly one-thirty. Then the trickle re-
versed itself and ebbed. Confident that no one
would notice her in the frazzled beige Malibu, she
kept watch for Mike's El Camino or the Game
Commission truck. For two hours.

Desire stymied gathers momentum. The longer
she waited for Mike's truck to roll into the parking
lot the more determined she was just to *see* him. If
she had had any notion where in all the blooming,
seeping, twittering woods of Allegheny County to
begin looking for him, she would have headed for
the hills right away. She decided finally that she
should drive out to his house. Chances of his being
there were remote, she acknowledged, but she
would never know without giving it a try.

On the road, every vehicle that materialized in
her rearview mirror looked as if it would become a
Game Commission truck. What she hoped against
hope would be Mike heading toward her turned
out to be a Pennsupreme dairy tanker. It nearly
swept her off the blacktop in passing.

If she had glimpsed Mr. Vogel in the lane she
might have stopped to inquire about his son's daily
route. He was nowhere in sight. The gnome in the
housedress and coke-bottle glasses who was setting

out primroses by the mailbox was more than Abby was prepared to reckon with; she sped by trying to look as if she were lost and possibly looking for the Turnpike.

The muddy tire tracks outside Mike's home were empty. By daylight, with the door shut and windows blind, the quaint cookhouse itself looked defiantly barren. Only the odor of apple blossoms was the same. She turned around in a patch of shiny new grass, hoping to leave visible tracks—her valentine to an unlettered lover. A wren called out and broke her heart.

Abby fled.

She was still thinking of Mrs. Vogel when she and Geoff walked into the reception downtown. Suffused with jealousy for the dumpy little figure who knew everything there was to know about Mike's childhood, she envied her living one knoll and a gross or so of apple trees away from him now. In the doorway she hesitated. Geoff firmly steered her across the threshold by her elbow. Fluent jazz and conversation surrounded them at once. It occurred to Abby that no one here cared a bit for anything more primitive than the *crudités* they were bathing in yogurt dip. To be sure, there was a certain element of hip funkiness to this building itself; the architects had retained a freight elevator for public access to this fourth-floor loft. Each new mob of party-goers came in smiling sportingly about riding up in that novelty. And the dangling tinshaded lightbulbs which were period for the building lent a chic "high tech" sort of vulgarity to the new gallery. But it was processed, a doctorate-level tribute to the city that macho built. The gruff old warehouse walls had been sand-

blasted clean and hung full of photorealism, post-
impressionism, dressed with little jewel-like spot-
lights as if the bricks themselves were semi-pre-
cious. The place reeked of artifice. And here stood
Abby, with the smell of fresh mud on her mind.

Come on girl, she urged herself. You can do this.
Start chatting with someone, you've done it before.
She had indeed survived countless small-talk festi-
vals in her years as a faculty wife, but tonight she
was in a delicate condition. The less she uttered the
better. If she opened her mouth she could not be
sure she would not give herself away as a sower of
wild oats. Her misdeeds were on the tip of her
tongue and like so many spilled beans they might
bounce—pollen, gravel, hops, semen bubbles,
pheasant babies—scattering on the vivid varnish
underfoot, bearing witness against her into every
corner of the room. She knew she was pretty in her
grey cashmere. She resolved to get by on looks
alone.

Maxine found them within the first five minutes.
First she chided Abby for not returning her phone
calls, then she kissed Geoff mockingly on his ring
finger. "Welcome to our humble city, world trav-
eler. Good Christ, Abby, are you sunburned or are
you just glad to see him?"

Abby smiled tightly. Sunburn made her blue
eyes startlingly greenish, she knew, but she was not
about to account for her two hours in the sun today.

"You've been hiding out from me, sunbathing or
something, when you could have been helping me
break in the new tennis court," Maxine accused
her. "Shame on you."

Geoff paid little attention to the frothings of

Maxine. But he did begin to watch Abby more closely when a succession of university friends and associates all said how long it had been since they had seen either Geoff *or* Abby.

"Sorry you couldn't make the party," came up a lot; they wanted Geoff to know it was not their fault if Abby did not get out while Geoff was gone.

"We missed you at choir practice," was Anne Fellows's greeting, accompanied by a small kiss in the vicinity of Abby's left temple. Geoff frowned slightly, then was led away by Arnold Fellows to "talk Foundation."

Dutifully Abby made the rounds, stopping by little groups to chat wherever someone snagged her elbow and drew her in. She heard who would be getting tenure and who would not. Chris Fairchild would not.

She heard what Previn said about the chamber concerts at the Hillman Library. She learned that Geoff was a candidate to become chairman of his department, and reflected for a moment that once upon a time such news would have propelled her and Geoff rejoicing into each other's arms, decorous arty party or not.

She also heard it said that Geoff would never chair the department—not as long as he spent more time gadding about than he did on campus. She heard his friends point out to his detractors that Geoff did mention the university by name when he was interviewed. She heard variously that she was pregnant, that she had been traveling with Geoff, and that she was doing everything she could to further her husband's campaign for the department chairmanship. When confronted directly with gossip she always answered

with a hearty *non sequitur* before moving on. Sounding dippy was her best protective coloration,
evolved over years of experience. But she was
growing quite tired of it. Smiling wearily, she decided to take refuge near Geoff.

Drifting up behind her husband she heard him
saying, ". . . When in fact, *she* is the one with
health problems. That's why she's been staying
home. Resting. Some form of dermatitis, I don't
know. It's a virus. It seems to sap her strength,
make her somewhat reclusive." He stopped then,
noticing that his listeners saw her behind him. He
turned gallantly to include her, but she intended to
keep moving.

"Yes, a virus," she nodded to the philologist
who put out a hand to detain her. "It's caused by
the same virus that causes asthma, ulcers and alcoholism."

The entire group looked at her as if she had gone
mad, Geoff included.

Maxine sailed up to the group laughing, "Abby,
you're too droll!" and rescued her. They retreated
to the sushi table together.

Not long afterward, Jerry Gerber rescued her
from Maxine. He distracted her from her inter-
rogation, announcing that he was famished and
that they had better hustle up to Mt. Washington
before their dinner reservations were given away.
He was right. They collected Geoff and said their
goodnights in short order.

High above the city they went in to dinner.

Hugo the headwaiter welcomed them exactly as
he had been doing for the last decade. Their cus-

tomary table for four was set for them by the windows. As always, Jerry helped Abby into her chair while Geoff automatically moved to pull out a chair for Maxine and was, as usual, reprimanded for patronizing her. They had their usual Scotches, gnocchi, veal scaloppine with multiple bottles of Valpolicella, all of it laced with the telling of Geoff's newest cosmopolitan adventures. Abby had heard most of them driving home from the airport. She may have had her head turned in the direction of the storyteller, but she was staring out the windows.

From up here downtown was pure sparkling magic, as usual. The rivers at the Point reflected light back from the expressways, the bridges, the barges, the buildings. And the fountain was turned on tonight—lighted from below, its tall shaft of water pluming handsomely in soft winds out of the North Side. Much was made, Abby thought, of the glamorous way the Ohio, the Allegheny and Monongahela garnished Pittsburgh's crotch. Justly so. The three rivers were always impressive, imposing—equally fascinating to visitors and local society. But the part she liked best was knowing there was always a fourth, hidden river down there. Not so articulate as the other three with their discrete banked beds, it was subterranean. The Wisconsin Glacial Flow seeped upward through amorphous deposits of gravel, but it was a live river nevertheless.

Deep, dark, constant, the Glacial Flow meant a great deal to Abby, and had ever since she found out about it. One drowsy afternoon when she and the children had waited in the car long enough for

Geoff, they strolled across campus to the Bureau of Mines for a little browse of the geology displays. Toby and Gabrielle had taken to the immense glossy coal nuggets at once, oohing and ahhing a succession of noseprints on every glass case. But Abby lingered over the cutaway physiography as if it were her family tree, pondering that underground river.

Knowing the source of Point Park's gaudy fountain gave it new value in Abby's eyes. To others its spouting water may be the principal jewel of the Renaissance City. But for her it was a totem, a reminder that life existed outside corporate and metropolitan channels.

Wisconsin Glacial Flow was her secret. That uncivilized river reminded her of Mike. And the thought of both kept her from screaming during dinner. Fortunately, no one wanted to linger over dessert; everyone had babysitters waiting at home.

Geoff was still talking about statistical mirages when Abby finished brushing her teeth—how important it was to have extensive primary sources so that, in his computations, he would not unwittingly round off computations which some other scholar had rounded off already. Abby rinsed her stockings, making the right muttering sounds of attentiveness. She assumed that when Geoff fell silent, brushing his own teeth, the monologue from the bathroom was only temporarily disrupted, that they might go to sleep lulled by anecdotes from Geoff's migratory census. She crawled into bed. Nothing happened.

When she opened her eyes, Geoff was standing silently at the foot of the bed, looking at her.

"You'll go stale, you know," he said, pulling on his pajama jacket. No doubt he imagined his voice sounded kindly. But Abby recognized the tone; he used it whenever her performance had not been up to snuff.

"Why?" she asked, dreading a lecture so clearly intended for her own good.

"I know, I know," he said, getting into bed. "You don't want me worrying about you, but I worry just as much as you do about me. You're not circulating."

"I am."

"Not enough," he objected. "Not when I'm out of town."

She took a deep breath. "Do we want you to be department chairman? Is that what this is really about?"

A grin of satisfaction brightened his face for a moment. "I'm not so worried about that. They'll probably have to make me chairman when they see all the grants I can attract to the University. If only to save face. What concerns me more is you. I'd like to know you're not lonely while I have to be away."

"What do you expect?" Abby began.

"I expect," and he pinched her cheek fondly, "that you will make it a point to get out of the house regularly. I don't want you in purdah just because your man isn't handy."

Abby's palms broke out in sweat, inducing terrible itching on the left hand. "I *go* out," she managed to insist.

Geoff's smile was gone; he was not fooling around. "Not with our friends, you don't."

"Who invites half-a-couple to dinner parties?"

"You are not to worry about that," Geoff said, bearing down. "I told you, go out without an escort if you have to. Have people in, if you'd rather. Someone has to keep after our obligations, and I certainly can't do it in flight. Besides," he added, "I heard Maxine prodding you. Obviously she thinks you're turning down invitations, too. You mustn't! It's not fair. You're making us outsiders."

Abby was incensed. "*I* have always been an outsider," she declared hotly. "I'm not so sure I care if we lose touch. Your colleagues and their wives only accept me . . . hell's bells, Geoff, even my own friends accept me only because we're on the same social circuit. Because of *you!*"

Geoff looked offended. "Can't you appreciate," he began.

"Appreciate, yes," Abby railed, surprising and scaring herself. "I always appreciate favors. But I resent being expected, required to do anything, show up or perform, by people who only bothered to know me in the first place for your sake. Maybe what I need is some friends of my own."

"Maxine is your friend," said Geoff, studying her face intently. "And you're neglecting her."

"Maxine," fumed Abby. "She is annoyed with me because I've caused a gap in her tidy little circle of reciprocal dinners. She can't figure out who's supposed to have who over next because the Mullens have dropped out. It's like a chain letter."

"She cares about you."

"She cares a great deal that you and Jerry and I are all close," Abby pointed out. "But we have to do things as a foursome because the wife is always included."

"Apparently *you* don't think so," Geoff bitched. "I don't care how you are frittering away your spare time, but it cannot be healthy if it excludes everyone who loves you."

He has no idea, Abby gloated, how much Mike loves me. How robust I feel. Mike loves me better than you ever did and he wants me with him every day. But she kept it trivial.

"I don't think being with people constantly is healthy, either, Geoff," she objected. "You sound like Maxine. She's always trying to get me to join some sort of class, to improve myself, finish my degree."

"If it's being short a degree or two that makes you fancy yourself an outsider," Geoff said, "she might be right. Maybe you should go back to school so that old Bachelors you're missing won't get in your way any longer."

"No! I have more experience and, probably, a better education than most of the teaching assistants you guys pass off on your undergraduates. I couldn't bear to be a student anyhow. Not after hearing the way you and Jerry talk about the women who come back to finish."

Injured virtue was one of Geoff's best acts, Abby noticed for the first time. "Who? Name one."

"Thea Kaltenborn," she shot back. "Thea might be unorthodox, but she's smart and works hard, and I positively quail listening to the contempt in your voice when you gossip about her. You'd probably talk about my papers that way, too."

"You're not like Thea in any way, shape or form," said Geoff. Abby did not trouble to correct him. "And I am truly sorry if you ever thought I intended for you to emulate her. She is a tough

broad. Bright as they come, I'll grant you. But sex-
ually confused, aggressive and," he added with disdain, "out for herself."

"But I'm not?"

"Of course you're not," Geoff approved
"You've got too much breeding. You're fine exactly as you are, Ab. You don't need a degree."

Breeding. Abby felt like letting loose a scream. It
was true, the last thing she needed was a degree.
But Geoff's chorus of "don't change a hair for me"
enraged her. She glowered at him. "Do you think
Mister Rogers likes me just the way I've always
been, too?" Steady, girl.

Fortunately Geoff laughed. She added: "Maybe
I'll invite him over for dinner one night while
you're gone. How about that? Do you think he'd
respect me in the morning?"

"That's not what I mean by circulating," Geoff
protested, grabbing her leg above the knee and
squeezing. It tickled unbearably. Abby dissolved
into shrieks and the ensuing silliness seemed to do
them both good. Their old habit of being good na-
tured with each other was still in effect, thank
heavens. What she needed even less than a B.A.
degree, Abby told herself, was an open breach in
her relationship with Geoff. She had always assumed she wanted whatever he wanted, but now
that she had secrets to defend, she found it more
urgent than ever that her husband should get
everything he wanted. His complacency would be
her best protection. Well, he had talked himself out
of tonight's grumpiness and seemed contented
enough.

Satisfied that for the time being she had deflected his disturbing new interest in her, she was almost optimistic. Geoff reached up and turned out the light. Softly, over the rustle of their matching blankets and linen, she ventured to have the last word. "I'm feeling my way, is all," she murmured. "Geoff, I promise you, I *am* trying to find the best possible use for my energy. I'm not abandoning ship really. I just need a little privacy, okay?"

"Whatever you need," sighed Geoff. "I want you to be happy."

He went to sleep soon after a brisk round of well-practiced orgasms for them both.

Abby lay awake. She grew cunning. She was going to have to cover her tracks if she wanted to avoid alarming Geoff again. I want you to be happy, he had said. Abruptly she understood what that really meant—I want you to be no trouble for me. She had no intention of troubling anyone so long as she could engage Mike Vogel unmolested.

Mike Vogel, Mike Vogel, she rolled the name of her lovely lover around in her mouth for a moment. Finding such a treasure had been accidental —anyone would grant her as much. But no more of that, she instructed herself sternly. She could not go on blindly feeling her way, creating accidents to get what she wanted. Accidents could not always turn out so favorably for her; she would have to have a plan.

A plan. She hesitated, knowing plans would cost her. Plans were deliberate; she would be admitting to herself what she was up to. One tremor of fear, or excitement, ran through her. She went ahead and concocted her plan. If she was discreet enough she could have everything she wanted. "No harm done" would be the cherry on top.

The next morning she took down the froggy cartoon from her refrigerator door. Later, when she saw Toby fishing it from the trash she said nothing, knowing it would surface next in his room. From that day until her husband left town again, Abby did not have a moment to herself. Geoff surrounded her with friends, squired her about town. He resurrected dormant associations one after the other, then praised her lavishly for the delectable meals she felt compelled to prepare for these new old friends. He took pains to include her in conversation, unless of course it was technical. He managed to get a lot of attention for himself by putting Abby's well-being first. As he was quick to tell anyone who showed the slightest interest, Abby was going through a difficult period of adjustment and needed lots of love. Which he alternately called support. Whenever they were temporarily alone he proposed sex, brought her drinks, rubbed her back. She was monitored like a bleeder.

Abby could scarcely tell whether Geoff's fresh devotion was punishment for her flagging attention to his interests, or whether he actually feared she might be straying from the fold. Either way, his attentions were burdensome. Thoughtfulness, on Geoff, was an unnatural act.

She kept reminding herself: he'll leave soon.

He insisted on making breakfast for the whole family his last morning at home. He did know a lot about appliances, Abby observed, but precious little about how groceries become a meal. Repulsing every offer of help, he finally served hot food to his wife and children and by eight fifteen the kitchen had become such a rubble of half-baked delicacies and artistic temperament that there was little to do but evacuate.

Driving Geoff to the airport Abby kept reminding herself, he'll be gone soon. As they topped the last big hill on the Airport Parkway she saw the sign she had always found so provocative; just at the crest in front of a vast sweep of sky it announced: Ohio and Points West. She felt like flooring the gas pedal, until she remembered there was no need to run away. In public, at the airport, she kissed him goodbye. Gladly. All she had to do now was to kiss his friends in public, too, from time to time. Triumphant, she told herself it was easy as pie, this plan of hers. She could do it indefinitely.

When Abby returned home Esther was nearly finished loading the dishwasher. They exchanged sympathetic grins. Esther sniffed into a bowl of yellowish liquid, then inquired, "What's this?"

Abby looked. "That's Gabrielle's," she explained. "I think she put five eggs and a pint of milk in there. She was doing quite well, actually, until Geoff threw her out of the kitchen. It seems she didn't know you don't put honey in omelettes. I thought Geoff was going to burst a vein."

Esther shook her head. "You had breakfast?"

"I did my best," Abby replied with chagrin. "Cream of Wheat is something I can barely force down."

"Me either," said Esther. "But I can salvage these goodies. What d'you say I add a little o.j. or sherbert, put it in the blender and turn it up to

'moosh' or something, and we'll have smoothies
for breakfast?"

Gratefully, Abby nodded. She poured two mugs
of coffee and, wobbly with relief, sank into a kitch-
en chair. They waited for Esther's breakfast to
wind down.

"Excellent!" Abby declared. She finished her
shake in a few enormous swallows, then got to the
serious business of breathing steam from her coffee
mug. "He makes me so nervous!"

Esther took things more slowly. After a few sips
she started carefully peeling cellophane from
today's pack of menthol 100's. When she got the
first one lit, she tossed the match hissing into the
sink and leaned back in her chair, exhaling, "Sure.
But you'll have some peace and quiet now. By the
time he breezes in from Columbia or wherever . . ."

"Colombia."

"You'll have the herb garden planted, a new
swimming suit picked out, and you'll be ready to
enjoy him again."

"Whew! I'd better be."

Esther looked at her and pursed her lips. "It's
like that already, huh?" she said.

"He never should have started going on these
long trips, that's all," said Abby.

Esther waited a few moments, digesting this sudden frank anger. She had seen Abby flare up before, but only over temporary annoyances. When
the two of them talked she had always relaxed, ru-
minating rather than complaining. "Keeps you off
balance, having him here and then not here, eh?"

But Abby leaned forward and delivered herself
of a confidence more dire than that. "When he's

not here, I don't miss him . . ." she began.

"You're a big girl now," nodded Esther. "Three times seven."

"And when he *is* here, I don't want him then, either." Abby pressed on. God, it was such a relief to say this. "I think the only reason I've ever wanted him was because I already *had* him. So I *had* to want him, the way you do with children. Sixteen years!" she gritted into her coffee mug.

"People change," said Esther. Prattle, but it kept Abby company.

"Not Geoff," she hissed. "I've been thinking about all these wonderful changes he's been going through. Or should be, anyhow. You know, since he's begun getting recognition in his field? All this hasn't changed him a bit. The only difference is that now he can be as manic in public as he's always been in private. Only he's not at home so much. Now I've had the chance to look at him with a little perspective. And you know what? He's a twirp. An over-achiever. All the enthusiasm in the world won't ever make him substantial. Or even thrilling. Let alone, loving. I don't like him, Esther," roared Abby, trying to make herself heard over the tears collecting in her throat. "He's not even my type!"

Esther patted the table thoughtfully. "Is anybody?" she offered.

With a rueful smile, Abby shook her head. "I'm my father's daughter all right. Round peg."

The housekeeper looked back at her from old, old eyes.

"This is ridiculous," Abby railed. "I mean there are battered wives out there who would give their eye-teeth for a nice husband like Geoff. He's decent. Reliable. What am I complaining about?"

"Maybe a little elbow room?"

"That's what I told Geoff," sniffed Abby. "That's all I need. I'm glad he's got to be in Colombia 'til the end of the month. Even if it does mean we'll never get the sundeck built."

"Forget the sundeck," advised Esther. "You don't need a sundeck. You already have a perfectly good patio. Could be what you need is some other place to stay."

"No!" she blurted before Esther could suggest anything further. "Don't start that! Good lord, I can't think of anything I'd rather *not* be than a libber. Some people aren't cut out for it. I'm certainly not. I can't imagine spending all my time with women. Squinting at men as if they were the enemy." She was babbling, concentrating more on the terrifying prospect of being pushed from her own nest than on what she was saying. She said, "I don't want to take care of myself!"

"Well," Esther summarized. She took their omelet glasses to the dishwasher and punched the start button. Almost as an afterthought, she turned back to Abby and shouted over the wash cycle, "It's not like you're ugly or ignorant."

"No."

"Plenty of men out there would like to take care of somebody like you. Have you thought of that?"

Abby gave a little hoot and said no. No deceit intended. Confiding to Esther about her infidelity would do no service to the truth when the truth of the matter was, there were some things these two women never discussed. The understanding which passed between them had always been more tribal than verbal. Esther faced enough unpleasantness when she scoured the drains of the Mullen household and swept its nether regions. That was Esther's job and she managed not to mind. But part of Abby's job was to attend to the unseemly details of her own behavior, and Esther seemed just as grateful to be spared the psychic hairballs and rubbish.

"I'd have to be crazy to leave Geoff," Abby remarked casually. Testing the sound of it.

"He'd be crippled from the waist up without you. You do everything for that man," said Esther.

"He's got two secretaries now," Abby corrected her. "One for each office. Not to mention a cinematographer, an editor, two teaching assistants, one agent, a computer and, when he wants it, the Foundation limo. He'll be needing me about next December, to buy Christmas presents for them, that's all."

"If you're *not* having an affair you should have your head examined," was Maxine's opinion.

"Um." Abby was the one who suggested they get together to make up the kids' Easter baskets. Dylan, Toby and Gabrielle should have traditional polychrome eggs no matter how many other traditions were secretly being by-passed.

"No kidding, Abby," Maxine went on. "You should find yourself a good shrink and go into analysis."

"Because I'm not having an affair?" said Abby, incredulous.

Maxine made a face. "Sure, go ahead and poke

fun," she replied. "But you are one very mixed up lady. We're all a little weird, face it. You, however, are especially peculiar these days and you're beginning to worry me. I'm not the only one. Ask Jerry. We both think the way you're withdrawing is not a good sign, babydoll."

After the Easter egg-painting incident, Abby took care not to expose herself to Maxine alone any more. Maxine tempted her too much, tempted her to tell all about Mike and demand an explanation.

The shrink was a good idea, though. The more Abby thought about it, the plainer it became to her that going to see a psychologist might remove some of the pressure. If it were generally known she was in therapy, her friends might stop trying to cure her. If at worst she came to be proven crazy, she figured, that verdict would provide her complete immunity.

"Do you think there's something wrong with me?"

From the front windows of her therapist's apartment she watched rain falling on the roof of Soldiers and Sailors Memorial Hall. She had chosen well. Anyone who knew Geoff would recognize the Mullen family car parked at the curb below. In addition, Dakota had an excellent reputation among the professionals attached to the University and was very popular. But what Abby liked best was that everything about the woman was cheerful— from her aloha shirt to the neon sculpture on the mantle spelling out "Powerlessness Corrupts."

Dakota listened for forty-five minutes, congratulated Abby on her powers of expression, and then explained what she could about dependency balance in marital relationships. No, she did not think Abby was crazy, but she definitely could benefit from additional meetings.

So Abby resolved to visit Dakota again sometime. And moved on, foxily leaving false trails.

She had not been to choir practice at church since Advent, when Geoff got that devastating good news from the Bessemer Foundation. But no harm done. Just now they were rehearsing Easter selections from *Messiah* and Abby knew "All We Like Sheep" like the back of her hand. Anne Fellows, Kit Fairchild, and the others welcomed her back cordially. It did her heart good to sing at the top of her lungs. Besides, the activity kept her moving around—and harder to pinpoint.

She asked Esther's Web to keep his eyes open for a clean used car. She truly did need a car of her own whenever Geoff was home. There were those future appointments with Dakota to consider, all sorts of business. Besides, it wouldn't kill Geoff, or her, for her to make a few major decisions on her own.

She filed the tax forms before April 15.

She finished moving Geoff's files into his office at the Foundation and stayed long enough for lunch with his new secretary. Lots of University people saw them eating at Stouffer's.

She stopped by the public television station to pick up her schedule for Pledge Week volunteer work. So did lots of other faculty wives.

Once these matters were arranged, Abby relaxed. She felt a student again, committed this time to learning the best way of being unhappily married. Her hand stopped oozing lymph. It slowly began to heal. Maybe there would not be stigmata after all, she wisecracked to herself. She felt wicked whenever she was in town conspicuously and deceitfully being Geoff Mullen's better half. But it was something she could get used to.

CHAPTER FIFTEEN

In the pasture below Vogel's farmhouse Abby was something else entirely. A simple woman with a simple task—to help the old man gather dandelion blossoms. A good morning's work. The pasture was knobby with new growth bulging out of old grass, milkweed, oxalis and clover, and pitted with groundhog holes so it was necessary to watch one's footing. Their feet would soon be glossy with dew, their cuticles stained a sappy green. Pickings were irresistible nevertheless. The lushest dandelions grew among old cow pies half loam by now and weathered scentless. Marsh marigolds were sprouting. Half-hidden under burdock an occasional violet nestled. Violets Abby hoarded in a shirt pocket with the notion of candying them for special desserts later on. But the main thing was to fill eight crackling brown grocery bags to their brims with yellow dandelion flowers. Easy and peaceful as cow pies.

Mr. Vogel meant to make dandelion wine. That was what he told her when she stopped her car by the fence to inquire about Mike. He recognized her from the Rising Sun, he said, but no, there was no telling where Mike was off to today. He consulted the sky. It was grey and gold with low clouds moving fast beneath high clouds, which left one thin spot where enough radiance gushed through to warm the whole pasture.

"Probably all the way up to Seifert's Gap," he concluded. "This rain's brought a lot of power outages up there. The river's cresting and Mike thinks it's the beavers again, cutting down power poles to repair their dams." Mr. Vogel was happy to leave such nuisances for youngsters like Mike to fret over, he allowed. As for himself it was high time he got on with brewing this year's wine.

"Do you ever eat the leaves?" Abby asked, reluctant to go away. "When I was a little girl we used to try to eat dandelion at least once every spring. My father said it was a tonic."

"We had a mess of 'em a couple of weeks back, Mother and I, but to my way of thinking they get much too bitter once the flowers set." He lifted the top strand of barbed wire invitingly, lowering the bottom strand with his heavy brogan. "You're welcome to all you can use."

Abby left her car in the lane and ducked through the fence. But not to gather greens for her own table. She only found a few succulent young plants whose flowers were still fat caper-like buds. Plainly Mr. Vogel was right—the meadow was entering its winey stage. She contented herself helping him with his harvest of flowers.

After a half hour she gave up stooping, and squatted to do her picking. The dew was slowly evaporating. As the sun rose higher a few groggy bees came moseying across bright tufts at her fingertips. They did not bother one another. The grocery bags gradually filled. The sticky patina on

Abby's fingers deepened, smelling wonderful.

Mr. Vogel warmed up his spiel on winemaking. He told her about adding raisins to the concoction; otherwise there wasn't always enough sugar to generate much alcohol and dandelion wine without any kick was, in his opinion, the worst swill in the world. Some people added orange peel, a practice he frowned on.

Bovine, they cropped their way down the hill. You have to have a good cellar with a clay floor, he insisted, if your wine is to have any consistency from year to year. That was his conviction anyway; he granted her that there were others who'd say it's all in the yeast, or in racking the stuff as soon as it finishes working. There was one bag apiece to fill when the sun broke clear directly overhead and the stable flies showed up.

By the time her bag was nearly full. Abby found herself working along a fencerow tangled with bittersweet at the bottom of the field. Mr. Vogel was twenty yards away near a limestone boulder. They were both out of sight and sound of the lane. She was straightening, ready to announce her successful take, when she noticed Mike striding down the slope. Loose in the knees, big hands swinging, it could not have been anybody else. When his father looked up too, he started trotting toward them.

They all recognized that they all recognized each other. Nothing else was clear. Mike was glad to see Abby, but surprised to see her in cahoots with his father. She could think of nothing to say; she was busy wondering whether it would be all right to hug him. Mr. Vogel seemed proud to show Mike this lady, his freshest audience, but did not know

what to call her. After three false starts it was decided who was presenting whom to whom and even
then Mike faltered in the introduction.

"Abigail Hays," she said upon accepting the
weed-green handshake that matched her own.

"Abigail . . ." Mike said after her, trying out the
name.

"What do *you* call her?" Mr. Vogel asked, catching the look his son exchanged with Abby. "Gail?"

"Abby," said Abby. She did not want the old
man to discover Mike had not known her name at
all before now. That much was deliberate. But
without actually intending to, she also kept the
name of Mullen from both men as instinctively as
a grouse hides her nest with leafy litter.

Mr. Vogel asked if she were any relation to that
clan of Hayses down near Steubenville. She said
no, and then they left it at that. Mike helped lug the
bags of flowers up the hill as far as the back porch.

They all waved to Mrs. Vogel who was airing
bedding on the second-floor balcony. She peered
down at them myopically, then popped inside. Mr.
Vogel extended an invitation for dinner, which
ought to be ready soon, but Mike declined. "She's
my girl, Pop. I'm taking her with me."

Abby blushed like an amateur.

"Maybe for supper sometime," Mr. Vogel
urged. "We owe you, for the picking."

Abby and Mike walked back to his Jeep holding
hands, drinking in the sight of clouds and sunlight
chasing each other over low mountain ridges
across the valley. Here and there a bit of white
shadbush flickered in passing sunlight, then the
calico pink of a redbud would glow, and fade, and
glow again. For the sheer joy of it Abby let loose a

strangled little whoop. Mike patted her fanny and helped her up into the truck.

He did not say where they were headed. She could observe what she wanted to know: the road was taking them toward the Laurel Highlands, further away from the little towns that studded Pittsburgh's belt of feeder roads. They were holding hands. The ride was bumpy.

"You're surprised to see me," she said when the Jeep had rattled over a rickety bridge.

The crow's feet around Mike's eyes crinkled. "I wouldn't have guessed you'd want to make a habit of this," he replied.

"I do," she said. "I want to go everywhere with you, see everything you do."

"You want to get laid in the woods."

"I want you all the time," she began to confess. "I think about it in the shower . . ."

He lifted her knuckles to his mouth, kissed them and said, "You are about as sweet as they come." And shooting her a mischievous look he added, "Why don't we go back to your shower and do it there?"

Abby was speechless.

"No, seriously," Mike was saying. "What's the matter with finding a nice motel, with a TV? A king-sized bed. Hell, I guess *you* get to do it on king-sized beds all the time. But what's the big deal about getting laid out of doors? When you could have nice clean sheets, a vibrating mattress. Huh?"

"That would spoil it."

"Spoil what?" Mike asked, still bargaining.

"The simplicity," Abby explained longingly. "Everything's so quiet out here. It even smells better. Smell that damp earth! The woods, the creeks, your father, even that roadhouse, it's all so much cleaner and simpler than the way I've been living my life. Do you know that practically every place I go in Pittsburgh has that same eye-stinging odor? It's wall-to-wall carpeting, draperies, it's the smell of synthetic fibers and it saturates every office, every lobby, every theatre and store. *This* smells right to me. This is the way we ought to be living. Near mud."

"Slumming."

"No," Abby protested. "Not at all! I think it's wonderful. I admire you for living here, for the way you suit yourself. All this seems like something I remember from a former life and I guess," she faltered, "I'd like to get it back, is all. I envy you."

Mike said nothing, thinking, until a short laugh erupted from him. "It's always greener. You know what you look like to me? A candy store. If I'd have thought it would get me somebody like you I'd have moved into a duplex in the South Hills long ago."

"That isn't where—" she began, then shut up.

"You look like those women, though. Everything tucked in and matching. Pop used to be a security guard at the mall over there and I saw them. I always wanted one," he confided. "I thought about those South Hills women the whole time I was in the army, when other guys had pin-ups of Kim Novak. I was still thinking about them when you showed up."

"Kim Novak was a spectacular beauty."

"Tell me," he said dryly. "My first wife looked like Kim Novak."

Uh oh. Abby considered what might be the best course through this knotty issue. Knowing perfectly well she would not have been invited into the farmhouse were there still a viable Mrs. Michael Vogel, she forged ahead, asking, "And now she doesn't?"

"Who knows what color she's got it dyed now," Mike tossed off. "She never could make up her mind. She left and came back so many times we might as well have had a revolving door. Finally I just changed the lock."

"You wouldn't do that to a South Hills lady?"

Mike was smiling again. "Know what it is about them? Women like that, you know for a plain fact they've always got on nice new underwear."

Abby burst out laughing. "That's really important," she hooted. "What a materialist you are!"

"Don't tell me you don't buy that stuff," he teased, eyeing her slyly as he turned his truck onto an old lumbering road. "I bet you have a whole dresser drawer full of soft, sleek bras and slips and panties in different candy colors."

She could not deny it.

"Maybe if you went without that stuff you'd find Hubby could buy you a place to live in the boon-docks."

"We thought about it once," she mused. "But when the children were pre-schoolers, maintaining a home in the country seemed more than we could handle." Lost in thought, she did not notice that Mike had parked the truck near a clearing among budding oak trees—only that he was watching her face intently now.

"I wasn't talking about a weekend house," he said. "I mean finding one of these old jobs the set-tlers built with stones they cleared out of the fields.

There're a couple of them about half caved-in in
the hills here. I mean really moving in and fixing it
up. Put in some decent insulation and a good
furnace, bird feeder by the window, and not come
out all winter long."

Abby could hear that he was speaking from long
years of hankering. Quite obviously he had never
owned a house. She wanted to take him in her arms
and hold him, not debate the dubious pleasures of
maintaining a furnace, grading a driveway.

"Wouldn't that be something?"

"Well," she said carefully.

"You'd love it," Mike insisted. "You could get
along anywhere. I can't speak for your husband. I
don't know him from Adam."

"It's the children I'd have the worst time convincing," she answered. "They have a lot of friends
in town, in our neighborhood too. And we're lucky
to have the University—not just the medical plan
—the museums and special programs too. I do
think the kids benefit from having plenty of stimu-
lation. Geoff would have to, well, we're part of that
whole university community. We would miss our
neighbors, really." He was studying her too closely
and she foundered. It was a recitation from memory.

"I went to Penn State for a while," said Mike,
jumping from the Jeep.

"You did?"

"Yeah. It was fun." He opened the door on
Abby's side and bowed low, Cinderella's footman.

Her breath caught in her chest. At her feet was a
white and green bed of trillium blossoms, twinkling
as the budding hardwood foliage overhead fluttered and filtered the sunlight. She sank to her

knees, tilted one flower up and gazed into the crimson star-burst of its fluted throat. It smelled like cress. She was tempted to sprawl there face-down. Ruffling the dense expanse of blossoms lightly the way a child ruffles his hands across a fuzzy blanket, Abby looked up at Mike. "This is perfect," she whispered.

He hiked his pants at the knee and hunkered down to face her. "Want me to undress you?" he asked. Then on second thought, "The ground's damp."

"Oh no," she said hurriedly. "We'd mash all the flowers. I only meant *it is perfect*. I'd like to come here for a picnic every sunny day this year."

Under the warm weight of his long, heavy arm, she walked with him to a sunny spot where a log rested on fallen limbs, high off the ground and dry as punk. Abby chose a seat with a backrest in the V of two limbs. It had pitchy spots but she did not care. Mike spread out his lunch on the bark between them.

By the miracle of picnic transubstantiation Mike's workday grub became a buffet of aphrodisiacs—peanut butter and bacon on white, pickled peppers, Fritos, a can of peaches he opened with his knife—all delectable. They were both hungry. Abby scooped a peach half from the can and munched it alternately with the dry sandwich. Devouring her portion as slowly as she could bear to, she watched Mike eat. And listened.

In a meadow just out of sight two or three cow-bird cocks were singing, gurgling trills which sounded more like fluid pouring from a bottle than a territorial song. The longer Mike and Abby remained silent, the more activity rustled to life right in the clearing where they sat. Small grey squirrels were cutting twigs for nests in several trees. Over near Mike's Jeep the ground was fairly red with blossoming twigs the squirrels had already taken from red maples. Mike made a sharp kissing noise. The closest squirrel froze, the incriminating goods still clamped in his jaws. Another one with a great fluff of tail was less inhibited. He was so busy nicking twigs away from the branches and dropping them to his mate below that he did not turn a whisker when Mike chirped at him. He simply continued to cut his quota of leafy sprigs and then, suddenly reversing directions on the branch, hurled himself headlong down the maple trunk, went skittering up another and vanished around the backside. Birdsong was all around—larks, warblers, the rasping randy hullaballo of a wild tom turkey.

Mike pointed out a tattered flock of white birds flying high aloft, almost out of range, and whispered, "Gulls. Migrating." Together they watched each thinking private thoughts about migrating.

While Abby was watching, head tilted back, Mike slipped from his seat to come kiss her throat just where a pale blue vein rose to her jaw. One of them moaned slightly. She held him close, which led to more kissing. Fondly they handled each other, feeling through their clothes like kids, smiling into each other's mouths. He removed her shirt and hung it from a splintered branch. She helped him with the rest, leisurely and affectionate. He would have stopped short of her shoes and knee socks because of the damp ground but, having sampled sunlit air with bare pores from armpits to knees, she was not about to deny her feet the same luxury. Stark naked she sat on the log, waiting. Rough pine bark dented her skin; she would have to move with care.

Unwilling to take the time for unlacing his high boots, Mike undressed by dropping everything as far as his ankles, effectively hobbling his feet. But they were proceeding slowly in any case. Abby hopped to the ground and turned around so he could easily reach her, resting her arms on the log. She cradled her face on her arms. The sun was warm on her back.

Surrounded by raw edges and not a little drunk with spring weather, they took the greatest imaginable care in coupling. So gingerly they almost laughed, so tender they were nearly in tears, Mike and Abby made love bent over a windfall pine until both their faces were shiny with sweat. Small adjustments were made: Abby sneezed, Mike blessed her and reached forward to brush the offending ant from her upper lip. Abby stepped atop Mike's booted toes to make herself taller. At last they found what they were looking for. Stupified with happiness they pressed on. Deaf, dumb and blind, the pair of them.

When they had finished Mike spread his hands wide on the log and leaned down to feel her back with his belly. They were sun hot and shade cool. Neither wanted to move. He breathed into her nape. Together they rested until he could no longer stay with her. Then he licked a bit of salt from between her shoulder blades and dropped away to pick up his pants.

Abby was not ready to get dressed. Instead she clambered up to her perch on the log once more.

"Good woman," Mike thanked her.

Exhaling deeply she lay down on the pine bark turning face, navel and knees to the sky. She was pale in contrast to everything but the rug of trillium. A bank of laurel bushes behind her was so green it was nearly black. Even the newest fiddlehead shoots of fern uncurling where her arm dangled down the side of the fallen tree were a vivid green. Eventually this spot would be cast in leafy shade, even at noon. High overhead the bronze buds of new hickory and walnut foliage had not yet grown together, however, and their bare branches simply funneled clean blue sky straight down on Abby. Her eyelids drooped in pleasure.

Opening a thermos, Mike straddled the log at her feet and drank coffee. He was watching her and she knew it, reveled in it. She basked, listening to him swallow.

She enjoyed the sensation of blood fanning out of her pelvic region to restore circulation in her extremities. She was aware of a pulse in the roof of her mouth. Only in childbirth had her body felt so vast as this, teeming, chugging, ticking with the same elements that made tides, seasons and eons. Now she knew where savages had got the idea that copulating in the fields would insure better harvests. She felt like the first woman. With her lover she might create the whole world, one crude act of piety after another. Rut until the crops flourished. And hold him hard and fast to her. This was what she wanted. Nothing else, or less.

Her stomach gave a little flutter of glee. "I guess this isn't virgin forest any more," she chuckled.

"Huh uh," Mike replied. "There's only one

stand of virgin timber left in the state." As he watched, sweat trickled down Abby's ribs, beaded up and dropped to the pine straw below.

Eyes shut, she coaxed, "Will you take me there sometime?"

"Sure," he said. Leaning close to kiss the inside of her knee, he murmured against her soft skin, "Abby?"

"Mm?"

"You haven't said a thing about prevention. The way we seem to be going, you know?"

"I'm not worried about it."

"Good," Mike said. "I figured you already had something worked out, being married."

That got a rise out of Abby. She sat up and eyed him, amused at his presumption. "For all I know, you may have had a vasectomy."

"I would never do that to myself," he said quickly. "Any more than I would commit suicide."

"I wouldn't commit suicide either," she agreed, stung. She inched closer to show him the tiny dimpled scar under her belly button. She wanted him to know how diligently she had pursued motherhood. She explained her laparoscopy and sterilization, how difficult the pregnancies had been because of her incompetent cervix and how important she had felt it was that she have children to give better definition to her marriage. She told him how deliberately she had gone about trying to conceive Toby even though her husband did not share her determination to have children, how overwhelming parturition had turned out to be and how, as soon as Toby was old enough to be going off to school, she went about trying to conceive Gabrielle.

Mike listened completely deadpan. When she finished, he shook his head once, then said, "I guess you knew what you were doing."

He doesn't understand, she worried. He supposes I have raped myself, that I'm an unnatural woman. She told him what wonderful, peculiar little individuals Toby and Gabey were, explained how it happens that sometime soon after children learn to distinguish themselves from their mothers the mother rediscovers she is something independent of her nurturing prowess. The more she talked the more silent Mike grew. She stopped, saying, "You don't approve."

He patted her knee almost absentmindedly. "You know what's best, no doubt," he said. "God knows you know all the words."

"You don't trust words at all, do you?"

"Sure I do."

"For instance?" she challenged him, longing for reassurance.

"Come on," said Mike. He threw her clothing to her and began to pick up their litter.

"No, really," she insisted.

Grinning wickedly he crooned a few syllables under his breath.

"What?"

" 'Come on sugar, let down your hair,' " he sang to her while she dressed, belting out the lyrics with a cheeky hillbilly yodel.

>   "Payday's burning a hole in my pocket
>   Band's a-stomping like hell won't stop it
>   We'll take off just like a rocket

Soon as you let down your hair . . ."

He sang to her all the way back to the main road. She hummed along where she could, marveling at the pungent lilt in his voice. With a little training he might have made a superb second tenor, she thought. But no, he already was what he was and that was something sterling. She was thrilled to be sitting beside him, jouncing along in a Jeep, serenading themselves as they chased the sun southwest toward Pittsburgh's bedroom communities.

"Take me to your most barren desert
A thousand miles from the nearest sea
The very moment I saw your smile
It'd be like heaven to me . . ."

"Now there's some *words* for you," said Mike after venting one final aboriginal warble.

Abby could not help smiling. "Country songs never cease to amaze me," she told him. "The lyrics are always such cliches."

"How do you think they got to be cliches?" was his reply.

He sang a song about going honky tonking while they jolted up the Vogels' lane. Abby sang harmony, regaling him with her Ph.D. paraphrase of the lyrics: "If you've got the tenure, dearest, I've got the funds." They laughed until they howled, neither of them willing to stop. He braked behind her car. They lingered in the Jeep, laughing and chatting. The light was failing. Mike offered to take her honky tonking so she could find out how it worked.

But Abby was in no position to accept. She had things to take care of in town.

They sat in the growing dusk. Just sat. There was nothing else they could bear to do. Nothing they could say. Abby put her hand on the door, then stopped. They looked at each other. Sucking in a deep breath between his teeth, Mike hauled her across the seat and crushed her against his chest.

CHAPTER SIXTEEN

"Not since Super Bowl XII," Web was saying. "Well, maybe a coupla-three times before that."

"Always," Mike corrected him. They were watching Roller Games on the Steubenville channel, impassively taking in the video portion of a grudge match. Stringy-haired women on wheels elbowing each other. Mike would have watched an aquarium with greater interest but as it happened a television set was what Gary kept behind the bar. Same difference: it gurgled softly.

"You're over-exaggerating," Web protested.

Mike snorted. "Oh yeah? Then what about the time we went to the Pirates game with Bink and Carl?"

"Which game was 'at?"

"Another round?" asked the bartender as he glided past on his damp rubber runner.

Mike nudged a glass forward and went on badgering Web. "You mean you don't even remember? That was the time Dock Ellis showed up at bat with his hair all done up in a hundred-some little pink curlers."

Web got a faraway look in his eyes, then began murmuring "Yeah" over and over.

Gary returned with two shots, two drafts, and a fresh bowl of chips. Mike picked up his shot glass, pausing first to sip about an inch off the top of his beer. "Uh oh," said the bartender. "Drinking depth charges tonight? I'm staying at arm's length," and he moved down the bar to fiddle with the TV.

Mike dropped the full shot glass into his beer and was drinking it, bottoms up, when Web let out a little yelp of surprise. "That's Esther's boss there," he told Mike, pointing to the television screen. Cooperatively, Gary turned back to the channel he had just riffed past.

Mike did not know Esther's boss from the Queen Mother, but he knew for sure who one of those two ladies was. If he had been turned loose blindfolded among all the women volunteering for Channel 13's telethon, he could have found the one that was his by touch alone. He did not say so. He simply dropped his chin into his palm and treated himself to an eyeful of Abby. She was looking perky, well-pressed, and delectable as high-bush berries.

"Esther says she's got two kids. You'd never guess it to see her, would you?"

Defending his favorite, Mike said, "So's the other. And *she* isn't exactly something the cat drug in, you know?"

Still at cross-purposes Web argued, "That one's a tad too young for me. Probably still tastes like peepee."

"Too young!" Mike roared. "She's older'n Esther for one thing, and I'll tell you true, she is just a little bit better than perfect."

"What do you know, Vogel?" and Web waved

him away. "That's stuff's so far out of your league."

Mike leaned meaningfully close to Web's elbow, pronouncing in no uncertain terms, "I've *been* there, Web. Okay?"

By then Gary was in the fray as well. Pointing to Abby so there could be no mistaking, he said, "Hey Vogel, isn't that the little stray 't's been in here a couple times? Yeah, you were dancing with her over noonhour once." On the television screen, Abby handed over a portable microphone to someone and, turning her back to the camera, stepped up through the bleachers to her phone, balloon and styrofoam boater in hand. "Nice buns," Gary observed.

Web was staring at Mike. "You've *been* there?"

"She's a damn fine lady," was all Mike would say.

"Well, I guess so," said Web. "That's Esther's boss! You got any idea about her old man? He's a professor at one of the colleges, not to mention galahading around with all those stuffed shirts in the big companies downtown."

Gary leaned on the bar grinning conspiratorially at Mike. "Never you mind about the husband, chumly. You stick with Sweet Buns. Maybe if you treat her right, stay on her good side, maybe she can help get you on TV. Boy, then you'd really have it made."

"Get off my back," Mike protested.

"You have a calling," Gary urged. "I can see it in your eyes."

"You think women in the audience could see it?"

"You'd be great," Gary nodded, and he indicated the vastness of Mike's success somewhere between the pay phone and the pool table.

Mike smiled into his glass. "I've always thought I'd be pretty good, now't you mention it."

"Bet your hiney."

"How about if I had my own show," Mike chuckled. "Now that'd be a switch. All dressed up fit to kill, and the wildlife watching me for a change."

"Better yet," Gary added, "be in the movies. That way you'd really make out."

"Movies. Yeah."

"You'd be a far sight better than that faggot they got playing Bond now." Another customer signaled to Gary from further down the bar and he drifted away, saying, "A man could make a potful that way, you know? Of course I'd be your manager. I'd get me a tux like Porter Wagoner's."

Someone switched channels and got a news show in time for the sports.

"The silver screen," Mike mused, constructing another depth charge for himself. "I could tell Tuckerman to go find himself someone else to play traffic cop for the nature-lovers.

The entire bar was now arguing what the real story was with the Bucs anyhow—all those hijinks at spring training camp and conflicting reports about contract holdouts. Everyone except Mike and Web.

Web had forgotten about the Bucs, Esther's boss and Channel 13. Reverting sentimentally to his collection of favorite drunk-driving stories, he yakked Mike Vogel to distraction: "It was Bink's car, but Carl was driving, remember? Oh my achin' back, every blessed one of us drunker'n a fart. Then this wirlygig light turns on behind us and I think it was you yelled at Bink to get rid of that jar of martinis. Wasn't it you?" Web was not discouraged by silence. He snickered woefully. "And when the cop pulls up behind us, his windshield wipers are slapping away, clearing martinis off his front window. Lord knows what woulda ever become of Carl if you hadn't been in uniform your own self. Bad enough as it was." But Mike did not appreciate the credit; he was still brooding over the shock of seeing Abby on TV.

Although it was in the university neighborhoods that Pittsburghers seemed most intensely to wish the city were New York, it was downtown that deserved the comparison. Unlike the Shadyside, Oakland and Squirrel Hill areas, downtown Pittsburgh had some sass to it. Like Manhattan it crowded all its transactions between rivers. The buildings loomed, the streets were always congested and every midday hordes of office workers picked their way through delivery trucks, trolleys, taxis, Teamsters, street vendors and window shoppers to lunch and back again. Oakland was contemplative, Shadyside boutiquey, Squirrel Hill victorian. But downtown where foundries, fish markets and federal agencies all functioned cheek by jowl Pittsburgh was a bustling city. Third largest corporate headquarters in the U.S., it had *Wall Street Journal* and *Business Week* bureaus, but it was also the county seat and it had the Orphans Court where couples in love or in trouble went to apply for marriage licenses. Sooner or later everyone had business downtown. Most of them seemed to be competing for space on the sidewalks when Abby arrived late one morning on an errand of love.

She felt mischievous this morning. And anonymous, since she had declined to dress up in her faculty wife uniform. Dressed in clean jeans and Lord of the Rings sweatshirt, she was devoting the morning to outfitting herself as Mike Vogel's lover. First, a sturdy pair of boots, the smallest size Stavros Army Navy had for sale. Also Army Navy —a smallish canvas ditty bag and a pair of aviator sunglasses that would not fall off even if she stood on her head. Next she had to find a five-and-ten.

Delirious with her plans she strolled around the corner enjoying a fresh spring breeze. The bobbing parade of passing faces was marvelous. Today the noise and the clubs offering "Live Music Live Girls Live" did not faze her. Everything was swell.

In Woolworth's she selected a cheap but service-able toothbrush, comb, razor, shower cap and hand lotion. These she popped into her new ditty bag. Next stop, Elizabeth Arden; no compromising on shampoo, protein pack and moisturizer. No one in the shop could possibly have guessed what she was up to. In her entire life until now she had never felt mysterious. She found it invigorating.

She came out of the Arden salon hungry, won-dering where she could get a good salad quick. The odor of Italian red sauce poured from every cafe and restaurant she passed. She stopped at a "Don't Walk" to look around. Everyone who was not working first shift at Homestead, it seemed, was out on Market Street today. Abby decided to wait until the lunch rush subsided before trying to find a suitable restaurant. Until then, she would indulge herself in the most exciting venture of the trip— choosing Mike's present.

She was entering a haberdasher's shop when she

met Maxine Gerber coming out. There was no getting rid of her.

Abby could not be cross enough to discourage an old sidekick. On the other hand, nothing was going to deter her now that she had made up her mind: she was going to find something beautiful for Mike before another day went by—no matter if battalions of busybodies dogged her steps. Already she was picturing Mike's eyes crinkling in surprise and pleasure. He would probably laugh. Practically bursting with glee, but poker-faced, she went inside followed by Maxine.

The proprietor recognized Abby, tactfully provided the minimal help she desired. She sorted through his warm weather inventory and chose, from the crackling towers of folded, pinned and tissued shirts, one classic blue shirt of English cotton and something more dashing—an oyster colored Italian one in rayon-linen blend with horn buttons. She was gratified to think she was giving that big lunk the first shirts he would ever have with sleeves long enough to cover his wristbone. Today she would not torment herself about how fine he might look in a good tweed sport coat; the shirts were titillation enough.

The proprietor looked at her over his bifocals. "On your charge?"

Abby said no and gave him Mike's two fifty-dollar bills.

When he ducked into a back room in search of change, Maxine caught Abby's eye. "Not Geoff's size," she observed in hushed tones.

"They're a gift," was Abby's excuse. That was the end of it until they cleared the shop.

Outside, Maxine grabbed Abby's arm saying,

"Of course they're a gift, my sweetmeat. Now I am taking you to lunch where I will ply you with ardent spirits until I know gifts for whom, and why and, if he's that big, how come I haven't spotted him in the crowd myself. Come along quietly," she said, leading the way toward Forbes Avenue.

"I thought I'd grab a salad and finish my shopping," said Abby.

Maxine was having none of it. "They serve salads at The Constabulary. They also have dark corners for confessing sins of omission. Besides, the house red is a damn good Napa Valley pinot."

Abby went along.

At The Constabulary men were required to wear coat and tie (which tended to channel lawyers and brokers in and keep the advertising designers out), but women were not expected to come up to the same standards. Maxine seemed disappointed that it took no wrangling to get Abby's sweatshirt past the headwaiter. She was somewhat consoled by the opportunity to argue for a better table. Eventually they were seated at her second choice—a booth vacated by a pair of gabardined youngsters who departed still talking about quit claim deeds. In rapid succession the table was cleared and re-covered, and their menus placed before them.

Maxine could not resist flirting with the waiter; this was one of the perquisites of emancipated women, she told him. Abby stayed out of it. She did not think any better of women for trifling with waiters than she ever thought of men for doing the same with waitresses, but she knew Maxine felt justified by fashion. She studied the menu. Better for her figure if she had bolted to McNatural's and ordered a sprout salad to go. Here she was, however;

she resolved to enjoy herself. It felt good to sit.
Abby ordered mussel soup when she learned that
was what perfumed the dining room so pro-
vocatively. There were live jonquils on the table.
Soon after there was crusty bread too and, once she
had half a glass of wine, Abby was willing to grant
Maxine this was like old times.

"Even if they torture me I won't tell them,"
vowed Maxine, unfolding her napkin. "So tell me
who he is. Immediately. I can't stand the suspense."

"If I don't tell you they won't bother torturing
you," said Abby.

"Aha!" Maxine crowed. "There *is* a man. I
knew you could do it, Abby! This is going to improve your disposition one hundred percent. I'm so
glad you've started looking after yourself. It'll keep
you from worrying so much about losing Geoff. I
won't tolerate a single morsel of guilt, either," she
added, poking a finger near Abby's face. "After all,
adultery begins at home."

"I'm not worried about losing Geoff," Abby
pointed out.

"But you *are* having an affair."

Slowly Abby was yielding to the urge to tell
Maxine. Lots of strange impulses were surfacing
these days. Talk could help her make sense of it.
Not that Maxine was her first choice for a con-
fidante, but Mike himself was not a man she could
persuade to discuss anything—especially not anything this important. " 'Affair' is not the right
word," she ventured.

"It's certainly *some*thing! You practically have
canary feathers sticking to your whiskers. Oh no,"
groaned Maxine. "Don't tell me you've finally

gone back to voice lessons and it's a platonic thing with some old relic of a singing coach. Please!"

"I don't know how to describe it."

"You could begin by explaining why you're buying his shirts."

Earnestly Abby leaned across the table and said, "Because. The only shirts that fit him are his uniforms. All his other shirts are these desperate floral polyesters that came in with leisure suits, and the sleeves are never long enough."

"God help us," Maxine intoned. "He's a cop."

"He is not!"

"Well, what is he?"

"He's the tallest man I've ever danced with," Abby began.

"Where did you meet him?" demanded Maxine.

"I met him, uh, out near the mushroom farm I took you to once, remember?" said Abby, equivocating for all she was worth. "He fixed a flat tire for me."

"Gallant."

"He's a little bit rough around the edges, but yes, actually he is rather gallant. And reserved, in a poker-faced sort of way. Except for when he laughs," Abby reflected joyously. "He has a wonderful way of bursting out laughing. You can just tell it comes all the way from his feet. And, oh, you should hear him sing!"

"He serenades you?"

"I wouldn't call it that. He just belts out a snatch of song every once in a while. Sort of as if he's used to being alone. Mostly it's songs I used to hear long ago when I would be riding in the Rambler with my father. His voice is quite good, come to think of it. But what interests me most is how, I

dunno, *exposed* he is when he's singing. It's so ornate! He puts in lots of syrupy trills and tremolo—
fit to pour his heart out—in these corny old
ballads, and the rest of the time he is utterly
matter-of-fact."

"An older man?"

"He may have five or six years on me," Abby
shrugged. "Not old enough to make any difference."

"I prefer them younger, myself," said Maxine.
"Get them while they can still talk about something besides work."

"He's not much of a talker, but he is quite
bright."

Maxine sighed, then said, "Who cares, really, as
long as he's sexy."

"Oh Max," Abby groaned. "You don't know
the half of it. He isn't sexy like a gorgeous little
hunk-of-dessert sexy. But I can't stay away from
him. He's overwhelming. You could put one of me
inside him," she said, indicating a Mike-sized hug.
"He moves things around. Very physical. He's like
the weather. On the other hand, he can also sit still
longer than anyone else I know. He seems to understand everything but he never explains himself.
He's very outdoorsy, but only his face and hands
are tanned. The rest of him is pale compared
to his hair, very dark hair. He never wears after-
shave or cologne as far as I can tell. He does smell
good though, rather like lumber shavings."

Maxine was impressed by Abby's outpouring.
"I'd say he's sexy."

"He is certainly passionate," said Abby, shaking
her head in wonder. "He makes *me* feel sexy.
Geoff always wants a light on and the radio, with

some elegant classical music playing. I know he
says it's life's little aesthetic ceremonies that distinguish us from livestock. But I've never been able to
shake the feeling that he has to have musical and
visual effects to make the whole enterprise
palatable for him. It doesn't seem to matter to
Mi . . . my . . . uh . . . friend . . . where or how we
do it as long as I will just let him hold onto me.
When we make love it is mostly silent, slippery
and," she tried to explain how elemental she felt in
Mike's arms, "it is not entirely unlike a struggle."

"Damn," Maxine breathed.

"You know what else?"

"There's more?" said Maxine, agog.

Abby had to get it off her chest, even though
Maxine would probably become hopelessly
bewildered. "He feels like family to me. He reminds me of the way I used to feel when I was a
kid, too young even to qualify as a girl. I remember
being a very rowdy little kid and a real scrapper.
Oh yeah, I know you won't believe this, but I
took no guff from any of the other kids in the sand-
box. There were families of brothers and sisters on
our block and I was an only, but I did just fine.
Daddy told me I would have to stick up for myself.
And I used to do it, too. I made all my own friends,
fought all my own battles."

"Your mother was telling me stories like that
last Fourth," drawled Maxine. "And I didn't believe her, either."

"Mother," said Abby with a snort. "She would
have had me rushing her sorority in first grade if
they had a tiny tots auxiliary. She could hardly
wait to start turning me into a lady. My father used
to try showing me how to make things, but she was

always calling me in from his shop or the yard or wherever we were working and trundling me off to ballet or voice. Pretty soon I stopped putting up a fight. And he never fought her for me," Abby veered abruptly toward tears. "The son of a bitch, he never fought her for anything. She civilized us both within an inch of our lives. She took all the fight out of him. I'm sure that's why he had those strokes. He was down in the basement working at his lathe, they told me, when he keeled over."

Abby knew the tears would spill over if she didn't stop at once. She drained her wine glass and managed a game smile. "Well, at least I managed to learn how to use my hands before the Cultural Curtain slammed down."

"So that's why you can't bring yourself to finish your Bachelors!" said Maxine.

"No. That's why I bake the best zucchini bread you've ever had."

Maxine looked her over with an odd little smile. "And you bake for this marvelous mystery man?"

Abby shook her head. "Come to think of it, I've only had one meal at his place. He cooked hash once in the middle of the night after we, uh, got very hungry. He doesn't seem to be one of those men who goes helpless in the kitchen whenever there's a woman around. In fact, he doesn't ask me to do anything—almost as if he doesn't want to rock the boat." Falling silent for a moment she rode the swells of Mike, of loving him, wanting him, having him.

Maxine was not so lulled. Her eyebrows were still way up there from the mention of midnight hash. "At his place, no less," she crooned. "That's a little on the bold side, I'd say. Aren't you afraid someone will see you?"

"Nobody is ever going to *happen* past," said Abby. "When I'm with him we're at his house way out in the country."

Now Maxine was in love too. "Do you go horseback riding? I'd give my last half-dozen affairs for one good fling with a country squire, go riding every morning before breakfast."

"I don't think he has horses," Abby replied. She furthermore had a hunch that was not the only reason she and Mike had not gone riding together. Mike had worked hard all his life, from what she could tell, and most of that outside in the elements. She seriously doubted whether he would deliberately belabor a large dumb beast over hill and dale for recreation. He would not have been trained to ride as part of his upbringing either. For real country people, she recalled from childhood travels among her father's clients, horseback riding was a stage farm girls went through before they were old enough to take up animal husbandry in earnest. A grown man would no more go riding for pleasure than he would go jogging for exercise.

"It isn't a place like Mother's A-frame in Ligonier," she explained. "Not a *home in the country*. It's where he lives, that's all."

"So long as Geoff isn't going to wander by," Maxine granted her. "What about Geoff, by the way?"

"What about him?"

"Now that you've discovered sex, are you prepared for the chance that he'll discover you?"

"He'll never guess," Abby declared. "In the first place, they would never run into each other. Anyhow, even if I were having an affair with Jerry right under your noses, I don't think Geoff would catch on. He comes charging in from these trips so intent on what we must accomplish together before he leaves again, the last thing on his mind is whether I might be unfaithful. Even if the notion filtered through his brain," she complained, "he wouldn't dream of mentioning it. The discussion would take too much time."

Maxine agreed. "I used to think Geoff would fool around himself, but I misjudged how ambitious he is. Dallying takes time and energy. And I daresay he credits you also with being too smart for anything so foolish."

"He doesn't really think I'm smart at all," said Abby.

"Of course he does. I think he trusts your judgment completely, maybe even irrationally, because you had the good sense to marry him."

Abby managed to swallow the most appalling reassurance she had ever been offered, then smiled. "So? No problem, right?"

But Maxine reminded Abby of her vaster experience in these matters. "The problem is going to be staying clear of him," she warned. "I know *I* always get sexier when I'm having a little something on the side. It's as if everything's in full operation, all the juices flowing, and then without really meaning to you end up spraying these, these signals all over. Even to your husband. Then he gets turned on. Look at you! Maybe it's because the scales have dropped from my eyes this morning, but you really look ripe and inviting these days."

"My hand has stopped itching. I'm not going around trying not to scream all the time."

"Still," insisted Maxine, "you think Geoff *used*

to crowd you? Wait 'til he gets a look at this!"

Burying her nose in her coffee cup, Abby tilted
the coffee far enough to touch her lips, and gave
the problem some thought. "I don't mind making
love to Geoff," she said after a while. "It's not
something I've been interested in withholding.
What I do with this man takes nothing away from
Geoff." Setting her cup down with an angry click
she added, "This is a part of me Geoff doesn't want
anyhow!"

Maxine was shaking her head. "Baby, baby,
oaby," was all she would say.

Abby drew one more little hobgoblin from her
supply of preoccupations—the most worrisome
one. "What I keep wondering is, this man is better
than Christmas and Homecoming and Judgment
Day all baked in one big gooey torte, but where
can it go from here? I think about that when I wake
up every morning. I mean, our lives are so mis-
matched. If we'd met in high school maybe there'd
be hope. But my God, to be with him I'd have to
give up everything and it would be difficult for the
children." Maxine was still shaking her head. Abby
rushed on, "No, really! I think you do have to
think about these things once you start."

"Save the fantasies for getting it on with your
country gentleman," her friend instructed. "You
mustn't be thinking in terms of couples all the
time."

"I have to," said Abby. "I'm married."

"Not the issue, believe me."

Abby frowned. "That's easy for you to say. You
never loved Jerry in the first place. You could leave
him whenever you want to. But Geoff and I have

been through a lot together," she said.

"And you feel loyal to him, after all," Maxine mocked her. "That's entirely up to the individual, my lamb. But I'm telling you, you don't have to put yourself through such agony. No one's demanding you make a choice between your men. Listen, something useful might be coming out of this. If you're so red hot to keep the flame for this fellow, then for a change you are finally going to have to get up the gumption to tell Geoff 'no'."

A pang of panic shot through Abby like dysentery. "What about?"

Scooping up the luncheon bill, Maxine leaned across the table toward Abby. "Tell the sonofabitch you're reserving some time as your own. If he wants to come and go free as the breeze that's fine, but he cannot expect you to drop everything whenever he shows up. You've got things to attend to, things he dealt himself out of a long time ago. He's not the only one with needs and interests, tell him. Let him be loyal to you for a change."

Abby thought about that. At her feet the ditty bag full of toiletries lay, waiting to be taken to a whitewashed cookhouse in an orchard. The last thing she wanted was confrontation with her husband. Why couldn't she just be in love?

CHAPTER SEVENTEEN

Mike liked his new shirts just fine. The same rainy Saturday when Jerry Gerber took Dylan, Gabrielle and Toby to a Chaplin festival at the Museum, Abby hurried out to see him with her packages. She had to let herself in. She heard him yell, "Pop?" when she knocked, but she did not find him until she got all the way in to the bathroom door. Water was splashing.

"Pop?" he said again.

Abby did not answer right away. She stood and stared. Standing in his bathtub, Mike was spraying a big oak rocking chair with water from a rubber shower hose. He was stark naked. Holding the hose high with one hand, he was scrubbing at the rocker's slats with a wire brush and trying to stand on the runners with one foot to steady it all at the same time. Curds of old varnish were washing into the drain. The place reeked of solvent.

He straightened for a moment when Abby came in, to rest his back and to give her a broad smile. "You alone?" he asked.

"Yes, but what—" she sputtered. She was amazed at the spectacle of this naked man so improbably refinishing antiques in his own tub, delighted to have the chance of seeing him naked in a neutral way, and horrified at his disregard for the hygiene of a tub where she intended to bathe sometime soon.

"It's a surprise," he said, going back to his task. "For my mother's birthday. Drove all the way to my great aunt Ramona's in Potter County to pick it up. Her cats had been at it."

She closed the toilet lid and perched there to watch Mike work. "Should I have called before coming out here?" she asked.

"Nope," said Mike, turning the rocker onto its back, scrubbing intently at its underside. "Come out any time. Sometimes I might not be here. Sometimes there might be company. But I'd always rather have you than not."

Spare of sentiment as his declaration was, it made Abby glad as if he had said, "Come live with me and be my love." Happy, she watched him sit in the rocker in the tub, scraping at old varnish. She helped herself to a sip from the beer can he kept handy. "What's this?" she asked. The beer tasted darkly of molasses or musk or something she could not identify.

"Bock."

"Bach?" she said, taking a closer look at the Iron City can.

"Bock," he explained. "It's a fifty-cent word meaning it's spring and they're cleaning out the vats down at the brewery again."

When he was finished with the rocker and was rinsing off, she held up the shirts for him to see. He whistled at the rayon one and, as soon as he had dried his hands, he put it on. He stood in front of her as her son might while she toweled his legs dry.

Having buttoned the shirt just one button shy of the collar, he rolled up the sleeves too, the same as always. Abby was about to correct him, explain about the long sleeves and why she had brought him these shirts in the first place, when she caught sight of his penis nosing out between the shirttails. She found it hopelessly touching. She said nothing.

He took the new shirt off to make love to her.

Afterward she lay in the crook of his arm and listened to the rain falling on his roof. She thought he was asleep, he was lolling so quietly. Comfortable, drifting.

"You're not in the book," she thought she heard him rumble.

She lifted her head, looked at Mike.

"Give me your number," he said. "I might like to call you one of these days."

"Oh please, don't!" Abby objected. "Not right now anyway. Geoff's coming home for a while and I wouldn't know how to explain if you called when he was there."

"He gone a lot?"

"It seems as if he's never home," Abby replied, lying down again. "Until he gets home. Then he acts as if he's never been gone."

Mike took her hand into one of his. "He shouldn't leave you alone so much."

"I guess he has to, though," she told him. "This is the biggest, well, it's really bigger than anything we even thought of trying for when he started out."

"What is?"

"The cycles project."

"Cycles?" marveled Mike. "Bikes? I thought he was a professor or something."

Startled into laughter, Abby enjoyed for one moment a sudden, ridiculous vision of Geoffrey Mullen as a motorcycle expert, biking hot as a pistol all over the world. "He is a professor, basically," she explained. "He's a statistician specializing in the study of cycles. He's made a lot of breakthroughs in systematizing the analysis of seasonal phenomena. People in his field have started basing their own research on his scholarship, so before his first book is even published he's having to plan a second edition. He goes to conferences to learn and ends up lecturing. He does field work, and the film footage he brings back is so good they want him to shoot more. Everything he does these days turns up more work."

"Film footage," mused Mike, eyes closed. "You mean movies?"

"Of migrating animals, that sort of thing."

"This is the guy who told you about the lemmings, right?" he interrupted once more. "I could show him some pretty weird stuff among the wildlife right out there, if he wanted. He wouldn't have to go off to Norway to film strange doings. You oughta introduce us," he grinned, baiting her. "Maybe I could help you both out."

"Oh perfect!" Abby gave a wry little laugh and rushed on with her story. "He wouldn't have time anyhow," she complained. "When he gets home he still has so much to do it would make your head spin. Corporate types are finding his data projections very valuable, too, so now he's constantly getting offers to work as a consultant. I guess he could do nothing *but* consult if he wanted to." She hesitated, then screwed up her courage and said it:

"If he were interested in staying close to home, he could consult every day in Pittsburgh and keep regular hours."

She wondered if Geoff realized that himself. She wondered whether she would ever mention it to him.

Four months ago she would have.

"You're sorta hard on him, don't you think?" said Mike with a little laugh. "I bet he's an all right guy."

"How would you know?" she teased him gently. "Maybe he's a leprous old wife-beater and cheats at cards to boot."

"Does he?"

"No."

"Anybody who's done so well for himself," said Mike, "I take my hat off to him."

"He's worked hard," she admitted. "Nobody could have possibly dedicated himself more to his work than my husband has. But it's not as if he gave up anything to get to this place. He hasn't wanted anything else."

"Boy, I envy him," said Mike, more to himself than to her. "To have an idea coming right off the mark like that, knowing what to go after from the start. Hell," he let his eyelids fall shut, "it's taken me all this time to start figuring what I *don't* want."

"I'm more in your camp," Abby answered with a little laugh. "Geoff, whew! Everyone we knew in school said he was going places." She was prompted then to relate how impressed with Geoff she had been when they met. Mike made companionable sounds. She fell to telling old stories about their courtship, mulling aloud the perplexing differences between the way things seemed then and the way she was coming to see them.

Mike did not offer his opinion. He seemed to be snoozing, one hand nestling hers and the other crooked behind his neck.

"We went through an awful lot when he was working so hard to get ahead," she continued quietly. "I remember we put off taking a vacation the whole time he was trying to get tenure. And then when he finally got it, we were still too broke to do anything on vacation but paint the house. I don't think anyone could blame him, really, for being so excited over all this recognition. It's just that our home, and the children—me too—we don't hold a lot of interest for him now. He's too busy living up to his potential."

Mike was breathing gently.

Abby told it to the ceiling, all but whispering: "I used to feel as if we were partners, both of us pulling for him to get ahead. But now he does everything himself. Or hires someone to do it for him. I guess I was hoping that when he got where he wanted he wouldn't have to work so hard and we could be together more. But it's just the other way around."

She thought about that for a moment, slowly realizing how much she meant it. How much she resented it.

"A friend of mine," she ventured, her voice small with wonder like Gabrielle's over bedtime stories. "A friend of mine says I ought to leave him. She says I'd be better off without him." She waited.

Mike stirred, stretched vastly and, gathering her to him, rolled onto his side. "Men and women," he managed to say through a yawn. "They're the only two sorts of people with special equipment to help bring 'em together. How come they can't get along better?"

Abby snuggled against him, reminding herself to be grateful for whatever time she could take to be with him. She could be sure of Mike. He wanted her, that much was obvious. Here and now. Again. Holding onto him, she thought of him as the rock of her life, the solid good, around which all this upsetting new flux would just have to flow.

Before she left, she scoured his tub and had a nice steamy bath with the new toiletries she had brought from town. Without mentioning it to Mike, she tucked her ditty bag of belongings behind the bathroom door where they would be out of his way until the next time. The important thing, she told herself as she dressed, was to keep things separate. Obviously it would not do for Mike to try reaching her by phone. Much as she longed to be in touch at every available moment, she would have to reserve the right of making contact for herself. And never—under any circumstances—must Geoff and Mike meet.

CHAPTER EIGHTEEN

Lilies of the valley were coming out. Uprooted. Abby put her children to work unearthing them too, a task the little churls attacked as enthusiastically as hogs rooting after truffles. In five years the lilies had taken over every good sunny spot in the flower beds behind the house. Enough was enough. Abby was determined to have a real garden this year. She paused, leaned on her spade and looked around.

Swiss chard would be as beautiful as any ornamental foliage, but it could also be pickled and eaten. Deer-tongue lettuce too. Radishes, peppers, beans both lima and snap. She wanted them clambering poles and prospering vertically while at their feet she meant to have carrots sprouting. Two sorts of carrots: Danvers Half Long and Tiny Sweet. Tomatoes, of course. This year she would no longer buy the pink prosthetic tomatoes trucked into her neighborhood Giant Eagle by carload lots. She was going to have her own fragrant red Beefeater, vulnerable Roma and juicy Small Fry. A few potatoes. Cabbages. And in a pretty border plenty of herbs—sweet basil, parsley, marjoram, tiny potted sets of thyme from the nursery.

Gabrielle had wanted strawberries but when Abby explained there would be no fruit the first year, she lost interest. Popcorn was a good consolation prize. There would be popcorn for chilly evenings when the fireplace was kindled, and for this year's Christmas tree. Sweet corn to take along to Grandma Hays this Fourth of July.

Gabrielle knelt among the clods of dirt where her mother was digging, singing a little homemade song about corn-on-the-cob pie. She was losing interest in helping Toby discard the noded roots of lilies, distracted by the novelty of seeing what wildlife existed under the flower beds. Her song was addressed first to one squirming half of an earthworm, then to a pillbug.

Toby was becoming impatient with his sister, but before he could lapse into spite and spoil their party, Abby sent him off to find windfall sticks from the woods across the street. It would be his job to cut them into three-foot lengths for bean poles. Toby liked his assignment; it required him to use the saw blade of his pocket knife.

The smell of spaded flower beds was powerful. Gladly Abby dropped to all fours and began chucking small pebbles into the heap of refuse with the lily roots. The sun warmed her back the same way it had while Mike made love to her in the forest clearing. Today, however, the soil itself was warm as well. Wrist-deep in it, she crumbled soft lumps of earth in her fists and relished the warm dark bed where her vegetables would grow. This was going to take a lot of work. Good for me, she thought.

"I don't know," she answered Gabrielle. "I think Grandma Hays has too many allergies for gardening. Anyhow, she doesn't even open her house in Ligonier until spring term is over. That's way past time for planting anything."

"Then I'll plant my Easter egg now," the little girl said, and rushed away. When she returned with a relic from her Easter basket, Abby dug a deep hole at once.

Cutting open the big sack of fertilizer, she tossed out generous spadefuls of the stuff and started turning it over, loosening and enriching the soil. "Sterilized Steer Manure," the package said. She hoped it was not from sterilized steers. The impulse came over her to drop everything, pile the kids into the car with a thermos of lemonade and go out to the Vogels for a trunkload of real live cow pies. To fertilize her garden, naturally. But there was no time for that. No telling when the phone call from Geoff might come.

He was supposed to be home sometime today. That was the reason Abby gave Toby for skipping church this morning: what if Daddy called from the airport while they were sitting around listening to Bach? In fact she was treasuring every last peaceful moment in the open. The last time she had spoken to Geoff he had said today would be the day and he would call. More recently the Foundation secretary said Dr. Mullen would probably catch a ride from Washington, D.C. in the Alcoa jet; if he did that it seemed logical he might go ahead and drive as far as Aspinwall with the board president. In that case, she would throw on a skirt, get her fingernails clean and run over by Hartlein Creek Road to pick him up. Either way, all she could do was wait for a call. In the meantime, there was nothing she would rather do with such a grand day than plant seeds. Almost nothing.

Around noon, she made up a tray of sandwiches and apple juice. Toby and Gabrielle enjoyed eating on the grass outside; besides, this way she kept their muddy shoes out of the kitchen. About twelve-thirty she went inside to call the airport, checked to be sure all flights from Washington were arriving on time, and brought out brownies for dessert.

She wondered for the thousandth time whether his plane had crashed somewhere. As always, she told herself there was no point in worrying that way; this time she acknowledged she was only worrying because she thought she ought. She could not picture Geoff dead. It was easier to picture herself in mourning, endlessly shaking hands. Geoff would look restless. He always did in a suit. Geoff would definitely look restless at his own funeral.

She wondered what would become of her if Geoff died. Suppose he did disappear in one of those tragic airline crashes which occasionally incinerate dozens of traveling entrepreneurs? It was unthinkable.

But still, what if?

It would be hard to make his loss comprehensible to the children, she knew that much. Of course she could manage. She had already brought the children through their whole lives thus far without much real involvement from her preoccupied husband. Where, she wondered, would the household money come from. His insurance and benefits from the university would not cover everything, not indefinitely. Quite probably she would have to find a job. At this point she ran out of ideas. Her education—foundered years ago on the tiny rock of her engagement ring—had been intended to train her in anthropology. She would have to go back to school before she could even think about working outside the home.

The Home. Abby straightened to have a look at the house. It was not so inviting as the prospect of her new garden.

Stretching white cotton string from one end of a freshly-turned plot to the other, she began hoeing shallow troughs where she and Gabrielle would poke their seed corn into place. She knew Geoff would never have agreed to start big horsey cornstalks growing in their lawn. He was the landscape artist in the family. This spring without his presence, his pruning and nipping, she felt entitled to cultivate whatever she damn pleased—even an unsightly truck patch.

Wryly she thought, it *is* unthinkable that Geoff would die in a plane crash. If he dies young, it'll be of apoplexy when he sees what I've done to the yard.

If he dies, she told herself, I'll sell the house. Find a place to garden even better than this. Move someplace where there were no zoning laws against keeping a coop full of chickens. Bantams. She knew how to deal with chickens. More than a few times she had gone out with her father to see customers of his laboratory and ended up helping vaccinate the noisy dirty things. Maybe she would study animal husbandry.

When both Toby and Gabrielle suddenly leapt to their feet and disappeared around the back of the house, Abby realized she had heard a car door slam. Brushing crumbs of earth from her hands, she went to see.

Geoff was walking down the driveway with Gabrielle in his arms, Toby lurching manfully along in command of his overstuffed suitcase. The sheer Norman Rockwell sight of them tugged at her fallopian tubes, invisible apron strings. Geoff was looking marvelous—smiling, suntanned. And wearing tennis whites she had never seen.

"Hello!" she smiled at them.

"Surprised, eh?" he said, and included her in the hug with Gabrielle.

"Well," reasoned Abby, "I was expecting you *sometime* today."

Geoff inquired about beer, inspiring both children to race into the house for the privilege of fetching one of those neat green pony bottles their mother had stashed there for Daddy's homecoming. Geoff took Abby in his arms and kissed her thoroughly. Together they walked around the back of the house.

He absorbed the news about the lilies of the valley calmly. Abby thought that was odd. He was making her nervous, but as she elaborated on her planting strategy, naming each row for seeds not yet sprouted, she forgot to feel self-conscious and simply told him with great pleasure what they had been up to all day. There was still a bit to be done: the tomato seedlings would have to be planted and watered before day's end. She explained about the three varieties.

"Gazpacho," Geoff nodded.

Abby smiled. "That's what I thought."

"Pesto sauce," he encouraged her when she showed him the sweet basil. "We can have the Fellowses over for fettuccelle with fresh pesto sauce. Should we get a pasta machine?"

"We're gonna have popcorn on the cob," exhalted Gabrielle, flinging herself at Geoff's shins. Toby was slowly making his way across the yard toward them with a beer bottle in one hand and a brimming pilsner glass in the other, utterly lost in the importance of his getting this drink properly delivered to his father. Abby dropped to her knees again, intent on getting the tomatoes planted before they started wilting.

"Here," sighed Toby. He plopped onto the grass at Geoff's feet, spent. Then he added, "I hung up the phone."

Geoff blew up. "You mean to tell me the phone's been off the bloody hook this entire day?" he shouted. "No wonder!"

Abby looked up, a sinking feeling in her stomach. Toby shrugged elaborately as if to say he was as baffled as the next fellow.

"No wonder I couldn't raise a soul when I called over here," Geoff fumed.

Abby murmured, "I thought it was strange we didn't hear from you."

"I must have called at least twenty times! How could you let something like that happen? Especially on a day when I am in transit and need to be able to reach home?" Turning to eye Toby and Gabrielle, he complained, "When are you kids going to understand the telephone is not a toy? It is a tool. It is to be used for conducting business. And to be hung up when you're finished!"

Toby eased himself out of sight as he had done when people shouted, since the day he could walk.

"I didn't do it," Gabrielle stoutly defended herself. "My wicked stepmother kept me in the palace dungeon all week long. I'm going blind," she gasped, tottering into the garden. Abby caught her gently and steered her onto the grass for an operatic collapse.

"I must have left it off the hook," Abby owned quietly.

Geoff gave her a look, sipped at his beer in injured silence.

"I was wondering about you by lunchtime," she maintained. "I went in to call the airport and they had no news, naturally. They couldn't tell me whether you were aboard any particular flight, but they did say all flights were running as scheduled."

"I wasn't on a commercial flight."

"How was I supposed to know that?"

"I instructed my secretary to tell you," Geoff huffed, finding someone else to blame. "I told her to tell you I might be coming in with some board members on a corporate jet." His final words shimmered royally in the air between man and wife, but when they dissolved, Abby found herself strangely unmoved.

"And if I had acted on that information," she said coolly, "what should I have done?"

Geoff turned sharply to glare at her.

"I stayed here all day waiting to hear from you," she added. And tried not to think, when I could have been elsewhere.

"Not that it did much good," Geoff spat back at her.

Gabrielle fled.

"I'm sorry about the phone," said Abby. Standing, she dragged the garden hose into position, ready to give her plantings a good soaking to start them off right. "Will you turn on the spigot, please? Then I'll be through here."

Stiff with injured feelings, Geoff got the water running for her. Abby watched him walk back to her holding his beer carefully away from his white shorts, and she thought how elegant he looked. She wanted him to feel better.

"I must have gotten distracted. The airline left me on 'Hold' for a very long time," she elaborated. "And I was fixing lunch, trying to mop up the dirt I'd tramped in on the kitchen floor. Thinking that I forgot to buy cucumber seeds. You know," she urged, "most days it wouldn't matter."

Geoff was unyielding. "I should think you'd get worried."

"I was worried."

"Not enough to drag you away from this eyesore you've been excavating all day. Not enough to come inside and make another phone call, try to locate me."

"This is not an eyesore!"

"The garden," Geoff corrected himself meanly. "You were still more interested in it than in my whereabouts."

She knew he would hate the garden all along, but did not ask herself if that was her reason for digging it. I have to live here too, she thought. He's never here anyhow. Except now, and tonight, and how many other nights to come? "Geoff, I was reasonably sure you were on a plane or in a car with Arnold Fellows. I was hoping for the best."

"I was at the Fellowses."

"And then you got a ride home. No problem. You're here now. That's good."

"I was at the Fellowses," Geoff repeated significantly. "For two and one half hours."

Abby looked at him in shock.

"Did it ever occur to you to call there, maybe ask if anyone knew where I was?"

"No," said Abby. "If you were with him instead of on a commercial flight, I knew you . . ." she winced. "You'd call."

"If you had bothered to call," Geoff told her. "Or if you had allowed me to call, you might have joined us. We had lunch there. Anne was expecting us, but of course Arnold was able to call her from the car. I couldn't reach you. So while I waited to get through, they invited me to a very lovely luncheon. We had cracked crab and asparagus with lots of butter and a tart little Riesling. We also had time for one set of tennis before I became so embarrassed," he finished vengefully, "I had to call a cab. They send their love, by the way. They're so sorry you couldn't join us."

"I'm sorry too."

But Geoff was not willing to quit. Something more than separate lunches was bothering him. Abby wiped the mud from her gardening tools, waiting.

"I mean, think about it," Geoff railed. "I've been gone—how many days? And when I get back, what's waiting? Not open arms, not so much as a message! For all the Fellowses knew, it could be my wife has run off with the milkman." Even Geoff had to smile at the absurdity of his reasoning. "I just wish I felt my coming home made a greater difference to you than it appears to."

Abby protested at once. "I *am* happy you're back, and I'm terribly relieved you had a safe trip. That's more important, I think, than whether I showed up at Arnold Fellows' house to drive you home. I don't want to fight. You just got here!" All the while she was wondering what had possessed her to forget and leave the phone out of service for so long. She wondered if the reasons could be read in her face.

"Does it make any difference to you?" Geoff's voice was cold.

"Yes."

"I don't think you're all that keen on having me around, to tell you the truth. I think you have more important things on your mind."

Abby glared back at him. Waiting until she could be sure of her voice, she said, "That is unfair, Geoffrey Mullen. Just because we got our wires crossed today!"

"Because you were too busy," he reminded her. "Too busy to pick me up, too busy to let me know what you were up to. Too busy to think about anybody but yourself."

He was dead wrong about that, though she could scarcely tell him so. All day long she had been thinking about him. About Mike Vogel, too. About the warm weight of Mike's legs across her, and how tonight Geoff would inevitably erase those wonderful tracks from her skin with the heat of his own.

"Okay! I was busy! I have been at your beck and call, and cheerfully, ever since we got back from our honeymoon," she pointed out. "So you lost face with Arnold and Anne because I wasn't waiting to play fetch the instant you touched down. I confess, I made you wait. So what? Everything else has been done on your schedule for sixteen years."

"Not everything."

"Yes, everything."

"The children came at your convenience," he

challenged her. "I wanted to have them later."

"We wouldn't have any children if I hadn't insisted. It was not convenient for you, and wasn't ever going to be," said Abby bitterly. "You were always too young, or studying too hard, or working too hard to help me raise children. What was I supposed to do?"

"I agreed that we should have children some day," Geoff defended himself. "But you stole them. Don't blink at me. It was nothing less than *stealing,* to go ahead and have babies when your partner wasn't ready."

Enraged, Abby threw down her shovel and yelled at him, "I did it for something to do. I had to have something worthwhile to keep from going crazy while you were studying to become whatever it is you are. So it was hard on you. I know you hated having to study with babies crying in the background, but I knew you were going to want grown children some day. And some day when you got your doctorate, and when you got your tenure, and were sitting pretty, I was damned if that was when I was going to start going to bed for nine months at a whack to make babies for us. I hoped if I started raising children when I did, and if they were partly civilized by the time you could take a breather, I thought," she roared through a tide of tears, "I thought all four of us could enjoy some time together. Well, you're busier now than ever, so who the hell are you to complain about my schedule?"

Geoff was staggered. He had no standard response to a counterattack from Abby; she had never quarreled with him. Maybe the odd bicker over some decision that had to be made. But never anything so unfair or so sweeping. And never yelling. Frightened, he glowered at her.

"In your absence," she informed him coldly, "I have been finding other things to do besides waiting for you to return."

How dare she condescend to him! To sober her, he made the most outrageous remark he could think of. "Perhaps you would like to strike out on your own?"

Abby denied any such thing. He was mollified to see how it agitated her. "Well then," he said.

She borrowed his handkerchief and, by the time he had helped her stow the gardening tools, he felt in command of the situation again. While she prepared dinner, he noticed she drank one of the beers she had laid in for him. Odd: she had recently acquired a taste for beer. She looked like a short order cook to him, standing at the stove and sipping from a bottle. But it seemed to be what she needed. Gradually, shakily, she got back to normal.

Dinner was pleasant enough; Abby and Geoff both enjoyed how enthralled the kids were with his anecdotes from Colombia. At Geoff's suggestion, they took the children to bed together, rather than sending them. He supervised Toby's bath and she oversaw Gabey's—a bedtime party with much shouting back and forth between the master bath and the children's. Geoff had as good a time as anybody.

But when the adults went to bed not much later, Geoff wanted to make sure he put a lid on today's eruption once and for all. He turned off the light and slid over to embrace Abby. "What do you suppose we've got here?" he murmured into her ear. "A touch of empty-nest syndrome? Should we think about having another baby?"

Wearily Abby stated the obvious. "I can't," she said knowing that she could not, and that he knew it too. But for the sake of peace-making she went along with his catechism.

"Why can't we?" Geoff said gaily. "Don't be so literal-minded. If another baby is what you really need, we can always see about adopting one. God knows there are enough homeless little kids in the world."

"No."

"Then what is it you need?" he probed.

Abby rolled over to face him, barely making out the shape of his face in the dark. "I don't think there is anything I could ask for," she said slowly.

Geoff was being patient. "Then what is wrong?"

"Nothing's *wrong*," said Abby. "Only I am beginning to fill in some of the empty places around you. Since you've been away so much . . ."

"Surely you understand why I have to take these trips?" he told her.

"I think I do. But I want you to understand that you aren't the only one with new interests. I may not always be able to drop everything just precisely whenever you become available for a little quick domesticity," she said as evenly as possible. "I think you ought to accommodate me sometimes, too."

She heard Geoff roll onto his back. She lay down too, and they lay side by side facing the darkened ceiling. Abby closed her eyes. Maxine's advice might work in Maxine's house. But not here.

The sound of Geoff trying to be understanding was, for a long time, the sound of one hand clapping.

"I'd like to hear about your new interests," he ventured at last.

You want me to trot them out on approval, Abby thought. But she had to say something; she did not want to prolong this rift until open war would be declared. "My garden," she began.

"Mm," said Geoff. She would have to do better than that.

"I'm thinking of buying a camera and taking it with me to the woods," she went on, improvising. "I've been driving around in the mountains and seeing some wonderful pictures."

"Suppose you were to have a flat tire out there?"

I already have had a flat, Abby smiled to herself in the dark. "I've been making some friends out that way. I don't think I'd have trouble calling someone who could help."

"New friends?" Geoff's interest perked up. "That's nice. Why don't you invite them here sometime? We'll have them for dinner."

"I'm not sure that's the best thing to do, Geoff. I mean dinner isn't."

"Why ever not?" he scoffed. "What sort of curmudgeons don't enjoy a good dinner?"

Abby hedged. "It isn't that. They're perfectly nice people—mushroom farmers, a retired couple, friends of Esther's."

"I suppose you're right."

They stared upward together, Abby hoping she had bored him into benign disinterest. But he was becoming annoyed.

"So. *Cavalleria rusticana* is your idea of recreation," he said. "Well, it's up to the individual. Just tell me, what is it you find in common with your maid's friends?"

"As much as I have in common with your friends." Then, hurrying to take the sting out of her retort, she added, "A few interests. But a few is enough. And to tell you the truth, spending a little time that way is rather restful."

"Restful!" Geoff repeated derisively.

On an impulse of longing for this companion of sixteen years to understand, really understand, something that mattered so much to her, she got up on one elbow and told him, "I can't begin to tell you how peaceful it is to spend time with people who don't intellectualize. And it's lovely to sit around with someone who takes me at face value, who isn't promoting a cause or evaluating me because I am Toby and Gabrielle Mullen's mother or that brainy Dr. Mullen's wife. I enjoy traveling incognito once in a while, just as myself. It's like airing out, going around nude in the open air on a sunny day."

"Oh, now don't get carried away," grumbled Geoff distractedly. With difficulty he digested her explanation.

Abby agonized silently, wondering if she had gone too far. Hidden behind the partial truth of her plea for understanding was a whole truth she was determined he would never comprehend. Friends of Esther's, indeed.

"What you're saying," Geoff informed her at last, "is that you need your privacy. Interests of your own."

Close enough. "Yes."

"Time alone."

"Yes."

"I can give you that," said Geoff. And then, as if it were his own idea, "It wouldn't hurt for you to get good at fending for yourself."

Abby said gently, "I've *been* doing that. Ever since Christmas."

Rolling up against her forgivingly, he urged, "Just don't get so good at it that you don't need me. Because I need you."

Abby returned his touch.

"I'm counting on you more than ever," he added. "There's an international symposium in Rome in June and they've asked me for a paper. But I don't dare go unless you'll help me out."

She had a hunch he was not about to invite her to help him write it, or to go along to Rome. "Why?"

"After spring finals the politicking for department chair really begins in earnest," Geoff reminded her. "I can't afford to ignore that, not if I want to be chairman."

Drowsily Abby mentioned, "You told me you weren't worried about getting the chairmanship."

"Not worrying doesn't mean I don't want it," he snapped. "I think I can get it if you'll just give me a hand. I would assume you'd want to anyway without being asked."

"What do you want me to do?"

"Circulate with me. Go to every party and every dinner even remotely attached to campus. It's the simplest way to campaign."

"But you don't need me for that."

"I certainly do."

"Why?"

"Because," he explained, "you're pretty, you're pleasant. And you're my wife."

Abby considered that for a moment. "Okay," she agreed. "I'll escort you to campus functions whenever you're in town."

But Geoff was not satisfied with her promise. "I want you to show up at these functions when I'm out of town, too."

"I don't care about partying when you're not here," she rebelled.

"Nevertheless. It's even more important that you do it then."

"Why?"

"If you're there you can represent me," Geoff spelled it out. "The sight of you in a gathering without me will keep those congested brains churning, wondering what I'm up to now. They'll remember me. And remember that they need me more than I need them."

"They do?"

"Sure," he crooned happily. "A man who travels in my circles will be in a fantastic position for attracting grants to the University. But only if they persuade me to stay. They ought to make it really worth my while. All they have to do is to make me chairman."

"There's nothing I can say . . ." Abby protested.

"You don't have to say anything. Just show up. You'll be a better representative for my case than I am, actually. Any place you go, wherever there's faculty, they'll see you and automatically be reminded of me."

"Maybe so."

"And that I am busy elsewhere."

Abby was silent.

Geoff stroked her, adding softly, "I'm not saying that's the way it ought to be, milady. Only that's the way it is."

Abby believed he was right. She also believed she

was being *had*. He was tightening his grip on her. Tonight she dared to make an effort at improving her status in their marriage. And tonight he was beginning to make even greater demands on her. She wondered whether she could possibly win. "I'll go along with the campaign plan," she told him quietly, "but I want you to be more considerate of my needs, too."

"I know, I know. You need outlets of your own. It's only fair," he said. And patting her cheek he added, "I wouldn't have it any other way."

Abby clamped her teeth together.

She truly did try to avoid comparing Geoff's lovemaking with Mike's. But her body was so very ready, having been recently groomed for this sort of thing. It was almost as if she had grown new nerve endings closer to the skin, a fresh supply of blood vessels. She felt nowhere near as sluggish as she might have become while her husband was away. Then the fatty layers that made her woman's shape might have doused the vitals underneath. But that was not the case. Her body was primed. And it was eager. Abby longed to use everything she knew by now. Things she had learned with Mike. But she did not dare. And so she settled for Geoff's idea of what she enjoyed. *Tarte maison*.

CHAPTER NINETEEN

Three days later she went white water rafting. The last hundred yards from the cars to the riverbank she could hear a roar of rushing water. It increased with every step she took and, chubby in her life jacket and long johns, she wondered whether she had not finally gone too far in trying to throw Geoff off her trail. Nor was she comforted by the sight of crash helmets on the heads of many of her party.

"Now I'm gonna put the fear of God in you," their guide announced. "That river is a living thing and it's moving right along, as you can see. Seven thousand cubic feet per second." The Tirhascamany River seethed brownly behind him, inspiring easily as much respect as an approaching locomotive. As he talked, Abby resisted the urge to clutch Thea Kaltenborn's hand for comfort. Instead, she focused on the flotilla of black rubber rafts tied up at the river bank.

"And whatever you do," the guide was insisting, "keep the bow foremost when you go through the rapids. If you start sliding through broadside you'll flip over sure as you're born. Among all those rocks is just where you don't want to be spilled out.

Got it?"

"What happens if I do fall overboard?" Thea demanded.

"Hold onto the raft if you can," the guide answered. "A kayak will pick you up."

"Cinch up those straps," said one of his assistants, pointing to Abby's life jacket. "When you fall out you'll be hitting the water something like sixty miles an hour."

Gloomily Abby clambered aboard a raft with Thea, the guide assistant, and three feminists for whom this was an assertiveness-training field trip. At once cold water from the floor of the raft soaked Abby's tennis shoes. She got her mind off the twinge in her bladder by helping to lash their gear fast to the gunwales.

A somber sky hung low over the rafts, drizzling mist as they cast off and bobbed into the current. Two guides in kayaks glided across their flanks apparently impervious to rushing water. Through the mist a wall of sodden dark evergreens loomed claustrophobically on either bank to shut the boaters into the channel of this flood. As her raft picked up speed, Abby saw an occasional pale birch flicker past on the murky shore. And then she could no longer do any sightseeing.

"Paddle," somebody yelled at her over the noise of thrashing water. She dipped her paddle into the river, feeling with a shock in her wrists how much strength she needed to make even a dent. "All forward," the assistant was shouting. "Shovel that juice."

Abby thought of him as a boyish Charon.

Paddling with more zeal than skill, they got their raft through a wide place with only one or two

boulders jutting up from the stream. Sailing between those obstacles and around a bend they
came up fast on their first rapids. "White water,"
Charon called out.

"Let's go get it," shouted Thea. The women dug
in, paddling hard as they could.

Abby thought of the release she had signed back
there on the porch of River Runners Unlimited,
thought how her children would not have a ride
home from school if she died today in the roiling
Tirhascamany. But the run across this first set of
rapids was exhilarating.

Yelling and laughing, water spraying into their
faces, they rode it out, paddles useless. "All forward," Charon called, getting them paddling
again. They jounced their way past tall rows of
waves standing up where a tributary was spilling
tons of upstream runoff into the river. It was there
that the raft ahead of them lost someone overboard
and Abby's raft swept into the lead, glancing sideways off a rock.

"Paddle!" They righted themselves just in time
to shoot another rapids bow first. Walls of choppy
water rose and fell at Abby's elbow as her raft
bounced through its turbulent roller coaster
course. Spume blew into her face. They were hurtl-
ing through a narrows now. Giving in, she opened
her mouth and let out her breath in one wild
whoop. Soaked to the skin and fast as can be, she
swooped downstream with her teeth bared in pure
joy.

In the next instant she heard Charon shouting,
"Hole!" and then they hit it, jolted into a swirling
depression of water. Abby was suddenly in it, the
raft gone.

Under water, she could not see a thing but her head was roaring. Mud burned in her throat. Kicking as hard as she could, she fought her way toward where she thought the surface might be. Once she did get a glimpse of white sky, a smack of raw air in the face, and then she was under again, tumbling against rocks at the bottom of the river. Next thing she knew, her head burst clear above water again. She caught a glimpse of one kayak—half-man, half-boat—bearing down on her position until she was sucked under once more. She needed air. Water was being driven up her nose, prying her eyelids open, pinning her to the river bed. And it occurred to her that she would die now. Without Mike, never having slept all night in his arms. Alone on the murky bottom of a river they might have picnicked beside on a better day.

"Hang on!" a man was screaming at her. He did not have a free hand, both hands clutching the paddle that steered him toward the hole where somehow she had boiled to the surface again. He fought valiantly to keep the nose of his kayak close to her flailing arms.

"The straps, grab hold!" Somehow Abby managed to claw a hold on the kayak's lug straps when next her head bobbed above water. Deftly he steered the boat—Abby clinging to its side—into a smooth stretch where Thea and Charon could safely pull her aboard their raft.

Abby expected to collapse on the floor of the raft, but Charon thrust a paddle into her hands and resumed shouting instructions to the five of them. She paddled feebly at first, her cold hands uncertainly gripping the handle. She was dazed. But soon the present effort of wrestling again with the river's surface restored to her a preposterous sense of normality.

The rafts pulled up for breakfast where the river widened into an unruffled flat stretch. It was Abby who jumped first to the muddy shore of the little island and caught a mooring line when Charon tossed one out. Then all the women were slapping her on the back, congratulating each other and shrugging off their life jackets. The guides prepared breakfast. Crouching over Coleman stoves, they fried pork chops and bread, sending columns of fatty steam into the drizzle. Abby strolled around, sipping scalding tea laced with honey, warming to the notion she would have another crack at this river after breakfast.

"You said you might bring your husband," said Thea. She was warming her hands around a mug of tea, too.

"I invited him. But he says he's missed too many department meetings as it is," said Abby with a shrug. "I knew he wouldn't come."

"It's a good thing," Thea remarked. "He'd still be looking for someone to blame because you went overboard."

Abby nodded, chuckled. "I wasn't expecting to fall in, in the first place. But anyhow, I had to give him the chance at least to come along. I'm trying to wean him gently."

"This is a husband you're talking about, a grown man."

"Weaning him of controlling me. You know, of always wanting to know where I am. I think he won't take it so hard if I let him think it's his choice when I go somewhere without him." She stooped to watch a leggy insect skating across water in the puddle at her feet. "I'm glad I came."

Thea stood looking down at the top of Abby's head.

After breakfast was gone, the rafts bailed out
and the gear stowed, their river expedition set out
once more. The day had brightened considerably
for Abby. To be sure, the sky was still a lowering
gauzy grey, but this leg of the trip was just difficult
enough that all hands had to keep lively and work
hard as their rafts slipped down through the green
enshrouded tunnel of Tirhascamany Gorge. Abby
worked up a sweat. She was discovering muscles in
her back and legs she had never been aware of before. She would be sore tomorrow, and the day after that. But she was also discovering how durable
she was.

By the time the rafts were pulled out of broad,
calm waters in front of McKittrick village's fire
hall, she was ready to stop boating. If not ready to
stop talking about it.

"Cocoa and cookies?" she offered Thea as they
helped toss their raft atop the waiting Land Rover.
Everyone in the parking lot looked the same—
flushed, bedraggled and satisfied. Each carload of
expeditioneers waved and tooted to the others upon
leaving—all beady-eyed with the glee of survivors.

When Abby and Thea pulled up to the curb in
front of Ellsworth Academy, Abby distinctly did
not look like the other mommies. "Oo-o, ick,"
Gabrielle rejoiced, smoothing Abby's muddy hair
across the shoulders of her sweater on the drive
home. "Mudder, dear Mudder, we'll call you."

"Later," Toby hushed his sister. He was de-
termined not to miss a word of what Abby and
Thea were saying. All the way to Farley Landing
Road the women talked about shooting rapids and

explained about cubic feet per second. The kids had lots of questions. Toby proclaimed the outing "Neat," and vowed to do it himself.

Once home, Abby let Gabrielle paint mercurochrome on their blistered hands and plaster them with Band-Aids. Toby stirred the cocoa. Not until Thea started talking about control did the children lose interest. "Pushing limits" and "testing one's mettle" meant far different things to them: they politely filled their fists with cookies and vanished from the kitchen.

Thea was explaining how the Graduate Women's Collective worked on campus when Geoff clumped in from the garage.

"You know Thea Kaltenborn," Abby introduced them. "My husband Geoff."

"Of course," said Geoff pleasantly. "You're the one who's suing the Allegheny Hunt Club, aren't you?" He kissed Abby hello. Inquiring "Drinks anyone?" he went to fix himself a Scotch on the rocks.

Thea called after him, equally pleasantly, "I am. It's a sexist organization."

Abby could tell that Geoff was trying to make the best of an irritating situation—that he was not enchanted to find she had actually taken him at his word about bringing people home with her. Especially people whom he did not care to know. He returned to the kitchen with his drink and, leaning against the edge of the sink, beamed at Thea. "I can see why you'd want to get in The Hunt. It's a classy operation. I had lunch there today. Believe me, if they'd make an exception in your case, you'd be so thrilled that would be the end of your class action suit."

Thea was momentarily speechless with indignation.

Geoff turned to Abby, smiling as he took in her disheveled state. Lowering his voice cozily he reminded her, "You're not forgetting we have a party at the Purcells' tonight?"

"I do not wish personally to become a member of that capitalist organization," said Thea at last.

"Sure you would," said Geoff.

"I don't believe I would," Thea said firmly. "Their admission requirements aren't up to my standards. It's a matter of principle."

"I know," Geoff bantered. "It's also a matter of principle to oppose private property when you can't afford any yourself. By the same token, I'm sure you're opposed to marriage and motherhood. Why not apple pie, as well? You don't happen to live in a bakery, do you?"

"Geoff," Abby objected. She knew perfectly well he was baiting Thea for something to do until she left, got out of their way.

"I am not opposed to motherhood," said Thea evenly. "Wifehood is another matter."

"Ho ho ho!" sneered Geoff. "Any woman should just go ahead and have babies whenever she wants, and the father be damned, huh? The man has no responsibilities, no rights?"

Abby bristled. So Geoff had not forgotten or forgiven: he would go on reminding her that she had fought with him about the children, that she had stood up for herself. And he would bring it up when they were not alone.

"It isn't fathers I'm opposed to," Thea answered. "It's couples. That Molly-and-me-and-baby-makes-three business. The nuclear family is the most anti-social element there is. It positively *breeds* selfishness."

"No doubt you think a woman is better off raising a flock of kids by herself," Geoff snapped.

"No."

Picking up cookie crumbs one by one and flicking them onto her placemat, Abby listened, wondering what they were really fighting for. She felt caught in the middle.

"I think extended families are best for children," said Thea. "A woman alone who has a child to raise is forced to seek out that sort of support group, either in the extended family or within her community. That is so much healthier than the couple. With a family at large, the child has more adult points of view to learn from, and the community frees up the woman so she can actually make more valuable contributions to it as a whole. The couple enslaves both child and parents."

"Malarky," scoffed Geoff.

"Think about it," said Thea. "Think about Mary and Joseph. Now there was a marriage made in heaven. Those two might have saved a lot of lives if they hadn't been so selfish."

"What are you talking about?"

Thea said, "I'm talking about the night the Roman soldiers came around to kill all the boy babies under age two. When Mary and Joseph got wind of it, they *might* have thought of the other couples who also had something to fight for, and *might* have gone around pounding on doors. If a resistance had been organized, that pogrom could have been thwarted. But no. Mary and Joseph split. They thought, well, we've got something special here so we'll sneak away quietly. The others will thank us later."

Abby went into the dining room to fix herself a Scotch, and to hide her smile over Geoff's obvious dismay.

She heard Thea conclude, "A couple is always less than the sum of its parts. Married men and women never amount to much as individuals."

"You remind me of a track coach I had in high school," said Geoff. "The old chestnut—I'm sure you remember it—which held that being with girls would ruin your performance the next day."

"Gynophobes we have with us always," Abby heard Thea sigh.

"Has it ever occurred to you that people who see gynophobes behind every bush are sexists themselves?" Geoff retorted.

Abby thought it was time to interrupt. "Anyone else for a drink?" she called.

"Excuse me," Geoff said. He hurried into the dining room, pushing aside the bottle Abby held out to him. In a stage whisper he told her, "Shouldn't you be cleaning up? I mean, I have to take my shower too before we go out."

"We haven't agreed yet that we're going to this function," Abby dared him.

"I told you about it last Monday."

"I know you did. But you wanted to go and I didn't," she said levelly. "As far as I know, that means we had no firm decision."

Geoff threw up his hands. "We can't discuss it while you're entertaining, can we? I'm going to take my shower." Popping his head into the kitchen for a moment, he gave Thea his most civilized smile and said, "By your leave, perhaps we'll finish our wrangling another time? Prior engagements, you know."

Abby took the Scotch bottle into the kitchen with her but Thea declined a drink. With something between admiration and curiosity, she told her hostess, "Maybe you're the strong one. Teamwork with somebody like Geoff Mullen has to be harder, actually, than paddling through white water."

Abby swallowed her drink with a shudder, then smiled at the faint praise. "There's a lot more to him than polish. Sixteen years, and some days I think I'm still getting to know him."

"I understand his sort perfectly."

"You do?"

"Yeah," Thea grinned. "He causes lesbians."

They laughed together for a little while until Abby started defending Geoff. Thea backed off, goodnaturedly allowing that it takes all sorts, then they congratulated one another again on their triumphal tour of the river.

When Abby had said goodbye to Thea she put the children's dinner in the oven to heat. Setting the timer, she stood by the stove thinking. The raft trip had given her a sense of accomplishment that would not go away. She had actually taken her life into her hands and learned to do something elemental. She had wrestled a river. The achievement tickled her so much she almost felt sheepish.

All right then, damn it, Abby overcompensated mentally. She probably ought to go along with Geoff to the Purcells. She could do that for him. A woman who could handle herself in white water should be able to do anything. And she stomped upstairs to get ready.

Geoff had cooled off in the meantime, seeming

by now no more interested in doing battle than she was. He came in and shaved during her bath, drawing from her a full recital of the day's shocks and strains while she soaked in hot water. "I imagine you *could* use some rest tonight," he offered. "You must be one huge bruise."

"I am," she said.

"Who could begrudge a poor waif an early bedtime?"

Abby flashed him a grateful smile, taking the bait.

And Geoff reeled her in right away. "Stay home if you like. That way you'll be sure to feel rested and lovely for the banquet at Gist Hall on Sunday."

Now Abby saw how Geoff's new policy of consideration was going to work. Much as he protested that he meant to be fair with her, happy as he said he was to see her blossoming this way, supportive as he sounded on the matter of her developing interests of her own—his pledges of generosity only meant open bargaining between them after all these years. Every inch he gave her was a yard he meant to take back in accommodation of his wants. He did not have it in him to let her have her own way.

She fought him by withdrawing: she went through the motions of giving in, keeping more and more to herself. Geoff must have sensed something was missing. He began to play dirty.

He told her how much he loved her. And needed her. He pointed out the sacrifices he too was making: he had put off an offer to fly to Caracas consulting for Koppers just so he could spend some time here with her. He pointed out that the social season was winding up, at its manic best as semester's end approached. He told her how well she looked in evening dress. He said she was indispensible to his happiness. And she knew in a way that it was all partly true.

So they socialized. Abby had her hair done and went with Geoff to vast gatherings where he had to put in an appearance, to intimate dinners where there was someone in particular he needed to cajole. On the days when dinners were scheduled at the Mullen house, Abby had Esther come in to absorb all other chores while she cooked up extravaganzas with the vaguely dogged good cheer of a Mona Lisa. She became sick of mousse, and Wellington. Her feet jammed into satin shoes, she began to fantasize about grazing through a simple salad.

On the evenings when they went out, Abby tried to have fun. All she had to do was show up. Geoff was the celebrity, after all. So long as Geoff was holding court, no one expected *bon mots* from a faculty wife. She amused herself on these occasions by making crazy throwaway remarks. She told a prominent patron of the Pittsburgh Ballet Theatre she didn't care how perverse the lyrics to disco tunes were, at least children were learning to dance and that was what counted, wasn't it.

Among a group of Montessorists she related a story she got from Mike—how certain insect larvae develop completely inside the mother during time of famine and devour their way out on maturity, leaving her a literal shell.

A medievalist gushed to Abby about recreating a fourteenth century fair—a cultural event for which he was trying to have Three Rivers Stadium donated. He said he thought The Society for Creative Anachronism had a marvelous opportunity to capture the imaginations of the ready-made audience of Steelers and Pirates fans. Abby suggested in that case the jousting should be done with chain saws instead of lances. But the man took his Dark Ages seriously. He informed her that chain saws were not "period".

Over dinner at the Chancellor's manse one night she was stuck with the most pretentious connoisseur on campus for her partner at table. Badgered beyond patience about the nuances of a certain ancient burgundy, she sampled the wine at last and pronounced it "Cute". Over brandy the same night she announced to a judge that she and Geoff had a marriage contract and that, "If we ever get a divorce, I will take the children and he will take all our friends. It's only fair."

Abby got away fairly well with guerrilla partying. Most people simply waited for her to finish what she was saying so they could tell her what they wanted to say. Those who did listen overlooked it. Word was out that Mrs. Mullen was in therapy these days and campus society in general has a soft spot for people who seek counseling. In a largely humorless gathering, some were even grateful for Abby's looney wisecracks. One young teaching assistant who was browning up to Geoff took it upon himself to tell Dr. Mullen, "Gee, traveling with you has certainly helped Mrs. Mullen find her voice."

Geoff replied that the shift was not in travel, but in the times: "Even my wife has become a libber," he claimed with a long-suffering smile. "It's epidemic."

It was what Abby tried to say in private, not in public, that finally tempted fate.

Late in May she accepted an invitation to a reception for all the volunteers at the public television station. The weather had taken a distinctly summery shift. Most volunteers would be dropping out to spend more time with their families now; an important club was breaking up. Abby decided to make a show of camaraderie. Going, and taking her husband along, was a good idea on the face of it. Geoff was gratified. He made a lavish show of being charmed to meet her friends. In fact, most of the volunteers were wives, friends and teenaged children of *his* friends—dignitaries from the University and from the corporations downtown. As Abby knew he would, Geoff turned out to be genuinely pleased with the opportunity. Once they had their wine glasses in hand and had sampled the hors d'oeuvres, she introduced him to the station vice presidents. In no time the men were discovering how many advisory boards and foundations they had in common. When Abby managed to disappear into the crowd, Geoff was chatting happily about the National Endowment.

She knew her way around the station. She knew enough to avoid the elevator, which would be full of evening-dressed guests descending to the basement for festivities in studio 31. She knew which stairwells would provide access to the office floors, which doors would have been unlocked because of staff members using the bash downstairs as their cover for clandestine rendezvous in other suites. She had a pretty good idea where the empty cubicles would be, how to get an outside telephone line.

Moving silently across the carpeted floors of the executive level in her thin-skinned evening pumps, she passed through a gallery of paintings. She knew they were works by the latest proteges of Pittsburgh Plan for Art: as a volunteer it had been her privileged duty to hang these paintings where people could see them while they waited for appointments in this or that suite. But no one had an engagement up here tonight except her. Portrait faces and still lives observed nothing.

She found her way to the office of the program guide editor. The door stood open.

"Hi there," she called to a janitor as she breezed past the secretary's credenza. Not waiting to see if he was watching her, she boldly took over the ell where, under piles of schedules and manuscript, the editor seemed to maintain a desk. She took off the jacket to her suit, rolled up the sleeves of her silk blouse. As if she belonged there she found an open ream of paper, removed the cover from the typewriter, rolled in a clean sheet and started with much authority to type. She must have been fairly convincing; the janitor failed to notice she was typing from memory the words to Hank Williams songs. He departed leaving the lights on for her and letting the door drift shut behind him.

At once Abby stopped typing and went to lock the door. Then with a sigh, she turned off all the lights and dialed out.

She listened to the flutter of Mike's phone ringing on the other end of the line. Soon his voice would be there. The very idea excited her. Listening for her connection to go through she leaned back in the chair, kicked off her shoes, put her feet up on the typing table and imagined that, after all these rings, she was probably calling him away from the bathroom. Or maybe he was outside, in the dark the same as she except for a single bulb on an extension cord dangling into the engine compartment of his truck. Tinkering with some gizmo. He would wipe his hands on the thighs of his jeans when he came to answer her call. If he was at home.

Unless he was in bed with company. Painfully she cleared her throat. When he came to the phone she wanted to ask him if he was with anyone, to tell him to wait right there, she was coming and he need never be lonely in his little house again. Nervously she recrossed her legs, feeling the warmth of skin newly shaved smooth under the cool sleekness of nylon stockings. Was he outside, or *out*?

Of course, she realized with relief. Mike would probably just go for a beer or two if he wanted company on a week night.

She did not have the number of the *Friendly* Rising Sun. Far too fragile to switch on the crisp business presence of an overhead light and look through a directory, she dialed Information. And then she had to ask another voice—the one that brayed "County Morgue" into the phone, if Mike Vogel was there please. But her courage paid off.

Mike came to the phone at once and Abby gladdened to hear the way he greeted her, "Where are you?"

"At a party," she whispered. "I miss you." On its silken lining her skirt slid as far as the tops of her thighs.

He wanted to call her back from the Rising Sun's pay phone, but she refused to hang up. She was not willing to gamble whether the TV station's switchboard would put through an incoming call at this hour. And when she pictured the switchboard, it suddenly occurred to her that the tiny red light for this office would be glowing. If the security guard was not getting stewed in honor of the reception downstairs, he would eventually notice that someone was making calls from this office. He might come up here soon.

Urgently, Abby hurried to transmit and receive with Mike all the love she could under these limited, filtered circumstances. She told him about the dreams she had been having. He said he had been afraid she had broken off with him to make her husband happy. Smiling sadly, she thought how she could no more break off with him than she could have broken off her fingers to rid herself of their rash. She told him how impossible it had been to get away, and how much anguish that caused her. He said four weeks was a long time. She was flattered to know he too had been measuring their time apart. If he realized it was four weeks, she dared suppose, maybe he had not been sleeping with anyone else meanwhile. "It's so good to hear your voice," she groaned. He asked her when she was coming out that way again. Allowing herself the pleasure of hearing him persuade her, she asked what he had in mind.

Fingering delicately the velvet hem in her lap, she listened to her lover describe the mysteries of Cook Forest, the remote stand of virgin timber where he wanted to take her before the tourist season got underway. She said she could go away with him next week, any day. To her delight, he added that his parents were asking after her, that she was invited to come with him to their house for supper.

The naivete of Mrs. Vogel's cooking for her—Mike's girlfriend—touched Abby. The sweetness of it stung in her eyes.

"I would like nothing more," she breathed into the phone.

And the overhead lights snapped on. Abby's stockinged feet fell to the carpet as she jerked her head around to see. She froze in position, telephone receiver gripped in her fist and tears standing deep in her eyes. It was not the old security guard she recognized standing in the doorway. It was the station manager, agape to find her here in the midst of his grand tour recitation. At his side stood Geoffrey Mullen.

No one said anything. Abby became acutely aware that she had taken off one earring and unbuttoned her blouse as far down as her bra.

Before Mike's voice could start spilling out of the receiver, she turned her back on the doorway and said into the phone, "I'll call you tomorrow, dear," Stepping into her shoes she heard him say goodbye.

When she hung up, the station manager began with a diplomatic frown, "We try to avoid making personal calls." Abby wiped her eyes with her fingertips. "Unless of course," he hurried to add, "if there is a family emergency."

She took her jacket and strode past them, saying, "My mother."

Geoff and the station manager lingered in the hallway admiring the paintings hung there, until she could vanish down the far stairway.

In studio 31 the reception was going full tilt. Abby hid in the fringes of a group of women who had Allistair Cooke cornered. Geoff found her there eventually and offered to take her home. Their goodnights were said quickly.

The drive home was silent.

"Who were you on the phone with?" Geoff asked. Abby was in a hurry to get into bed, but he stood by the armoir fully-clothed, sipping a fresh Scotch and watching her with an unkind smile skittering around his mouth.

"My mother," Abby repeated.

Geoff made a face. "Women don't take off their shoes to phone their mothers."

"I do."

"Not you," Geoff contradicted her blandly.

"How would you know what I do?" Abby flared. "You didn't invent me. I'm not some jazzy little datum you can chart and predict. Go be an expert on somebody else's time."

The sober, appraising look he gave her made small hairs on the back of her neck stand up. "Pretty touchy."

"I'm sorry," she said. "I am very tired." She was scared.

She reached up to turn out the light on her side of the bed. Gently he caught her hand and held it captive between both of his. She stared back at him. "I think it's time we got away together," he said.

"Okay, good." Anything.

Geoff was beginning to look quite pleased with himself. "I'm going to take you with me on that trip to Caracas next week. We'll have three days— no, five. That'll be Memorial Day weekend so we can take five days." He was nodding enthusiastically, pleased with his calculations. "We might as well take six and I'll fly straight from there to Houston and you can catch TWA home."

It was not fair. After Memorial Day weekend, Mike had indicated, Cook Forest would be teeming with Winebago families. Abby shook her head. "Does it have to be next week?"

"That's when I told them I could be in Caracas."

"I've been asking you to take me along on one of these junkets ever since you went to London and Norway. All of a sudden," she wailed angrily, "it's now or never."

"What's wrong with now?" Geoff asked.

"What was wrong with now, earlier?" she countered.

"It was not the right time before," Geoff argued. "I had too much else to handle on those earlier trips. It simply didn't work out before now."

"Now I don't have nearly enough time to get ready. Thanks a lot."

"You can buy some clothes down there. Whatever. A trip is a trip," Geoff reasoned. "What do you care, as long as we can spend a little time alone?"

Abby turned over and jammed her fists under the pillow. "Some other time," was all she would say.

Geoff did not sleep in the master bedroom that night. He unpacked a lot of paperwork from his attache case, spread it out on the dining room table the way he used to in the old days, and paced the rooms of the first floor. After four o'clock he switched from Scotch to coffee. And when morning light began leaking in the window behind the sink, he called Abby's mother.

"I don't know how much she told you last

night," he began, "but Abby's having a very rough time of it lately."

Mrs. Hays said she was very surprised to hear this. But, she explained, she had not been on the phone with Abby since last month when they had that ridiculous fight over Gabrielle's birthday present.

Geoff hesitated, thinking.

"I believe she's having a nervous breakdown," he ventured, enlisting her mother as an ally. "Crying jags, uncharacteristic behavior. Yes, she's seeing a therapist. But I have to be gone for a few days next week and a few more right after that, and I thought it would do her good to have you around. Frankly, I'm very worried. Can't you come stay for a while, keep an eye on her?"

CHAPTER TWENTY

This time Abby brought a change of clothes along with her. Not to mention a picnic basket. The working man's grub they had shared in the woods earlier had been nice enough, but today she intended to treat Mike to a properly-planned luncheon alfresco. She had prepared a feast. Cornish game hens roasted with rosemary and butter, then chilled overnight in a pair of matching crocks with gherkins and small red potatoes. Slaw: she had axed a whole pale head into shards before bedtime, sprinkled it with dilled vinegar and this morning early, lovingly slathered it with sour cream. Forks: not her wedding stainless Danish but two worn and baroque forks of silverplate she kept in a kitchen drawer, reserved until now for cooking. Beer—two kinds, both from eastern Europe via her delicatessen, and glasses so they could smell the beer. Apples, almonds, gingerbread baked this morning and swaddled in a tea towel. And the thermos which she paid Donna to fill with coffee at the *Friendly* Rising Sun while she waited for Mike to appear. She would leave her car out back with the empty cases of bottles all day, and all night.

Mike was providing the fresh air. Today, at

long last, they were alone together in his truck again, moseying their way north toward Cook Forest.

They puttered through little crossroads towns so backward that the filling station had only one moon-faced gas pump. Where the post office was in back of a variety store.

They stopped beside the road to buy a box of strawberries from a fat young woman who was crocheting together panels cut from Budweiser cans. She was making a vest, she said. The berries only lasted a few miles down the road. Made greedy with the smell of fresh fruit Abby and Mike dusted their strawberries off as best they could and, one at a time, crunched them into juice.

They stopped at a railroad crossing and dizzied themselves reading names on the rolling stock as it passed: Great Northern, Erie Lackawanna, Rock Island Line, Chessie, Penn Central, L&N, Chesapeake and Ohio, even one outlandish boxcar labeled Alabama State Docks. Then the caboose passed, abruptly revealing farmland again.

They passed three men in shirtsleeves and Sunday hats arguing in front of a John Deere tractor dealership.

They passed a ramshackle blacksmith's shop where "Antiques" and "Goats Milk" had been sketched in silver spray paint across the rusty tin roof.

They caught a glimpse of a scarlet tananger perched, swaying, on the tip of a cattail reed.

Abby counted at least five barns sporting enormous blue advertisements for Mail Pouch chewing tobacco on their sides.

As they drove further into the past, Mike told

Abby about the virgin forest ahead of them. He told her about the wolves and bears and elk which used to inhabit the woods when all of western Pennsylvania was virgin forest. George Washington came out here on a surveying trip, he claimed, and marched his company through woods so deep they did not see sunlight for two weeks.

Abby asked him about the trees. "White pine mostly," he said. "With hemlock and laurel underneath. Some hardwoods too. Oak—lots of oak—walnut, hickory. Too dark for anything else."

"That's funny," said Abby.

"What is?"

"You know, in fairy tales the forest always has little streams and flowers and roots and berries. In case any heros get lost there, I guess. So they can survive until the spell wears off."

Mike gave it some thought. "Cook's too dark for flowering stuff. Oh, I guess there might be a few wortleberries, pawpaws."

And it *was* dark. When Abby first jumped down from the truck she reached for the picnic basket, ready to hightail it into this legendary forest for a legendary lunch. But Mike suggested they look around first, saying, "Maybe we'll decide to eat somewhere else." They hiked into the forest on a trail made slippery with browned needles. Unsure of her footing, she kept her eyes on Mike's bootheels. Not until he stopped halfway up a domed slope did she realize he had led her off the trail: they were standing in the middle of the closest thing to nowhere her commonwealth could offer.

What had been a sunny day now splintered into a few pallid shafts of sunlight quivering eerily between massive columns of darkness. Nothing growing here except old, old evergreens, older than her grandparents, older than the United States—and not so much as a wortleberry bush. A clump of blackish hemlock shrubs crouched at the feet of some gigantic pines uphill from them. But there was little else to see at eye level—only those towering presences which forcibly drew her attention up, up, where instead of the heavenly blue relief of sky she saw only spiny pine branches converging into ancient darkness overhead. For one twanging moment she glimpsed herself in proportion to the past.

And to the future. "They'll still be here long after we're gone," she whispered.

"I guess," said Mike. "The ones that aren't struck by lightning. That's nature's way of keeping up with the weeding." When she moved closer to him he put his arm around her, murmuring, "Still want to eat your lunch here?"

Later she asked, "Were *all* the woods really like that?" Shaking out her pretty yellow tablecloth to cover a trestle table, she served their lunch in dappled sunshine. She had dozens of questions.

"Sure," said Mike. "For a while."

"What happened to them?" Abby gestured past the well-groomed little grove where the Park Service maintained picnic grounds. "Did the settlers cut them down to make cabins and pasture?"

Mike's mouth was full: he made a noncommittal gesture. It occurred to Abby that the two of them had entirely different views of mealtime. Her set was in the habit of garnishing food with conversation. He, on the other hand, was well brought up enough to know it was rude to talk with food in his mouth and so said nothing until he had eaten his fill. She dawdled over her food, savouring the sight of his face, the warmth of the sun, gurgles from a nearby creek.

"I'd rather be here than Caracas, Rome or France," Abby told him. "Of course, even if you did insist on going to Dubrovnik for an opera festival I'd be happy to do that with you, too. Anywhere you like. But I do dearly love being here.

"My husband thinks I'm going crazy. You know what he did, that bastard?" she grinned happily at Mike over a fork laden with slaw. "He called up my mother, without even talking to me about it first, and asked her to come stay with me while he's gone. As if she'd be any help! If I *were* having a nervous breakdown she'd prescribe fresh fruit. I'll never forget the last time I went to her in tears over something—I think it was the time they made me retake my college entrance test. Mother said, 'There, dear, you see? You've been drinking too much coffee and got yourself over-stimulated again.' She's the sort of person who would attribute hepatitis to a failure of the will. The great anthropologist! Completely fascinated with human beings, as long as they've been buried a hundred years or more. I called her back and told her I didn't think it was a very good idea. She was happy not to come. We don't get along famously, a thing she knows perfectly well herself. I swear she only bothers to keep in touch because she's so big on having grandchildren." Abby licked at a drumstick pensively.

Mike complimented her on her cooking then and she stopped to ponder that milestone. So much between them already. So much more to look forward to. She wanted it all. Every minute Geoff was out of her hair she wanted to spend being happy like this, with Mike. Any time Geoff was out town, she could.

Now she contented herself with eating in silence.

Mike was nearly finished when she dug in, but there was something terribly satisfying about sitting on a rough board sucking chicken bones while her man talked to her. He had answers for all the questions she had asked.

"It was timbering took out all the forests but those few acres," he told her, jerking his thumb backward. "They cut them down for the mines, some for railroad ties. Mostly for the coal mines, though. It takes a lot of timber to shore up all those shafts and tunnels. What they'd do was, they just cut down an entire forest and then put it back up underground. My grandpa told me by World War I there was hardly a tree left standing in Pennsylvania."

Abby considered this denuding appetite for coal, then recalled the wooded spot where they had made love over a log. "Not *all* of them?" she protested.

"Yeah," he nodded.

"But there are woods all over the place. Up at Ligonier . . ."

"Some governor. reforested in a big way. Pinchot. He used to be a forest ranger, I think."

Abby broke into a gratified smile. "Maybe more politicians ought to be forest rangers. You're a noble lot."

Mike reached across the table and ran his finger lightly around the smile on her lips. "You are a beautiful woman." It was the tenderness in his voice that made her feel beautiful.

"Seriously," she said.

"I'm not so noble."

"You are! You're taking care of something precious for all the rest of us."

"I do it to be outside," Mike shrugged. "I'd quit this job in a minute for something better. But not to be governor. I've got no interest in becoming a bureaucrat. It's bad enough working for bureaucrats."

When they had finished the coffee with their gingerbread, Mike went down to the stream and, rinsing out her thermos, brought back a drink for Abby. The water was delicious, achingly cold and fresh. "It has a flavor," she marveled.

"Iron."

After lunch they put in a few hours on Mike's job, stopping by woodlots both on private property and on state Game Lands. Abby filled out the checklist on Mike's clipboard according to his instructions, listening drowsily to the sound of his voice while he explained what they were doing. The afternoon was sweltering and they sweated like stevedores. They stopped once for hot fudge sundaes at a Dairy Queen. In a shady patch where trees converged and made a tunnel over the road, she watched Mike dig a few sassafras roots out of a moist dirt bank. She lent him her tea towel to keep them cool and dark on the ride back. They rode slowly with the truck windows up while on dusty dirt roads, roasting themselves, and fast with the windows down on macadam two-lane, tangling their hair. Kiddish, they necked in a dark booth at the bar where they stopped for a beer.

By the time he turned the truck toward his parents' orchard, Abby was so engorged with love that

there was not a sophisticated bone left in her body.
She was prepared, today, to spend an evening with
his parents.

She was scarcely prepared for suppertime, however. No sooner had they arrived at the Vogels'
house when Mike excused himself and disappeared
into a bathroom. Holding a tea towel full of roots,
Abby was left to accept all the attention, greetings
and questions. Plainly Mr. and Mrs. Vogel had
been spending their day waiting for the kids, as
Mike's father kept calling them. Abby told what
she could about the remarkable things they had
seen and done, trying to keep a certain recurring
giggle of overjoyed lust out of her accountings.

Mrs. Vogel comprehended the sassafras as a
present from Abby, took the bundle in one hand
and Abby's elbow in another and, saying how
thoughtful Abby was, led her away to the kitchen
where longingly she overheard Mike reappear and
sit talking with his father.

The kitchen was redolent with ham, green beans
and dumplings simmering in one pot on the back
of the stove since morning. Abby's hot fudge sun-
dae reared up on its hind legs. "We've been snack-
ing all afternoon," she said. "I'm not sure I can do
justice to your dinner."

Mrs. Vogel agreed that ham and dumplings
could get pretty heavy on a queasy stomach. Abby
said she might feel best having just a little salad,
and Mrs. Vogel beamed: she said there was plenty
of salad.

Salad turned out to come in three varieties. One
was raisins, carrots and walnuts thoroughly
swamped in mayonnaise. The second was
macaroni. And the third consisted of red Jello

studded with celery, pineapple chunks and tidbit-sized marshmallows. No greens anywhere in sight.

Abby ended up drinking a pot of elderberry blossom tea while the Vogels had their supper. She enjoyed watching them, appreciated the fancy plates and serving bowls set out because she was company, was touched to see that Mike had combed his hair with water when he washed up for supper with his parents. No doubt it had been this way since he outgrew his highchair.

For dessert there was tapioca pudding, coffee, and Army stories.

As darkness started creeping up to the house from the creek, they all stacked the dishes in the sink and moved out to the porch where they could properly watch fireflies. Mike finished his Army stories on the glider with Abby nestled under his arm against his ribs, and when Mr. Vogel's answering story died down, they contented themselves with the incoherent epics chirped out by peepers down beyond the porch. Mrs. Vogel started reminiscing then, sitting side by side in the squeaking swing with her husband. First about their courtship on this very swing, then about the night Mikey scared the living daylights out of them by starting to be born while they were still way the hell and gone out at Hagler's Dam fishing for catfish. Then she recalled her pregnancy and soon enough ended up encouraging Abby to go ahead and have her children before too much more time gets away.

Abby hedged. She had treasured every pensive moment of feeling single in this island of twilight and she was loathe to disturb anyone here by intruding with the facts. "I'm almost thirty-seven," was the most she was willing to say.

Mrs. Vogel assured her that she was none too old, and that it was high time Mike started a family. No one contradicted her. Abby was grateful, however, for the conspiratorial fondle Mike gave her in the darkness. Mrs. Vogel's assumption that she was Mike's for keeps left her tense and needy.

The talk veered off toward more concrete things, such as the new fireplace in the living room and the old furnace in the basement. Tomorrow's weather. Last winter. Whether indoor-outdoor carpet should be laid on the porch floor. Abby shrank from giving an opinion about the porch; she had not yet gotten over her disappointment in finding that the Vogels were covering the plank floor in front of the new fireplace with yards of smelly new nylon shag. (Mrs. Vogel had wanted wall-to-wall carpet ever since seeing a televised tour of the White House, and now by golly the floor wouldn't get so cold in winter any more.) Abby listened politely, then inquired how the dandelion wine was working out. Mike's father said it would be ready for her to sample by Thanksgiving.

The very notion scared her. Thanksgiving was too far away from May; its distance implied certain fearsome events in the meantime which she would have to face up to and go through one way or another. She would have to do something about Mike. It was agony to think about.

When Mike stood up, stretching, she hurried to her feet too. Saying their goodnights they did his parents the courtesy of implying Abby would be heading for home now: both understood that no matter how greedy for grandchildren that generation becomes, they do not welcome evidence of unhallowed fornicating.

As they walked into the lane together, she turned back once to wave goodnight and saw the porch light go out. It wrenched her heart. She felt orphaned by being unable to promise Mrs. Vogel babies.

Catching up with Mike, she tugged mutely at his arm. He stopped, folded her against him and kissed her soundly. That was what she wanted. His mouth went hard against hers. They ground teeth against teeth and still it was not enough. Abby was nearly frantic with need.

"You looked so good," he growled against her cheek.

"What?"

"At the table. Easy and sweet as could be, sitting at the table with Mom and Pop. Sunburned like some good-hearted girl down the road I could have married right out of high school."

"I am like that," she wished, holding herself against him as if she would crawl inside.

"No you're not."

"I am. When we're together that's exactly who I am."

"You," he breathed, nuzzling her scalp. "You're supposed to be living it up at some snooty place on Mt. Washington with wineglasses that're too big and coffee cups that're too small. You are a faculty wife."

"Don't," Abby begged him. "I don't feel like that. I just want to make love with you and be happy ever after."

Groaning a little, Mike kissed her. "Wouldn't that be something," he whispered.

She whispered back, "Keep me here. Let's disappear together and never be heard from again.

Squirrels and spiders'll nest in the doorway so no one can ever find us."

Mike kissed her until they both wanted to be out of their clothes and then they hurried up the hill to his place hand in hand.

He stopped her right inside the kitchen door. Abby was intent upon getting into his bedroom, turning down the covers, taking their clothes off and settling down to a mind-numbing marathon of lovemaking. But she got no further than the braided rag rug at the doorsill before he turned to block her progress. Deftly he undid her jeans and gave her a look, waiting for her to step out of them. She obliged him, then tried to lead the way into his bedroom. He held her fast.

"Not here," she smiled at him, explaining the obvious.

Nothing was obvious to Mike except the single flaw about Abby—that she was still wearing panties. He pulled them down and immediately knelt to press his big warm face against her.

"Wait," Abby urged. He had kissed her this way once before and the salty memory of it lodged in those tissues still—surprising, moving her. She had wanted more ever since. But not in the kitchen. Undignified as it was she wanted to concentrate on every nuance. "Let's go lie down first. I can't manage, standing up."

"Not if you're talking, you can't," she heard him say.

Persisting, he overwhelmed her.

She found she could manage perfectly well after all. Planting her feet, she gripped the countertop with one hand and Mike's hair with the other. White-knuckled, cursing silently through gritted teeth, she forced upon him what he demanded. She let him get a full taste of this ferocity that was so new to her. She did not worry about his comfort. She did not care. She was magnificent.

When she finished he rocked back on his heels to laugh up at her, vulgarly showing his shining wet face. She could see herself there.

Faculty wife, he had said; a woman in her position. Now Abby laughed too. A woman in her position—in this kitchen, right now—had just faced herself and she knew she was no hothouse plant, no matter what he said. She was kin to him. Whatever coarseness in her allowed this sort of carrying on, it was made of a willful fibre she had not realized was in her. She might as well stop worrying. She felt sure of herself, even with this disconcerting man who insisted upon going down on her. If after all these years she could find someone who did that for his own satisfaction, if she could find this marvel of a man to love her, then she could do anything.

He stood up. Full of gratitude she reached for him. But he walked away, carrying her jeans with him as far as the bathroom. "Oh no you don't," he was saying. "I wouldn't want to scare you."

She left her shoes on the rug and followed him. He was stripping, dropping his own clothing where he had dropped her jeans. "What do you mean?" she asked.

"I've been sweating all day," he said.

"So have I."

Mike turned on the taps in his tub and brandished the shower hose festively. "I know," he said. "Come on, let's slosh off."

All elbows and knees they washed each other in

his bathtub—a process Abby found to be as comic, sloppy and touching as getting her children bathed. Something about it must have touched Mike as well, because he went on sitting on the edge of the tub when he had finished scrubbing his feet. Letting the water sluice down his shins, he studied her face almost sadly. "I worry about you sometimes," he said at last.

"Whatever for?" she wondered.

"That I won't be able to live up to what you expect."

"I don't expect anything from you, dear heart," she rushed to reassure him. "I love you exactly the way you are."

"But I'm none too sure I could make you happy, you know?"

"You make me very happy."

"Okay," he nodded. "Maybe today I do. What about later, though? When a woman starts moving in little bags of cosmetics, you gotta be pretty sure she's not happy at home. The next thing you know she's bringing clothes here straight from the cleaners instead of taking it home, leaving it in my closet, and pretty soon papers are being served for the divorce hearing. Then suppose we got married. Are you sure it would be an improvement?"

Too quickly she assured him she was perfectly happy with her present arrangement.

"I'm not, to tell you the truth," Mike said. Absentmindedly he trained a stream of water from the hose across her breasts. "I worry about your husband. Poor guy. Sometimes I think about how I'd feel if it was him beating my time with you."

"Geoff is getting everything he wants from me," said Abby. "It doesn't happen to amount to very much, but in point of fact he does always get what-ever he feels he needs.''

Mike looked up at her with an ironic smile, saying, "Well, if you're not worrying why should I? More for me, that's all.''

Abby loved him for being jealous, and managed to ignore the restless undercurrents in his voice. She was no more conscious than he was that his concern for her was fundamentally an instinctual maneuver; as they grew closer he would naturally have to shift positions slightly if he was to keep an eye on the door. That he wanted her to himself was enough for her. "You're all I've ever wanted," she declared.

"Am I?" he dared her tenderly.

"Yes," she murmured. Now it seemed terribly true.

"Sometimes I think I have a better idea about that than you do," he told her, and helped her out of the tub. "You're only just starting to find out what you've got. Not to mention what all you want.''

Abby dried off beside him, then hung her towel neatly over the door knob. "Do you really mind that I brought some toiletries?" she asked.

"Hell no," he yawned. "It's nice having somebody's tracks in here besides mine. I don't much care for it when Mom lets herself in to tidy up. You should've seen the ruckus we had when I wouldn't let her put up pissy little cafe curtains in every goddam window," he chuckled.

They got into bed as people do who belong to-gether—exchanging a few syllables of easygoing chatter left over from the bathroom, pulling the covers down neatly and one of them sitting, the other one rolling, with a sigh, onto the sheets.

"I think it's nice the way you and your father talk," said Abby.

"It's getting better. For years we couldn't talk at all," he answered.

"At least he waited around for it to get better," she said jealously. "My father died a little over a year ago."

"Umnh. That's rough," said Mike. "I don't think Mom could take it if Pop died before her."

"My mother could," Abby recalled. "But they'd been separated since I started junior high."

"No kidding?"

"Lots of people get divorced."

"But that was *then*. It used to be that everybody stayed married no matter what. Unless of course the old man had a weakness for three-and-a-half-year fishing trips."

"No," said Abby. "I think they broke up because he wasn't an intellectual. She was always telling us he could have been a brilliant doctor, when I know for a fact he didn't even bother finishing veterinary school. He embarrassed her. She thought he was a failure because he had no interest in being a scholar. He just liked livestock, and being out of doors. She said the grounds for their divorce was mental cruelty, but she was the cruel one. He never got over it when she took me and moved out. He died of hurt feelings. No, really. I think it was because he was so angry from then on that he finally started having those strokes."

"More than one? How many did he have?"

"I don't know. I found out he was having them when I noticed one time—I think at my daughter's christening—he had to pick his one hand up with the other to reach into his left pocket." She inched closer to Mike for comfort.

He collected her in a big, yawning hug and held her until she could feel the chill of that memory get drawn out of her by the vast warmth of his skin. She relaxed. Tonight she did not need to be on guard, to perform brilliantly, nor even wake up in time to go home. Tonight she could suit herself. Snuggled against Mike, she found herself being aroused again.

She resolved to give him the sort of pleasure he had given her, to take the lead this time and see firmly to it that he was gratified as she had been. He looked willing. Lying perfectly still, unsmiling, he closed his eyes. He simply let her do things to him. Whatever she kissed, caressed, pinched, seemed to be perfectly all right with him.

Until abruptly he got to his knees.

Whatever he wanted was fine with Abby, and she lay down to let him take over. There was a blunt, busy earnestness to his actions now.

"Touch your breasts," she thought she heard him say, so she opened her eyes. That *was* what he'd said. "Hard."

Abby was shocked. Only recently had she got up enough courage to touch her own breasts in private for the recommended periodic checking after lumps. She had never touched herself anywhere in the presence of another: she had learned that tenet of etiquette at her mother's knees. Touching breasts became permissible in later years, of course, but it still seemed indecent unless subcontracted to a male, or at least an infant.

Mike's hands were busy elsewhere.

"Go ahead," he urged her quietly.

"I can't."

"You can. They're yours, aren't they?"

Self-conscious, wanting to please, she bargained, "It doesn't turn me on."

"It does me," was his answer. "Let me see you do it."

So for him she did it. Awkwardly at first, her eyes riveted to his in hopes of being excused at the last minute, she did it. Not for her own pleasure but caught up in the fervor of this vulnerable tyrant bending over her, asking her to help him take her by storm. He was completely rapt. In sympathy for his touching hunger she manipulated her own body along with him. Still embarrassed, she found herself becoming as urgent as he was.

Soon all she knew was how much good this was doing her. He kept up with her until her breath came in big gulps of amazement. Then, suddenly engulfed in tenderness, she was a small dim body delivered, contracting quietly, on the solid ground of his bed once more. He collapsed beside her.

It was nearly too much for both of them. Neither managed to utter a word after that. They comforted each other incoherently with a few good-night hugs and pats, then rolled over rump to rump for rest.

Dozing off, Abby wondered if this was what trust always felt like.

Mike was a lonely sleeper, a thrasher. He abandoned himself completely to the anti-world of sleep. In that realm, it seemed, he had to ransack a full store of dreams and set them all ablaze before morning. A bleak yelp escaped him occasionally. Sometimes he appeared to rest. But most of his vital signs took the form of mute violence.

During the night Abby surfaced once. Before she
opened her eyes she knew where she was. A sun-
warmed lumber smell came from Mike nearby and
she recalled drowsily that she was with him—not as
her dream suggested in Cook Forest, but in his bed
in his small house on the far side of his parents'
orchard. That orchard outside was a physical presence for her even in darkness, and to her it felt
cozier than having a nightlight. Her eyelids drifted
shut once more. Tonight she was one of the little
ones herself, bathed, loved and tucked in. She
drifted back to sleep but her pores stayed alert for
some time after, sensible to the heavy form beside
her, the textures against her skin. The quilt at her
cheek smelled of people's homes, of cotton and
cider and lullabies—a dozen other ephemera besides. Something in the dark inside her here could
recall life as it was when she first observed it. Life,
therefore, as it was meant to be. Before synthetic
carpeting, before computers, before 747s, before all
those post-war beads and trinkets for which her
generation traded its children's birthright, there
was a cotton quilt on a little bed where fairy tales
were read aloud to her. In those days life had certain blemishes, of course. Already it had Howdy
Doody, and disappointment. But they were part of
life as she knew it and so had had their own quirky
beauty. Then everything started changing faster
and faster, so fast she could hardly see any change
at all, and the changes came to feel so unnatural
she could hardly bear them.

An owl in Vogel's orchard called out in the
night. The sound of it swallowed up Abby's
dreams, easing her into smooth blank peace.

In the morning she woke up feeling more confident than she ever had in her life—more even than the day she survived white water rafting down the Tirhascamany. Her lover was corny and easygoing over coffee; she was able and daring. All was right with the world.

After breakfast she kissed Mike goodbye out behind the *Friendly* Rising Sun. Driving toward Farley Landing Road she chortled to herself thinking how lucky she was to have finally wised up. With a little finesse she could juggle all the contradictions—maintain a home for her family as well as a lover for herself. She was doing just fine. So long as she had Mike's orchard to resort to, she could go on indefinitely balancing the equation of her marriage. Today, for example, would be simple.

She would change clothes, call Esther and pick up the children at Maxine's before lunch, make a major grocery run this afternoon, and be ready with sauerbraten and homemade bread to welcome Geoff back tomorrow.

CHAPTER TWENTY-ONE

Geoff was there when she got home. He had left a rental car parked recklessly in the driveway.

Abby's heart was pounding when she walked into the kitchen and found him sitting at the breakfast nook browsing the mail. Not that he said anything ugly or suspicious. Rage was fairly smoking out of him in dry-icy waves as she bent close to give him a hello peck. But he was aggressively calm.

"I came home early," he said. It was a brilliant opening bid, since anything she could possibly say in direct response would certainly incriminate her.

Least said soonest mended, some old wife inside Abby's head advised. "Well," she said heartily.

Keep moving girl, she told herself. She carried her Design Research shopping bag straight upstairs and emptied yesterday's clothing from it into the hamper. She caught a glimpse of herself in the mirror: not too white-eyed. Buck up, keep moving. In the kitchen once more she began banging cupboard doors, making a grocery list.

"Up and out pretty early yourself, weren't you?" Geoff said.

"Yes."

He was watching her microscopically.

"I'll have my list ready in another minute," she ventured. "Want to go along?"

Instead, however, she ended up driving behind him all the way into town so he could return his rented car. He did so, brusquely. On the return trip, she postponed her visit to that nice Italian-German deli in East Liberty. She had little choice: he got behind the wheel of the Gremlin before she could offer him her keys, and started driving toward Farley Landing again.

"Wait," she protested. (This was admitting into evidence dangerous material but it could not be helped.) "Let's stop by the Gerbers now and pick up the kids."

She expected he would favor her with another of his crystalline looks, be surprised, and demand to know why their children were in someone else's care. She did not have a detailed plan in case he questioned her. She simply intended to imply she had dropped Toby and Gabrielle off to play with Dylan while she ran errands.

But he did not ask anything. For a long time he said nothing. The Aspinwall off-ramp was behind them before he said, "The kids aren't at the Gerbers'."

"Of course they are, Geoffrey. I took them there just . . ."

"I don't think I care to hear when or why you took them there," he replied. "Suffice it to say they were not at home when I got there last night. Nor, it goes without saying, were you."

Panic: "We . . ."

"I called Maxine," he went on. "After rattling around in the house alone for a while, with no note from you, no message, no nothing. So I assumed you'd run over there with Toby and Gabey."

Geoff pulled up to their garage door, yanked on the hand brake, and when they both got out of the car he slammed his door hard. Smiling across the car roof at her with a hideous smile, he bellowed, "And sure enough, you had!"

On the far side of their woodlot Abby could hear the neighbor's power mower running. She was painfully aware that Kit Fairchild might be dropping by, or that someone else might bicycle into the drive looking for coffee and a chat or to borrow the pruning hook. "Let's not fight in the driveway," she said as evenly as she could. "And please don't yell at me."

He stalked around the car shouting, "My *children* were there, but my *wife* was not."

"Where are the children now?" Abby asked.

"Oh no you don't! I picked this fight and I'm picking the subject. I'd like to know where in bloody hell you were last night!"

"I was out late."

He said, "I know. It was after ten o'clock when I drove up to Ligonier, so I know perfectly well you were out late."

Abby was incredulous. "You drove all the way to Ligonier looking for me?"

"To talk to your mother. We stayed up half the night talking, worrying about you."

So, he could not know for sure whether she had spent any time sleeping in her own bed last night; he likely had breakfast with Mother and drove back early this morning. Abby decided to tough it out. Her spine was stiffened further by the indignity of Geoff's complaining to Mother about her behavior. "So where were the children while *you* were tattling back and forth in the mountains? And where are they now?" she demanded.

"I'll tell you that when you tell me where you spent the night."

"Don't be absurd," she said. "What matters most is the children."

"You didn't seem to think so last night. In fact, I happen to know you haven't seen Toby and Gabrielle since yesterday morning when you unloaded them on the Gerbers. That much I have from Maxine herself. So I doubt if it's crucial you see the kids at precisely this moment."

The skin was crawling on Abby's hand. "Where *are* they?" she insisted.

Geoff half-turned away, elaborately bored and disgusted. "For God's sake, Abigail, stop badgering. Toby and Gabrielle are safe and sound in Ligonier with your mother. Where I want them to stay," he added over her protests, "until you and I have had all the discussion we need."

"You dragged them out of bed . . . ?"

"They were not in their own beds," said Geoff.

"Dragged them off in their little peejays to my mother's?"

"I feel they should stay with your mother for the time being."

"Why? So you can browbeat me at your leisure?"

"There is no need to scare them out of a year's growth just because we're having contractual disputes," Geoff said sarcastically.

Abby countered, "Let's not dispute."

"We have to come to some sort of understanding."

"I thought we had an understanding," said

Abby bravely. "I was going to be more accommodating about your professional comings and goings, and you were going to stop blowing up over the service I do or do not provide at home."

"I found my own ride home this trip," he reminded her furiously. "I did not impose upon you at all. But that is not the issue."

"If the issue is my free time, I still think you're being unfair."

"I want to know precisely what you were up to yesterday and last night."

"Geoff," she maintained, shaking her head wryly, "I am not going to tell you."

"Why not?"

"Because it is petty of you to ask. It'll only make you mad. I don't want you yelling at me again, and besides, it's none of your business."

"None of my business!" Geoff raged, yelling again. "I'm your bleeding husband."

"And I am your bleeding wife. But I don't extort from you detailed accountings of your days and nights away from home." For one bizarre moment it appeared Professor Mullen was going to smack her face.

"It *is* my business," he shouted at her. "It is indeed my business *now,* no matter how finicky you want to be about your privacy and your space and your needs and all the rest of that consciousness-raising tea group claptrap. I'll tell you why. Your free-spirited devil-take-the-hindmost behavior has probably cost me the department chair!"

"That is unfair. And silly."

But she could see the bombast draining out of him before her eyes. "Of course it's unfair and silly," he said. "True nevertheless. When I went over to the Gerbers last night Jerry told me."

Too concerned not to argue, Abby said, "How would Jerry know? He's not in the department."

"Maxine was playing doubles with the Fair-children, of all people, when Chris—that twit—just happened to drop the news on her. Irving Purcell is the new chairman."

"Oh Geoff, I'm so sorry."

"Are you?" he said meanly. "Thanks."

She resisted the urge to take him in her arms as she would have one of her children, to hug him and rock him because it was such a sore hurt. Instead, she said, "I am sorry. I know how much you were counting on it."

"But didn't care enough to help me."

"What are you talking about?"

"Philandering! I'm talking about good old-fash-ioned cuckoldry. Faithlessness. Abby, your wretched randy behavior has damn near ruined my career."

"Stop it!"

"Surely you can't think your conduct has done me any good on campus?"

"Oh, come on now," she replied. "Even if I spent last night dancing on the tables in a Liberty Avenue strip joint, that doesn't make your wife de-partmental business. Besides, the voting for chair-man must have happened before yesterday if Chris told Maxine about it yesterday at tennis. I am truly sorry you weren't voted in, but you can't blame the election on me. I did everything in my tiny little power to help you."

"Acting the hussy is not what I call help," Geoff said dangerously.

"Even if the University did evaluate faculty

wives' comportment on a pass-fail basis, I assure
you I've done nothing that could tarnish your
image." Abby turned to go into the house.

"No? What about that little display at the party?" he demanded, following her.

"What party?"

They fought in the kitchen, they fought on the
stairs, they fought in the bedroom, the bathroom
and downstairs again in the living room. The more
he argued the more convinced Geoff seemed to become that it was Abby's making personal phone
calls from an office at the television station party
which had cost him the chairmanship of his department. He harped on that error relentlessly. It was
something Abby would not defend.

Geoff was driving her to distraction, kept un-
balanced as she was by the fear she was somehow
to blame for her children being out of reach. Drawing a long trembly breath she announced, "This is
completely out of hand now. I'm going to pick up
the kids. When we get back, I'll fix us something to
eat. And when we've all had our dinner like normal
human beings and they've been put to bed, then we
can talk some more. If you must."

But Geoff had her car keys with his own, in his
pants pocket. He was not about to hand them over.
Crazily, the notion crossed Abby's mind to lunge
at him—wrestle him to the carpet if necessary—
grab the keys and be off. When she realized the
anarchic break in their relations that would pre-
cipitate, she decided against open struggle. Besides,
he was bigger than she was. There was nothing to
do but wade through this fight, let Geoff berate
her, until his chagrin at losing the chairmanship
began to drain off. Until he was finished assigning

blame, there was no point in trying to restore any order in their lives.

Abby listened to her husband's tirade without answering. She moved around. Out of the freezer she concocted a good-looking supper neither of them could eat.

She called her mother's summer house, prepared to insist that Mother drive Toby and Gabrielle home tomorrow. But Toby answered the phone and begged to stay: his telescope worked so much better in the dark skies of the Laurel Highlands, and Gabrielle caught three crayfish today.

She listened to Geoff take a call from his cinematographer. Apparently there was excellent material to be filmed in South America. She heard how cordial and intimate Geoff's voice was while talking business with his colleague. And how cold his voice was when he hung up and told her he was going to bed. He was obviously exhausted, barely holding on to righteous rage with the last vestige of his energy.

Abby realized she was exhausted too. Exhausted by the unaccustomed strain of fearing her own husband.

Throughout the entire sorry childish fuss about his departmental ambitions and during the power struggle over the children, Abby's composure was seriously eroded with fear. She was unreasonably afraid that Geoff would find Mike and forbid him to have any further dealings with his wife. She knew it was insane because Geoff would never run into Mike, but my God, what if he did? What if he went completely Byronic and got himself a dueling pistol? What if he shot Mike? She decided to go to bed and try to sleep before her frayed imagination could impose any further lurid notions upon her.

But she was not meant to sleep that night. Tired as she was, while crawling into bed she remembered the basket from her picnic with Mike, and was wide awake again. The picnic basket was still in the trunk of the car; within it remained all the romantic rubbish from luncheon for two in the forest. No telling when she could discreetly get that stuff into the kitchen and put it away, or whether Geoff would find it first. Then Esther called: she was sorry to bother them so late at night, but the whole side of her face was blowing up with toothache and did Abby know a dentist who took emergency calls? Abby suggested the university hospital emergency room at Presby. And then Geoff refused to come to bed after all.

He sat up in the chaise longue near Abby's side of the bed, complaining that he could not be expected to sleep. Abby could feel him watching her in the dark. She tried not to think about Mike or the picnic basket for fear he could read her mind. She stared back at the place where she knew Geoff was sitting, concentrating on her.

His confidence must have been severely shaken by losing the chairmanship, she began to realize. Only the unfamiliar discomfort of having doubts could have turned Geoff so vicious. He was always in command of his situation, always able to predict his next best move. That was why he was torturing her with these accusations: frustrated at having his ambitions thwarted he had to put himself in control of something. So it was to be Abby. Her pain he could manipulate. Geoff was dangerous in this condition, she told herself. He would not likely hurt the children or herself physically, but he might insist on keeping them uprooted. Or using them against her somehow. She hated to think what rash thing he might do if he were not mollified.

Please, she begged nameless powers. Let me get through this one and I'll never tempt fate again. That was it—she had to steady herself. If she could be firm then Geoff would let himself wind down.

"I'm sorry about the department chairmanship," she ventured softly, knowing his eyes were still completely open. "But think about it this way. Irving can't possibly last much longer without retiring. And if he does, even if he lasts another decade, he'll have to go on sabbatical in seven years and they'll be needing another chairman. You can take the job then." Her voice sounded to her like the voice of an actress in a badly dubbed foreign film.

"Probably be too busy to deal with it by that time," grumbled the voice of Geoff, badly miscast as the hero of her sophomore year. "I certainly *hope* I'm too busy."

"With your consultant business idea?"

Tentatively, the old habit of togetherness began to develop once more. Talking about work appealed to his vanity, soothed his temper as it always had. Abby had become a good listener because of that long ago.

"I may leave the University anyhow."

"Aren't you being a bit hasty?" Abby suggested.

"No."

"There are always other universities," she offered.

Tartly he reminded her that if anyone did any speculating about his professional future, *he* was the one most qualified to do so. She was welcome to listen but not to prattle. "There are one thousand seven hundred twenty-one other universities, to be exact. Not counting colleges, seminaries or Kent State."

"All right."

"I'm no longer sure I'm so attracted to the musty joys of teaching, anyhow. As it is, I've scarcely had time to spend with my students the last couple of years. Why should I be looking for another university—possibly even more hide-bound than this one? I'd much rather see what kind of study I can scrape together around this Amazon River Basin thing. Funding," he mused, "is the first hurdle. As usual."

With a kind of grim amusement Abby supposed that only couples who are irreparably wed to their marriages can drift like this between ferocious battle and speculative chatting. Now that we've taken up fighting, she decided, we're probably more married than ever. People such as this toss out neither bath water *nor* babies. We hold onto everything, she concluded. Even each other's jugulars. So she relaxed about the children. And took heart from the intractability of her bonds.

"What Amazon River Basin thing?" she asked.

"They're cutting down the rain forest there."

"For teak?"

"To make work and bolster the Brazilian economy as much as for the lumber, really. But for whatever reason, it's falling fast. That's a lot of change. The rain forest shelters millions of different species of plants and animals, not to mention some nearly Stone Age people. But we'll all be affected by it. When that enormous ocean of trees stops processing water, its absence is going to change weather cycles everywhere."

"Can't somebody do something?" Abby asked.

"It's considered an internal matter by the Brazil-
ians," said Geoff. "All I can do is make the study.
While there's something left to study."

So he will be wanting to fly to Brazil soon, Abby
thought. Leaving me to my own devices. She began
calculating how much time that would mean she
could spend with Mike. Already her hasty promise
never again to tempt fate was forgotten.

Maybe Geoff was right. Safe for a moment, she
allowed herself to consider his point of view. Was
she so innocent of doing harm to his career as she
claimed? Abby acknowledged her peculiar view of
his job situation: if he had won the department
chairmanship he would not be able now to go
dashing off to Brazil. The promotion would have
kept him close to campus all semester long. Maybe
she did not want that. Loyally now she tried on the
cloak of blame which he had flung at her: perhaps
his setback at the university *was* her fault. It might
have grown directly out of her secret enthusiasm
for having him travel out of town. She wondered
how many Freudian slips she had made, how many
disasters other than the occasion when she allowed
herself to be discovered stocking-footed in a dark
office talking intimately on a business phone. She
had created so many of the accidents which developed into this exquisite affair with Mike, that
perhaps she was also to blame for any accidental
blows to Geoff's career.

Without realizing it, she allowed her own in-
stincts to be shod and gartered and trussed once
more by Geoff. She was beginning to feel guilty,
dancing to his tune.

Not for a minute had she wished her husband
any harm, Abby told herself. So many years al-

ready she had stood by him—to deliberately hurt
him now would feel as if she were doing damage to
the entire family.

So many years. But then she had become
isolated from him. Had begun believing that nothing she could do would affect him. (At first that
notion was painful for her but lately it was all too
encouraging.) She was ashamed of how angry she
had made him. Whatever else she may have felt,
she was sure she owed him something better. She
had no idea where she would be today if she had
not had him, not had the children she got from
him. She did not want Geoff to be upset. Perhaps
if she could help him feel better, she might feel better about herself.

"The papers I've read say the rain forest is already one-third gone," Geoff was saying enthusiastically. "Neville says it's worse than that.
He's flown over it. He was calling from Brasilia."

Brasilia. Abby had studied it in architecture class
—the brilliant new city invented completely by
architects and erected on the brink of primeval forest. A forest that would never happen again. "Are
you going to have a look?" she asked.

"I ought to. To determine whether it's worth the
trouble to shoot any film, or just grab the study
and run. Neville is hot to shoot, but he says crew-
ing the film won't be easy. There just aren't many
men down there who can handle the wilderness and
speak English both. It's either-or. But we ought to
try. It's a unique opportunity."

"How long do you think you'd be gone?" she
asked.

"Nevertheless," Geoff continued, "I shouldn't
go. I hardly think you're in any condition for me to

leave you behind. Not alone."

"I would like to go with you."

"Running off to the tropics will not solve your problem," he snapped.

Geoff had no intention of letting her make amends, Abby realized with a dull thud in her guts. He did not care how much effort she was making to remember tonight what they owed one another. He was too intent on punishing her any way he could for whatever iniquities he fancied she had committed against him.

"I want to see you straighten yourself out before we start planning any second honeymoons on Foundation funds," he was telling her. "I want to know why you've been fooling around behind my back. Why, and with whom, and I want to know as soon as possible that you're over it. When all that has been discussed and resolved between us, then we can talk about a vacation. As for now, I have work to do. And so do you."

"My work can all be delegated."

"No sir!" Geoff snapped. "I want you to knuckle down, confront this destructive behavior in yourself. *That* is your work!"

How she was feeling did not concern him; it was results he wanted. Abby's good intentions blew up in her face. Bolting upright and switching on the bedside lamp, she cried, "Geoffrey Mullen!"

"Yes?"

"I know I may seem a little weird to you these days," she began.

"Impossible, actually."

"But it does not help in the least," Abby fumed, "for you to be tormenting me with your fantasies and suspicions and schedules. It isn't fair!"

"I recommend caution in shifting the blame," he told her coolly. "Any therapist worth his salt will tell you that progress is out of the question until you own up to creating your problems in the first place."

He wanted nothing less than surrender now. Not accommodation. Every last detail of her life was to be entrusted to him. As in the good old days. After sixteen years of good old days the only valuable she could call her own was the time she had spent with Mike Vogel.

Geoff had no specifics about how she had spent her time and it enraged him—this independence of hers. She could silence him with two words, by giving up "Mike Vogel" for him to annihilate. Then he would be happy again, would have something to forgive her for. She would be conquered, annexed once more as when they first married. And peace would reign once more in the Mullen master bedroom.

All he expected was that she confide in him. But it had been too long since he had taken any interest in her confidences and she no longer trusted him. At this late date she would not begin again, not by betraying her affair.

"Okay, I admit it," she said. "I am a difficult, selfish person right now. We've all had a lot of sudden change in our lives, and I'm not dealing with it as well as you and the children are. But I am trying. And after all I've put up with from you, the least you can do is to show a little forbearance while I find my sea legs."

"I am trying to help," Geoff insisted.

"By prodding?"

"Listen," he spat. "I've been as solicitous and

patient as I know how to be with you. Yes, I have! I've been ignoring your weird behavior patterns since Christmas. Talk about difficult! Delirious is more like it. You are becoming completely out of line with the sunny, candid young woman I married. It's spooky. I can't make any sense of you any more."

"I'm perfectly miserable right now, if that's any consolation to you."

"Of course not," Geoff said. "I don't enjoy having you sulking, slinking in and out of the house looking dark and secretive and neurotic. It's unhealthy. For both of us. Whether you choose to admit it or not, we are in serious trouble as a marriage. I am extremely upset. You're not the only one who has needs around here, after all. And no, gallivanting about peering over my shoulder in the Amazon is not going to help either of us. The children . . ."

"*Now* you're worried about the children!" Abby remarked, shocked at his gall.

"Can you really say you're the best possible mother?" Geoff demanded. "In this preoccupation, or funk, or whatever? In a pig's eye! I'll go with you to see your therapist if you like, or stay up nights hashing it over between ourselves if you prefer. But you have got to straighten yourself out. I've about had it."

Abby hugged herself nervously. She refused to acknowledge his veiled threat about the children.

"Look at you!" he accused her. "You're perfectly miserable with guilt."

"I am not guilty," she protested. "I've done nothing to you. It's more a matter of what you're doing to me. I may have been feeling sort of wounded, but that doesn't mean I . . ."

"Wounded. Okay, now we're getting somewhere. You feel wounded. What can I do to help? Get you a powder, a shrink? A lawyer?" he threatened.

He would never admit his part in the conflict between them. As blameless as the "observers" and "advisors" for the United States in Vietnam, he would only make things worse if she depended upon him for anything. If she meant to survive this undeclared war, she would have to fight for her interests in a way that made sense only to herself.

"I'm not sure there's anything for you to *do*, Geoff," she replied at last. "If you'll just try to be fair."

"That goes without saying."

"I *am* very upset and confused these days. Truth to tell, I guess I have been ever since our pleasant set of routines caved in. I am not crazy, though."

"These things are all relative," Geoff observed dryly.

"I guess it's something I can only work out for myself."

"Please do."

"At my own speed," she added.

Geoff threw up his hands. "I shudder to imagine what your own speed might turn out to be."

"Don't you ever get tired?" Abby asked. Tired of having to be right? she added silently. Tired of taking command, inexhaustibly. "I'm weary."

Her husband said nothing.

"If we try to get some sleep now," she begged, "we can get up first thing in the morning and go get the children."

"Interesting priorities you have."

"Here we are, living in one place," she pointed out. "And our children are stranded some place else. What could be more important than that?"

"What's most important to me," said Geoff, affecting a Viennese accent, "is finding out the precise nature of your problem. *Are* you having an affair, or simply wanting to?"

"Geoff, stop it!"

"Come on," he taunted her. "You can tell me. Good grief, woman. If you can't talk to me, who can you? I'm the closest relative you've got."

"We are *not* related," said Abby in amazement. "I'm more closely related to Gabrielle, do you realize that? You and I aren't even third cousins!"

The flicker of teasing died out of Geoff's voice immediately. "Abby! Calm down."

"Anyhow, the single greatest problem I've got right now is that you have removed our kids from the house. I want them here where they belong."

He said, "Time enough to drag them into this when we know what your problem is, and have it well on the way to solution."

"Don't blackmail me," she said. "Please. You're making an emergency out of a squabble."

"Are you going to be hysterical?"

"I need support, not coercion."

He thought about it, or seemed to. Then he said, "Okay, perhaps we can have the children here. If you'll stop sneaking off every time my back is turned."

Who the hell did he think he was, making decisions like that single-handedly. *"The children live here!"* she reminded him furiously. "And I can't keep my mind on anything else when I don't know what their situation is."

"Now you know how I feel," Geoff smiled at her. It was the cold smile of a man who would willingly sacrifice a family to keep his wife in hand. (Abby wondered whether she could ever let him make love to her again.) He added, "How do you think I manage to concentrate on my work when I have to be concerned about your whereabouts, and Toby and Gabrielle besides?"

Abby doubted whether Geoffrey Mullen's concentration had ever veered for one moment from work to his children. His self-righteousness incensed her. But she refused to fight with him about the children. She did not dare let him know how much his attitude toward them distressed her for fear he would use them against her further. Poor kids, she thought. At least they weren't hearing this awful business. When they were safely back home, she would make sure Geoff found nothing to fight her about.

"I'm sorry to upset you," she told him, curling up around a vivid urge to vomit. "All I want is to have some harmony in my life."

He studied the shape she made on the bed.

"But we can't leave our babies in Ligonier every time we're worried about something," she added, pleading as un-hysterically as she could. "They're part of us."

"At least there's one thing you can make up your mind about," Geoff granted her. "I suppose that's a step in the right direction. All right. If you feel so urgent about it, we'll take a drive out there tomorrow and pick up the kids."

Abby felt the fresh air of relief on her face.

"But if you've been seeing another man—" he started to add.

"Why do you keep harping on this?" Abby quickly defended herself. "Hasn't it ever occurred to you that there are little things I like to do by myself? Perfectly ordinary things? I like to talk to Thea Kaltenborn, for example. But I reserve her company for times when I'm here alone. There is no reason to include you in what Thea and I do together. It's obvious you don't care for her at all. Yes, we exclude you. But that doesn't mean we're having an affair, does it?" She stared at him defiantly.

"Maybe not," Geoff replied after a long time. Turning off the light at Abby's side, he walked around the bed and got in beside her. When the rustling of their covers settled, his voice came from some place far over by the glowing green hieroglyphics of his digital clock. "But I'm not a fool, you know. So why do I keep thinking you're being unfaithful to me?"

Unfaithful. Worse than that, she had been *faithful* to a man whose qualities she had taken for granted since college. Now that he was beginning to show her what he was really like, Abby dreaded to think what she would have to become in order to render herself faithful to him from now on.

Lost in thought, she neglected to deny his accusation.

"Whoever it is," Geoff continued, "I must ask you to stop meeting this person. When you are doing that, you can't be concentrating on solving our problems together, can you?"

Abby dreaded what she felt she had to do. But it was the only sure way to change the subject.

"I refuse to spend another minute on your fantasies," she said into the dark and made him hear her smiling. "Let's work on mine for a while now."

Deliberately, fighting back something outrageously like tears, she put her hands on him. She stirred him up, felt her cold hands warming on his flesh. She did not want to make love to Geoff, but she had to. Not even wanting to lie in the same bed with him, here she was bellying up to him. Everything they had ever enjoyed together she threw into this concoction tonight and flambéed it with the spark of her private panic.

That secret element of Abby which was panic seemed to goad Geoff's id. He bore down on her especially roughly.

Abby knew she was being unfaithful. But the infidelity she felt was to Mike Vogel, and because of it, ironically, she suffered at last the full measure of guilt her husband expected from her. She should be with Mike. Sick with guilt, she made love to her husband as if her life depended upon it.

Mike Vogel came home drunk and angry that same night, getting angrier by the minute as he foraged around his kitchen for something to eat. He had had another row at work with Tuckerman and was fed up with the supervisor, the Service, the State and himself besides for getting buffaloed into sticking with the whole dumb-ass operation for as long as he already had. He had half a mind to quit tomorrow.

A colander tumbled, clanging, onto the linoleum when he dug out his frying pan. He kicked it savagely, and it ricocheted off the stove before coming to rest near the cupboards again. When he went to retrieve it, he found something shiny on the floor nearby. He picked it up, puzzling over the sheer prettiness of it—a membrane-thin camisole Abby had sloughed when she was out here last. Pink on beige, silk on nylon, it was embroidered with tiny scallops and the monogram *aMh*. Confounded with alcohol and a sudden pang of wanting her, he pondered the middle initial. He supposed her middle name was Marie. Or Marilyn. Or, he snickered happily to think of the bawdy companion he was discovering inside her ladylike shell, could be Maybelline.

He would get the underwear back to her the next chance he had. Meantime he would put it some place safe, where he would not forget it. Outside among the cricketsong he found his motor pool Jeep and, folding the underwear as neatly as he could, he tucked it into his glove box.

CHAPTER TWENTY-TWO

All the way to Ligonier Abby was busy thinking. Hard to tell what was going on in Geoff's mind. He was driving, keeping his eyes on the road, but he managed all the while to generate the ostentatious good cheer of a winner. She was not so sure he had won. What was clear to her was that she must come to a decision.

Eyes teary with sleeplessness, she stared through her sunglasses at the patchwork of woodlots and pastures whizzing by in glaring June green, and worried. The process was almost soothing, the dangerous suspense of pretending there was no problem finally over. It was as if one shoe had been dropped, in the king-sized expanse of their marriage, the day Geoff began his new career and left her behind with the other faculty wives. Last night the other shoe had fallen. After hours of quarreling and unfriendly sex, morning brought the blessed opportunity to move ahead and make a decision, any decision.

She could not have Geoff grabbing the children and spiriting them away whenever he saw fit to punish her, that much was certain.

She would be bereft if she had to give up Mike Vogel.

She knew things about herself now she should have known long ago, good things.

The children and Geoff aside, she had never felt better in her life.

Geoff and the children could not be *aside;* they had practically raised each other.

Geoff was right; she was not behaving like the girl he married.

She could never give up Mike.

If she persisted in seeing Mike, Geoff would surely catch her and all hell would break loose. Geoff was right; that would be bad for the children.

Geoff was behaving like a child.

If she did not start behaving like a wife, he would make her be single.

Geoff thought she was community property. Everything in her head was supposed to be so much equity they shared.

She did not enjoy sharing with Geoff. She hardly knew him any more.

It was as if she had known Mike all her life. She knew him the way she knew the nose on her face, the flavor of her own saliva. To forget him she would have to have brain surgery.

To forget Mike would be to forget herself. The nice new self she had been growing of late.

But Geoff expected her to do that. For their sake as a family. She could see the sense in his point of view. For a few happy months she had childishly hoped to have both chocolate and vanilla—to indulge herself in an affair, yet maintain responsibly a hearth for the three people who depended upon her. She wanted it all. She could not bear the thought of giving up Mike.

But she was no runaway. She could not take up with a handsome scamp from the *Friendly* Rising Sun just because he asked her to dance or because he made breathtaking love to her, because she liked his father or because he knew creeks by name and the personal stories of individual birds. That was no reason to fall rashly in love with someone. Except—those were the best reasons she had ever had.

Still, she could not hope to hold out, to keep Mike over Geoff's objections. Geoff would be probing at the unknown quantity, her love, until she got it out of her system.

Her guts ached to think she would never be with Mike again. But they were tough scarred guts which had been through far more than ever showed on her face. She had willed them to function for her in defiance of the odds. Now in this grave situation she would have to rely on them to absorb further hurt. She could do it. What her guts could not do was to have children with Mike. Anything else, not that. So it was settled. Or so it seemed to Abby. She already had two babies. She had taken to bed more than twice in her struggle to validate her marriage with children, and she had barely survived it. Now that she had, she could hardly endanger them all. Besides, she could not rationalize all the pain she had put herself through if she traded it for a bachelor who warbled hillbilly songs in her ear.

Giving up Mike meant giving up. And that is what Abby resolved to do.

Seeing Toby and Gabrielle again did Abby's pinched heart good. They were exuberant over the appearance of their mother and father, crowding against them to show off jarsful of half-froggy tadpoles and Polaroids of themselves standing beside thoroughbreds at Rolling Rock. Abby liked watching them, liked hugging them and smelling the fuzzy baby skin in the napes of their slim necks. They liked the presents Geoff brought them; they liked the brownies Grandma Hays was serving between meals because Geoff and Abby were here; they enjoyed telling Abby how late they had stayed up last night. But they were not keen on going home just yet.

Geoff and Abby spent the day with them. Gabrielle could hardly wait to climb up on her mother's lap and show her how Grandma was teaching her to read. Abby felt the small bones of Gabey's buttocks digging into her lap. Something in her own bones responded with inarticulate joy. Holding the book upside down Gabrielle recited:

There was a young woman of Niger
Who smiled as she rode on a tiger;
They returned from the ride
With the woman inside
And the smile on the face of the tiger.

The kids thought it was a hilarious bit of verse. They laughed and punched each other happily. Then Toby followed up with a limerick that could never have been blamed on his grandmother, and soon afterward he led them out of her house to meet the kids in the A-frame down the road. Kids who had the best possible recommendation—their own electronic Pong game. Playmates, special treats—the summer could be great for Toby and Gabrielle if only they would be permitted to squander it in the highlands with Grandma Hays.

Abby watched them, wanting to snatch them home this instant.

In the end it was decided the children would stay with Abby's mother a while longer. Talking in terms of July Fourth weekend, Abby and Geoff headed back to Pittsburgh. The air was sulphurous in the direction of town. The back seat was still empty, tomorrow uninviting.

An extremely subdued Abby took up the business of tending her home and garden once more. Not once did she allow herself to picture Mike's face or think of his voice. She went around sore with the effort of not thinking about him. She had plenty to do, she reminded herself: she had to weed among the tomatoes, save her marriage, have the cat spayed, stand in for her housekeeper who was disabled by dental abscesses. At every moment she was engaged in not having an affair—so she could get her mind clear—busy not dwelling on that. To help herself, she cleaned the basement from top to bottom. For Geoff's peace of mind, she went to see her therapist.

Geoff was constantly underfoot. Staying close to home for days at a time, he was noticeably patient, conspicuously waiting for Abby to make progress in working out whatever her disability was. He stopped going to the office. He said he was leaving the Gremlin free for her to drive on errands, to make trips to consult Dakota; he said he could make his business calls and draft budgets from the house as easily as from the Foundation offices. Plainly, he thought he was being magnanimous.

Abby thought he was watching her every move.

Dakota had a third opinion, which was that Geoff was avoiding campus, that he would not show his face at the University until he had another project grant firmed up and ready for touting. Da-

kota understood university society and dissected it
as minutely as other Pittsburghers studied the
Steelers' summer training reports. She knew Abby
was just marking time in their sessions together.
That was all right: fifty minutes with a taciturn
client could be restful. Only once did their discussion grow heated—when Abby in passing accused Geoff of cruelty because he was fighting with
her.

"For the first time in our whole married life,"
she complained.

"Well, fan my brow," Dakota mocked her. "I
wouldn't condemn any marriage on the basis of
open quarreling! It's about high time, I'd say.
Fighting is a sign of life after all these years."

Abby tried to explain why she felt victimized.

"Of course you're being victimized," Dakota
said briskly. "And you will continue to be, as long
as you remain passive."

"What do you mean?" Abby asked, afraid she
knew the answer.

"Assert yourself, woman," said the doctor.
"You have to make things happen your way."

"I was doing that," Abby wailed. "Sort of. Until
I started having, mmm, interests of my own at least
he only ignored me. But once I took up outside
activities, moving around, you know, then he
began taking pot shots at me. That's all the good
asserting myself's done."

"You know sailing, right?" Dakota pressed her.
"Without motion your control surfaces are useless,
right? If you don't have any direction you're dead
in the water. Make a decision, then go for it. Don't
just go limp in the face of trouble. Of course he'll
run right over you. If you won't fight for yourself,

who will? Goddam, I get so tired of hearing women complain about being victimized when they haven't a clue as to what they'd like to be instead!''

Warming to the subject, Dakota denounced Abby for creating accidents instead of making decisions.

That hit close to home. Openly angry at last, Abby defended herself by complaining bitterly about the decision she had already made. The wretched, aching decision not to "see another man".

"I don't mean decisions like that," Dakota prodded. "Decisions *not* to do things don't count. Make a positive decision, for crying out loud."

Abby knew she was right. While the sting of it was still fresh, Abby resolved to be positive. She would actively decide upon making her marriage work. She went home determined, and terribly unhappy.

Nighttime was the worst. She had to resume lovemaking with Geoff on some sort of regular basis. Being lonely in bed corroded her sense of purpose and seemed to give Geoff a martyr's upper hand. She appealed to her own sense of reason: a reliable regimen of good domestic sex was probably what they needed most right now. Neither she nor this touchy opponent she was trying to remarry would be able to sustain any sort of decent humor without it. Maybe it would actually make them feel close.

They managed with precarious success. But Abby's conscience bothered her. She could not get over the feeling she was a cheat.

Mike Vogel did not even know she wasn't seeing him any more.

Rolling over to her side of the bed, she resolved to see Mike one last time. To tell him out of courtesy that they could not be together from now on, and why. Much as she hated to do it, it was the only honorable reason she could think of to see him one more time.

She owed them both that much, she thought. The excitement accompanying the idea scared her.

Finally one morning while Geoff was in the shower, Abby hastily called Mike's number. Keeping her voice poised as if conversing with Maxine (in case Geoff cheated and turned off the water suddenly), she said to the presence on the other end, "Can you do lunch today?"

By lunchtime she was as shaky as a semi-finalist. Dressed in sophisticated linen and wearing as an amulet the ugly gold medallion Geoff had brought her from Norway, she waited at the *Friendly* Rising Sun for Mike. He looked very tall in his Commission uniform.

"I can't see you any more," she blurted when he had kissed her mouth inside and out.

"Sure you can," he laughed down into her face. "You're here, aren't you? And what a sight for sore eyes."

Abby was painfully aware that Donna and the bartender seemed glad to see them together again; they watched every step of the way as Mike walked her to their old booth. Donna brought the usual without asking. At the sight of the familiar battered glass mug Abby choked up. She had not meant to become one of the regulars again. She had intended, on meeting Mike, to emphasize the distance between them. He sat beside her in the booth, put his arm around her blocking out the view from the bar, and turned her showdown into a homecoming.

She longed to curl up in his lap and sob herself to sleep. Fortunately she had memorized her farewell speech. She kept it simple. Every time she said "commitment" he smiled at her. And every time he did that regret ran down her legs like seminal fluid and made her weak in the knees. He shook his head dubiously when she mentioned such things as "relationship" or "dependency".

But "husband" he understood.

He did not make it easy for her. He took it like a man. He reminded her how much she liked being with him and asked her to reconsider. He asked her to look at him, lifted her chin and told her she was the best news he had had in years. Wrenchingly, he confided a crazy notion he sometimes had that maybe they could have found a place to live together. He looked so miserable at the thought of losing her that she almost forgot her own sense of loss feeling sorry for him. But in the end he let her go.

When she slid from the booth she looked up at him, saying softly, "You don't believe I can do this, do you?"

"I guess a woman like you can do whatever you have a mind to," he answered. He was too sorry to remember the little item of hers he had meant to return next time they met.

He walked her to the car, opened the door and put her in behind the wheel courtly as a prom date. When he leaned through the window, kissing her ever so gently on the lips, she was tempted to blurt out her feelings. She longed to throw off this terribly mature pretense and yell, "Trick or treat" or "April Fools"—that she was his. Maybe "Allee allee in free!'' Fortunately he went straight to his truck after the lapse of that one kiss. He was out of the parking lot before she got her own car in gear.

Abby went home, woebegone, to forget him and forgot instead her appointment with Dakota.

In a dark mood she spent the afternoon bikinied in her yard, picking beetles from the squash plants Geoff detested and dropping them into a jar of kerosene. Freckling, sweating, she did not cry. It's over, she kept repeating. I'm making progress.

Theoretically, it *was* all over. No one in here but we Mullens, just Geoff and Abby as it was in 1964. Fiercely willing the old contentment back, she went through well-organized days and nights staring straight ahead into the past. She planned elaborate diversions for two, as in the past, and made her schedule revolve around that of her husband. She made every effort to devote herself to him once more. But nothing, as usual, would ever be the same again.

It was Geoff who kept the issue of Mike alive in the household. Not by name, certainly, but by implication. Much as he encouraged Abby's reversion to "your old fun self," he teased her mercilessly. Granted, he had never proven her guilty of any particular wrong; still, he enjoyed rehearsing for her how generous he had been about whatever unmentionable stage she had been going through. Since that was all behind them now, as she said it was, he insisted she tell him everything, "even if it only amounted to one single momentary failure of willpower." He tried to persuade her there was nothing to hide, nothing to defend any more, because it was all over and so did not matter anyhow. Except that it seemed to matter a great deal to him.

He wanted names. In bed he fantasized aloud. It turned him on so much he failed to notice she was becoming more and more silent.

In company Geoff struggled openly with Abby, trying to goad her into revelation. This passed for humor if the evening was sherried lavishly enough and if there were a certain number of encounter-group veterans present. Failing that, he simply theorized about sex in extravagant ways, drawing others into his preoccupation. Abby ignored him as much as possible. This was easiest on nights when she happened to be the hostess—she could bustle. Try as she might, however, she could not feel her old fun self.

One night their oldest friends Maxine and Jerry Gerber left early. They claimed to have babysitter problems, but Abby knew better. Near despair, she wondered how they had endured this long. How could anyone enjoy themselves with Geoff's pornographic paranoia lurching around the edges of the dinner conversation like an old family ghoul. When they were gone Geoff helped carry coffee cups into the kitchen.

"I think Maxine is sleeping with Chris Fairchild," he announced.

"What on earth makes you think that?" asked Abby wearily.

"My nose tells me these things."

"Poppycock."

"Oh ho ho!" said Geoff, easing into second gear. "You think it's only women who enjoy the advantage of intuition, eh? Well, I happen to have a pretty good feel for that sort of thing myself."

Abby put the Kaluha away and, refrigerating the cream, said, "Do you now?"

Flatly Geoff answered, "I knew when you were having an affair, didn't I?"

Abby turned away before he could read the disdain in her eyes.

"Or maybe you still are," he persisted. "Maybe I'm all wet about the timing, but there has, without question, been an affair." He followed her upstairs.

Desperately Abby stopped and looked him in the eye. "I am not!"

"Not what?" he prompted her.

"Not having an affair. Not having anything but a tough time."

"Okay then," Geoff breathed. "If it's over then why can't you tell me about it? Come on, Abby. It'll help you get over this abysmal mourning thing you're involved in. You've got to talk it out." Trying to keep it light, he burlesqued her mother's voice and added, "If you don't start talking again soon you'll lose your tongue and become autistic forever and ever."

"Geoff," Abby begged him to stop. "I don't feel like free-associating with you all night. I talk when I feel I ought to. What do you think we're paying Dakota for?"

"Just tell me who it was," he pushed her. "You've got me looking funny at every man we know. Excuse me, every person. I even asked Maxine. She told me to go to hell, naturally. Was it Maxine? I'll understand. There's lots of that going around these days. Politically chic."

"Stop!" Abby snapped.

Geoff defended himself with injured innocence. "I'm trying to help you. I want you to get this stuff off your chest once and for all so we can get back to normal. I can't speak for you, of course, but *I* used to be happily married. And I'm not exactly impressed with the progress you're making with Dakota. She's costing me a bundle and not showing me very much. Sometimes I think you two sit up there and talk about the future of cinema or something. I worry about you!"

"You couldn't care less. You are trying to worm your way into my head for your own satisfaction."

"I am trying to share," he explained hyperpatiently.

Abby collapsed onto the edge of the bed and leaned wearily on her elbows. "Me too, Geoff. I've been trying too. I know we've always said we share everything with each other. Ever since sophomore year I've been sharing bed, board and bank account with you. I've shared your car, your germs, even your graduate studies with you. God knows, you have enough degrees for both of us. I've been sharing myself with you ever since I was too young to know who I was. And now, now, I'm beginning to see I did that sharing entirely by myself. That's right. Turns out this stuff we've been sharing is completely yours. I'm not part of a team. I've been a wholly-owned subsidiary all along and didn't know it. You share nothing. Even the gifts you brought me were for yourself."

"You say that to me after I've supported you for sixteen years?"

"You have not supported me," she laughed harshly. "I supported you. All you did was bring home money."

Abby realized with a shock that she might make things worse by defying him, but it felt grand. She sank back, staring up at the ceiling for a moment. "Anyhow," she added, eyeing the blemished patch of plaster she had come to regard as her personal totem. "Your salary has not bought you access to the innermost reaches of my mind. I do have worries of my own. I refuse to worry about how to make them comprehensible to you. Not on demand. And that's final."

Geoff glared at her, furious with betrayal. She was supposed to be repentant, not standing up to him.

"Maybe it *should* be final," he said. "I don't think we can go on living together if this is the sort of malice you're harboring."

"Baloney," Abby heard herself saying. She was ready to fight with him if necessary. She felt resigned to hacking out a place for herself to stand in this marriage. It was a marriage from which all the love was eroded, but if they both grew up and started working on it right away they might salvage enough security from which they could eke out separate satisfactions and take care of their offspring together. She had avoided fighting too long. Now she saw that despite themselves they had only been surviving a long witless honeymoon. With some struggling they could become a mature American family—a Mother and a Daddy hanging in there until the children finished school at least. It would not be so dreadful, really. It would be better than no family at all, which was what she had had as a girl. Obviously it was what nature intended, and quite likely would be an adequate hedge against a world of unknowns. If it was good enough for her, no doubt it would be more than enough for Geoff.

"If you want to move out," she challenged him, "move out."

His face clenched. "I don't think I'll be moving

out, if it comes to that," he told her.

"Good, now let's forget it."

"If there's going to be a separation," he continued, "I feel the guilty party should have the inconvenience of finding another place to live."

"I reject this guilty-party business," said Abby.

"Besides," said Geoff, "I'll need the house for entertaining. You don't even like to entertain. It happens to be expected of me, though. And to tell you the truth, I've always had an idea I could be at least as good a cook as you. Maybe more so, since dinner and conversation have a certain civilized appeal. For me. I can't speak for you, but I get the feeling lately you're aggrieved somehow if I ask you to prepare anything with more panache than a casserole. So be it. Find yourself some suitably bohemian flat where you can be happy. Express yourself, eat from take-out orders. Have all the privacy you want. Wade around knee-deep in grievances if that's to your liking."

"Geoff, I won't dignify this with debate."

Abby assumed she should handle this outburst with calm. She wanted to grab him by the throat and scream: Look here, I have given up my lover to make this thing work with you and if you don't at least try to help I'll cut your heart out. But she did not want him to feel he must defend any of his wild pronouncements. So she tried to overlook them.

"Suit yourself," Geoff said, and clammed up.

She had no idea how much she risked in letting him glimpse her strength. Maybe she could have saved her marriage by continuing to act like damaged goods.

But the fat was in the fire. So seething was Geoff's rage that neither he nor Abby could have guessed what he was going to do.

Esther was down on her hands and knees laying carpet tiles in the trailer living room when Web came home that night. She had got a special price on them because there were not many of each color but she figured if she put them down in sort of a checkerboard it would look okay; now the checkerboard was driving her crazy because she was working herself into the middle of the floor and only had three reds to put down right smack beside each other.

It was hotter than the hinges of hell—had been all day. The dentist's office where she had spent two hours that afternoon had been air conditioned, which only made the trailer seem hotter. And her teeth still hurt.

Web left the door open. He pinched her behind, saying, "Better not point that thing at me unless you intend to use it."

Esther was in no mood. He almost had his arm removed for his trouble before she noticed that he had brought ice cream. She quit fretting over her design project right away. Web got two soup bowls, loaded them with ice cream—one with wet nuts and one without—and brought them with spoons to Esther.

They sat outside on the lawn chairs to eat. From the trailer across the way came a succession of terrifying shouts, gun shots and crashes; Brenda was probably watching "The Rockford Files."

"Finally found a good car for Mrs. Mullen," Web told Esther.

"What?" she asked around a painfully cold lump of ice cream.

"A Camaro."

"Camaro?" Esther complained. "With two kids to haul around she needs more like a station wagon."

"She can put the kids in the back seat if need be, and the trunk's plenty big enough. I wouldn't put anybody's wife and mother in a station wagon. Not safe. The damn things don't work right, especially not a used one. Anyhow, on the money she told me, I was lucky to dig up this car. I thought the best I was gonna be able to do was find an MG or some other beat-up two-seater."

Esther was dubious. She was fond of Abby and had always more or less hoped she could talk her husband into buying her a Cadillac. Maybe he would be famous soon, buy her one next year.

"It's a convertible, top in decent condition," Web said. "A sixty-nine. Nice clean-looking thing. I'd've wanted it myself, it's such a good car, except it's only a six. If it'd had a V-8 I'd be sitting on the title right now."

"What color?"

"Yellow."

"A yellow convertible," said Esther slowly, beginning to enjoy the idea. "That'll be a nice surprise for her. She'll like it."

"I can get the keys on Monday," Web said. "Want to drive it to work? You can just pull up to her house really casual in it."

"I can't," said Esther. "I'm getting the rest of my root canal on Monday."

Web said not to worry, he would work something out.

CHAPTER TWENTY-THREE

Monday was no picnic for Mike Vogel. Hunched over a bowl of chili with the lunchtime crowd at the *Friendly* Rising Sun, he crumbled a pack of saltines, stirred them in, and pondered just how fed up he was. Most of the weekend he had been half horny without much he cared to do about it until he gave up and went home Sunday morning with an R.N. that lived way the hell over in Braddock. For a chaser he spent the better part of Sunday sipping from a bottle he brought home with him, got carried away and ended up mooning over that fine woman with the candy-colored underwear. Now there was one that would have been worth spending the weekend with, but she had deserted him to go back to her husband. Useless. Today she was still gone and he had a hangover besides. Fine way to face a morning of necropsy.

He had tried to get out of it. Who wants to spend Monday morning gutting diseased deer, he reasoned; even a handjob like Tuckerman ought to see the wisdom of postponing that awful business. But no, the supervisor had some high-powered pathologist from Penn State's animal disease laboratory and today was the only time he was free to help Mike analyze his district.

Queasy and sullen he had spent the morning amid the stench of post mortems, taking a gander at fibromas, parasitic lung worms, liver fluke infestations, and horrors without names but likewise suspected of contributing to the severe mortality which the deer in this district were suffering. There was no point in spending the whole day at it: by the time they were ready to break for lunch they had enough information to decide on planning a doe hunting season this fall. Only an out-sized deer population and an overgrazed range could have led to this much pathology. Tuckerman and his Ph.D. pal moved on to another district and left Mike to handle the paperwork.

But he did not feel like knuckling down to paperwork for the afternoon. He did not much care to sit indoors at a typewriter on a day like this; he hadn't much cared for working in the field this morning either; come to think of it, he hated his job most of the time. He was sore as a split toe. The way he looked at it, he was not much good for anything the rest of the day.

That was why he did not tell Web to get lost when he took the stool beside Mike and started spraying genial chatter all over his right side. Web had the afternoon off and was looking for someone to run an errand with him. There would be plenty of cold beers afterwards if Mike was interested.

"I gotta deliver a car and I need somebody to follow me over, bring me back," Web was saying. "Not far out of the way. It's the Mullens. You know."

Mike did not know. The name meant nothing to

him, but he was ready for any old excuse to knock off. He would rather have gone home first to change out of his uniform and get the El Camino, but Web had a wild hair and had to get it done now.

He got into the Jeep and followed Web to Farley Landing Road. While they were in that neck of the woods they might as well stop by Wayne's Wayside afterward. The Bucs were in Los Angeles today and that was as good a bar as any to watch the game in.

Much as it went against the grain Abby had to start looking for an apartment. It would have been easier to stay—in fact, with dread in her heart she had told Geoff more than once they must stay together and make this thing work—but he was crowding her out. He was at home constantly, all the while refusing to discuss anything with her. There was only so much time she could spend in Dakota's office; there was also such a thing as too many luncheons with volunteers. She had nowhere to go.

From the night he announced that she ought to move out, Geoff was continually developing evidence that he needed the place and she did not. He staged elaborate retreats for his Foundation staff that sprawled through every downstairs room, claiming that here they could brainstorm freely, away from the turmoil and telephones of the offices in town. He kept the telephone hot with incoming and outgoing calls—person-to-person calls, conference calls, overseas calls—all top priority and Abby could play receptionist or stay off the line. He agreed to let a film crew from the public television station begin a documentary about his newest project, so Abby should not have been so surprised to come upon a pair of youngsters on the floor of the darkened master bathroom, up to their elbows in black bags changing sixteen millimeter film magazines. They had more business being there than she did—she could always use the powder room downstairs—but they were M.F.A. candidates in Communication Arts.

When no one else was underfoot, Geoff left his papers, print-outs and reference materials strewn anyway on every available surface. At night the telephone was still tied up, only now it was the feed line for his personal computer terminal. When Geoff's access time to the University computer came around he obviously had no time to haggle with Abby.

She could find no way to get through to him. There was no question of fighting to save their marriage, to solve it or even to dissolve it. He was ignoring her, "concentrating," he said, "on matters I can fathom."

In the meantime, she decided to get on with life —whatever she could muster of it.

Trying to remember what that might be, she stood watching the man of the house early one humid afternoon. He needed a haircut and looked magnificent. He was working alone in the breakfast nook, or going through the motions. The Pittsburgh Pirates were playing the Dodgers on Esther's little TV set, and Abby suspected Geoff of watching the game more than the luminous numbers of his calculator, but he was damned if he would be found not working when she was present. Daring to use the phone, she enlisted Maxine to help with

the odious chore ahead of her. Then she told him
she was taking the car, and left.

Following Maxine's advice, they started looking
among the tree-lined avenues of Squirrel Hill. Ignoring Maxine's advice, Abby insisted on looking
at everything. They saw the quaint one-roomers in
converted mansions with Deco woodwork and me-
dieval plumbing; they saw new singles flats with
weathered barn board in the living-dining area and
tinted mirrors in the shower; they saw sedate Vic-
torians with gas-burning fireplaces and ten-foot
windows long since jammed on layers of paint. As
they shopped their way toward Shadyside they
even looked into whole houses and halves of studi-
os. Abby was dumbstruck by so much new information. It was Maxine who started getting down to
cases.

"Huh-uh," Maxine turned down the ninth landlord. "I don't care how chic it is. Without a dishwasher, it might as well be Bates Motel."

"Wait," Abby cautioned Maxine. To the landlord she added, "I wouldn't mind having a dishwasher, but if this is the only unit you have with
three bedrooms, I'll consider it anyway."

Maxine got between Abby and the landlord,
nudging her past a corner into the living room.
"Why does he need three bedrooms, you ninny?
It's the kitchen that worries me. If he doesn't have
any conveniences he'll let the dishes stack up in the
sink until they rot, then buy new ones."

"I'm not looking for an apartment for Geoff,"
said Abby. "It's for me. And the children, of
course. That's why I need three bedrooms. I didn't
mind putting Toby in a room with the baby, but
not any more." She was considering, as an after-

thought, that she should look for apartments in East Liberty and Point Breeze too: that way Toby and Gabrielle might be able to walk to school.

But Maxine was having none of it. "You are not moving out of your house," she argued. "Think of how it'll look."

"I'm not interested in appearances."

"You'd better be. If you move out, it will look like your fault," said Maxine. "Appearances count for a lot in court. May be the only things that do count."

"We're not going to court," Abby objected.

"How do you know? That may be your best bet."

"I just want him to stop fighting with me so I can think," said Abby. "If one of us has to move out, then whatever seems fair . . ."

Maxine was having none of it. Hustling Abby out of the apartment she took her directly to the Encore where she could spell out in air conditioned gloom, over a martini rocks, the etiquette of separations. In the first place, she explained, whoever brought home the biggest or only pay check was obligated out of simple decency to take on the burden of renting a new place. She also explained that Abby was letting Geoff push her around because she harbored feelings of guilt she would not admit to, that Abby must see a lawyer as soon as possible, that if Geoff moved out getting a divorce would be easy on the grounds of abandonment. On the other hand, she explained, if Abby did want to keep Geoff but just bring him into line, then seeing a divorce lawyer would help anyhow. Geoff would probably come to see the merits of an open marriage contract rather than face a divorce suit. In the long run everything would be more manageable if she stayed put now. Maxine had a dozen more consumerist aspects of this conflict she wanted Abby to grasp. But Abby was a listless student.

She did not care about hedging her bets or the long run. She did not want to bring Geoff to heel. She was not even sure whether she wanted Geoff. What she wanted most of all was to know where she was going to live, to get her children settled into that home with her wherever it was, to resume some sort of routine so she could stop fraying and start trying to get a grip on her own feelings. She told Maxine so.

"Next to municipal bonds," Maxine scolded her, "marriage and divorce are the two most important financial decisions you'll ever make. Try to think of this as a sort of bond issue, not an emotional bloodbath."

Ordinarily Web would have had reason to expect Mrs. Mullen to be home during the day. But when he sashayed into the driveway, gunned the motor once for the benefit of Mike in the Jeep behind him, and got out, it was some guy who came outside from the house.

"Mrs. Mullen about?" Web inquired.

Geoff shook his head. "I'm her husband. I'll be happy to give her a message."

"Well," grinned Web, indicating the jaunty yellow convertible. "This here's for her."

"In what way?" Geoff said stiffly.

"It's all hers," said Web, at a loss for any more intricate explanation. "She asked me to find her something to knock around in, something in the range of fifteen hundred dollars she said she was

willing to go for. And this is what I found. It's a
good car."

Geoff kept looking from Web to Mike and back,
less interested in the Camaro than the two strange
men. "I was not aware that my wife has been looking for a car," he smiled.

"She is," Web nodded firmly. "And I can see
why, with you doing as much gadding about as you
have to." Now he had Geoff's full attention. "If it
was up to me, though, I'd let her take the Gremlin
and use this one for myself. It's practically a
collector's item. You'd look good in it, too. Don't
you think a man ought to have a convertible at
least once in his life? Esther says the missus will
want it, though."

"Oh, you're Esther's husband!" Geoff said, the
light finally dawning. He shook hands with Web,
saying, "I don't believe we've met. I'm Geoffrey
Mullen. Glad to meet you at last."

"Not her husband," said Web, jovially returning
the greeting. "Let's just say her old man. This is my
buddy Mike Vogel."

"How do you do," they said in unison.

Something about the introductions rang a bell in
the back of Mike's head. But he could not discover
what it was.

Web opened the hood and all three of them were
treated to a view of the very clean, well-appointed
engine compartment. "New battery," Mike
pointed out.

"Yep," said Web. "The paint isn't bad either,
considering the type conditions we got here every
winter. Second paint job. The guy told me he had
it done three years ago this spring."

Geoff got in behind the wheel, pushed the seat

back and sat, elbows locked, sampling the feel of the convertible around him. It had been a long time since he had talked about cars with other men except in terms of leasing versus purchase. "What kind of mileage has it been getting?" he asked.

"Said eighteen, but I suspect she'll get twenty or better after an overhaul," said Web. He pointed to the odometer in front of Geoff. "Soon time for a tune-up."

Mike leaned in closer to read the gauges over Geoff's shoulder. "That's been set back."

Web protested, "Guy said he hadn't touched it."

"There isn't a man alive who's owned a convertible for six years and only put thirty-nine thousand miles on it," Mike rumbled. "Even if he saved it for summer Sundays."

Geoff looked into the sunburned face appraisingly. This man spoke with authority when he bothered to speak. Geoff admired that. On an impulse he opened up to him. "My neighbors had an old Packard convertible when I was just learning how to drive," he said. "It had the longest hood I'd ever seen, and a customized dash of burl veneer. I thought I'd die if I didn't have one of those beauties to tool around in some day. Naturally," he concluded with a shrug, "by the time I had any earning power worth the name, classics like that had gone way out of range."

Web and Mike shook their heads appreciatively. They all agreed cars were not being made like that any more. Each man took his turn then telling tales of the first car he had ever driven, the first car he ever paid for with his own money, the first near-miss ever survived in a speeding car; eventually the first date in one of those cars came up for dis-

cussion as well. Mike mentioned that his love life
as a kid improved when automatic stick shift options freed him from two-handed driving. Then
Web reminded them of those steering knobs guys
used to have with pictures of half-naked females
sealed under the plastic. So Geoff advanced his
theory that since the proliferation of personal auto-
mobiles following World War II American men
had become a nation of left-handed lovers, all because so many boys had begun their first tentative
gropings toward full sexuality parked in lovers
lanes with their right arms behind the shoulders of
a girl in the passenger's seat.

They all laughed, having a good time getting to
know each other. There was a fine delinquent
mood to lounging in the Monday afternoon sunshine this way. There were clouds too, but the
thunderheads were not going to reach critical mass
until evening. Humidity beaded up and rolled
down the ribs, grasshoppers and cicadas twittered
itchily in the grass, but at least the sky was limpid
blue.

Web dug a six-pack from the floor of Mike's
Jeep and peeled a can from it thirstily. "Anybody
else?" he offered. Mike and Geoff each took one.

Something about drinking beer from cans, leaning against a Jeep, relaxed Geoff. He had not
enjoyed this sensation since his fraternity days
in college. Since then he had never allowed himself the luxury of hanging out; from
graduate school on, he was concerned with goals
and always felt the need to persuade or compete
with any men around him. Today was different, a
throwback; he certainly did not need to compete
with or persuade these roughnecks about anything.

It occurred to him that he still belonged to the fraternity that counted most, and could participate at will: whether it be jump-suited gentlemen splurging champagne on each other over a winning car at Lime Rock, tank corpsmen spending their weekend passes in West German *biergartens,* or bikers pouring Four Roses from the communal bottle into their beer cans, it was men that a man could get close to. It was men that a man could count on.

"Sure," Web was saying. "Esther wants to get married some time. But right now she's getting her little sister through stewardess school. She's worried about saving up some money for it. I tell her, hell, long as we're together there's no big deal about going legal."

"Then you've been together a long time?" said Geoff.

"Let's see, how long has it been?" Web grinned sideways at his companions. "That depends. I count from the first time I got my finger wet, but she'd probably say it was when we started sharing housework."

There was an embarrassed moment of silence in which Geoff looked at Mike because he expected Mike to laugh, and in which Mike looked away because he felt sorry for Geoff. Mike figured Geoff had not heard anything like Web since he left the navy or Guard or wherever he did his service. Not that he came off like a pansy or anything, but from his haircut to his loafers he had the look of a man who prefers certain niceties.

Geoff upended his beer and finished it, which gave him time to think of something to say. "I think you're right about the car," he said when he could look Web in the face. "All things considered it's probably a pretty good deal. Shall I write you a check?"

"No," said Web. "It'd be easiest if you went out to Gladney's place and gave him the check yourself. He can give you the papers that way, and whatnot."

"Gladney," Geoff repeated thoughtfully.

"Yeah, Crank Gladney. I don't know what his given name might be, but he's easy enough to find without it. You know out by Vandergrift where the new industrial park's going in?"

Web was having trouble giving Geoff directions, so Mike obligingly opened his glove box to get out a map; together they would figure out once and for all how Geoff Mullen was going to find Crank Gladney.

Abby's chemise tumbled out onto the floor of the Jeep.

Mike paid no attention at first, busy as he was with smoothing the map over the Jeep's hood. Geoff saw it. The smile fading from his face, he picked up the silky pink-on-beige garment with its *aMh* monogram. He looked from it to Mike.

Mike smiled sheepishly—a smile which implied that a man's girlfriend was liable to do anything, even leave her undies in a Jeep—and, taking it back from Geoff, he tossed it into his glove box.

There was no point in being angry at Mike. Geoff knew perfectly well the man did not know he had been discovered, so he could not have intended this affront. He probably did not know she had a husband, or even a name, Geoff imagined. The very thought enraged him.

Dark impulses shifted slightly in his belly. Now he had what he had been looking for. Evidence;

better yet, the upper hand. The element of surprise. With Abby's unwitting lover a known quantity at last, he would be able to analyze the situation within fairly close tolerances and come up with a long overdue course of action. He invited the men inside for another drink.

"We were heading over to The Wayside to watch the Bucs on their big screen," Mike said. "You're welcome to join us."

Geoff assured them the Pirates game was playing on the TV set in his kitchen. In the end they all went inside where he mixed up generous highballs.

Web devoted himself with tipsy concentration to the baseball game on Esther's TV.

Geoff and Mike only saw occasional fragments of it, glancing at the screen whenever they heard another megagasp from the crowd—the early warning system for possible homers. Meanwhile they leaned against appliances and chatted. Geoff asked Mike dozens of apparently offhand questions about himself, flattering the man into volubility. While he listened, he sized up Abby's surprising lover. And thought.

Originally Geoff had intended to snap Abby out of her self-indulgent, depressive funk with his threat of separation. According to the way he understood himself, telling her she would have to move out was simply his way of upping the ante, a way of bringing her to her senses. But to his dismay, she seemed all too willing to consider his suggestion seriously. Right now she was probably having a ball whining to Jerry's awful wife about moving out, or poring over the rental section of the *Post-Gazette* with that shrink of hers. It was a shame, really, that she had gotten so carried away

when all along he just wanted the old Abby back.
Stupid, how she was changing almost for the sake
of change. Now he knew how Jehovah must have
felt, he wryly told himself, when that dippy pair in
his well-appointed Garden of Eden insisted on
educating themselves.

In Geoff's opinion their marriage had been a
genuine idyll for Abby. She should have been happy with her situation: he had let her have the run of
the place, had made sure he was upwardly mobile
enough to guarantee her ever-improving well-
being, had been considerate—goodness knows had
doted on her and showed gratitude for all the ways
she made his life pleasant too. But she had gone
sour on him about the time everything else began
improving. It was almost perverse.

Mismanagement was probably the key here, as
in the Garden. It was an error of judgment on his
part to leave her to her own devices when he might
have taken her traveling with him. In too much
spare time she became restless, curious, malcon-
tent. And now it seemed that even the healthy and
brisk sex in their marriage did not satisfy her.

Underthings scattered all over town. There was
no excuse for that. Geoff's ire mounted once more.
So his Guid Wyfe was now a member of the Me
Generation, willing to expose him to all manner of
unpleasantness. So be it. With any luck, her lover
would still be here when she returned. In which
case Geoff was willing to arrange what promised to
be an edifying confrontation. He would show her
unpleasantness.

He had to hand it to Mike Vogel; there was a
fascinating man inside that civil servant's uniform.
He heard about Mike's ongoing war with off-road

vehicles, his devotion to being outdoors, his contempt for bureaucracy, and his longing to match wits with what he called real wilderness.

"Hot damn!" Web hollered. The crowd at Chavez Ravine was on its feet as well. A brilliant triple play put the Pirates into the ninth inning one run ahead. Mike and Geoff watched the slow-mo replays from every camera angle while Web and ABC's color man told them what they were seeing.

When the whooping died down, Mike turned to Geoff and inquired, "I bet you don't work for any bureaucracy."

"In a way I do," said Geoff. "I'm a teacher."

Mike recognized false modesty when he heard it. Out of courtesy he asked a few more questions and was rewarded with some pretty impressive detail. Geoff told him about the new research project he was planning along with a film he meant to make, all in the wilds of Brazil.

Here's a guy with something on the ball, Mike was thinking. Then he heard Geoff mention his study of cycles. The bell rang again, only this time it was followed by a jangle of panic sending adrenalin to his extremities. Abby's husband studied cycles, she had said. He remembered with horror that Web's Esther worked for Abby, but it was not until he was trapped here in this kitchen that he made all the connections and realized that Geoff Mullen was her husband.

He looked around, instinctively measuring the steps from where he stood to the nearest exit. There was a pair of her silly girly shoes standing empty by the door. That Polaroid stuck on the refrigerator door must be the kids she had told him about. And there was Abby's husband, talking and asking him if he knew anything about the massive lumbering projects that were underway in the Amazon Basin.

Geoff Mullen hadn't the foggiest notion who he was talking to, Mike reassured himself. Might as well hang loose until some occasion for leaving gracefully presented itself. "Can't say that I do," he answered. "But it sounds like the same thing they did to all the forestland in this area back around turn of the century."

With another jangle of fear he remembered the initialed chemise in his glove box outside, and knew that Mullen was indeed onto him. Yet here he was, befriending him nice as pie. Mike had heard there were marriages like this—where the wife went one way and the husband the other, and they still agreed enough to have kids, house, Winebago and all. It was not something he understood, but he was in no position to argue. He had to hand it to Abby's husband: he was being a real gentleman about this whole sticky business.

He thanked his lucky stars Abby had already broken off with him before today. He might be in a delicate situation but at least he could look old Geoff in the eye with a clear conscience as of now. And it was not like he had taken anything away from a man he knew at the time.

"It's different in the Amazon," Geoff was saying. "They're not thinning the forest. They're leveling it."

"That's what they did here, too," Mike told him, treading water.

"You don't say?" said Geoff with real interest. He asked Mike a lot of questions about the felling of Penn's Woods and, while he listened to the answers, his professional juices automatically started flowing: so the action in Brazil was not un- precedented. He could see the point of view of his Amazon study broadening. He congratulated himself on talking to this practical man; so many good ideas came out of conversations with people such as this, if one just knew where to find them. The man was full of surprises. Geoff smiled to himself.

Abby still had not come home by the time the first Pirates game was over. Web wanted to get home before the second of the double-header started and was pressing Mike to hit the road. Geoff decided there was no point in trying to detain them. He was losing interest in anything so sophomoric as a showdown anyway. Besides, he had taken a liking to Mike Vogel and did not especially want to embarrass him.

Geoff strolled outside to see them off. He looked up at the thunderheads casting greenish twilight over the driveway. Better put up the top on Abby's new old car, he decided. Waving goodbye, he leaned across the side and heaved on the canvas contraption of the roof. The germ of an idea was beginning to take hold in the subsoil of his mind.

The telephone rang and he hurried inside.

CHAPTER TWENTY-FOUR

Abby almost had herself talked into an apartment in Shadyside by the time she got home. She did not share Maxine's appetite for the adversary challenges of marriage, or for the marketplace of divorce. But there was something to be said for Maxine's claim that her own apartment would do her a world of good. She was shocked to find herself planning the move, considering that it was Geoff's idea to separate in the first place. But perhaps she truly could benefit from a trial separation. As Dakota had observed more than once, jumping from one man's bed to another and back was not the best way to find a sense of direction. And Maxine swore the only way Abby could get some much-needed rest was to be alone. On the other hand, anything Geoff and Maxine agreed upon could not possibly be all good.

She was somewhat frightened. No Mike *and* no Geoff? Withdrawing from both relationships at once was a large order. Geoff had always been around, even when he was out of town, because his clothes and colleagues and appliances and preferences and his twelve-year-old Scotch had remained steadfastly close to her.

And then Mike. She was not over Mike. At home, not seeing him was painful enough. She was pretty sure junkies did not cure themselves by dropping the drugs *and* dieting at the same time. But she was a grown woman—a fact she kept reciting aloud all the way home. Ought to be able to face the supposed enormity of her own desires. Alone.

Precarious with unaccustomed martinis, aghast at the lowering sky and where the time had gone, she eased into the driveway at Farley Landing Road. Company, she thought, noticing the yellow Camaro. We'll have to wait until later to discuss anything so troublesome as an apartment.

But Geoff was alone in the house.

"Art Fellows just called," he informed her when she came into the kitchen. "We've got all the money we asked for from the Foundation. Plus matching funds from a federal agency—that's for research and consultation only, not the film—and the Audubon Society besides."

He was dicing cheese and chives, stirring up a vast omelette. He asked her if she wanted some. Vaguely, she nodded. This was not the turbulence she had been expecting.

"What does the Audubon Society have to do with your work?" she ventured, trying it his way.

"Well, of course there are countless species of tropical fowl in the rain forest there. Or, will be until it no longer exists," he said. "But there's more to it than parakeets. When you stop to think, birds, trees, flowers, fish, creepy crawly critters, fungi, all the exotic stuff that grows there is a kind of genetic bank for the rest of the world. There are only three major rain forests on the globe and when

they're gone, numerically most of natural history's genetic options will be gone with them.
No more variety. Nothing to go to when we need a
new hybrid legume or an experimental host for developing some new vaccine. The stakes are con-
siderable.

"Art said the proposal we pitched them
absolutely knocked them out." Briskly Geoff
slashed the pillowy omelette across the middle and
while it was still sinking, shoveled it onto two
plates. They ate standing up leaning against the
kitchen counters.

Brazil was the only subject Geoff was willing to
consider. He showed no interest in the ticklish matters Abby mentioned. In fact, so flatly did he de-
cline to discuss her thoughts on finding an apartment that somehow the very idea of separation
now seemed to be her fault alone. She pressed him
once, asking, "Have you reconsidered my moving
out? Because if you have something to add on the
subject I would appreciate hearing it."

"It doesn't matter for the time being," was all he
would say. "I'll be off to Brasilia in a matter of
days and you'll be alone for some time regardless
where." He was polite, preoccupied, and utterly
impervious to her efforts toward an understanding
of any sort. He did tell her about the Camaro outside, gave her the keys, told her how to find its
owner if she wanted to buy it, and mentioned not a
word about the man who followed Web into their
driveway this afternoon.

He was not even nasty when he pointed out that
Abby's having a car of her own would make it easier for him to get to and from the airport without
relying on her. He simply would not give her an

inch. Nor would he fight.

Abby sat up alone all night, queerly feeling like a guest in her own living room. She was not going to cry. She had to think of something. Mostly she listened while thunderstorms prowled the length of the Allegheny drenching the little towns on its banks with cloudbursts. She opened a window to sniff the dark warm scent of earthworms flushed to the surface by rain. Her garden, its vines clinging to spindly poles, corn stalks thrashing in the wind, looked by the occasional bluish flare of lightning like a colony of lepers, dervishes and beggars. She pictured instead the slow fanning of carps' tails, soothingly safe under water as the big fish swung along the river floor, and felt less buffeted for a while. Before dawn the house cooled. She wrapped around her shoulders an afghan Esther had given her last Christmas and went outside with a flashlight to prop up what the storm had blown down.

Geoff's disposition did not improve with the weather in the days that followed. There was something macabre about the high spirits he displayed around home—far worse than a huff. There was nothing Abby could complain about. He quit prodding her to confide in him. He went out on errands (she never knew where but she had relinquished her right to comment on that), sometimes dressed in tennis shorts, sometimes in coat and tie, and returned at odd hours of the day. He received and placed many phone calls. She assumed he must be assembling logistics for his trip. Instead of nattering relentlessly about work as he would have if he were truly as happy as he pretended to be, he kept every detail to himself. The effect was to make him seem secretive. He asked nothing of her, a mystery in itself. And there was an end to their hypocritical lovemaking—not so much as a quickie to help him relax before sleep. Abby could not have felt more alone living with one philodendron in an efficiency. The most she seemed able to do was to stay out of her husband's way. She did the housework while he was out. It kept her safe in a voodoo sort of way.

He was scheduled to leave for Brasilia Sunday evening. By Saturday she could not stand the cheerful treatment any more. To get a reaction out of him, she suggested they invite Arthur and Anne Fellows over for brunch the next day.

"I'm not sure," said Geoff, making a great show of deliberating. "I've told them you're leaving me, so it might look strange for you to invite them to an impromptu farewell party for me on their way back from church."

Abby was flabbergasted. "You told them that? Geoff, we haven't even discussed it since last week! I'm not sure I'm moving out, or you're moving out, or any such thing. What possessed you to say that?"

"I had to have some way to account for your behavior lately."

"What about my behavior?"

"For one thing," Geoff said too casually, "that display at the TV station. You remember what you did there, I suppose, since it cost me the promotion. For another thing, your boyfriend."

She tried to stop him before he got himself into that state again. But it was no use.

"After we're separated, you and he will be able to go about doing whatever it is you do with more

discretion," Geoff went on. "More to the point, it
will explain to our friends your disregard for my
standing in the community. Even if it doesn't excuse it." With a tight little smile he added, "Do me
the favor of seeing a divorce lawyer while I'm out
of town, will you?"

"Why?" she demanded, shivering.

"To get a legal estimate of your situation."

"My situation is that I am considering a trial
separation," she said. "To please you. Isn't that
enough?" There was an eerie sensation of rugs
being pulled out from underfoot.

"I know what you're considering," he leered at
her. "More shenanigans. Suit yourself. But give me
the face-saving courtesy of a divorce, won't you?
I'd rather not have to take the initiative on this."

Trying to penetrate his phony civility, she
shouted in exasperation, "Will you listen to me?"

He put on a listening face.

"I've been trying to talk to you about this separation idea of yours," she told him. "We haven't
even talked about it. How can we contemplate
divorce when we haven't come to any sort of agreement on a trial separation? I can't believe you
mean this. But even if you do, there are more sides
to this question than yours."

"Your boyfriend's?"

"Our children's," she countered, silently shouting: *And mine. Don't you go creating pandemonium
in my life too! I can barely stand all the confusion
I've put there myself!* Her voice went on, a
burlesque of calm reasoning: "Stability may not be
a priority for you these days, but it is absolutely
essential for the kids. You have no business being
highhanded about anything so important. This is a

home you're talking about—for four people! I'm willing to talk about how to solve some of our problems whenever you can take the time. We'll discuss it in detail—certainly not in a rush just before another of your big trips. We can come to an agreement together."

But Geoff was slowly shaking his head. "Divorce doesn't work like that, my dear. If a couple can agree on getting a divorce in this state, the courts figure they can agree enough to stay married. You and I know that's not true, don't we?"

"Well . . ."

"We can't even come to an understanding about acceptable conduct with regard to certain bodily functions."

"Stop it!" she cried.

"You stop it."

They stood staring at each other in the middle of the kitchen. Abby had no way of guessing her husband had found Mike Vogel on his own. Mike had been transformed into a cherished niche in her imagination since she had stopped seeing him in the flesh, a wishful thought not even she herself entertained on many occasions, so he was utterly unthinkable as an acquaintance of Geoff's. She assumed Geoff was baiting her again with this accusation—out of malice but out of left field, too.

As firmly as she could, she told him, "I am trying to find out how we can continue this marriage, Geoff. I am not having an affair."

"Maybe you've had it, maybe you're having it," he shrugged. "The details no longer interest me. But I do think you should have a divorce to go with it. Make a matched set."

"No."

Geoff stopped pretending he was anything less than hopping mad. "If you won't file a divorce suit," he pronounced the words sharply into her face, "then I'll have to do it myself. And I don't want to do that."

"Then don't."

"Don't, is right! If you force me to open that can of worms, Abby, I promise you I will end up with custody of the children."

Abby could not believe he wanted so much as a divorce, let alone the job of handling two kids on his own. "You wouldn't do anything like that."

"I would rather not have to. We'll see," said Geoff. "The court will no doubt award me custody anyway."

"They would not," she assured him. "The mother is always preferred."

"Except in cases where the plaintiff can prove adultery. And I can prove adultery by you. I have evidence."

"You can't be serious!" she said right away, then wanted to bite her tongue. Geoff's face turned ugly with frustration and rage. He advised her to watch how serious he could be, then stalked from the house.

There was no doubt that he was serious.

His rantings about adultery and evidence notwithstanding, she knew Geoff Mullen well enough not to take him literally. Never, if his very job depended upon it, would he do anything that would make him look ridiculous; he would not send detectives to spy through Mike Vogel's windows and make infrared pictures, not even if he knew where to send them to do it.

In her ignorance she felt a twinge of sympathy

for Geoff. He was certainly beside himself about something. And whatever it was, she had better remain calm until he got over it. True, she was no longer sure she wanted to stay married to him. But she was appalled at the thought of being thrust into single parenthood on Geoff's angry say-so. She was not ready, the children were not ready and, she was convinced, her husband was not ready. If they were to have a separation they could live with, she would have to see him through this fury of hurt feelings he was writhing in now.

She sat beside the computer terminal and telephone in her kitchen until dark, trying to make sense of Geoff's rampage. There could be little doubt that he blamed her for the pain, confusion and chaos they were both experiencing. Abby had changed—that had been his complaint all along. She knew perfectly well she was changing, and why, so maybe this *was* all her fault. Maybe if she had never ventured to please herself without pleasing him, magically everything would still be the same. It was her fault. She had taken that ride on the tiger of her own free will, never mind whether she was entitled to the pleasure.

Abby questioned whether she would ever feel guilty enough about it to suit Geoff. She did feel too brittle to risk arguing with him any more tonight. He would be leaving for Brasilia tomorrow. That was just what they needed. A cooling off period.

She shuddered at the thought of spending this dank, threatening evening alone. Guilty as she felt already, there was no further point in not seeing Mike Vogel. By phone she arranged to meet him. Then she hastily scrawled a note to Geoff saying

I'm out at Esther's. Don't worry. I'll see you before you go. A. and left Farley Landing Road in her yellow Camaro.

Mike had quit his job yesterday and it did him a world of good. This Saturday night he was not getting drunk at the *Friendly* Rising Sun. He had one beer, daydreaming benignly about being in movies, and went home for supper. He was in fine spirits. It did worry him somewhat when Abby called, but her voice sounded wonderful in his ears.

Without saying why, he agreed with her they should not meet at his place. He did not suggest the *Friendly* because he was no longer sure that was discreet either. No motels: Abby was right, in that direction lay madness. For lack of a better idea, he ended up suggesting the drive-in across from the Turnpike overpass.

Bruce Lee was kicking out a villain's trachea when Abby pulled away from the lights of the ticket booth and puttered hesitantly through the aisles looking for a vacant stall. She took the first one she found. Next obstacle, finding Mike. She knew his El Camino would be the only one with a bumper sticker saying "Fish and Game Commission Personnel Make Better Lovers," but she was not looking forward to stumbling through the flickering shadows of the theatre looking for it.

Not because she intended to listen to the movie, but from some vestigial habit, she leaned out to claim the speaker for her car. Mike was standing there. Miraculous as it seemed that he had found her in the dark in a completely strange car, Abby did not give it a moment's thought. Love made lots of strange occurrences possible.

He got in with her. "God, it's good to see you
again." And to touch you, and smell, and kiss, and
taste.

What Abby intended when she called Mike was
something different. She intended to get alone with
him long enough to have a heart-to-heart talk.
Their circumstances had changed slightly since
they were last together and she felt there would be
no harm in meeting him. Just to talk. Just in case
she was indeed going to have a divorce forced on
her, she wanted to explore whether and how Mike
might fit in sometime later. When everything was
settled, of course. She wanted to find out whether
he cared about her so much that he could wait until
her situation was secure, and then whether he
would be willing to get seriously involved. It was
possible, she had reminded herself. He did not
seem precisely the domestic type, but then she had
not thought of herself as the wild adulterous type
either, so there was merit in keeping an open mind
about this. If Mike was willing to spend evenings at
her home in the company of her children, then she
would begin to know whether he was a person she
could take permanent interest in. This was her idea
of being reasonable.

All that became immaterial once she got her
arms around his neck. Nothing could have felt better. Or more painful. The relief of being with him
again put in stark contrast the galling ache of
everything she had gone through in trying to give
him up. It was blood returning to circulate in extremities that had to sleep, a shot of rum on an
empty stomach. Loony with happiness she held
onto him. He had missed her too, she could tell.

After endless squirming, grief-stricken kisses, incoherent clutching, muttering, touching, greeting, they became aware of a kid bringing pizza back to his car next to them and they tried to straighten up. The kid was demonstrating far greater composure than these adults. His biggest problem appeared to be acne. Abby's was being in love. Mike was having trouble finding his voice.

"We have to stop carrying on like this."

"Yes. We said we wouldn't. But."

Mike cleared his throat and got his voice back in its usual lower register. "It's kind of funny," he said, "kissing Geoff's wife."

He had never called her that before and she did not like it. Come to think of it, she realized, Geoff's name had never crossed Mike's lips before. Abby went rigid.

"I know you're trying to make it work with him, like you said," Mike told her, taking her hand. He leaned back and stared out through the windshield. "I don't want to make things hard for either of you."

Abby laughed wryly. "I'm sure Geoff would appreciate your considering his feelings."

"I think so. He's a pretty nice guy."

"You don't know the half," she said.

"Well, no," Mike allowed. "But I'm starting to get to know him."

"You've met him?" Abby was trembling now.

"Sure," said Mike. "You mean he didn't tell you? That's what I thought you wanted to talk to me about."

"Michael," she began, groping frantically for whatever fragments of anger she could find to help her. "I asked you never to try to get in touch with me. I asked you to leave my homelife completely alone. Did I have to specify, don't introduce yourself to my husband? Do you have any idea how much damage you could be doing?"

"It's not my fault," he said. "You gave me the wrong last name. Look," he added, feeling her shaking and feeling very sorry about it all. "You're really rattled. I've got a bottle in the truck. We'll have a drink and I'll explain. It's not as bad as you think."

"It will be when he finds out how you happen to know me."

"He's already onto us. Now wait a minute, hold on sweetheart. It's not that bad. He's really a classy fella. He's being very cool about everything. Hasn't even mentioned it."

Her eyes wide, Abby whispered, "You told him."

"No. Abby, I would never do a thing like that."

"Then what were you talking to him about?"

Mike opened the car door. In the eerie light from below the dash she could see him trying on a smile of reassurance. "I'll tell you about it. But I want a drink before we get into all that. Wait. I'll be right back."

He stepped out, quietly making his way across the gravel to where his truck was parked.

In a sudden fit of rage, Abby put the Camaro in gear and backed out of her stall, tearing out by its roots the speakerful of Bruce Lee's righteous shrieks. As she spun wildly through the aisle a few cars tooted their horns after her. One of them may have been Mike. But she stopped only long enough to pay the man at the gate her damage fee; he said it happened all the time. She did not stay to chat.

She flung a five-dollar bill toward him and drove through the exit.

Out on the road she hesitated for an instant, then turned the wheel sharp right and hightailed it toward Esther's. She had never visited Esther in her trailer but at the moment it seemed the only refuge she could expect.

"Look who's here," Esther said to Web when she let Abby into the living room.

Web stood, accepted Abby's handshake because there was no cap on his head for him to tip, then quickly went back to his recliner near the TV.

"Do you want something to drink?" Esther offered. "Coke? Ice tea? I know, listen. I've got a couple cans of strawberry margaritas in the freezer. Want one of those?"

Abby ended up with a bowl of ice cream and wet nuts. She hugged it between her hands to feel her palms burn with its coolness. She could not say why she had come. She stared at the matching portraits of Web and Esther done in pastels at Disneyworld; she recalled discussing possible frames and was interested to see a gilt-flecked white French provincial had been the choice. Already Web and Esther were beginning to resemble each other. Abby and Mike would never look alike if they waited until the Orphans Court crumpled into dust.

Esther did her best to make Abby feel better. She offered her the other seat that had a good view of the TV and sat facing her to crochet. She told in lurid detail about her root canal surgery. She convinced Web to give up the evangelist he was watching and tune in a movie with lots of can-cans and musical numbers. At last she put down her crocheting. "Have you ever thought of having a perm?" she asked.

Abby and Web looked up from their separate meditations upon the can-can. Both of them said pensively, "No."

"I didn't mean you," Esther dismissed Web with a chuckle.

Web was not about to be dismissed as a joke. "Lookit," he begged to inform her. "I might get a perm. Plenty of guys at work are doing it." But Esther was on her feet, smoothing Abby's hair away from her face, bending in close to look and leaning away to squint as the hair fell into place once more. Soon Web excused himself on the grounds that it was half-past two.

Abby flatly refused a body perm. She did accept the offer of a trim. She had never submitted to an amateur haircut before, but never before had she so needed a kindly laying on of hands. This was Esther's invitation for her to unload whatever was worrying her, besides. Tucking a tea towel around her collar, she handed over her comb and told Esther, "I don't really feel like going into the whole mess. I just need someplace to stay tonight."

"You can have the sofa," said Esther. "Want this layered here on the sides?"

They took their time. Abby mentioned the threat of divorce specifically, custody questions in passing, adultery in the legal sense only, and men in theoretical terms—free-associating aloud. Esther stood behind her, above her, out of sight most of the time. Simply a friendly contact in the region of her scalp. *Tsk*ing occasionally she helped Abby outwait the night.

Lights winked out everywhere in the trailer park except at Esther's place.

"I'd be worried about Toby especially," Abby said once. "Divorce can be such an upheaval for children, I'm told. He probably won't stand a chance of growing up to be a normal American man if we get a divorce now."

"What's so important about being a normal American man?" Esther complained soothingly.

They ruminated in silence again.

"I feel obligated to provide Toby with a male role model," Abby ventured. "I wonder if I'd have to think about getting married again. I'd hate for him to grow up effeminate or a bedwetter or something worse that would make him a complete outcast." She was exorcising fears, not expecting Esther to respond.

But Esther could not hold her peace indefinitely, any more than a barber can resist commenting on the weather. "That's not gonna save him," she said past the hair clips in her mouth.

"What?"

"You getting married. Every boy that has a father already feels like an outcast. Until he's big enough to catch the eye of some other woman besides his mother," Esther maintained.

In spite of herself Abby laughed. If Esther believed that, then there must be something to Freud after all. "I guess that is the biggest attachment—mothers. They all want to go back to the womb. Even the grown ones, eh?"

"Nope," said Esther. "They care much more about men than they do about women. Grown boys don't care a hoot about wombs. The only thing a man really wants to get back into is his father's good graces."

"Do you think so?"

"Sure. Why do you think they make themselves experts on sports?" Esther explained. "So they'll have something in common with the old man besides Mom. When he's still a little kid Mom gives him plenty of attention and so the old man has to keep threatening to knock his block off, to keep the upstart in line. By the time the guy's on his own, most of 'em have figured out a way to make other women take a liking to them. But the charm don't work on Dad. They can spend about their whole life trying to get in good with their fathers. That's how come they're such hero-worshippers. All those guys have heros. Makes up for Dad. Whereas it's different with girls."

Esther finished the haircut and started a pot of coffee. "Wanta see Richard Widmark?" she asked.

Abby did not have much to say, but she was not ready to be left alone to sleep. Nursing their coffee mugs, they used up every old movie until there was nothing left in the TV but a test pattern. Abby nodded off while Esther was rinsing their mugs. She dreamed she and her mother had a big custody battle in court; her mother won Toby and Gabrielle, and Geoff got custody of Abby.

She woke up abruptly, still drooling on one of Esther's throw pillows, to hear Web defending himself. "I told Vogel who the car was for," he was saying. "How am I supposed to know Mrs. Mullen don't want him over at her place? He told me once that he knew her. For all I knew, she mighta been glad he helped me with her car. Mr. Mullen didn't seem to mind." Esther must be cooking breakfast —no, lunch. Unless she was in the habit of feeding

Web spaghetti for breakfast. Was it that late already?

Abby sat up. The living room sofa was only inches from the bar which served as dining room for the trailer, and at once she was in the thick of it. Web did not bat an eye when she appeared. "I thought you'd be the one at home last Monday, not your mister," he told her.

So that was how Geoff managed to get next to Mike. Trust Geoff. What made him so ruthless, she realized, was that he considered himself civilized. Too civilized to permit himself any confrontation unless manipulation did not work. So much she had learned about him in the last few months: he would never have marched off to defy her lover as she once feared, guns or even eyes blazing, but having stumbled over him in the driveway he would of course contrive his own separate friendship with the man. Hoping to pre-empt any further claims by her. She knew that Web had not wronged her. Neither had Mike; he would not have gone to her home looking for a confrontation with her husband. Confronting her husband was her job.

"Web," she said, combing fingers through her hair. "I like the car you found for me. Don't give the rest of it another thought."

The look Esther gave her across the steaming cauldron of pasta was equal parts pity and reassurance. She smiled back at her, drawing what courage she could from that homely countenance.

Abby said goodbye as soon as she had washed her face.

She headed for home at seventy miles an hour to pack her clothes, to move into Mike's house, to call a lawyer—who knew exactly what decisive

gestures she was going to make. She was hell-bent
on getting home before Geoff left for Brazil so she
could tell him to his face how unscrupulous and
cruel she thought he was. Let him threaten
divorce, she fumed. She would prefer that to waiting around for him to invite Mike home for dinner
with the Gerbers some night—a thing he might do
just to torment her. That was where she drew the
line on sharing, once and for all.

Mrs. Rainey crossed her mind as she pulled into
the driveway. Suddenly Abby comprehended the
silent middle-aged drudge from the South Side who
had made herself famous once last year before she
was hustled off to the penitentiary. Now she knew
why the woman had been able to lean across the
supper table and plunge her steak knife into Mr.
Rainey's heart. Abby could feel rage at her husband in her own fists.

She took the stairs two at a time. Geoff was in
the act of packing her new camera into his hand
luggage when she stormed into the bedroom. "He's
mine," she said, grabbing the camera.

"All right," said Geoff. He started stuffing neat
rolls of socks around his portable tape recorder.
"Abigail!"

She flung the camera into an empty suitcase
where it landed with an ominous clunk and tinkle.
"He's mine. Leave him alone, you bastard." Geoff
pulled the suitcase to his side of the bed and Abby
pulled it back. She tossed the nighty from under
her pillow into it. Then she opened a drawer, starting to heap her underwear in on top. Geoff turned
away, trying to work around her, and moved toward the bathroom to pack toiletries.

"I found him. I was the one who understood

how worthwhile he is," Abby was shouting, beside herself with rage. "You're such a pretentious snob you wouldn't have given him the time of day if you ran into him on the street. You would never choose to know a man like that if it weren't for me. You don't deserve to know him!" She grabbed all the toiletries away from him, shoveling them into her shower cap and tossing it into the suitcase she had commandeered.

"I suppose we're discussing your paramour," Geoff replied. He opened the closet and took out the remaining suitcase for himself—this one tailored in cream-colored vinyl for ladies. Opening it, he began transferring shirts from a drawer into it.

Abby grabbed at the pile of shirts, pulled out one article and, holding it up to find a misplaced blouse of her own, yanked it away to add to her pile. Frantic with indignation she was packing everything she could get her hands on, barely able to keep time with the torrent of words pouring out of her.

"You've got everything else, you greedy bastard. Can't you at least leave my transgressions to me? God almighty, do you have to horn in on the only thing I've ever attempted by myself? You think I'm so terrible for getting to know another man. Well, if I have to take the blame for him at least you could let me keep him to myself. Don't you have any sense of decency?"

Smugly Geoff nodded. "Then we *are* talking about Mike Vogel."

Abby had already piled the suitcase of her choice full to overflowing. Now she was tossing objects into Geoff's suitcase willynilly—the digital clock from his side of the bed, a clothes brush, a picture from the wall—disrupting his packing and making a mess. "Of course, Mike Vogel," Abby wailed. "I'm paying for him. You saw to that starting the day you sneaked our kids away. By God you've been getting your pound of flesh, so I want you to leave him alone. He's mine. Have you got that?"

"He's my friend too," said Geoff.

"I doubt it," replied Abby wrathfully. "He probably listens politely when you talk. You know so little about people that the absence of viciousness passes for affection in your book. Mike would not be interested in your thin-blooded cocktail-party sort of friendship."

"Maybe you're right," Geoff shrugged. "But I don't think so. Mike and I hit it off pretty well. Some days I think we have more in common than you and I do."

"Such as?"

"Mutual respect," he offered in a first swipe. Then, "Admiration."

"You respect him?" Abby protested. "He . . . You're the one who called Esther a rustic! You're just patronizing him."

"Mike Vogel has a lot of guts. At his age, to start a new career," Geoff said, bewildering Abby further. "He is his own man, besides. The kind of fellow you could drop out of an airplane over Death Valley and be invited for coffee and lunch when you come back years later to rescue him. He knows how to solve problems at the elemental level —enjoys nothing more. That's what I admire. One doesn't often meet a man like that in faculty lounges," Geoff grinned at her.

"This makes him your buddy?" Abby scoffed.

Geoff nodded. "I think he'll be an asset."

Still confounded by how much Geoff knew about her lover, Abby missed that last point. She was busy mulling the unlikely possibility that Mike would give Geoff the time of day. "And what does he see in you?" she demanded.

"Ask him yourself when he gets here."

"What?"

Geoff consulted his watch. "He'll be here in another ten minutes or so. You can ask him then whether I have anything to offer him."

"What do you mean?"

"Just what I say."

"Geoffrey Mullen," breathed Abby dangerously. For the second time she thought of Mrs. Rainey. If Mike Vogel showed up here today she would, well, the only thing to do would be to dash outside to meet him in the driveway before Geoff could speak to him, throw her suitcase into the truck and run away with him as fast as they could go. Later, when Geoff was safely out of the country, then she could decide whatever seemed most sensible in the settling of living arrangements. She had no idea she was panting.

Forcing her suitcase shut she staggered downstairs with it. Geoff had said Mike was coming here. Surely not. Geoff would say anything he could to keep her off balance, she reminded herself. Most likely she ought to wait until Geoff drove to the airport, then have a long shower and try to tidy up a bit. She found a bagel, split it open, slathered it with peanut butter and, leaning against the kitchen sink, bit down on it hungrily. Her jaws were still locked in the first bite when she saw Mike's El Camino pull into the driveway.

Abby was electrified at the sight. Carrying no

more than half a bagel she raced outside and plunged through the pole beans straight for Mike's truck.

He leaned across the seat and opened the passenger's door for her.

"What are you doing here?" she asked, sliding onto the seat, ludicrously careful about keeping the peanut butter side up.

Mike looked as miserable as she had ever seen him. His face was murky with worry and apologies which he did not have the brass to make. His shave was shiny new, his fresh haircut a tad too short for the suntan on his neck. The only sport coat he owned partially hid her magnificent Italian gift shirt. A tie was stuffed into his coat pocket. From the sinking feeling in the pit of her stomach she knew what he was doing here.

"Picking up Geoff," he said.

"He can get himself to and from the airport," said Abby.

"I'm going with him," Mike had to admit then.

"All the way to Brasilia?"

She knew it was all the way to Brasilia. She knew it the same way she knew Geoff's secretary had expedited a brand spanking new passport for Mike, the same way she knew his suitcase lay under the tarp back there in the bed of his truck.

"I'm going to work for him," said Mike. In a sheepish attempt at levity, he grinned and added, "I've always had a hunch I was cut out for pictures."

Numbly Abby kept repeating, "He's hired you. I can't believe it," until Mike became a bit touchy.

"He thinks I have a lot of potential, Abby. He respects the work I've been doing for the Commonwealth and, come to find out, being unit manager on this kind of film shoot shouldn't be a whole lot different.''

"That's insane," she protested. "It is! Why is he bending over backwards to find you a job when he ought to be calling you out for a duel, or hiring someone to kill you, or at least plotting with a lawyer to divorce me? What the hell kind of husband . . . ?" she trailed off, helplessly. "At least he might have had the courtesy to slug you."

"Geoff's a gentleman."

Abby looked up at him sharply, not bothering to argue the point. "Stay here and fight for me!"

"You're the one that said we weren't going to see each other . . ." he reminded her.

"For *a while,* I said."

"We weren't getting anywhere, you know that," he said softly. "And I surely am sorry to say it, but you were right. Since that's behind us, I think it's pretty cool of Geoff to forget the whole thing too."

"Are *you* going to forget it?"

As close to begging as he would ever come, Mike urged her, "Abby, this is the kind of job opportunity the guys in Harrisburg don't even dream about."

"You can't do it," she muttered.

"The last thing I'd want to do is embarrass you."

Gripping her bagel for dear life, Abby looked him full in the face and said through gritted teeth, "That is not why you can't do this."

"Why?"

"Because it's not right," she told him. "God's blood! Because I love you. Because you let me howl my brains out astride your belly. Because there are things I've never so much as pronounced in the master bedroom that I've done with you in

broad daylight. Because I'm better with you.
You're mine!"

"Abby."

Tears were coursing down her chin now, forming
drops and spattering warmly onto the fabric covering her breasts. "Because the smell of you is all
over me. Because you make me feel beautiful. I get
homesick for you. I do! Because you love me too.
Don't deny it. You nearly died of joy face-down on
me and, say what you want, that creates a certain
impression of devotion."

"You've been having things pretty much your
way," he started to reason. But she was having
none of his bargaining.

"You cannot run off with my husband," she
bayed, crazy with grief and betrayal.

Mike looked at her as if he thought she might
assault him. "It's the best job offer I've ever had."

"He won't treat you any better than he treats
me."

"He's pretty fair."

"He is not fair," said Abby. "And neither are
you. It's not fair for you to show me so much
sweetness, let me hear you sing and yodel stupid
cowboy romance songs and get silly. It's not fair to
let me fall in love with your family. You can't
throw back your head and laugh until I'm bursting
with pride over some goofy remark I managed to
tickle you with. You can't groan into my neck as if
I were the only breath of fresh air in the whole
flaming furnace of your life *and then leave me for an
opportunity!* It isn't right. You know that, too.
You'll never make it as far as Moon Township.

"If you try to leave, God will descend in the
form of a big retriever and bring you back to me in

his teeth." She could not go on.

Laughing helplessly over the pathetic wreckage of her love, she wiped at her tears and, looking through the windshield of the truck, saw Geoff dressed to the nines stepping out the kitchen door with his luggage.

Mike said nothing. He turned on the ignition.

Sucking in a breath through her teeth, Abby got out of the truck.

As Geoff passed her she muttered, "If you don't take him with you he'll be satisfied with me." It was her last plea, but not loud enough for Geoff to understand. He turned back to look at her for clarification. For clarification she slapped her bagel sticky side down onto the windshield.

When Mike's truck pulled onto Farley Landing Road Abby was walking slowly toward the house licking peanut butter from her knuckles.

CHAPTER TWENTY-FIVE

Geoff had won, Abby freely admitted it. She was so defeated it was all she could do to feed herself a couple of times a day. The most assertive act she could muster was to call Esther postponing the usual visits for housekeeping; she could not bear to pull herself together enough to face anyone who cared about her. She puttered around in pajamas watering and weeding the garden for hours on end. As the vegetables began to ripen she ate them— more to keep them from falling onto her tidily hoed rows of soil than because she was hungry. She did not bother to answer the phone. She did not have to.

Abby was no longer that problematical thing, a faculty wife. Just as well, she kept telling herself; it was work she was not cut out for. No faculty wife, no game protector's wife, no fishwife, no little mermaid—she was finally the worst thing she could imagine. She was independent. Any curiosity she may have had was more than satisfied. She knew all about independence now. It meant having neither husband nor lover, no home, no strings, no help. She felt completely alone in the world—a colony emancipated too soon, a sack of puppies tossed out of a passing car. She had no one to answer to, no one to take care of, and could not have possibly felt less liberated. She did not have so much as a calling. She tried to picture her husband and lover together somewhere in Brazil—witnessing and documenting the demise of a great forest. The last Eden on earth, and Geoff would not do anything to try to stop the felling of that prehistoric timber. He would only study it. She ought to try to rally a mob of activists who would bully the United Nations into stopping the destruction. Maybe that was her calling: she might as well save the planet because she did not have anything else to do. But then she remembered how long it had taken her to round up thirty-some pledges for the Rehabilitation Center in her former life as a volunteer.

Her truck patch was the most she could manage right now. It seemed to be the only thing she could call her own. One night she took Toby's sleeping bag outside and slept in it beside the Swiss chard. That night it rained.

In the morning she cried piteously the whole time she was wiping mud from the sleeping bag, the whole time she struggled with the soggy thing draping it over lawn chairs to dry slowly in humid sunlight. It was not until she saw in a mirror the mess she had become that she sobered up and stopped crying. Something enraged her for a moment. She breathed on that small lifesaving spark of anger until it grew large enough for her to identify in the glass: with her eyes swollen she looked more like her father than ever.

Her father was dead. He had deserted them when Gabrielle was just tiny and now after all this

time he was still dead. He had not come back and
would not no matter how long she waited. Abby
was furious with him for that. She blamed him personally for the stroke that caused his death. He had
thrown himself into the dynamo of love when his
wife took the child Abby and moved out. He had
not *had* to grow sick and listless and overweight,
but doing so suited him. It made him more believ-
able as a victim. And the woebegone face in
Abby's mirror bore a terrible family resemblance.

She was not going to let that happen to herself.
Not for husband or lover. "No indeed," she whispered.

It was not Geoff or Mike she could never forgive, it was her father. Her forgiveness would not
do him any good. She found the brass container of
his ashes amid the rubble on her dresser and rolled
it between her palms. Poor Daddy, she thought.
She might as well forgive herself, and give his re-
mains the burial they deserved.

It only took an hour to straighten the messiest
corners of the house, shower and comb out her new
haircut. Assuming she would recognize the right
place to scatter her father's ashes when she saw it,
she locked the back door, put down the top of her
jaunty yellow convertible for the first time, and followed the Allegheny north and east away from
Pittsburgh.

Whenever she came to a fork in the road, she
took any branch that seemed to go out of the way.
A couple of times she was fooled by what looked
like a back road and ended up being dumped into
the brick-paved streets of some backwater
borough, but she persisted and soon was given her
choice between potholed macadam and puddled

dirt roads. She took the dirt roads. At first they were rutted two-lanes between pastures, then the vegetation grew taller and began to encroach. At the same time the road became one lane. When the bushes began to make their way down the banks, sloshing noisily against the side of her car, she stopped.

Putting the car keys in her pocket and tucking the brass canister under her arm, she waded through a sort of frowsy hedge, ducked under an old barbed wire fence to find herself on a railroad track.

The iron rails were rusty with disuse. Between the ties milkweed and burdock bristled up through the cinderbed providing perches for hundreds of odd little moths and butterflies. Best of all, both sides of the track were lined with overgrown black-berry bushes.

Abby followed the track, tottering along the bal-ance beam of the rail, browsing the bushes. The blackberries were small, sweet and superbly juicy. Right away her fingers were stained a luxurious purple. Delicious.

Daddy used to say where there were wild berries there were snakes. But she did not see any. She did hear running water. As she followed the track deeper into the ticking, chirping, rustling shade of the summer woods, the sound of a creek grew louder. When it broke into a roar the woods dropped away on either side. She was standing on a short trestle of filigreed ironwork spanning—far below—a steep and rocky creek. What creek, she wondered. Could be a feeder for the Tirhascamany, in the waters of which she had learned that not all danger is fatal. Or Raccoon

Creek—but would it come this far south? Whatever its name, its pedigree was certain enough: any
water moving through this terrain was in the long
run Allegheny River water.

Abby wasted only one moment wishing she had
found this place long ago. She sat down gratefully
amid the din of creek splash to rest.

After she had been there for some time, she noticed out of the corner of her eye that a rock was
moving. No, it was a box turtle. The turtle
crouched on cinders just beyond the far end of the
trestle, excavating with her hind feet. Stretching
out each scaley foot alternately she scooped dirt
from the flask-shaped hole and pushed it to the
side. She had all the time in the world. Abby
watched. When the hole at last achieved some un-
specified turtley standard for nests, she stopped
digging and began laying whitish leathery eggs into
it. There were seven in all, more or less oblong as
far as Abby could see. Backhoeing then the turtle
covered the nest with cinders, smoothing it over
tidily, and lumbered into the brush.

Abby felt the cinders. They were quite warm
where sunlight struck them. The eggs would incubate nicely.

Fluttering in and out of the shade below she
could see a chubby bird chasing gnats along the
creek, but any birdsong was lost in the sound of
rushing water. Once she saw a raccoon sidle out
onto the rocks and wash something in a pool below
her feet. Other than that, and a constant flurry of
butterflies, she had the place to herself.

She thought about her situation calmly for the
first time. With a wry grin she acknowledged what
satisfaction her father might get from knowing she

was breaking up with Geoff; he had disliked him heartily. Well, she sighed, now she was up to date with everybody else—formerly married. With overpopulation and birth control, marriage had finally become as sophisticated a technique as every other process of civilization—it was a project one invests in for a time, then cuts one's losses and drops out for another more promising project. Only diamonds were forever; betrothal meant until further notice. A habit of waste was spreading from the economy into human contacts. Everything was plentiful, people seemed to feel, so nothing need be husbanded. Not even intimacy.

Even though she had come to know that Geoff was not something she would keep, she also knew he was not disposable. The sharp instrument of adultery had uncovered much that was wrong with her marriage and she did not want to salvage it once she understood how it worked. But she was losing something. With a pang of regret she admitted she had been comfortable in a way that would not happen again. She could not say which seemed more wasteful—having spent sixteen years in ignorance or giving it up now. She did know there was no going back. She was no longer ignorant enough or weak enough to be Geoff's wife.

She was now a take-charge woman, she laughed bitterly over the gurgling creek, in a world where more than enough taking and charging had already been done. The future was no longer a hazy upwardly-mobile glow; it was distinctly rickety, fragile, limited, and quite possibly the only bargain she could strike with its inhabitants was in the form of her genes. Her two nice kids.

Standing up, knees crackling in a manner suspi-

ciously middle-aged, she unscrewed the lid of the
brass jar. She looked around. The sun had slipped
behind the wooded hills already and the creek was
swathed in dark shadows. She would not be able to
watch her father's ashes all the way to the surface
of the water. But she would know roughly where
they landed. They would land in the midst of a
second-growth forest that was thriving beautifully
not far from a city full of steel mills. She upended
the canister.

That was the last scattering Abby intended to
do. Reclamation, she told herself with satisfaction,
begins at home.

"They're good kids," Abby mused aloud when
she and her mother had put them to bed in the
guest room. "Those kids are the only piece of professional work I managed to accomplish since I
dropped out of school. Geoff is not going to take
them away from me, not in court, nor any other
time."

With her father properly buried Abby no longer
required her mother to feel guilty, either, and the
two women surprised each other by fighting only
marginally in the wee hours while Abby explained
candidly her situation. The older woman was sympathetic in a way Abby had not expected, coming
up with her own explanation for the episode with
Mike. Listening to Abby describe the mysterious
painful hankering she had felt for a man who
would not even talk to her, her mother said it was
precisely because they were *not* equals, not con-
fidantes, that an attenuated hopelessness had been
able to build up and lend the affair so much passion.

Abby only shook her head on that score. Trust Mother to have an academic explanation. She was more inclined to think of Mike in Dakota's terms —an accident she had caused because she did not want responsibility for admitting she felt trapped in her marriage. It did not matter now. What most concerned Abby was finding a new way to live.

Her mother was glad to have Abby back in the family. Half expecting to be refused, she offered her prodigal daughter the use of the summer house all year long if need be.

CHAPTER TWENTY-SIX

"Will the red ones lay red eggs and the brown ones lay brown eggs?" Gabrielle asked her mother.

"No, Ducks," Abby winked. "They'll all be bright yellow because that's the only color Leghorn chicks come in."

"Yellow eggs." Gabrielle pondered that while Abby finished spreading a deep layer of wood shavings on the concrete floor of the old potting shed. Water founts were ready, feed troughs were disinfected, clean, dry awaiting their Chick Starter feed. The electric brooder was in place and when fifty cheeping, clambering chicken babies arrived tomorrow Abby's fledgling poultry business would start its first experimental phase. Gabrielle found the prospect excruciatingly exciting. Abby suspected her of thinking the chickens would be pets.

"Yellow on the inside, of course," she warned her daughter against eventual disappointment. "On the outside their eggs will be ordinary white. But there won't be any eggs for five or six months, Gabey. They'll have to grow into pullets before they can start laying."

At the door she switched on the brooder, its thermostat set to warm the room to ninety-five degrees. Then she switched out the light, closed the door and followed Gabrielle through the entryway outside into swirling snow.

The next day while Gabrielle was telling everyone on the school bus (much to Toby's embarrassment) that her mother would be selling Leg Horn Bullet Eggs, the electricity at the old stone house went out.

Abby had no way of knowing until it was too late. The snowstorm did not disrupt electrical service in town and when she picked up the big warm boxes of chicks at the hatchery all seemed well. But the weathered wiring at her mother's house gave way where the power fed from the main line through the transformer, and the potting shed-chicken house was dark when she drove up to its windows with her delicate cargo.

She kept the heater running in the car while she dashed from shed to house and back to the shed again, trying to figure out what to do. The shed was still quite warm and the thermostat on the brooder said just a bit more than ninety-five degrees. Her phone was working. When she raised Penn Edison at last they promised her a repairman before lunchtime. Risking that the power would come back on before the temperature indoors dropped too low, she took the boxes of chicks inside the shed. Kneeling, grinning with happiness, she scooped tiny fuzzy beady-eyed birds two handfuls at a time onto the clean shavings. All released onto the floor, they milled moronically about, climbing over each other and looking around their new home.

The repair truck did not show up until eleven. The shed was cooling by then and Abby knew the chicks would not be able to tolerate much of a drop in temperature. One chick was dead already, whether from cold or simply part of the natural attrition the hatchery told her to expect, she did not know. But she was not about to lose any more of the little things to hypothermia. Mouth set, she carried the dead thing with its snakey-looking eyelids as far as the house and left him on the white mound of the compost heap to be covered with more falling snow. Inside, she got out one of her mother's old coats, the once-grand Shagmore with its shawl collar and commodious sleeves. The house was cold too, but that was no problem: unlike chicks, her kids would thrive happily in front of a fireplace. She put on the enormous coat and went outside.

The chicks took to her plan cheerily enough. When she had lain down in the crackling fragrant litter and opened her coat to them, they bounced across to her and climbed right inside, cheeping all the while. It felt wonderful. She was a hardy pioneer, a founding mother, a brooder. She had won this battle, at least, with the elements. She and the chicks became so cozy she was tempted to nod off to sleep, but she did not: someone had to shoo the stupid little things into motion regularly so they would not pile on top of each other in her armpit or the small of her back suffocating each other. She was proud of herself. As an enterprising sort she might not be long on power, but she had gut enough to stand between her livestock and disaster. She was chuckling to herself when she heard the door to the entryway bang open.

The man from the power company laughed too when he saw the woman in the oversized coat teem ing with lilliputian birds. He was a neighbor, it turned out, and yes, he thought his wife would be happy to know where she could buy fresh eggs come summer.

When the thermostat forecast good conditions indoors for chicks, Abby slogged through the snow to the kitchen. Toby and Gabrielle would need hot food as soon as they finished that long walk up the lane from the school bus stop. The school bus. Abby shook her head and got out the pot she used for making cocoa. Toby was learning the vilest language possible riding in the back of that wholesome-looking school bus. But he was not turning into a bed-wetter. For that matter, neither was Abby.

EPILOGUE

The custody battle Abby dreaded so long was not much of a battle after all. Geoff was deprived of his adultery evidence when Mike Vogel moved to Aspen to live with a Sierra Club lobbyist—a gorgeous young woman he met in Brasilia.

Much as Geoff disliked the sound of it, he agreed to sue Abby for abandonment instead. It was the only other grounds available to them in the Commonwealth of Pennsylvania. The divorce itself was such a gruesome experience that when Abby and Geoff were finally shut of lawyers they tended to look on each other more kindly—in a remote sort of empathy. Predictably the judge ruled that the mother must have the children, although privately Abby and Geoff agreed on a policy of joint custody. What this meant in divorce (as in marriage) was that the children saw their father occasionally.

Short of dying and going to heaven, the best possible thing happened to Geoff that could happen to any intellectual: he was interviewed on a BBC television news program which played to approving scholarly notice on every public television station of the United States except the affiliates in Dayton and Fort Smith.

When Geoff sold the house on Farley Landing Road and moved to Cambridge, England, Abby put her share of the equity into her expanding poultry investment. Raising chickens was hard work and dirty, but it appealed to her more than clerking in a boutique or getting a real estate license.

The adversary system of contact between men and women did not make it easy for Abby to find a new companion. But she was in no hurry. Legally she was still married when the tall ships sailed into New York harbor on Independence Day, 1976. The adversary system of divorce died even harder than Abby's marriage. She was arguing Plymouth Rocks over Leghorns with a feed salesman on the radiant spring morning in 1980 when Governor Dick Thornburgh signed into law the new "No Fault Divorce" bill.

Don't Miss these Ace Romance Bestsellers!

74b

D. E. STEVENSON
ROMANCES

"Finding a re-issued novel by D. E. Stevenson is like coming upon a Tiffany lamp in Woolworth's. It is not 'nostalgia'; it is the real thing."

—THE NEW YORK TIMES
BOOK REVIEW

ENTER THE WORLD OF D. E. STEVENSON IN THESE DELIGHTFUL ROMANTIC NOVELS:

01965	**Amberwell**	$1.95
24088	**Fletchers End**	$1.95
48470	**Listening Valley**	$1.95
54725	**Music in the Hills**	$1.95
73325	**Rochester's Wife**	$1.95
76180	**Shoulder the Sky**	$1.95
86560	**Vittoria Cottage**	$1.95
95048	**Young Clementina**	$1.95

Available wherever paperbacks are sold or use this coupon

74a

There are a lot more
where this one came from!

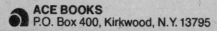